THE LAST EAL

Matthew Baylis was born in Nottingham in 1971, educated
in Liverpool and Cambridge and currently lives in London.
His first novel, *Stranger Than Fulham* was published in
1999. After working as a literary agent in London he became
a storyliner for 'Eastenders' and went on to become a free-
lance journalist and screenwriter. He was involved in a
British Council project to create the first pan-East African
soap opera and is currently working on a venture for
Cambodian television. He is also currently working for the
BBC, adapting Catrin Collier's series of novels for the
screen.

ALSO BY MATTHEW BAYLIS

Stranger Than Fulham

Matthew Baylis

THE LAST
EALING COMEDY

V

VINTAGE

Published by Vintage 2004

2 4 6 8 10 9 7 5 3 1

'A Study of Reading Habits' from *Collected Poems* by Philip Larkin. Reproduced by permission of Faber & Faber Ltd.

First published in Great Britain in 2003 by Chatto & Windus

Vintage
Random House, 20 Vauxhall Bridge Road, London SW1V 2SA

Random House Australia (Pty) Limited
20 Alfred Street, Milsons Point, Sydney
New South Wales 2061, Australia

Random House New Zealand Limited
18 Poland Road, Glenfield,
Auckland 10, New Zealand

Random House (Pty) Limited
Endulini, 5A Jubilee Road, Parktown 2193,
South Africa

The Random House Group Limited Reg. No. 954009
www.randomhouse.co.uk

A CIP catalogue record for this book
is available from the British Library

ISBN 0 09 927355 1

Papers used by Random House are natural, recyclable products made from wood grown in sustainable forests. The manufacturing processes conform to the environmental regulations of the country of origin

Printed and bound in Denmark by
Nørhaven Paperback, Viborg

To Sophie Parkin

Acknowledgements

The Ealing films themselves have been, and continue to be a great source of inspiration. In addition, Charles Barr's excellent *Ealing Studios* (Cameron & Hollis 1999) provided some invaluable insights. Anyone interested should also look at the Ealing screenwriter T.E.B. 'Tibby' Clarke's autobiography *This Is Where I Came In*. Thanks also to my Mum and Dad, whose taste for the unfashionable has always been a guiding influence, and to the Bannisters, for the Latin and the spare room.

The Captive Heart

'If you wouldn't mind coming through to the Interview Suite,' says the young detective. He's standing at the cell door, fresh-faced and earnest, sporting a tie with cartoon characters on it and a button-down shirt.

'So it's just that, then? Just an interview?'

'Not exactly, sir.' He looks pained to continue, as if this is the unsavoury end of a job he otherwise adores. 'I'm afraid you're in quite a bit of bother.'

This confirms it for me: I am asleep; this is just a dream. I have two distinct images of the police, and they are nothing like this. There is the Ealing Studios version, in which the forces of law and order are a bevy of large-bellied Santa Claus types, who nab miscreants with a sorry shake of the head, asking, 'Why did you have to go and do that, son?' Then there are the modern, urban-drama cops. That leather-jacketed, sideburned tribe, who have weekend access to their kids, and a thousand euphemisms for the things that can happen to a pretty boy in prison.

But not here. In this dreamscape, the business of being flung into the cells is more like checking into a five-star detox clinic for overworked executives. Soft voices ask how you're feeling, between offers of tea and homeopathic remedies. Every detail of your forthcoming ordeal is explained, in clear and priestly tones. *Now then, Alastair, we're just putting these plastic handcuffs on you. These are for your own safety and comfort. Now then, Alastair, this is called a custody suite and we're just going to lock you up in here for a few hours . . .*

I am sitting on a black plastic mattress in Custody Suite One, listening to Capital MaxiChart FM on the tannoy overhead and ignoring a printed brochure next to me entitled *So You've Been Arrested?* I am tired to the point of soreness and – as only rarely happens in dreams – I think I know why.

I was fighting in the street. Perhaps in the dream, perhaps before the dream began. Someone, an angry man, had his hands around my throat, squeezing so that little bubbles of light were dancing at the edges of my vision. I managed to fend him off with a sharp knee to the midriff, just as I was losing the battle for life. He fell down and I ran on, neither looking back nor caring, not easing up until I was on the Ealing Road and could see the Westlines coach ahead, boys trooping onto it, with their morning-hair in damp resentful spikes. Then I saw the panda car. Two uniformed policemen standing talking to Ann. She turned and pointed towards me. The policemen followed her gaze and I froze in my steps.

Then I was sitting stunned in the back of the car, and the policemen were doing complicated things with their radios. And Ann bent down to the passenger window. Hers was a dawn face – without its usual Gothic make-up, it had a puffy, scrubbed look, like a freshly beaten arse.

'See they've caught up with you, then? Can't say I'm surprised.'

'Did you do this, Ann?' I was asking her, straining forward angrily in my seat. 'You did, didn't you? You did all of it!' But she wouldn't answer me; she just smiled her thinnest, most distant smile. Then we were driving away.

Now we are down in the Interview Suite, I sit forlornly at a table while the young detective prepares tapes. He then leaves the room for a few minutes, returning in the company of an older, craggy-faced, pipe-smoking individual who looks like a Geology lecturer. He wears a corduroy jacket with leather patches on the elbows. They both stare at me as if I am an exhibit.

I start explaining things in a fitful voice. 'You see – that woman – Ann Gorley . . .' I start. 'She's got a grudge against me, so she's made it all up.'

'Made it up?' the young one echoes, arranging Polos, pens, rubber and ruler in front of him, like a small girl about to do her first exam.

'Well, not exactly made it up. I mean, it's Davenport's telescope. And I'm definitely not the person you're looking for – not intentionally anyway. I don't even really think *she* thinks I am. She just hates me because I won't be her boyfriend. That's why she's been doing all this.'

Silence follows. I watch the younger detective painstakingly write the words *Telescope* and *Boyfriend* on his notepad. The Geology teacher simply stares at me, through the filmy eyes of a much-loved dog.

'All what, Alastair?'

I'm about to explain, when the Geology teacher emerges from his trance and holds up a hairy-backed hand. 'I don't want to interfere, Gerald,' he says. 'It is your collar. But I don't think we're going to get anywhere like this. Remember what I told you. Come in late, get out early.'

Gerald chews his bottom lip. 'All right, Philip,' he says, sulkily. 'You're the boss.'

'It's Gerald's turn to stare and crunch Polos while Philip opens a folder and turns it round so I can see it. It's got my name written on the cover.

I had a Maths teacher who used to claim that one day, when I was least expecting it, there would be a soft click inside my head, something akin to a shot of morphine. After the click, I would understand everything Maths-related: simultaneous equations, mensuration, statistics. I would be free and happy; I would like him and come to his lessons to learn more. It never happened. But now, as I look down and realise that these people, serious police people, have a folder with my name on it, there's a click. The gritty edges of my vision recede into clarity. I understand things – horrible things. The lights grow brighter. The floor seesaws beneath me, just once, then is still. Because I am not dreaming at all. This is happening.

Philip seems to understand what's going through my mind. His face wrinkles, becoming a sort of benevolent item of luggage. 'Just start at the beginning,' he says, gently. 'Then perhaps we'll see if we can help you.'

'But I don't know where to begin.'

'You could start by telling us about the forged references.'

The Man in the White Suit

'Not sure I can appreciate the cost-effectiveness of a *constant* supply of hot water to the lavatories, Bursar . . .' The headmaster glances up, seeing me in the doorway. 'Alastair!' he exclaims, waving me into the office. He holds a slim hand over the telephone receiver. 'In fact,' he continues, 'you're a young man – perhaps you could assist with a small problem?'

'Of course.' I cross the carpet, new shoes squeaking.

'We seek to ascertain, as a percentage, or a vulgar fraction – strictly ball-park – what proportion of teenage boys willingly washes their hands after micturition.' The headmaster stares at me keenly.

My heart gives a soft flip – as upon opening an exam paper to discover you've studied the wrong poems. In some depth. 'Mick who?'

'After they micturate. Urinate. Pass water. In my experience, the average boy just doesn't, does he?'

'Doesn't urinate?'

'Doesn't wash his hands! They just don't, do they?'

'Erm . . .'

'Did you? When you were a boy?' The headmaster is not going to give up on this.

'Do I still get the job if I tell the truth?'

The headmaster is silent. Martha used to call this habit

of mine 'gabbing on'. Meaning I can be relied upon to make the joke that's the least understood in the circumstances where it will also be the least welcome. That I'm the usher-in of all conversational shibboleths and behemoths, the boyfriend you leave at home. Or chuck out.

The headmaster briefly returns to the telephone, promising the bursar that they can have a *serious natter* about the hot-water issue later on. As I take a seat, he shuffles papers, bringing my c.v. into view, and also a small pot of moisturiser, which he stows hastily in a drawer. He casts an eye over the c.v., then clasps his hands together. He has long, steely hair and looks quite like a mid-morning TV talk-show host.

'My apologies. Perhaps we might commence now. Tell me,' he glances up at the ceiling, 'why do you want to teach at Lorry's?'

'I've heard a lot about the school,' I begin.

'Really?'

'I was having lunch with Amjit Sammaddi the other day. You know, the media . . . erm . . .' I stop, wondering how to describe Sammaddi. He is a media mogul, a broadcast Effendi, Khan of the Information Tartars.

'Sammaddi? The gentleman who's put in a bid for the old Millennium Dome?'

'Has he?'

'So I gather. And Mr Sammaddi was conversing with you about the school?' The headmaster coaxes, while seeming not to believe me.

'Well, his wife was,' I add, lamely.

The week before, I'd been walking down Kensington High Street after a particularly disheartening encounter with Darren Krajic, my ReStart counsellor at the Hammersmith OneStop JobShop. And I bumped into Tara.

We'd shared a desk back in the days when I worked for a vanity press. More accurately, I'd worked at the desk while Tara enjoyed the privileged position of being the boss's daughter, so was more often to be found under the desk, asleep. After falling in love with an Indian poet of unspeakable literary badness, she had run off to marry him. This poet – Mr Sammaddi – had turned out on further inspection to be the twenty-ninth-richest man in the world. They were back in London, Tara told me, so that he could buy the *Evening Herald*. And she didn't mean just one copy of it. Tara had insisted we have lunch together.

It was during this lunch – taken in the Miramont, a canopied Chelsea affair specialising in the sale of bad food to Euro-Sloanes – that Tara had decided I needed help. After listening to Tara's own, dizzying account of how someone I didn't know called Nosher had just been caught trouserless on the billiards table with someone else unknown to me called Chuffy at a place I'd never visit called Lummers, I'd been encouraged to tell her what was happening in my life. Out of pride, I'd kept it pretty brief. Telegraph-style: *Quit job editing TV magazine stop. Finished with Martha stop. Two are related stop.* And Tara had said, 'Poor you! We'll have to see what we can do.' She was always like that – a slender, foxy girl with a surprising streak of kindness.

Later, just after the waiter had brought over a dish called 'Pork Rinds on a Russian Bun', and we had all independently discovered that there was nothing Russian about the bun except for its being freezing cold, Tara had a thought. She started rummaging through her Prada handbag. 'I've just thought of something. *F. exciting*,' she declared.

Sammaddi rolled his eyes at me – the only communication we had during the meal. He passed the rest of the time flaring his nostrils and sending e-mails from his palmtop computer. I got the impression Tara often invited people to lunch and that these lunches prevented Mr Sammaddi from doing what he loved most. Which probably involved money.

'What is it?' I asked, as Tara pursed her fulsome lips, having found nothing in her handbag except a spare pair of tights and an American Express card.

'Boy I bumped into the other day,' she said, removing a strand of her dark, straight hair from her mouth. 'Davenport. Lord Chertsey's son. Do you know him? He teaches Classics at Lorry's.'

For Tara, the whole world is just a big marquee in the grounds of some country house (possibly Lummers). And, given time, provided the champagne keeps flowing, everyone will come to know everyone else, if they don't already.

'I don't think I do. And what's Lorry's?'

'Boys' school in Ealing, lovely. Anyway, they're after a new English teacher, Davenport says. Last one was found dead on Ealing Common in a Versace frock.' She leant over to impart some darker details, lowering her eyelids with theatrical fervour. 'When they pumped his stomach, it had just malt whisky and sperm in it. Isn't that too brilliant?'

I ignored this edifying detail. 'I'm not a teacher.'

'Oh, Davenport's been there for f. yonks and he couldn't teach a baby to dribble. Anyway, you've got to give them a call. Right away. Lend him your moby, Amjie.'

Sammaddi did not seem keen to lend me his mobile,

but later on, after we'd parted on the King's Road, I did what Tara said. Rather suprisingly, they invited me in for an interview. And here I am.

'I didn't realise you'd worked for Sammaddi,' the headmaster says, glancing vaguely at the c.v. 'A reference from him certainly won't do any harm . . .'

'No, I didn't mean I'd worked for—'

He interrupts, blinking serenely like some weathered saddhu. 'Our founder would have approved. Being himself a man of business.'

Steven Harpenden – this is the headmaster's name – is tanned, mid-forties, slender as a ginseng root, with eyes the colour of lapis lazuli. He smiles at me frequently – smiles whose brightness matches the dazzling white of his linen suit. I can imagine him saying, in his pasteurised, virtually accent-free accent, 'Do you mind if I screw your girlfriend?' And I can imagine myself lending him my last pound for the Durex machine, so that he can go and do it.

'The founder. This would be St John Lorimer?' I ask. I pronouce it Saint John Lorimer, because that's what the sign outside the school says, in big gold letters.

The headmaster gives a little wince. 'We pronounce it *Sinjun Lawmaah*,' he corrects me gently. 'But then you wouldn't have known that. And why should you? I probably committed a similar error at my own interview. In fact, I'm sure I did.' He gives a short, embarrassed laugh. 'I myself attended a secondary modern in Welwyn Garden City.'

I make a murmur of surprise. 'Oh yes,' the headmaster continues. 'Lorry's might once have been founded on principles of elitism. But nowadays we see ourselves as providing a key service to the community.'

He is at pains to point out that this service does not

merely extend to those members of the community who can afford the fees. The girls from the local convent school already use the old tennis courts, he tells me proudly, and when the new sports centre is completed it will be open to the public at weekends.

Tea follows, and a series of amiable enquiries, no more taxing than those a visiting vicar might ask the youngest child of the house. Then we leave the headmaster's light, pine-panelled office, its walls hung with framed awards from Harvard Business School and the Koniginsuniversitet Rotterdam, and cross a little courtyard where a fountain tinkles gently.

Before us is the main building, a nineteenth-century sandstone affair, nestling alongside the Design and Technology Centre, which is the kind of glass-and-steel wigwam that only architects truly appreciate. Behind lurks an ugly, Lubyanka-style rectangle, fittingly housing the Maths Department and the gym, and next to that, skirted for no apparent reason by a wire fence, is an odd, low 1930s block, white-painted, with a few small outhouses. It doesn't fit in with the rest of the school at all, and looks more like some former outpost of government-sponsored research. I can picture white-coated boffins inside it, cracking codes and curing the common cold.

'Oh, that's not one of ours,' the headmaster says. 'That's the old Ealing film studios.' And then, when I make a surprised noise, he adds, 'You're fond of film, I take it?'

'Hmm. I mean yes. I am. Some of them.' A thought strikes me. 'I like Ealing comedies.'

There's been a season of them on Channel Four. And they're the only kind of telly I still love. I can't stomach the truthful grime of the kitchen-sink any more, the miscarriages and the bickering couples. But I can still self-medicate with the black-and-white laudanum of Ealing Studios, with its honourable spivs and its eccentric dowagers, its little communities battling to outwit White-hall and Progress and all the other forces of darkness.

When I was eight years old, my mother went into hospital to have some operation that made people wince whenever its name was mentioned. My father, a distant figure who forgot my name as frequently as he forgot the date, was left in sole charge of me. I remember this as a glorious, bathless era, a time of late nights and chip-shop suppers. They were reshowing the Ealing films on TV and my father, forlorn and confused without the ceaseless chatter and dizzying efficiency of his wife, let me sit up with him in the front room. I would fall asleep well before the end of each film and until recently could recall only slivers of the plots and the dialogue. Intermingled with the sketchily remembered images of rioting crowds and umbrella-wielding dames is a heady, comforting smell – the vinegar of chip-wrappers, the earthy odour of my father's green sweater as I dozed in its folds.

My mother came back, the Ealing season ended and my father withdrew again to the upper reaches of the house, signalling his presence only with a long, throaty cough that set my teeth on edge as I hit puberty. But ever since, the merest mention of the word *Ealing* has had a certain power, to recall a brief, sweet interval of togetherness, of belonging – of all the things, in fact, that Ealing films were about, although I never knew that until now.

'Ealing comedies, eh?' The headmaster gives a forgiving smile. 'Well, I'll have to take you at your word.'

He leaves me puzzled by the musical fountain, wonder-ing what he meant, and pads off in his suede loafers towards the main building. He beckons to me to catch up.

The building we are entering, he tells me, is the oldest part of the school – the original Lawson Manor. It was the grand dream of a manic-depressive architect with a passion for Regency flourishes and a bank manager who did not share that passion. Completed, it stood empty, declining into a rotting hulk until an enterprising businessman bought it at the end of World War One. That was the school's founder, St John Lorimer.

The interior is cool and dark. Last term's notices – advertising the Judo Club and hockey trials – flutter as the door shuts behind us. Outside the staff room, a portrait of the founder hangs on the wall. St John Lorimer is a heavy-jowled individual, radiating the kind of smug *bonhomie* found usually in pub landlords who know a thing or two about horse-racing. He died, the headmaster relates, aged forty-nine, of a perforated bowel.

He leads me down the marble-flagged main corridor, a parade of classrooms on our right, and high varnished boards lining the left-hand side, painted with the names of long-dead scholars. He's saying something about the 'fertile congress of tradition and modernity' – which is in evidence all around. Outside the Computer Room stands a memorial to those boys who fell in World War Two. And a bronze bust of old man Sinje, fatter and even more delighted with himself, keeps watch over the new auditorium, seeming with its circular seating and pine floors like the parliament of some deeply enlightened Benelux democracy.

In the library we find a willowy young woman hunched over a desk in the middle of the room, engaged at a task so meticulous she doesn't even look up. Her fingers can be heard skimming across the keyboard of a laptop.

'. . . a shelving in-load of thirty-three cubic metres,' the headmaster is saying. 'Borrowing ratios stand at four units per boy per term, but that's only ever going to be a low-end average. I recently attended a symposium on library resource management in Hilversum, where our Dutch cousins are unsurprisingly rather blazing a trail . . .' He waves a hand towards the woman at the desk. 'And, of course, our Miss Gorley is doing what she can to upscale the multi-user connectivity.'

She looks up. She's about my age, white-faced, long-necked, with black hair cut into a severe bob. She does not smile — in fact, she looks like one of those girls who are into not smiling as a way of life.

The headmaster introduces us. Her name is Miss Ann Gorley. Still unsmiling, she holds out a hand. Her skin feels as chilly as I'd expected. On her middle finger she wears a heavy silver ring with a skull on it, pure Camden Market. This is her only adornment: a concession, I assume, to the sober surroundings of the workplace. I suspect she goes pretty Gothic at the weekends.

'Alastair is hoping to join us,' the headmaster explains.

'As a teacher?' asks Miss Ann Gorley, in a vaguely Northern accent.

'I hope so,' I say, with a giddy laugh and a backwards glance at the headmaster. He in turn inclines his head as if to suggest that, whatever the outcome of the interview, I will remain a trusted friend.

The headmaster and Miss Gorley begin a private conversation, leaving me to look at the coat of arms on the wall above the door. It features the obligatory griffins and stags rampant and something that's either the Font of Wisdom or a small saucepan. I suspect Sinje himself designed it, on the back of a racecard or a menu.

'Mint ball?'

'Sorry?' I look down and notice that Miss Gorley and I are alone. She's proffering a little paper package. 'Where's he gone?'

'SAH?' she says, blinking tired, heavy-lidded eyes. 'Gone to get you a hard hat. Wants to show you the Sports Centre.'

I get a sense, from the way she says the words, that Miss Gorley has a healthy contempt for sports centres. Which makes her all right in my book. I perch on the edge of her desk and take a sweet. 'SAH?'

'Everyone's supposed to call everyone else by their initials. So he's SAH. And I'm ARG.' She crunches the sweet and adds, 'Aaagh.'

'Unfortunate.'

'I don't mind,' she says, softly. 'I expect the boys call me something worse.'

'Where you from?'

'Oldham,' she says. 'You?'

'Southport.'

'My granny's in a nursing home there.'

'Everyone's granny's in a nursing home there.'

She laughs, a slightly mournful noise exposing a set of large but perfectly straight teeth. One of those little gestures that make you realise how pretty someone might be, when they're not trying to be anything.

'So do you like working here?'

She blinks, as if the idea of liking anything much is a little foreign to her. 'I wouldn't do it unless I was desperate.'

'Maybe I am desperate.'

'You might be if you stay.'

Miss Gorley reminds me of those haunted girls who were always to be seen doing their essays, intensely, in the

University Library, whatever hour you went in there. That was the only time you saw them – except during rain storms, when they went outside and got deliberately drenched, presumably picturing themselves in a Kate Bush video. She wears a long floaty skirt and a dark top, and keeps a bunched-up tissue up her right sleeve, as if tears or a heavy cold are never far away. The idea of having a conversation with someone like Miss Gorley is so bizarre as to be quite enjoyable.

Regrettably the headmaster returns at this juncture, bearing two yellow plastic helmets. 'Time for the jewel in our crown,' he says.

'How do I look?' I ask Miss Gorley as we head towards the doors, putting the helmets on. She says nothing, merely bends her head and continues tapping the key-board.

A sweeping gravel walkway takes us right to the main gates. Beyond them lie the assorted charity shops and specialist coffee-houses of Ealing Green, hazy in the hot sunshine. There's a small field to our right, dotted with a couple of cricket nets. In its top corner, a building is taking shape. Wooden boards lie over the grass, smeared with concrete and the tracks of wheelbarrows. We walk across them to the building site. Swarthy, curly-haired men are digging the earth, alongside yellow machines that sputter and chug.

The Sports Centre is to be the headmaster's own mark on the history of the school. There are already tennis courts and a swimming pool situated an unpractical distance away – over the other side of Ealing Common. This was adequate in former decades, when Hangar Lane was still a lane and the pupils could travel to the sports ground on bicycles, with only the odd baker's van or errand boy for company. But nowadays, the route is a roaring motorway and not a term goes by without a memorial service for some squashed child and threats of litigation from the grieving parents. The Sports Centre will solve these problems in a swoop, offering every imaginable on-site facility from hockey to Tae Kwon Do, and establishing the school as a multi-tasking beacon of physical culture.

The headmaster stops as the boards give way to chewed earth. We stand next to a grey Portakabin, where my escort sniffs the air and smiles. 'Look on my works, ye mighty, and rejoice!'

I give him a sideways look, trying to decide whether this misquotation of 'Ozymandias' was a deliberate interview trick. But before I can say anything, the door in the Portakabin opens and a man steps out. He's a ham-faced bullock with closely cropped white hair. Something about his movements, fast and forceful, suggests that he is intending to punch someone. The workers on the site seem to be the object of his fury, but when he sees us he slows down and smiles.

The headmaster greets him with considerable reserve and introduces him as Mr Warren, the site developer.

'Call me Bunny,' he says, shaking my hand. A gold bracelet gleams from beneath his white cuff. A small groove curves underneath his left eye – a scar or a wrinkle, I can't be sure. But I recognise a Liverpool accent when I hear one.

The headmaster is thinking along the same wavelength. 'Alastair is practically a kinsman to yourself, Mr Warren.'

'Wha?'

The headmaster ups the volume. 'Alastair comes from the same region as yourself.'

'Southport,' I clarify.

'La-de-dah,' Warren returns. This is what Liverpool people always say when they meet someone from Southport. Even if both are lost in the Gobi desert at the time.

'She's coming on beautifully, Mr Warren,' says the headmaster.

'Who? Oh yeah,' Warren says, somewhat dismissively, taking off his dark glasses to squint at the site. I suddenly notice his pink eyes and white eyelashes. 'Some of these lads are a bit relaxed, though. I don't know where he gets them from sometimes.'

'Where who gets them from?'

Bunny Warren ignores the headmaster and winks at me. 'Southport, eh?' He gives it the full scouse treatment: *Sowpawsse.* 'Went to a few parties there. Me brother was the drummer for the Hurricanes, y'know. Before they became the Merseybeats.'

'That's super,' the headmaster says, with the dismissive air of an adult being handed a plasticine space-shuttle. 'If you'll excuse us, Mr Warren . . .'

'I went to one of Johnny Fontana's parties once,' Warren continues, leaning close to me so that I can smell his aftershave. 'Roger McGough was there an' all. Oh aye. And Ringo. He had this great philosophy, right?'

'Yes?' says the headmaster, uneasily. I see him glance at his watch.

'He could have any bird he wanted, yeah?' Warren continues, winking at us. 'Johnny, I mean. So one time, me and me brother's in his house. And he says, "Come in here, lads." It was like this big lighthouse, right. By the sea . . .'

'I know the one,' I interject, excitedly. 'It's by the golf club.'

The headmaster looks at me disapprovingly. But Warren is encouraged. 'That's it, lar. And we go up top, right. Into the lamp room. And there's these two birds. You know . . .' Warren pauses, to lick his lips and lower his voice, '. . . *getting it on*.'

The headmaster coughs and I stare at the ground to avoid catching his eye.

'And Johnny says, "I can't be bothered nobbing them any more. *So I just get 'em together and watch!*"'

He sniggers loudly, nudging me. I dare a glance at the headmaster, who is doing a lot of pained blinking. He clears his throat.

'Not sure I quite follow you, Mr Warren. What was this man's *philosophy* exactly?'

Later, when Warren has left us and is shouting at his builders, the headmaster is still confused. We're walking towards the gates and he's undone the top button of his shirt. It's as if the encounter with Warren has knocked him off balance and he's itching to get back to his air-conditioned office, to some corner of the cosmos he can control.

'Sometimes I find our Mr Warren a little impenetrable,' he confesses. 'I mean, what precisely *was* this Fontana gentleman's philosophy? Are we meant to surmise that he was some sort of Epicurean?'

'I don't think he meant it was a philosophy. I think it was just a . . . you know, a smutty story.'

'Come again? Smutty?' He looks at me keenly. 'You mean "in poor taste"? Pornographic? But what was smutty about it? Wasn't this musician simply someone who enjoyed watching ladies dancing?'

'I'm afraid not.'

'But these "Merseybeaters" were, I assume, some sort of musical ensemble . . . ?'

With as much discretion as I can muster, I explain what Warren meant. The headmaster's expression passes through bewilderment to horror and then contentment.

'That's really most impressive,' he announces, over the roar of a passing juggernaut.

'Is it?'

'You took a difficult concept and you rendered it entirely comprehensible to me in seconds. Exactly the skills we're looking for here.'

'Oh. Erm. Thanks.'

'I don't doubt you'd have fared as well explaining it to a classroom of teenage boys.'

I do doubt this myself, because I know something about teenage boys. But I keep quiet.

'It's basic Burnham scale,' he continues. 'I'm afraid we can't offer any better at the moment. The Sports Centre has rather swallowed up our available funds.'

'I see,' I say, not seeing anything. Then I realise I'm being offered a job. Which might pose a problem. 'I should have explained earlier. I don't exactly have any qualifications. I mean, I haven't got a teaching certificate . . .'

The headmaster waves a dismissive hand. 'Lorry's philosophy is to offer on-site training to the right, results-driven individuals. All right?'

And I suppose it is. It's a start, at least.

'Just one thing. If you could get me that reference from Amjit Sammaddi before the start of term . . .' He looks at me. 'Is that going to be a problem?'

'No problem, Headmaster. None at all.'

The Ladykillers

Such joy has not been seen in Ealing since the Lavender Hill Mob got away with the gold bullion, since old Mrs Wilberforce saw off the Ladykillers and the Titfield Thunderbolt rode again. I've got a job. I can find a flat, one that doesn't — as all the *Loot* adverts suggest — entail sharing with twelve non-smoking, fun-loving Kiwis or require me to be a cat-friendly vegetarian prof. female.

I haven't felt this good since I walked out of *TV Forum*. I felt liberated then, too — a great giddying gulf of freedom which, complemented by several pints of lager, concluded with me being sick on the new sofa.

Martha was fairly cross about the sofa — a polar-white creation from Heal's which she'd taken three days off work to get delivered. She became even more cross next morning when, as the stain on the sofa turned from green to yellow, I told her why I'd got so drunk. She didn't understand. 'I thought you loved that job,' she said, while attacking the sofa with a damp sponge.

She was right. I did love that job. Once. *TV Forum* was a magazine aimed at that section of the populace who not only watch television, but depend upon it as newsreaders depend upon daily disaster. I used to be among them. But things happened. Martha happened, for a start.

It wasn't just Martha. My love affair with the soap opera

was placed under considerable strain by the business of editing a magazine featuring such monthly highlights as 'Win a Day with the Emmerdale Wardrobe Team'. It was further battered out of existence by the necessity of spending my days in an airless cube at the back of Kwik Save on the North End Road. An office within whose walls my task was to marshal the efforts of one dyslexic sub-editor and one shy publicist into saving the life of a magazine that began with a circulation of six thousand and finished with one of just six. I found this to be a form of slow death. By the time the magazine's proprietor, the rarely present Mr Ridout, announced that he was cutting my salary in half, I was already frothing at the mouth in my desire to leave. So one lunch-time, clutching my customary offering from the Marks & Spencer sandwich chiller, I decided not to go back to the office. I went to the pub and stayed there. I took control.

Unfortunately there were other things I could not control. Because Martha was changing too. The Heal's sofa was the perfect emblem of all that Martha had begun to stand for. Our tiny flat in Fulham was crammed with objects like the sofa — costly, over-designed things of beauty that we spent all our Saturday mornings choosing and queuing for, alongside every other childless couple in west London. Objects that cost so much we were slightly afraid of them once we got them home.

Martha became very serious. Even though we were living together, I still thought of ourselves as being in that state people call 'going out'. But then I found we weren't going out any more. We were perpetually going *to* things or to *do* things that at least one of us didn't much want to. There was no time to spend Saturday mornings under the duvet, because there were curtains to be bought, dry-cleaning to be dropped off, colour schemes to be frowned over. There were evenings to be spent in the company of other couples, who were as earnest about their careers as they were about being couples.

She got better. That's what happened. When we first met, she'd been recovering from a difficult time. And I hadn't: I just didn't like going out much. I liked watching television and if I went out at all it was to the sort of pubs *Time Out* never mentioned. I thought this – with its take-away pizzas and its all-night video sessions – was the life Martha wanted, but it turned out to be just the sort of cloistered, greenhouse environment she needed to repair herself before a rather drastic relaunch.

The relaunch kicked in a year ago. I discovered that soap operas had the ability to send me into a coma, while Martha discovered a new anti-depressant with a zingy name like Zoloft. She sold the little country cottage left to her by her mother and purchased a small, bright place in a mansion block near Turnham Green. I took some time off work and painted it, while Martha took a temping job on a magazine called *Putney Properties*. It was there, working on this publication devoted to the praise of the 311 bus route and the fine dining opportunities of the Earlsfield Village Conservation Area, that Martha discovered a hidden talent for selling advertising space.

This description underplays the miracle that was Martha-at-work. With a headset clamped to her ears and her auburn hair drawn into a fierce ponytail, Martha could have convinced the terminally ill to buy running shoes. And Tim, the new boss of *Putney Properties*, recognised Martha as being their hottest property and took her on permanently. She became Head of Sales, lost weight, had her thick, scatty hair restyled in a straight wispy fashion that made her look like most girls in London and gradually, imperceptibly at first, she stopped being mine.

I watched the wardrobe filling with Burberry skirts and knee-high boots and I was happy for her, at the same time as being pricked by a sense that something had gone missing. It was hard to work out what it was. We were still having sex – we were having it with such alarming frequency, in fact, that I sometimes wondered if she was trying to get pregnant. But she wasn't. It was just a good way of ensuring we didn't have to talk.

There'd been a time when we used to sit on the balcony of the flat and watch the winebar over the road. Martha had devised a points system based upon close observation of the gilded clientele. You got five points for a signet ring, ten for a pair of red cords, fifteen for a navy blazer. It went right up to fifty points for one of those quilted riding coats that are normally found only on the Italian aristocracy.

Then one evening, in a period when Martha was spending increasing chunks of her life selling advertising space to estate agents and our conversations largely consisted of toothpaste-scented grunts at the start and finish of each day, I'd been sitting on the balcony watching the winebar, and I watched as Martha – wearing a tan-coloured trouser-suit – stepped out of a soft-top Mercedes with a boggle-eyed individual who reminded me of a prawn. I continued to watch as they entered the winebar, and as they proceeded to drink a bottle of Chablis and eat some Thai crab-cakes. Then, as the spring light was fading, they came out again. The prawn didn't kiss her, but I'd tried and failed to kiss enough people to know that he wanted to.

When she came home I tried not to say anything. But

in the end, fuelled by the dregs of a bottle of Lagavulin, I finally capitulated and asked her, in a wavering voice that sounded as casual as Mr Chamberlain announcing the German invasion of Poland, who the bleeding sodding hell she'd spent the evening with.

'That was Tim,' she said, brightly. 'My boss.' And as I choked on the whisky fumes she added, 'You'd like him, you know. He's really down-to-earth.'

Presently, 'down-to-earth' became Martha's mantra. To me it meant dull as dried cowshit but to her it meant sensible, hard-working, get-ahead. These were the qualities she lusted after. These were also qualities I've never had in great supply, so I shouldn't have been surprised when the lust dried up as well.

Then I quit my job and showed no signs of being penitent either about it or the sick-stained sofa. I imagined Martha would show some sign of being angry, or at least bothered, but she was too busy. *Putney Properties* was relaunched in handbag-sized format and there was a party to celebrate.

I wasn't invited, but I turned up anyway, wearing a white shirt and a pair of black trousers because, due to the strange workings of fate and an earnest letter from my bank, I'd gone along to a temp agency that morning and got a night's work as a waiter.

As I passed through the crowds, bearing a tray of damp hors-d'oeuvres, Martha did, at last, become angry. Her shame practically fizzed in the air around her. She did introduce me to a few people. This included Tim, who was wearing a corduroy suit of the nastiest yellow and had only one topic of conversation, which had something to do with why Riga was rapidly becoming the new Reykjavik. I also met his wife Kitty, who was a corkscrew-haired, intense sort, like some cellist who sat up all night cutting her arms. Tim seemed to believe I was walking round dressed like a waiter as a sort of good-natured joke, but one on the verge of becoming tiresome. Kitty, on the other hand, believed I was a sort of bug that fed on mucus. It was an opinion that Martha − in spite of the glassy-smiled enmity that existed between her and Tim's wife from the second they met − came to share.

A sit-down meal ensued, during which I tipped a bowl of lobster bisque over Tim, and ignored the Duke of Kent. This rounded things off nicely. By the end of the following day, I was in the spare room. By the end of the following week, I had acquired a long-dreaded prefix. I was an 'ex'.

But now I don't care. I sit on a wooden bench on the little green facing the school and the sun warms my blood. So this is Ealing. W5. One of those London postcodes I'd always shivered at − like N22 or SE6. Redolent of wet winter Sundays, lonely dinners bought from newsagents and carried home in thin candy-striped plastic bags. But here, in the lunch-time sun, Ealing looks like somewhere a man could be happy. It's more like a village than a London borough. The green really is a green. It's got an old-fashioned signpost in the middle, pointing to Étaples, which is the twin town. There are trees along the street − chestnuts and sycamores, the trees of a suburban English childhood. It feels like home, even though I've never lived anywhere remotely like it.

It would be easy to slip into a reverie. Even easier with lager in front of me. And as I bear left, down quieter residential streets towards the common, I realise why I feel at home. It's because Ealing, W5, still seems to have more than a little in common with the films they made here, in the Forties and Fifties. Ealing's England was a village. A village under threat from bureaucrats and capitalists and the many-horned beast of modernity. Even in *Passport to Pimlico*, when the subject was a south London bombsite, they made it seem like a little community, complete with its clip-round-the-ear bobbies and its dippy old dames. This place could be the backdrop to *Pimlico II*. The sounds of local industry are all around – the chip of a workman's hammer performing a duet with some starlings. I can imagine some announcer saying, in tones of polished Wedgwood, 'Here is London, the finest city in the world.' In a pub round here I could find Terry-Thomas being a devilish cad, Alastair Sim lisping darkly over a warm pie.

I find a pub at the end of the road – the MacKendrick Arms – painted fire-engine red; it looks cool and enticing. There's one old tortoise spilling Guinness over his demob suit and nobody else. My drink comes in an old-fashioned stippled glass with a handle. I haven't been served with a glass like this since I was under-age. I take it into the darkest reaches of the pub, a large, cornerhouse construction, with high ceilings stained tobacco-brown. On the walls are gloomy renderings of unknown aristocrats, advertisements from obsolete brands of cigarette.

And in a corner scarred by the wounds of poorly aimed darts, I discover the pub has more than two customers. Supping a pint of cider and blackcurrant is the slender librarian, Ann Gorley. I think about backing off, but she hears my footfall, looks up and very nearly smiles. 'How was the interview?' she asks, quietly.

'I got the job.'

Ann closes her book. 'I knew you would. He's been looking for an MCS teacher since the start of the summer.' She leans back into her seat, pointing at me, for an instant, a pair of uniquely cheerful breasts. 'And you're the only one who got the guided tour.' She takes out a cigarette – Embassy Numbers. 'I know because I've been stuck in that library all summer. Computerising the catalogue.'

'MCS?'

'Media and Cultural Studies,' Ann replies, diffidently. She pronounces it *culcheral*. 'Are you thinking about sitting down?'

Grasping this as an Oldham-style invitation to join her, I pull out a stool, still confused. 'What's Media and Cultural Studies?'

Ann frowns. 'You're the one teaching it.'

There must be some mistake. 'I'm an English teacher.' I correct myself. 'I *will be* teaching English.'

'They're not looking for English teachers. They've hired the new one already.'

I trawl back fretfully over the interview. It must be said, nobody ever mentioned English, or any other subject. It seemed more like meeting a new landlord – just a formality to ascertain whether or not I breed pythons or collect spanking literature. The only mention of English came, in fact, from Tara, who evidently got it arse-over-tit.

'Heck,' Ann pronounces, taking vague satisfaction in my plight. 'What'll you do?'

'Hide?'

'Don't worry. Anyone can teach MCS.'

'But what *is* it?'

It emerges, from Ann's scathing summary, that Media and Cultural Studies is a new variant of General Studies. It is a hugely popular option both at GCSE and A level, as the course work entails watching videos and reading the odd popular novel.

Ann regards the introduction of MCS as typical of the headmaster's managerial style. It is the academic equivalent of the Sports Centre – impressive on the surface and ultimately pointless. A moron could get an A in Media and Cultural Studies, she says, without being taught.

'Good news for me, then,' I point out.

'Oh, don't worry,' she warns, after tipping the last of her mauve concoction down her throat. 'They'll find plenty for you to do. It's that kind of place.'

'What do you mean?'

'The only reason anyone sends their kids to that school and not the comp down the road is snobbery. That's what it is. A snob factory.' Ann's liquid brown eyes grow bright as she warms to her theme. 'The kids aren't going to get a better education. They're possibly going to get a worse one. But their mums and dads don't care. They just like the idea of them wearing a blazer with a little coat of arms on it. Learning Latin. They think they're getting a slice of tradition. No matter that every single tradition in that place was invented by someone in nineteen-flipping-eighteen.'

'All traditions have to be invented sometime.'

She blows smoke at me, momentarily stumped. 'You know what I mean.'

'Well, yes, I do,' I concede. 'I went to the same sort of place.'

'Me too,' she says. 'We didn't go on holiday for five years, just so my dad could afford the uniform. And where's it got me?' Now she blushes slightly and looks down at her knees – embarrassed, perhaps, at having been so frank with a relative stranger.

'Why don't you leave if you don't like it?'

'I—' her voice cracks. She clears her throat. 'I don't

know. Anyhow. You mark my words. They'll hire you to do one thing and you'll suddenly find yourself taking the Year Nines for Social and Personal Development. They've got me doing the cross-country next term. I'm supposed to be getting into shape.'

She underlines this point by stubbing out her cigarette in the ashtray. It occurs to me, and not for the first time, that I quite like Ann. I even like her name – an honest, simple moniker, Ann, not like all these Amethysts and Hippolytas you find down here. In her presence, I can almost forget that I've been hired for the wrong job.

'Fancy another?' I ask. 'Or have you got an aerobics class?'

She looks away again, as she did when I asked her if she liked the hat. I don't think Ann Gorley goes in for jokes.

Nevertheless, I stride to the bar in jaunty manner, aware that I've just done what I've always thought impossible, even as and when it happens. Namely, get talking to a passably attractive woman, and persuade her to have a drink – a thing both trivial and vital.

I glance back at Ann. She's fiercely smoking a fresh cigarette and examining her knees again, pale face bent intently downwards. Ann is what we at school would have called a 'three-pint girl', referring to the amount of alcohol she would need to be bought before being willing to move onto more physical pursuits. In retrospect, the term seems pretty ambitious. It would have been more accurate to call any girl you fancied a 'ten-pint girl', in recogniton of the amount of booze you would need to sink before you could proposition her, and cope with the rejection.

When I return from the bar, Ann is scribbling in the front of her book. She stops as I put the drinks down and the cover curves slowly back. It's the collected poems of Philip Larkin.

'Fond of Larkin?'

'He was a librarian and he died of throat cancer,' she says, as if that was all the answer required. 'It's a present for a friend. In Bradford. He just got stabbed.' She says this with casual nonchalance, as if her friend had just won six quid on the Irish lottery.

'Sorry to hear that,' I say, to which she shrugs.

'He's OK. He dresses a bit alternative, so he's used to it.'

'And you're sending him the collected poems of Philip Larkin to cheer him up?'

'I couldn't think what to get,' she says, defensively. 'What do you send someone who's just been stabbed?'

'Elastoplast?'

Ann stares at me, blinking her long-lashed eyes in disbelief.

It's my turn to blush. 'Sorry,' I throw in, hastily. 'I just seem to say things sometimes . . .'

She tips her head to one side. 'You're seriously weird, you know.'

I've been wrong about Ann. Watching the way her swan-white neck tails gracefully into her wine-dark shirt, noticing the smile lines at the corners of her mouth. She is not quite pretty. She is really rather beautiful.

'I knew someone else like you. Always making weird jokes. He was a Capricorn. What are you?'

'Roman Catholic.'

'That's a joke, right?'

Over the ensuing hour, I discover a fair amount about Ann Gorley, if not quite reaching a point where I can ask her why she is permanently glum. I do discover, however, that she is the daughter of a policeman and a dinner-lady, and that she liked university (Bradford) only marginally more than she liked school. She spent her adolescence in her bedroom, she says, *readin'* and ignoring her delinquent sister, Tamsin.

'See much of them now?'

'Hardly,' she says, wanly. 'That's the point of it, really. I mean, what did they spend all that money for? I can't even be in a room with them without having a row.'

'Row about what?'

'Oh, you know. They're just all so *narrow* up there.' She makes an odd, shrewish face. '*Reenie from the hairdressers saw you and she said I didn't know they let punk rockers go to university.*' The face disappears. 'I *mean*. As if I'm a punk! And who gives a stuff what Reenie in the hairdressers thinks?'

'Well, quite.'

'They put a notice in the local paper when I got my 2:1,' she goes on. 'And whenever I go up there I spend half the time on the phone, trying to book a seat back to London. What was the point of that?'

I can't think of an answer. In my head, the same phrase bounces back and forth. *I knew someone like you, too.*

She's sharing a flat round the corner, Ann tells me, with two Australian girls. She'd been about to move in with someone called Danny, who used to teach at the school. He was the man she said was like me, apparently, the one with the jokes. Her mouth turns downwards at the mention of Danny, and although she says nothing else I get the impresison he did not live up to his promise.

'What about you?' she asks, as we come close to finishing our drinks together, me on my first, she on her Lord-knows-what.

'I was living with someone,' I say, thickly. 'Martha. But she just threw me out.'

Ann flexes her eyebrows in a hieroglyph of surprise. 'Did she?'

This is enough for a strange thought to trot onto the stage, make a twirl and then exit the other side. That Ann Gorley is indicating she might have a *sort of a thing* for me. And even if she doesn't understand my jokes, a flicker of excitement now passes upwards, from my feet to the crown of my head. I think I might like Ealing.

'Do you fancy it, then?'

I snort into my pint. 'Wh–what?'

Ann gives a click of her tongue. 'Were you not listening to me? I said, do you want to come back and have some lunch?'

Ann's definition of lunch appears to be like that of Fleet Street columnists in days of yore. After we leave the pub, we cross a short patch of common and then turn onto the Uxbridge Road. There's a parade of shops by Ealing Common tube, and here Ann goes into a branch of Thresher's. She takes two bottles of Chilean Sauvignon from the fridge.

'Is that lunch?' I ask.

'Last night's tea,' she says, as she pays. 'I'm replacing them before Daisy and Sandra notice.'

Ann's flat stands further down the parade, above a restaurant faint-heartedly entitled 'Pizza World and Curry World – the best of both worlds'. According to Ann, the mozzarella naan is worth trying.

'I've got to sit in this aff,' Ann tells me, turning her key in the door, a little blue-haired troll attached to her key-ring doing a somersault. 'There's a new duvet coming from Heal's.'

'All by itself?'

'It's Sandra's. I promised I'd sit in for the van.'

'Nice of you.'

'I was dyeing my hair last week. Couldn't find a towel, so I used Sandra's sarong. It went a bit of a funny colour. So I sort of owe her one.'

If that wasn't enough, then the flat's interior confirms my suspicion that Ann is the gooseberry in this domestic arrangement. The walls are decorated with framed posters – from dire films like *Muriel's Wedding* and *An Officer and a Gentleman*. On the coffee-table (Conran vase, no ashtray) sit glossy magazines – *Modern Weddings* and *She*, and the inevitable *Putney Properties*. The air smells of scented candles. There is a note tacked to the refrigerator. Ann puts her yellow Thresher's bag on the work surface and pulls this note off. She reads it, grimaces and throws it into the pedal-bin.

'*Hew's been jrinking moi woine?*' she whines, in a parody of the note's Antipodean author. Then she picks a corkscrew from the draining board. 'Honestly,' she murmurs, pulling one of the bottles from the bag. 'Well, that settles it.'

'Who was that – Sandra or Daisy?' I ask.

'Oh, that'll be Daisy,' Ann grunts, easing the cork from the bottle. 'Sandra doesn't even *drink*.'

'She sounds fun.'

Ann fills two highball glasses to the brim and passes one over. The wine is cold, and it briefly answers the gathering stickiness in my mouth.

'Dee-licious *and* nutritious!' I am rephrasing a recent commercial for tropical juice. Ann simply squints at me, baffled. I should have realised she wouldn't know the commercial in question. Girls like her probably pass their evenings listening to Celtic ballads on a battered tape-recorder.

She takes a bag of Doritos from a cupboard, scattering them wantonly about the worktop as she puts them down in front of me. Then she withdraws a tub of hummus from the fridge. The lid is marked SANDRA in felt pen.

'Now they'll both have something to complain about!' she says, with a gawky grin.

'Not too fond of the flatmates?' I remark, as we sit on the sofa.

'It was two other girls at first. They were Aussies, too, but they were all right. Dead alternative, you know. But then they went off to Cambodia. I was going to move out and all. In with Danny.' She pauses. 'And then I didn't. and Sandra and Daisy knew the other two somehow – you know what they're like, they all know each other don't they, somehow? So I just thought they'd be all right.'

'They don't sound particularly all right.'

'No, they're not.' She lets out a long sigh. 'It was, like – I'm the one who's inviting them to come and live with me, and suddenly I'm the odd one out . . . Anyhow, I just stay in my room most of the time.'

'*Readin*?' I ask. She responds by biting her bottom lip with her front teeth and I regret teasing her. 'Must get lonely.'

'Yes,' she replies, pointedly. 'It does a bit.'

Embarrassed, Ann picks up *Putney Properties*. The inside page features the grinning plankton-face of Tim, plus two thousand words by said plankton on the subject of Cambodian food. This is where I decide to get very drunk.

By the time *Countdown* has begun – which is the next time I am truthfully conscious of my surroundings – there are no cigarettes and only a trickle-remnant of the wine. Ann and I are next to each other on the sofa, me angled slightly in the crook of the arm so I can see her and the television. She has her feet up defiantly on the table, the long skirt drawn back to her knees, flashing a length of smooth, pale shin which keeps bothering me. I'm foggily still aware of that moment in the pub – a reedy little voice that echoes again, whenever I catch sight of the crimson tip of her tongue or the sketchy outline of a shifting breast.

One of the contestants on the television is engaged to be married, a revelation that brings a burst of applause from the audience. Ann greets it with a horsy snort. 'Sandra's getting married,' she observes drowsily, indicating the short stack of bridal magazines, upon which the two wine bottles now rest. 'To Trent. He's a manager at Carphone Warehouse.'

I give a grunt and shift slightly, looking at Ann, who is blinking at the television screen.

'I would have married him,' she says. 'Danny. I would've married him. He was . . .' She frowns. 'He was from Wigan, you know. A sweet lad from Wigan.'

'Why didn't you?'

'He had a bit of a drink problem,' she says, ruefully. 'And . . . a few other problems.' Then she straightens herself, readjusting her rumpled top. She gives me a curious, sideways look. 'D'you want to?'

'We've only just met.'

'Did you want to marry *her*? Mabel? Maud?'

'Martha. I think we were just after different things,' I answer carefully. 'We had a lot in common once. But it was just because we were in a funny sort of situation. And when that was over, we didn't really have anything in common any more.'

I hope Martha sees it as charitably. All I can be certain of for the moment is that Ann thinks it very moving. She bum-shuffles along the sofa so she is right next to me. I can smell her – something fresh, like citrus fruits. And wine on top of that – which can be a fine smell, on someone you've started to like.

'And what were you after?' she asks, huskily. She blinks her wide sad eyes just once, slowly.

I realise I am now staring right down the soft valley of her cleavage, and twist my eyes away to the television. My heart is pounding, pumping the accumulated confusion of a dozen cigarettes and a bottle of wine into my centres of reason. I focus on the screen. The contestant who is engaged to be married has just won ten points with the word APPROPRIATE.

I know who Ann reminds me of. She's like Martha when we first met: Martha in her pre-Burberry, pre-sales-target days. A gawkiness going beyond the body and into the soul, into the way she keeps saying too much, too soon, and then being sweetly embarrassed about it. Possessing this in-built allergy to the upbeat, the positive, to all who might dub themselves team players and self-starters. It's the mist-shrouded mystery of the miserable girl, the seductive gloom of the sixth-form rebel from three doors down your road. This is what makes Ann so appropriate.

I plant a kiss firmly on Ann's sticky lips. It makes a comical smacking sound. She looks surprised, blinking as if newly awoken. 'I was starting to think you didn't fancy me,' she murmurs. She pulls me to her with surprising force, then we sink down into the smoky depths of the sofa, just as the word FLACCID appears on the television screen.

I feel her lips raining soft blows on my face, and I wrestle with the silks and velvets covering Ann from the light. One hand trails the smooth warmth of her thigh, the other is inside her shirt. I had dimly wondered, during fallow points of the preceding afternoon, what girls like Ann wear underneath their shirts, had worried vaguely that I might be confronted with some Mary Shelley corset construction, all hooks and bows. Instead I am touching bare breast, that puzzling combination of soft and firm. The shirt slips away, her flesh pale and smooth and not, to my relief, marred by silver studs or tribal markings.

'Oh God,' she moans throatily.

'Mmm,' I answer, contentedly, moving my other hand further up her skirt. Suddenly, I am pawing at the cushions, as she rolls out from under me and lands with a soft thud on the floor.

'Wha?'

She staggers to her feet, supporting herself with the coffee-table. One of the wine bottles falls to the floor. She stands before me, swaying dangerously, her face an ashen grey. 'Wazzat the bell?'

'I didn't hear anything.'

'It's not been working prop'ly. I'll have to putha door on catch or delivery man carn ger . . .' she mumbles, the words trailing off into a toxic hiss. She hiccups and weaves towards the door. I sit upright, my stout member twitching irritably beneath my trousers.

'Couldn't we leave it a few minutes?' I ask, tetchy at having my lust thwarted for a duvet delivery. 'Five, say.'

'No,' she insists, thickly. 'I've fuggorrit twice already. Jusswait there.' I rub the back of my head as she gropes out of the room.

There is a painful bang from the hallway and then an

equally dreadful silence. I wait for a moment, and then, when nothing happens, stumble to my feet. Bear-like, breathing gluey flumes through my nose, I lumber to the doorway.

In the hall, Miss Ann Gorley lies like a twisted star on the carpet. There is a decadent indignity about her, a queen punched to the floor at her own coronation. I shamble across to her and haul her upright by one wrist. Her small head lolls back dangerously on its long neck and there is an angry red mark on one cheek.

'Ann?' I shake her gently. Her head drops to her breast, crow-black hair flapping sideways. I shake her slightly harder, panicking now. 'Ann!'

'Wha?' She opens a bleary, accusing eye.

'You had a bit of a fall,' I explain gently, sounding like a nurse enquiring about recent bowel movements. 'Are you all right?'

Ann lets out a gassy belch and tells me to fuck off.

I ignore this and kneel down to her level. I put a hand on her leg, shaking her again. 'Do you want to stand up?' I ask, loudly.

Ann shuts her eyes and shakes her head.

I give a long sigh. This is one of those moments where we apprehend the true nature of God. Not the touchy-feely God of the Gospels; this is the God who plagued the Israelites, a bearded Philip Larkin in a long nightdress. A malevolent Old Fart who takes pleasures in stuffing things up most regally.

'Aw Christ,' Ann moans. She hunches her knees up, turning her face to the radiator on the wall.

'Ann—' I begin.

'Jus' sod off!' she screams at me. 'Go away! I never wanna see you again!' Then she gives a single sob before falling silent. She remains that way, numbly facing the wall, rocking gently, no matter what I say, until I pick up my jacket from the sofa and let myself out. The delivery man is outside as I stumble onto the street.

Meet Mr Lucifer

'**Y**ou could have Cordy's room while she's in Zanzibar. I don't know much about the other girls. One of them's a Haskayne. The Norfolk Haskaynes, of course, not the Lancashires.'

'God forbid.'

Tara gives me a stern look as she taps her cigarette. 'You know, if you gave people a sparrow's fart of a chance you might find they weren't like you thought at all. Cordelia's *very* down-to-earth.'

'Please don't say that.'

'I'm trying to *help*, Alastair.' Tara looks away irritably as a waitress comes over. We're sitting, on an unreasonably hot September morning, in the FullaBeenz coffee-shop on Ealing Broadway. 'Oh, hello. I'd like a cake, please.'

'We don't do cake,' says the waitress. 'Just drinks and sandwiches.'

Tara gives me a baffled look.

'She means a Coke,' I interpret. Tara's life currently consists of a triangle, the corners of which are formed by Rajasthan, Eaton Square and Monte Carlo, and living within it has made her sound posher than ever.

While the waitress goes off to discuss us loudly with her colleagues, I remind myself to be extra-nice. After all, Tara did offer to come and meet me when I rang her up. She's never stopped trying to help. It's just that I'm in a quite unhelpable mood. I've got my staff meeting in half an hour and I'm feeling sick.

'It's good of you to try and help. I've actually got a flat already.'

'Have you?' She crosses her legs, revealing nut-brown ankles and a pair of jewelled sandals. 'Round here?'

'Well, it's not a flat, exactly. More of a B&B. Mrs Danischewsky's. It's all right.'

'Polish?'

'Irish.'

'Of course. Silly me.' She wrinkles up her nose. 'And you got the job. Well done.'

My mind hovers like a carrion crow over this festering subject, because I got the wrong job, a job I know nothing about and a job working alongside someone who recently drank herself unconscious as I was trying to seduce her. But over the last couple of weeks I've settled on a basic head-in-sand approach to that one.

'Well, that's why I wanted to see you . . .' I start hesitantly.

'And I thought it was because you still loved me,' Tara says, skimming my hand with her own. She doesn't mean this, of course. It's just her way. She's always been one of those girls who regard flirting as a basic courtesy.

Other things about Tara have changed. She used to favour little black cocktail dresses at any hour of the day, but now she wears linen *shalwar kameez*, and her hair is done up in a sort of pre-Byzantine bun. This must be to please Mr Sammaddi, who is the principal reason behind our meeting.

'I need a reference from your husband,' I blurt out. 'There was a bit of a mix-up at the interview, you see, and the headmaster sort of got the impression that I'd . . . you know . . .' I trail off into sheepishness.

'*Well*.' Tara raises her eyebrows and lights another cigarette. 'You're your father's son, aren't you? False papers and all that. I'm surprised he couldn't have fixed you up a little job with some of his friends.'

'I wouldn't want one, Tara, even if he could.'

'All right, Alastair. No need to get shirty. I'm in the same boat as you, remember. Both got our little skeletons. And, Lord knows, *someone* never lets me forget it.'

'Someone?'

'Amjie. Every time we have a barney he brings it up. My rotten little father and his dubious publishing outfit. "Just remember what you were doing before I picked you up from the gutter" − all that.' She leans closer. 'Compared with me, darling, you're descended from a hero. If I were you, I'd be dining at Quaggers every night on the strength that Daddy was a spy.'

'Do you want to say that a little louder?'

She dips her head. 'Sorry, Allie.' She looks up. 'Sorry. You want a reference. Shouldn't be a problem.'

'Really? You mean he'd do it for me?'

'Do you mind not blowing your smoke over me?' A small blonde with a pert nose leans across the aisle. She's wearing a sort of tweedy Forties suit with a beret.

Tara surveys her coolly. 'We're sitting in the smoking section, actually.'

'Well, I'm not,' replies the tweedy blonde. 'Actually.' *I'm nhat*. A husky voice with a trace of the transatlantics.

'Well, I can't help the properties of smoke, can I?' Tara asks loftily.

'Any more than you can help being a snotty bitch. No, I guess not.' The blonde girl picks up her coffee cup and stands. She ignores Tara and trains a pair of cold green eyes, pebbles from the bottom of the Baltic, onto me. 'Good luck,' she says. 'You're going to need it.' She moves seats. I watch her skirt moving against the backs of her knees.

'God, I hate the bloody English sometimes,' Tara says.

'I think she was American.'

The blonde girl has only just sat down again when a car horn sounds from the street outside. She looks out of the window, where a chunky man is sitting at the wheel of a battered old Mini. Her face turns from irritation to joy in a split second and she runs out of the café to greet him.

'You seem to think she's altogether rather fascinating.'

'No, I don't.'

'Well, stop staring at her arse, then. Honestly.' Tara opens her handbag and withdraws an electronic organiser. She taps a few keys and then looks at me with a solemn expression. 'I'll see what I can do. But you'll have to do something for us. That's the way it works, lover.'

'Of course.' I say this, but actually the comment surprises me. Tara's never been like this before. Some of Sammaddi's business acumen must have rubbed off on her.

She proceeds to tell me something that surprises me. Namely that her husband has recently tried to buy Eton College and been turned down. Now he wants to buy another English school. Any one will do, she says, as long it's faintly posh.

'He's been in a terrible mood ever since Eton,' she says. 'Absolutely impossible. Keeps finding fault. Won't eat. Headaches . . .' She stops herself. 'Anyway, I do love him, Allie, really I do, but he's going to make a terrible tit of himself if he tries to buy St Paul's or Winchester or something. He'll just get turned down again and get even more depressed.' She takes a deep breath. 'That's where *you* come in.'

'I'm not sure how.'

'You can help him to buy Lorry's. Don't you see? The place is practically bankrupt. So Davenport says, anyway. Amjie could put in a nice low offer and rescue the place and then he'd be a jolly good chap.' She pauses, a misty, sad expression passing across her feline face. 'That's all he wants to be, poor lamb: a jolly good chap.'

'Well, how am I supposed to help him?'

'Well, you could, you know, get us some inside gen. Accounts, financial info . . . that sort of thing.'

'But that's industrial espionage, Tara! It's insider dealing. Or something. And if this Davenport knows so much, why can't he get you the info?'

She sighs, patiently. 'Number one, because Davenport's strictly old-school-tie. It was *his* school and he simply adores the place. And, number two, because . . . well, he'd never do anything to help my husband. Bit jealous, you see. Always had a library crush on me up at Durham . . .'

I interrupt her. 'I'm sorry, Tara. But I just can't do it. It's illegal.'

She gives me a look longer and dryer than the costliest Martini. 'So, I believe, is obtaining false references to work in a school.'

'Yes, but . . .' I run out of arguments.

Tara smiles at me sweetly, leaning forward and squeezing my hand. 'I knew you'd see it my way. You always were such an understanding boy.'

I run through the gates as the bell tolls. The first glimpse of the school – its brooding stone buildings and its sweeping drive – skewers me with assorted doubts. I felt just this way when I was in my last year of junior school and my parents drove me past St Mungo's, the Jesuit–run stockade where I was shortly to serve a seven–year stretch. They'd said things like 'You'll be coming here in a few months.' And I'd kept silent in the back, thinking, No, you're wrong. I'll never be old enough to come here. And I think these things still, now fully grown and stubbled, one of Mrs Danischewsky's paying guests.

I like Mrs D, who comes from County Clare but married one of Ealing's sizeable Polish contingent. She's one of those Irish ladies who seem to be permanently enjoying a private joke. And her house is handy for the school. Twenty minutes' walk – ten or so if you can find a bus. But that doesn't mean I want to stay there. Much as I like Mrs D, there's something sad about the communal feel of life in her house – the lingering smells of womanless men, the flowery counterpanes. Sometimes, it's just a little too *Ealing*, too much like that lodging house Stanley Holloway and Alec Guinness share in *The Lavender Hill Mob*, a place where men pay the price for not being very good with women.

As I run past the playing field, the albino site developer, Bunny Warren, is on the short steps to the Portakabin. He wears a fluorescent yellow vest over his rudely checked suit, a white helmet on his head. He waves as I run past the building site. Shovelling mortar a little way down is a gang of curly–haired, Balkan–looking men. They are bare–headed and, unlike Warren in his protective armour, toil merely in faded denims. A couple of them glance up almost fearfully as I approach and then, seeing that I am more or less no one, continue their labours.

Entering the main school, this morning's poached egg reconstitutes itself into a peach–stone of dread. The corridor smell – disinfectant and a million shoes – hits me. I know the feeling that comes with this smell. It's the one that came when you smelt the interior of your pencil case after a long absence; that gripped you as you tried on a new term's anorak in the final days of August.

The heat of the early September sun has turned the staff room into a greenhouse. As I enter, it's like stepping from an aeroplane onto the tarmac of some impossibly tropical country. Forty faces turn, sunflower-like, to greet the pink flush of my face.

The staff are draped about the room in attitudes of deep boredom. There are not enough armchairs to go round, so those lower down the food chain have adapted coffee-tables and stray cushions to their needs. The floor is a forest of arms and legs, the air rich with the odour of teachers – spilt coffee and ancient jackets, dry-cleaned but once a term.

I peer through the fug, scanning the faces for one I dread. The dark-fringed face of Ann Gorley has visited my dreams for the past week, a bruised eye squatting on the china-whiteness like a Technicolored reproach.

The headmaster is standing next to an easel, upon which he has made many complex drawings. He waves me into the room, smiling. 'Just squeeze in there for a moment,' he suggests, pointing to a bare patch of floor. 'I'm sure LSD will show you his notes.'

I slot myself next to LSD, a thick-set young fellow in a hairy green suit, who affably waves a sheaf of printed notes in my direction. I stare at the notes. A header at the top of the page reads THE HAT PARADIGM – CHALLENGE STRATEGIES FOR THE MILLENNIUM MANAGER. Someone, presumably my neighbour, has been drawing cobwebs in the corners.

'Lawrence Davenport!' he hisses, holding out a hand.

His face, flanked by copper-red curls, somehow contrives to be handsome as well as very fat. So this is Lawrence Davenport, son and heir to the Earl of Chertsey and fancier of Tara. He rolls a pair of brown eyes supportively at me, as the Head recommences his lecture. I tune in.

'And finally, the Brown-hat response. As you can see on page ninety-two, I have borrowed a little cartoon from *Tribune*.' The headmaster pauses. I glance around me. In the entire room, only one man, a small, grey-bearded creature with furtive, private-looking eyes, thumbs busily through his notes. Nobody else moves.

'Brown-hat takes a problem . . . sorry, a *challenge*, but in trying to implement his challenge strategies he only unearths all the other problems . . . er, challenges, around it. I'm sure,' and here the headmaster gives a scheduled laugh, 'we have all been guilty of this in our time.'

The little bearded man – one of the few staff sitting upright in his chair – gives his wad of notes a disagreeable flick. 'I really don't see what this has to do with teaching the lads.'

The headmaster meets this inflammatory statement with a beatific smile. 'Page forty-four, AS. Page forty-four. Where are you on your Belief Spiral?'

'For God's *sake*, Headmaster!'

'Itself, if I may say so, AS, a classic Brown-hat response. Now, shall we try a little Green-hat?'

'Yes, but—'

The Head holds up a slim hand for silence. There's less of the TV talk-show host about him today. His grey hair has been cut and side-parted, and he reminds me of the muscular types who used to model thermal underwear in 1970s catalogues.

'I've let things run on. As the Dutch epigrammist Cees Noteboom said, "Spend too long on the pannekoeken and the snerp will grow a skin." There's still a great deal to process.' And with that, he begins to fold up the easel.

Davenport leans in to me. 'That's Scarsdale. Deputy HM,' he murmurs with beery breath, motioning to the bearded man.

As I feared, the head's next piece of business is to make me stand up and then introduce me to the room. 'This is AKS, who will be teaching MCS,' the headmaster says, before turning to me with a faint bow. 'Perhaps you'd like to say a few words about yourself?'

I clamber to my feet. In a thin voice, sounding like some swotty cousin you were always being unfavourably compared with, I mumble something about being very glad to be here, and looking forward to meeting everyone in due course. Few of the staff – except for Davenport, who smiles, and Mr Scarsdale, who shoots me a suspicious stare – even look up. I sit down, relieved. Relieved because, unless she is lurking behind or underneath some furniture, Ann Gorley is absent from this morning's proceedings. And this pleases me a lot.

There is one other new teacher joining this term, Mr Smaut – a fresh-faced graduate with a Christian symbol on his bomber jacket. He manages to do a passable imitation of the Mekon: mostly forehead, with his face occupying that tiny area normally taken by a chin. He now takes the stand and gives a barely audible version of what I just said.

Scarsdale, bristling in the corner, appears to take immediate and great exception to Smaut, though it is hard to imagine a less offensive creature. 'Did you say your first name was *Adam*?' Scarsdale enquires. His voice has a bleak estuarial twang to it: Essex or the chilliest reaches of the Northern line.

Mr Smaut answers in a soft whisper.

Mr Scarsdale tuts sharply, undoing the top button of his mud-brown jacket. 'No middle name?'

Mr Smaut shakes his head, this time with a hint of apology. I feel quite sorry for him.

'Well, what are his initials going to be?' Mr Scarsdale asks, of the entire room. 'If he signs a notice AS, people are going to think he's me, or *that one* over there.' He jabs a rude finger in my direction. 'Or I'm either of them. It's hardly on.'

'Maybe he won't put any notices up,' Davenport offers, cheekily. 'Far as I can see, Scarsdale, you're the only one who ever does.'

'That's not the point. What if . . . here, Mr Scarsdale waves a furtive little claw in the air for inspiration, 'what if he started up a club or—'

'Are you *intending* to start any clubs, Mr Smaut?' Davenport interrupts with an air of playfulness that does not pass unnoticed among the other staff, who rub their mouths and smirk into their notebooks.

Mr Smaut shyly ventures that he is quite interested in setting up a Christian Union.

'Well, you can't. We're non-denominational,' rasps Scarsdale, unkindly.

This proves too much for the headmaster, who has hitherto observed the proceedings with studied detachment. '*Mister* Scarsdale,' he says, reproachfully. 'Thank you. I have applied a little Green-hat thinking to the challenge in hand. I went to the trouble of downloading a printout of your last pay-slip.' He withdraws a folded piece of paper from his shirt pocket. 'You are, are you not, Mister Arthur *Richard* Scarsdale?'

Scarsdale flushes under his beard and mutters something.

The headmaster continues. 'Then we have the solution at our very fingertips. Mr Strange shall sign himself AKS. Mr Smaut will now sign himself AS. And the master *formerly* known as AS −' he smiles warmly at Scarsdale, 'that's you − will henceforth sign himself ARS.'

Davenport titters softly to himself as the headmaster folds up the pay-slip and returns it to his breast pocket. Scarsdale exits the room, fast and furious − an event causing no more than a ripple of surprise. As the door slams, the headmaster clasps his hands together in an attitude of composure. 'Other business,' he says, brightly.

I try to concentrate, but as the headmaster moves away from detailing the manner in which the first year is to become known as Y7, and onto the subject of whether sarongs are acceptable wear for a Dress Down Friday, my attention begins to wander. I wonder about Ann Gorley − if she's suffered some calamity, or if she never makes it to the staff meetings. Perhaps librarians don't come to the staff meetings. Perhaps she's found a new job, gone back North, got back together with Danny. I just hope we don't have to see each other again.

My attention returns round about Item 6.6.7, which deals with the introduction of a new period into the timetable, the 'I'm Not OK' hour, during which the boys can approach a designated member of staff in confidence, about their problems. Or, failing that, work quietly in their classrooms.

'Fuck about in the library, more like,' observes Davenport, *sotto voce*. I grin back.

The headmaster catches my eye. 'That's tremendously kind of you, Alastair. I was just going to say that I wanted to kick things off with one of my younger team. So that's splendid. I've got some literature back in my office.'

The headmaster goes on to say that, as a feature of his new 'culture of approachability', he is declaring an open-door policy in his office, so that every member of the school – boys and staff alike – may feel empowered to pop in and have 'coffee and a natter' with him. Or at least an appointment to do so.

I'd better book one straight away. I rub my forehead in alarm, wondering how I'm going to acquit myself as the school's new therapist. I barely understand the curriculum, let alone the psyche of the adolescent boy. I glance for support to my only ally in the room, Mr Davenport, but he is studiously resetting his watch.

The headmaster is now running through the school rules, some of which he feels are long overdue for *perestroika*. Whistling in the corridors, for instance, is an anachronistic vice – defunct in an age when most boys are plugged into MP3 players. Similarly, the ancient prohibition on eating chips in the streets. 'I think we had better say chips, burgers or other types of snack,' declares the headmaster, with the self-satisfied manner of a Gorbachev sweeping aside state monopolies, 'excluding gum – bubble or chewing – which is permissible outside lessons as long as the residue is disposed of in an approved manner and in accordance with EC recycling protocols. Any objections?'

After an hour or so, proceedings are concluded with a promise to issue every member of staff with a pager before Prizegiving Day. Nobody, apart from me, treats this with more than weary indifference. After a somewhat limp cry of 'Forward, Team Lorry's!' the headmaster announces that there are sandwiches and fresh coffee in the canteen. This provokes a different reaction. Everyone jumps to their feet with smiles, lively chatter buzzes around the room and there's a sudden scramble for the door.

Davenport claps a hand on my back. 'Come on,' he says, briskly. 'Scarsdale will eat all the effing salmon if we let him.'

The canteen has a pungent odour of vinegar – less like a bottle has spilt somewhere and more like whole kegs of the stuff are used daily to swab down the floor. But nobody apart from me seems bothered. The staff assume a joyous, liberated air as they munch on sandwiches and swap jokes, standing around in little knots, or seating themselves at trestle tables set with big pots of hot coffee.

'Aah, AKS,' the headmaster cries, just as I'm about to take an extremely tempting cream slice from the trolley. 'I trust that wasn't too bewildering. And thank you for volunteering to take the counselling sessions.'

'Well, I—'

The cream slice disappears into the face of Davenport.

'I did want a brief natter with you about your references. I've been unable to trace this Mr Ridout person. The last time I tried, my call was diverted to a gentleman at the NatWest bank who said he was rather keen to contact Mr Ridout himself.'

'Oh dear.'

'I'm not so concerned about that. It's the other reference I'm keen to see. From Amjit Sammaddi? If you could ensure that it's desk-side soonest?'

'It's what?'

The headmaster blinks at me, baffled, as if I'd admitted

to not owning a set-square or knowing who the Chartists were. 'Desk-side, AKS, desk-side: on my desk.'

'Well, there might be a small—'

The headmaster bends down and squeezes my shoulders in a manner that is quite upsetting as well as not being clear why. 'Don't stand here talking to me,' he exhorts, breathing peppermints in my ear. 'Go and mingle with your team-mates. *Bond*. Establish networks of mutual reciprocity.'

After a few half-hearted attempts to join in other people's conversations, I find myself ghettoised in the corner with the other new teacher, Mr Smaut of the mighty forehead. Smaut proves to be a great pain, because he speaks only in that hushed murmur most people reserve for art galleries and the sites of recent accidents. In addition, he has the habit of starting to say something every time I open my own mouth to speak. My thoughts are turning to escape, through a window if necessary, when the tree-stump presence of Davenport appears at my elbow, with a tray of sandwiches.

'You're Tara's friend, aren't you?' Davenport asks as soon as we are alone. 'She said you might be applying for a job.'

I nod and smile.

'You fucking bastard,' is Davenport's suprising response to this.

'Pardon?'

But Davenport's not looking at me. Instead he is disgustedly thumbing his way through the plate of sandwiches. 'That *shit-stain* Scarsdale,' he confides, in a low voice, 'always does it. Every September. Stages a walk-out so he can get up here first and eat the bloody salmon.'

I comment that the atmosphere between the headmaster and his deputy suggested considerable animosity.

Davenport agrees. 'Scarsdale wants his job,' he tells me. 'Christ knows why.'

'You wouldn't yourself, then?'

'Rather be a sodding librarian,' Davenport declares. 'Speaking of which, did you hear about our librarian? Miss Gorley?'

'No?'

'Had a bit of a fall, apparently. Broken some bones. Might not be coming back. Bad show.'

'Awful,' I agree, breathing an uncharitable sigh of relief.

'Nice girl,' Davenport muses. 'Bit odd. Intense type. Sort of girl, you know, looks like her idea of a great night is a flask of cold Lapsang and a Russian novel. All right, though.'

I try not to think about Ann Gorley and focus upon my new companion. I think Davenport is going to be my friend. He is nearly as wide as he is tall, and he is not particularly tall. He is also ruddy-faced and prone to winking, like those seedy cavaliers you find on the walls of steak-houses. He says *rum* for 'room', and probably, should the subjects arise, *tuthbrush* and *Rumseaagh*, whereas poorer mortals would content themselves with 'toothbrush' and 'Romsey'. But he lacks entirely the pained aloofness of those high-borns you see goose-stepping up and down the King's Road. I know why Davenport is Tara's friend – because, like her, he combines two qualities very few people can: posh and nice.

'Haven't seen Tars properly in yonks,' Davenport reflects, sadly. 'She's always got that odious poet with her. You know – the Indian?'

'Her husband, you mean? Amjit Sammaddi? Yes. I met

him.' I am doing my best to sound worldly. 'He's buying the *Evening Herald*, you know.'

'Is he?' Davenport looks as if he had been wearing a monocle which has just popped out from his eye. 'Well, more fool him. My father says it's going down the pan. And more fool Tars for picking a chap like him. She was always much more fun before she met him.'

'She said you'd met at university. Durham, wasn't it?'

'Spot on,' Davenport says. Then he sniffs the air in a sheepish fashion and says, 'Six years up at Durrers. Then straight back here. Rather sad, isn't it?'

Returning to work at your alma mater doesn't strike me as being better or worse than what I've done, rootless and holed up in some B&B at an age when most people are getting engaged. 'It's good to stick to your roots,' I say, encouragingly. 'If you've got any.'

'More like tentacles in my case,' Davenport murmurs, glumly twirling the thick gold ring on his little finger. He seems prone to violent changes of mood.

Fortunately this new mood is interrupted as the disagreeable leprechaun Mr Scarsdale scuttles across, balancing a clipboard, an ancient briefcase and a plate of salmon sandwiches in his hands. 'Davenport,' the old man hisses. 'I'm getting up a petition!'

Davenport distractedly takes the clipboard from Scarsdale's hands.

'I'm opposing the Head's decision to make me use the R,' Scarsdale explains. 'I'm going to take it to the Governors.'

'I don't see the problem,' says Davenport with his mouth full.

'A-R-S!' the bearded man spells out. 'Arse? Imagine

55

what the lads will do with that! Arse. *The* Arse. Arsehole. Hairy Arse. Arse Wipe . . .'

He would clearly like to carry on, but Davenport places a restraining hand upon his arm. 'I've been signing things LSD ever since I started here,' Davenport notes. 'And the boys just call me Ginge. So I shouldn't worry. What do the boys call you now?'

'Shit-head,' replies Scarsdale solemnly.

I give an unintentional cough.

'Well, then,' replies Davenport, comfortingly. 'Lorry's boys have great respect for tradition. I should know, eh, Alastair?'

Before I can reply, a short, curvaceous woman with an unruly mass of dark ringlets drops her handbag on the floor next to us. Its contents spill everywhere and the woman, in bending to recover them, adds her own spectacles to the tangle on the floor. We – Davenport, Scarsdale and I – bend down to help her recover them.

At last, she sits at the trestle with us, breathless and apologetic, fumbling with a series of dark cardigans and shoulder-throws. Cloaked in these fringed black garments, and staring wildly through the greasy lenses of her glasses, she has the air of an inefficient witch. But one you could find yourself fancying. She is introduced to me as Rosie Kastrafitis, Maths.

'How went the hols, Rosie?' Davenport asks, casually. 'Any fun?'

Rosie launches into a long account of a journey to visit relatives in Cyprus, which was marred by illness, family feuds and every other disaster short of hijack. I consider fetching more coffee, but it seems a little rude. By the time Rosie has listed the final tragedies of her holiday (her mother's suitcases ended up in Aleppo and Rosie was detained at Customs), Davenport is openly yawning and Mr Scarsdale polishing his spectacles with the end of his tie. I try to change the subject, by asking if she lives close by.

'I was sharing with these Irish girls,' she tells me, 'but one of them stole all my CDs and when I called the police they all ganged up and said I was a heroin addict and I ended up being strip-searched and when I got back they'd had the locks changed.' She gives Davenport a pointed look. 'So now I'm not sure what I'm going to do.'

'Awful,' I sympathise.

Rosie Kastrafitis laughs as if I'd just said the wittiest thing ever. 'Oh, don't feel sorry for me,' she says, tossing her hair about, her lips parted. 'I'll manage. I always do.'

Davenport shrugs as she moves off, her shape a slowly gyrating, erotic egg-timer of scarves, pashminas and ponchos. 'I suspect our Rosie was hinting she'd like to rent my spare room.'

'I'm sure you'd like that,' Scarsdale observes drily. He puts on his spectacles — a large lensed apparatus giving him the overall appearance of a bottled curiosity in some medical museum. 'Always had a soft spot for her, haven't you?'

'Most certainly have not,' Davenport says hotly. 'The girl's a walking disaster. And an energy sponge of the first order.'

'A what?'

'Oh, you know, Scarsdale. One of those types — spend a few minutes with her and suddenly you've lost the will to live.'

'The gentleman doth protest too much, methinks.'

'Think what you like,' Davenport snaps. 'Frankly, I'd rather rent my spare room to a Mormon.'

'I'm sort of looking for a room myself,' I venture boldly. 'Not that I'm a Mormon or anything.'

Davenport treats my comment to no more than a vague jowly nod, as if my looking for a room and his own search for a tenant were mild coincidences, beneath civilised attention. I am embarrassed.

The embarrassment increases as my companion stands up, stretches himself and says he ought to be 'tootling along'. There's been no outward change in his manner, but I watch him shamble out, feeling I've been dealt a snub. *These people*, says a smug interior voice. *In two minutes, you were tugging your forelock. But then you got above yourself, didn't you?*

As Davenport ambles away, I notice Scarsdale now looking at me across the table in a way that's not very pleasant. At some point in the intervening seconds, he has swapped the foetus-in-a-jar spectacles for a fresh piece of eyewear that might look better on a young studious girl, but not much. 'So you're this Strange, are you?' he asks.

While I am confirming this, he withdraws a folder from a cracked leather briefcase resembling the skin of a leper, and takes out a copy of my c.v. He reads the document, clicking a retractable biro on and off all the while, as if itching to write 'See me' somewhere. Finally, he emits a baleful hiss and demands my teaching certificate.

'I don't have one. The headmaster said—'

'Ho, let me guess,' Scarsdale interrupts. 'On-site train- ing to the right results-driven individuals?' I nod and Scarsdale gives a final dissatisfied click of the pen-top. 'And did he tell you who'd be responsible for the training?' I shake my head. Scarsdale jabs a thumb uncouthly at a small printed timetable taped inside the folder. 'MCS,' he grates, 'fifteen periods a week, coloured pink. Same as English. Any idea why it's got the same coloured ink as English?'

'Because they're a bit similar?' I venture.

Scarsdale repeats this to himself, the way teachers always did when they asked you where your tie was and you answered, 'In my pocket.' 'Media and Cultural Studies comes under the domain of English,' he spells out. As his temper rises, his London accent becomes increasingly brutish. I'm reminded of Dickie Attenborough as the diminutive gangster in *Brighton Rock*. 'So I'm the 'ead of Department, see? *I'm* your boss. Not Mr Harpenden. OK? Me.'

'Pleased to meet you.'

Scarsdale ignores this, which is probably for the best. 'He had no business interviewing you,' he tells me, charmlessly. 'None at all. But then, that's just typical. Ho, yes. King of the Hill, isn't he, when it comes to shaking hands and meeting the parents and conning a few cheques out of them so he can build his . . .' He stops himself, a muscle twitching within his beard. He tosses me a photocopied booklet. 'Since you're here, you might as well read through the syllabus,' he snaps.

'That would help.' But any sarcasm is lost on Mr Scarsdale.

I glance through the booklet. It's much as Ann Gorley suggested – a course that entails little more than watching a bit of TV and reading a few books. The course is broken up into modules, which have rather intimidating titles. There's 'Troubled Pasts: Songs and Poetry from Northern Ireland', which sounds as much fun as walking down the Falls Road with steel weights tied to your scrotum. Then there's 'Gazing Ahead: Visions of the Future in Fiction and Film' and 'War and Peace: British Cinema

1939–1959'. But if these titles give me cause for concern, I'm more relieved to read the sample exam questions. It seems like the Board went out and had a boozy lunch on the day they were dreaming up the final exam. One question reads: 'What views of the future have been presented in the books you have read?' Another presents the yawningly unchallenging challenge: 'Do you think old films can have a message for modern audiences?' A cinch, in other words, whether the boys should happen to be extremely dim or otherwise. I am cheered up. I can do this.

'It all looks very interesting,' I answer, carefully, closing up the syllabus booklet and placing it on the table between us. 'Are there any sort of textbooks I could be having a look at?'

Scarsdale looks as Evelyn Waugh might have done after an hour or two on a Club 18–30 holiday. 'Of course there aren't any textbooks!' he spits. 'It's a donkey course. A complete joke. Just tape stuff off the TV for your sixth-form set. Read a few sci-fi novels with the Year Tens. And I'll do the Irish poems. We'll review things after a term or two.'

'OK,' I reply, in an eager, hopeful tone. Put like that, Media and Cultural Studies doesn't sound too terrible.

'Just so's we're absolutely clear . . .' Scarsdale says, leaning across the table. He's now assumed a 'we-don't-think-much-of-Lunnen-folks-round-here-see' tone normally reserved for the point where the pub landlord in the Thirties film suddenly stops being charming and warns the hero not to ask any more questions about what he saw in the orchard. 'If I had my way, we wouldn't be teaching the thing at all, and I certainly wouldn't have hired someone whose last job was editing a magazine that nobody's ever heard of. But we'll have to make the best of a bad lot, won't we?'

'If you say so.'

The thought strikes me that it would be nice to make the best of Scarsdale's beard by removing it slowly with a piece of blunt glass. I dismiss this satisfying notion, thank him and rise to leave. I'm close to the canteen doorway when Scarsdale calls after me.

'One more thing.' I turn round to face him. 'You might have a chance here if you don't get mixed up with the likes of Davenport. If you don't manage to ruin yourself, he'll do it for you.'

The Gaunt Stranger

Back in the porch of Mrs D's, my door keys have sneakily teleported from the pocket where I always store door keys into some pocket where I never store anything because I didn't know it existed. I'm just mounting a second search, when the front door opens in front of me. A milky youth of seventeen or so stands there, holding a slobber-ridden dinosaur in his hands. This can't belong to him – I assume it's one of Joe's. Joe is the serious-eyed toddler Mrs D seems to look after on a more or less permanent basis. There are always reasons for Mrs D looking after Joe, entailing various cousins who are poorly and further cousins who have to make urgent trips to lawyers and dentists and Ballykelly, but I listen to these explanations, as I listen to much of what Mrs D tells me, politely, and not understanding quite why she's telling me.

'Coming in?' the youth asks, softly.

I've met the other residents – mostly commercial travellers, in for a night or two and always out by the time I get up. So it's not clear who this boy is. Maybe he's another relative of Mrs D – like the earnest Joe, part of the endless genealogy of niece's cousin's brother-in-law's boys. But she's never mentioned this person. And she's a woman given to mentioning most things. I know all about her sister being a martyr to psoriasis.

I thank the boy, who hovers in the hallway, taking a thin grey jacket from a peg. He gives me the unsettling sensation of having stepped into a black-and-white film. Not only is he wearing black jeans and a grey jumper, but his neatly cut, side-parted hair has that half-tone quality, impossible to call a colour. If he were not wearing trainers, he might be a studious boy-detective from a 1940s flick, off to do brass rubbings and in the process unmask a gang of swarthy smugglers. I wonder if I'm dealing with a ghost.

'Someone called for you,' the boy says, touching his thin nose. A bland, Southern accent, not too posh, not trying to sound like a Yardie and equally bearing no relation to the Western brogue of Mrs D. 'She brought this round.' He indicates a low elephant table next to the staircase. On it stands a cardboard box. I recognise familiar objects within. A souvenir ashtray from Speke Hall and an Elvis mug which, before Martha put it in the new dishwasher, used to illuminate upon contact with hot beverages.

'Martha was here?' I ask, eager for details. The boy frowns and seems about to say something. But at this point, Mrs D can be heard coming up the driveway with the pushchair, a mixture of religious song, rustling bags and traffic impersonations from Joe preceding her. The noises seem to throw the boy off track. He nods vaguely and steals away into the kitchen.

Upstairs, in my chastely narrow bedroom, I unpack the box and forget all about the ghost in the hallway. This is not hard to do – the business of seeing your possessions gathered together in a box that once contained family-sized bottles of fabric softener raises its own sorrowful spectres.

There's my video collection – a recent phenomenon,

consisting of a few dozen old films on Woolworth's tapes. My St Mungo's scarf – a striped bumblebee affair which was always too itchy to wear and was redeployed in Fulham as a draught excluder. A T-shirt brought back by my parents from Switzerland and appropriated by Martha for sleeping in. I nearly sniff it, but some fragment of dignity prevents this.

I try to see the box as a good sign. It marks a closure, the end of my life with Martha. I won't keep it, I decide, or any of the things in it. I'll take it out to the bins at the side of the house. Then I can face the future.

Until now, I've only thought mechanically about the new job, been on auto-pilot and in that state done all that's necessary: found lodgings; purchased – from the Amnesty International shop – a smart fawn-coloured overcoat to match my new shoes, before realising that I still lack a decent suit.

Shaving in the mirror each morning, to a background of little Joe's squawks and bubble-blowing, I've also practised teaching. I've perfected a reasonable, authoritative approach, which sounds a little like Radio Four. I know my foibles – a tendency to speak too quickly, to sound rasping if I raise my voice – and I've worked on them.

But the real business lies in the distance. Legends of ineffectual teachers, carried off mid-term by ambulance, never to return, are something everyone shares. How will I silence chattering, rebuke the impertinent? There are such things as 'natural teachers'. Brother Constantine, my old headmaster, he was one. Rarely raised his voice, he was trusted, ex-pupils came back to visit him, and he didn't even have a nickname. Did Brother Constantine start like me, nervously praying for guidance? Or was he just born a teacher? What if I become the stuff of legend, stretchered, frothing at the mouth, from some Babel of boys?

The boys. I've not considered them much either. They occupy the same space in my mind as my funeral and giving up drink – inky future-points that will blot the present if I let them. What am I going to teach them? I've glanced at the curriculum and seen something about visions of the future, something else about old British films. I remember what Scarsdale said about taping stuff off the TV. But the video recorder belonged to Martha.

Then, as my thoughts return to Martha, and via her to the box on my bed, the route ahead twinkles in a sudden shaft of glory. I look at the labels on the sides of the videotapes. *The Magnet. The Blue Lamp.* I've got dozens of films. Sitting at home – in my old home – while Martha was out being proactive and confident in the winebars of south-west London, I taped that whole season of Ealing films: *Whisky Galore!, Hue and Cry* – even the more obscure titles like *Cheer, Boys, Cheer* and *Frieda*. The whole collection has found its way back to Ealing and I was about to throw it away, not realising that it's my lifeline.

I decide to celebrate the new beginning with a cup of tea. So I head downstairs, past the china clowns and pigs in the alcove. On the table in the hallway, on top of a grubby pile of bean-stained bibs and colouring books, is something else for me – a note scribbled in biro. Perhaps I missed it when I picked up the box.

Ginge here. Sorry don't always catch on – mean about sp. room. Want to meet up in MacKendrick Arms this l/t? Turd pub but only one no 6 Form. About 1?

The Happiest Days of Your Life

'**M**r Scarsdale, being fellated by a PVC-clad Ann Widdecombe, while Captain Birdseye takes him from behind.'

Davenport, looking like a fat emperor in his purple dressing gown, is hunched on the floor feeding scraps of last night's pizza to the dog. He looks up, shakes his hair and nods. 'Missing a trick there. Replace Captain Birdseye with Ann Widdecombe's identical twin sister. Have to have some sort of device strapped to her, I suppose. Or perhaps not.'

'You win,' I concede, stuffing books into my bag. It's twenty to nine and there isn't time for any more of our early-morning routine. 'I'll buy the first round tonight.'

Davenport, now picking flakes of mucus from his dog's eye, gives a grunt of dissent. 'No sesh in the Mack tonight. You haven't forgotten, have you?'

'Oh God.'

'I'm doing this for your benefit.' He puts the last piece of pizza into the dog's jaws and then straightens up. My housemate is wearing nothing under his dressing gown, just a pair of striped boxer shorts which, regrettably, leave little to the imagination.

'I've got it all worked out,' he continues, excitedly, reaching for the orange juice. 'I'm meeting Corky in the

66

Chelsea Farts at eight-thirty. You come along too. And then we sidle off to this gallery thing in Flood Street. Meanwhile you have met the lady of your dreams and are on your way to the Seventh Realm of Nirvana.'

'I wish you'd tell me who she is.'

'That's right, Cinna,' Davenport croons, crushing the dog's cheeks between his hands. 'Silly man wants all the mystery taken out, doesn't he?'

He looks again at me, eyebrows knitted into a skein of disapproval. 'She is a young professional like yourself. That is all I will say.'

'She doesn't teach at our school?'

'No. She's a local girl, but she doesn't teach anywhere.' Davenport muses privately for a second or two. 'Dresses a bit odd sometimes, I'll tell you that much. But then, you're hardly Beau Brummell yourself, are you?'

'What's that supposed to mean?'

'I'm simply saying you'll have a few things in common. You've both got funny accents.'

'What's funny about my accent?'

'Oh, Alastair, sod off, won't you? I want to be on my own for a moment or two.' His face assumes the pained expression of a tired parent. 'Is that too much to ask?'

I move into the hallway. After a month of living here, I'm used to my friend's sudden changes of mood — particularly in the mornings. Davenport's waking mental state has much to do with the mood in which he went to bed on the preceding night, which is almost always one of boisterous high spirits. Last night involved an attempt to make cocktails shortly after the *News at ten* — an experiment not limited by there being nothing in the house except Dutch lager and lemon squash.

Cinna — a cross between an Irish wolfhound and an

Alsatian, and embodying the stupidity and violence of both breeds – senses someone out in the hallway and, despite knowing it is me, starts barking.

Davenport answers the dog in an indulgent tone. 'Yes, boy, thank you for telling me. You're calling for reinforcements, aren't you, my gorgeous feller?'

The next stage, I know, will involve Cinna hurtling out into the hallway in attack mode, jaws gnashing and claws skittering on the tiled floor. If he is lucky, he will get a grip on the hem of my once-smart overcoat and then we'll be here for easily another ten minutes, me trying to entice him to release me with all manner of doggie chews and soothing entreaties.

To bypass this, I shout a word of farewell, nip smartly out of the front door and begin the journey to school. In the porch there's a short postcard from my father, written in the intricate, spidery hand of someone who's spent a lot of time using invisible ink. I read the card as I head down the driveway. Its message is short, wishing me well in my new lodgings. It also says that my father is setting up a local Neighbourhood Watch scheme, but that he's having trouble getting people to join.

Local MP was the rudest [reads the latter section of the card]. Slammed the door in my face, practically. I blame Thatcher. No fan of Bolshevism, as you know, but at least we had some sense of community before she came along. Mother says are you keeping warm . . .

It does strike me that, whatever cankers might be eating at the heart of civilisation, Mrs Thatcher cannot be blamed for the failure of my father's Neighbourhood Watch. If people are reluctant to join, it might have more to do with the fact that, as an ex-spy who speaks fourteen languages, my father is something of an unknown quantity in our neck of the woods. Merseyside is not where you'd expect to find the man who surreptitiously brought Dubcek to power. Which is, of course, exactly why P. P. Strange, my father, chooses to live there.

I pick my way down the driveway with caution, strewn as it is with damp leaves from the chestnut tree. At the gate, I glance back at the house. It stands alone, a white-painted, veranda'd villa at the end of Balcon Road, backing onto the school's old tennis courts and the swimming pool.

The house represents, as with many of Davenport's gestures, a touch of grandeur which he has neither the resources, nor the worldly nous, truly to carry off. His ownership of it is akin to the way he will sometimes go into a pub, call for champagne and then, should it be brought, suddenly find he doesn't have any cash. Only a Hollywood stuntman would contemplate standing on the veranda, and few of our windows have been wiped this side of the Macmillan government. In the grounds sits a rusting Mini Cooper, which Davenport says he is licensed to drive.

But Davenport says lots of things. He says he has a girlfriend. Possibly this is the Corky person I am to meet tonight, possibly not. Davenport is vague on this subject as upon all others, and nobody ever comes round to the house. That bit, at least, is understandable.

I do *like* Davenport, though. He is moody, illogical and the possessor of the sort of High Tory opinions that would get him lynched on the average university campus. But while he might scream at you for leaving the milk out of the fridge and call you an unconscionable cunt for using up the last of the hot water, he might just as easily make you a three-course feast when you've had a dog's arse of a day. When I first moved in, I was struck down with a case of flu straight out of the pages of Dostoevsky, and Davenport's response – without words, without a hint of wanting thanks for it – was to lend me his second-best hip-flask and fill it with his very best brandy.

I could almost do with a swig of that brandy now, as a Vladivostock-style wind blows from the common and into my very gums as I trudge to the bus stop. I always get the bus these days. Nine times out of ten, the bus makes me very late, but I endure this because I like looking at one of my fellow passengers.

I first saw her on the day of the staff meeting – in the FullaBeenz – the girl who was angry with Tara. She's a small blonde, thirty or so, with pixie features and high cheekbones, and a few times a week she turns up in the middle of the 291 wearing some outfit that could have come straight from the pages of a yellowing *Picture Post*. Her face is pink and fresh, and she's always reading a book with fierce concentration. This is invariably a crime novel of a certain, distasteful forensic character, replete with dismembered seamen and morbid discharge.

I have theories about the Bus Girl, all of them endowing her with some job that's more diverting than my own. She's an actress, for example, scouring the literary canon for heroines she could play. I expect she'd play them very well. That doesn't mean I fancy her. I've never gone for pointy noses, even if their owners do have very interesting green eyes and little disarming patches of pink on the cheekbones. And I never stare at the girls I fancy. I ignore them, because someone once told me that this was the best way to make them interested in you. Judging by the lack of success I've had with this tactic of seduction-by-disdain, this someone must have been a hell of a lot better looking than I am. But still, you stick with what you know.

The bus arrives and I barge the doors, withdrawing a handful of loose coppers, crusty tissues and conkers, all of which fall through my fingers and onto the floor. Various people groan and sigh – irritated, but not quite to the point where they might do anything to help. Once I've recouped about a third of what flew forth from my pockets, I pay the driver and squeeze into a wafer of space, next to a damp youth with a cough like a lost hyena.

Last night, I was re-watching *Passport to Pimlico*, a film I'm showing to my sixth-form set after lunch. And it occurred to me, as lovable Mr Pemberton fell down the open bomb crater, how often the Ealing writers used clumsiness as a device to make their heroes likeable. Ealing's men are perpetually dropping things, falling down open manholes, standing on stray roller-skates and receiving nothing but love in return. I wish it could be like this in life. Instead my own untreatable apraxia – whenever I stumble and fumble – seems only to make enemies.

I grit my teeth as another burst from Coughing Boy goes straight to my ear-drums. I shift position slightly and descend into my usual commuter trance.

'Do you mind?'

The voice comes from somewhere below and to the left of me. It's the Bus Girl, beret-less and her golden hair arranged in some complicated Forties film-star roll on the top of her head. I didn't notice her in the crush. Today the book is an old penny-shocker type, entitled *The Case of the Creeping Death*.

She isn't speaking to me, but to an acne-scarred straphanger next to her, in a suit whose pin-stripes speak of many things – city bonuses, weekend skiing trips, great arrogance. He blinks irritably.

'Not much, sweetheart. Do you?'

A few people around us smile sheepishly. But Bus Girl sets her mouth into a hard line.

'Can you stop banging into me?' The same American twang I noticed in the FullaBeenz – just barely audible in the way she says *stap*. 'It's really annoying.'

The pin-striped man shrugs and ignores her. Gradually, the interest dies away. I try to catch her eye, but she buries herself in her book. I look at my feet.

'Are you doing this deliberately?' She's snapped at him again as the bus turns a corner and we all veer to the left.

'It's the bus,' the man says, all mock innocence. 'I wasn't doing anything.'

'Yes, you were.'

'Not my fault if you're having a Bad Hair day, darling.' The man grins at the onlookers. 'Or maybe it's the wrong time of the month . . .'

There are a few intakes of breath, mine included. The patches of pink on her cheeks turn a shade darker.

'Listen, pineapple-face. If you rub that thing of yours against me one more time I'll fucking pull it off!'

There's a ripple of laughter. A spontaneous noise of approval from the tall black girl by the doors.

It's the man's turn to go red. 'In your dreams,' he says, oafishly, just as the bus stops and the doors swing open with a hiss. The atmosphere is an electric soup. The bus driver is not letting the new passengers on, just leaning out from his cab and staring down the aisle. Everyone wants Bus Girl to make the next move – hopefully with a pair of pliers. But she doesn't. She swears under her breath, slams her book shut and storms off the bus. I follow her – but it is my stop.

As the bus pulls away she stands there, catching her breath, a faint glimmer of moisture in her eyes. This time, I succeed in catching her glance.

'It's not even my goddam *stap*!' she says. 'I'll have to walk now!'

'I'm sorry about that.' She looks at me now, her eyes still alight with fury. 'I was on your side back there.'

The green eyes narrow into a fine beam, three thousand volts of unadulterated contempt, aimed straight at the soft tissues of my brain. 'You were on my side, were you?'

'Well, yes,' I falter, with a faint laugh. 'He was a twat. Wasn't he?'

'If you were on my side, *buddy*, why didn't you say something?' she demands hotly. 'Why didn't you *do* something, instead of standing there admiring your reflection like you always do?'

Assemblies at St John Lorimer's are occasions of immense formality, veiled in all the pomp and mysticism with which some Micronesian tribe crowns its king. At 8.45, a bell will ring and two black-gowned prefects take their stand by the entrance. At 8.47, the headmaster rounds the corner from his office and the prefects fling the doors wide. The school rises as one while the headmaster mounts the stage. As he puts his notes upon the lectern, the boy in the lighting box directs the spotlight onto him. Harpenden surveys his dominion, letting the spotlight play on his tanned skin. He nods. The school sits, with a mighty whoosh of trouser fabric.

There follows an edifying parable, cobbled from some handbook to which all teachers, everywhere, have access. I recognise many of their naughty protagonists from my own schooldays: the assorted little sods who cried wolf and said why bother.

After this, the headmaster sits on a leather chair, while a piece of nasty music is played. As the boredom of the boys reaches its peak, the headmaster stands again to read out the notices. The first part of the notices consists of congratulating boys for the honours they have received; in beating Dulwich College at fencing, for instance, or in proceeding to the finals of the Capital Radio 'Build a Hovercraft' contest. The second part consists of bollocking them for the things they have not done.

The only respite from this routine is Friday morning's Master's Assembly, when a teacher is given rein to conduct his own, free-form address to the school. Last week Davenport stomped disdainfully onto the stage and made the boys listen first to some breakneck techno music, then to The Inkspots, in order to show them that their elders do not necessarily know better. This piece of sedition was upstaged by Mr Scarsdale, swooping down upon some romantic fifteen-year-old who had his girl-friend's scarf knotted round his wrist.

This morning, the evangelist Mr Smaut has dragooned a group of first years (or Year Sevens, as we are meant to call them) into enacting a moral playlet, concerning the perils of computer games. Tucked away at the back, I'm finding it almost impossible to hear and see the tiny, mumbling figures on the stage. So I'm watching my colleagues instead.

As the play reaches its conclusion – this being that computer games induce neglect of friends, church and homework, leaving the players open to further vices, such as crack and devil-worship – I glance along the row and note that not one of my colleagues is paying attention. To my left, the curvaceous Rosie Kastrafitis is filling out an insurance claim, having parked her Fiat Uno dangerously close to the building site last week. She wears a thick, foreign scent, making me think of slightly horny postal clerks in Central Asian cities.

I was disappointed when Davenport said the mystery woman wasn't a teacher. Because, some mornings, like this morning, I've glanced at Rosie Kastrafitis, at the fluffy curls on the back of her neck, and the way her unironed skirts ride up to reveal a healthy portion of matronly thigh, and thought I wouldn't mind. Though not quite enough to do anything about it myself. Lust can be an honourable feeling. But this Rosie-lust is not. It's a tremulous, weedy feeling – the whine of some mosquito that we cannot sleep through, but can equally not be bothered to get up and kill.

Rosie, perhaps sensing my gaze, looks up from her forms and gives me a shy smile. Davenport, seeing it himself, kicks my ankle. He thinks it very amusing that Rosie smiles at me like this. Sometimes he imitates it when he's in his cups. Possibly, I think, remembering how Mr Scarsdale teased him on the day of the staff meeting, he might be jealous.

To distract myself, I look away from Miss Kastrafitis and down the auditorium to somebody who doesn't arouse me in the slightest. Several rows down, sitting with his form – a collection of cowed-looking fourteen-year-olds – is Mr Scarsdale. He scans his row continually, looking for signs of wrongdoing. Today, this action is hampered somewhat by a thick, white neck brace, which Scarsdale has been sporting since last Wednesday, when he – allegedly – slipped and fell on a patch of untended lasagne in the canteen. It is rumoured that he now has one of the city's costliest silks mounting actions against the school.

Davenport, squeezed uncomfortably into a seat right next to me, wakes from what appears to be a very pleasant dream and licks his lips. He smiles at me and then frowns. 'Hope you're going to put something smart on tonight, old chap,' he murmurs out of the corner of his mouth. 'That tie's strictly below-decks.' He gives me his lost-monocle squint. 'You'd better not be trying to back out again.'

I still don't understand why Davenport is so keen, so desperate even, to fix me up with a date – unless he's just fed up of having me around the house. But I am nevertheless looking forward to this evening. My teaching career has, as yet, not been marred by any disasters, but it's still such a novelty as to leave me whimpering with fatigue at the end of each day.

I've not become the target of the boys' scorn; indeed, some of the younger ones are prone to greeting me in the street – even at weekends, in the bloody shopping mall – with shrill cries of 'Sir! Sir!' But there are tensions I never imagined. There is the continual noise, that clamour of shoes and shouts, slamming doors and scraping chairs, that rings in my ears long after I've turned off the bedside lamp. There is the smell – the reek of confined youth – that I find impossible to purge from clothes and hair. And there is the matter of my supervisor, Mr Scarsdale, whose supervision consists of sitting at the back of my lessons two or three times a week and taking detailed notes. None of which he passes on to me.

There's also the fact that, in becoming a guardian to the young, you surrender your days to the most tedious and insane preoccupations. I'm still recovering from yesterday's lunch-time. During which, starving and impatient, I had to resolve a bitter feud, which began when a slow boy called Spofforth swapped a SIM card with the deadly Whittaker twins, and half an hour later realised he'd received nothing in return.

As the headmaster reads out the notices, I locate another reason to look forward to the weekend. The first of the school's new 'I'm Not OK' counselling sessions, chaired by yours truly, is to take place this afternoon, in the Deputy Headmaster's office. Scarsdale has successfully campaigned to force these sessions out of the timetable and into the realm of extra-curricular activities, from four till five p.m., to be precise, an hour when I most care to be rushing homewards with a few cold cans under my arm and least care to be anywhere near the human boy. I'd managed to forget this until the headmaster read it out. It does not help that Davenport sees fit to accompany the news with a great deal of playful nudging.

The nudging continues, to such a degree that I'm only half-concentrating as the head moves on to announce the return of a much-missed member of staff. 'I trust,' he says, 'you will all join me in welcoming Miss Gorley back to her duties. In fact, I think a school cheer might be appropriate.'

'Christ, she's back,' I murmur involuntarily. Davenport shoots me a curious look.

I gaze fixedly at the stage as Ann limps onto the podium and gives bashful waves, her silver ring glinting in the spotlights. The boys erupt into loud cheers, accompanied by wild clapping. From the rows containing the sixth form, a few wolf-whistles are added to the mayhem – at which point, Mr Scarsdale stands up.

'*Don't spoil it!*' he shouts, pointing in the direction of the whistlers. A bitterly short man, Scarsdale possesses the sort of voice God used when casting Near Eastern nations into oblivion. The cheering turns, in an instant, to fearful hush. I can hear my heart beating. Ann is peering across the hall, her brilliant white teeth biting down on her lower lip. Her sights have homed in on me alone.

As Assembly ends, and the boys rush for the exits, eager to savour a few minutes of the open air before lessons begin, I am among them, pushing and shoving my way towards the door, elbows stuck sharply outwards to fend off the competition. I don't care if it's an unseemly way to behave. My concern is to put as much distance between myself and Ann as possible. She's walking up the aisle towards me.

There is a bottleneck at the doorway, but I'm making some headway by charging at the boy in front of me with my shoulders. The knot of tightly jammed boys is about to give, when another godly bellow from Scarsdale rends the air. 'You lad!'

Lad? The knot vanishes, the heaving boys shuffle apart and I stand alone, the centre of a guilty circle as Scarsdale trots towards me up the aisle.

'What did you have for breakfast?' demands Scarsdale, furiously. '*Hooligan Flakes*?'

I sigh. In four weeks, Scarsdale, whose many pairs of spectacles are clearly not the spectacles they once were, has accused me some eleven times of being a pupil, and on three occasions rebuked me for walking on the grass. Davenport is running a sweepstake on how long I will last before my parents are called in.

As the boys around me slip away, smirking, I sigh again.

'I'm one of the *teachers*,' I point out. 'Mr Strange, remember? We've met a few times.'

This makes little difference to Scarsdale. He wanted a word with me anyway, he says, donning a pair of half-moon glasses which lend him the look of a little Yiddish-speaking tailor. I notice with annoyance that Ann is now very close.

'Can't it wait?'

'No, it can't,' Scarsdale replies. 'I'm about to go and check the sixth form for hair gel.'

'Well, what is it?'

'These counselling sessions of yours,' Scarsdale says, narrowing his beady eyes, the eyes of some especially mean-spirited turkey. 'You've got to rename them.'

I say distractedly that I quite agree. I don't much care, and not just because they aren't *my* counselling sessions. Ann is next to us now, some new, musky perfume announcing her presence.

'I think "I'm Not OK, *Sir*" would strike the right note,' Scarsdale says. 'And I don't want you using my office. The Geography Room's free. All right?' This last utterance is a challenge rather than a question, and when I say nothing to it Scarsdale follows the direction of my glassy stare to its source, Ann. 'Miss Gorley,' Scarsdale says warmly. 'Glad you're back.'

With a stiff bow, a courtly dipping of his beard in the librarian's direction, and a disproportionately poisonous glare in my own, Scarsdale is gone. I look around. Ann and I are alone in the auditorium. Her smile fades along with Scarsdale's departing footsteps. She has only a little eye-liner on, but enough of it to make her seem like some avenging presence in a vintage horror film. Around her right eye, however, there is still some evidence of bruising. My awkwardness is so strong I can smell it.

She opens her mouth to speak, but before any sound comes out, a scholarly voice interrupts from behind.

'AKS. Might I just have a brief natter?'

I swing round from Ann and find myself looking at the headmaster, resplendent in the sort of eggshell-coloured suit which, if not quite fit for a king, would certainly be within the price range of the average duke.

'I'm sorry to sound tiresome on the subject, but I still haven't received your references . . .'

Cheer Boys Cheer

I spend most of Friday mornings in the staff room, filling
out forms that ask me to rate my pupils' performance on
a scale of one to five, and further forms that ask me to rate
my own performance at filling out forms. I've only one
class to teach, the period right before morning break, but
this is undoubtedly the worst. Form 4L is a notorious
grouping of fourteen-year-olds who keep up a steady hum
of chatter as I attempt to teach them the subtler points of
Brave New World, and bolt for the Tuck Shop several
minutes before I have finished doing so. Officially we are
now supposed to call them 10L, but this is a form to
whom the usual rules do not apply.

Davenport calls them 'the Ferals', a term that not only
sums up their refusal to join civilisation but is also a fair
appraisal of their collective smell. They come to me
directly after PE and, being at that age when showering is
viewed as so not cool, they resolutely stink.

I teach them doggedly, talking just above the level of
the chatter, and standing close to the open windows. I
drink Scotch when I mark their essays, which are
desultory and grudging in tone, knowing that the Ferals
will do badly at Media and Cultural Studies. But they will
do equally badly at everything until they are released into

life, when, I suspect, many will flourish as slum landlords and pornographers.

I have acquired this cynicism swiftly and it does not extend to the other boys I teach. Nor did I go down, in the case of the Ferals, without a fight. After my first lesson with them (during which I sent the entire form out of the room, twice) I tried to speak to their form teacher, a Mr D. Laycock, but subsequently discovered that he was the man found dead on Ealing Common. They are currently under the nominal supervision of the headmaster – which means being under no supervision at all.

After my failed attempt to contact Mr Laycock, I tried having a man-to-man word in the ears of the most unruly class-members, hunting them down at break-time so as not to embarrass them in front of their peers. Their response to my lecture was to fix me with a sort of streets-of-Trenchtown stare, kiss their teeth and mutter various phrases like *Babylon* and *ras claat*. Which would be forgivable if these were deprived, south London teenagers, but less so when you consider that at least two of them have mothers who make documentaries for Channel Four.

This having failed, I approached Davenport for some advice on controlling them. He smiling at me serenely one break-time through the crush of the main corridor, thought about it for a second, then said this: 'Go for the little PFT on the front row. The swotty one who's always got a tidy pencil case and copies down everything you say. Even the jokes.'

'Go for him?' I queried.

Davenport nodded. 'Rip the absolute living shite out of him,' he said. 'If you want the toughs at the back to respect you, bollock the PFT.'

PFTs, in Davenport's unique system of classification, are

boys who deserve Points For Trying. They work hard and worry about tests. There are other types, too. DGPs (Daddy's Got Pots) are rich boys, to be shouted at with extreme caution, since the daddies in question are usually in the process of paying for a rowing machine or donating some wartime engravings to the History Unit. NTBs are slow boys – Not Terribly Bright; while RQBs – Really Quite Bright – are the effortlessly clever.

PIA boys, meanwhile, are those boys whose parents would prefer, on principle, to send their children to local state schools, but are too nervous of the end product. The typical PIA parent does something at Radio Four, or is a psychoanalyst, and Davenport, with the aristocrat's natural hatred for the bourgeoisie, tolerates all but them. PIA parents are always on the telephone saying that the school is stifling their son's individuality, and hence the initials – Pain In Arse. 'Send the little bleeder to Bedales, then,' Davenport is given to grunt after such clashes with a PIA parent. 'But of course they couldn't bloody afford it, not with their sodding villas in Tuscany.'

Davenport's advice about bollocking a PFT was passed down with such assurance that I swallowed it whole. I spent the second and third lessons with the Ferals seeking out my target. There is indeed a boy who sits in the front row, whose work is neat, if uninspiring, and who scans my face for the duration of every lesson. Peter Histon is his name. He is a slight, but large-headed boy with protruding eyes. On charitable days, I think of him as a goldfish – at other times, when I've spent too much of the night previous in the MacKendrick Arms, and the world subsequently seems irritating and grotesque, Histon seems more like a foetus, with barely formed hands and pale veins at his temples. But in spite of his low aesthetic appeal, and his reedy voice, I bear him no ill will.

Today's lesson, however, sends my charitable principles straight out of the open window and replaces them with a philosophy that is purest Jungle. I've found and photocopied an article in the *Independent*, all about the former Soviet government's attempt to re-educate left-handed children. I pass these around at the start of the lesson and ask the boys to read them. Ten minutes later – during which time I've confiscated the latest issue of *Knave* and dissolved a violent bag-fight – I ask the class if they have any comments.

One boy, a whippet-thin, freckled creature from Gunnersbury, is actually waving his hand. This pleases me. I glance briefly down at Peter Histon, his mouth opening and shutting in silent, fish-like concentration.

'Sir, it's like off *Logan's Run*, sir, isn't it, sir?' says the freckled boy at the back. A sigh catches in my throat. It's a reasonable, if useless, comment, and it ought to be encouraged. Especially as this particular boy, Spofforth, has never volunteered anything in a lesson so far.

'Yes, Spofforth, it is a little like *Logan's Run*. But what is the specific relevance to *Brave New World*?'

'Sir?' Spofforth looks at me blankly.

'*Brave New World*,' I say again, more loudly.

Spofforth shakes his head, mystified. 'Is that the one with Samuel L. Jackson in it?'

The class explodes into laughter. Spofforth glares hotly around him and punches a few of his neighbours. I call for quiet.

I continue calling for quiet throughout the lesson until, five minutes before the end, a chorus of watch alarms signals the impending arrival of break. I am interrupted mid-sentence as boys begin packing up their bags. I've had enough. I look down at little Peter Histon on the front row and see, to my profound annoyance, that even he has started to zip up his pencil case. A hot snake of anger flicks from my rectum to my jaw.

'Going somewhere, Histon?' I demand, imperiously.

The class, shocked at this unfamiliar tone, falls eerily silent. Histon ignores me utterly, now leaning down to the side of his desk for his bag.

I swallow my saliva, feel my pulse throbbing. Now is the time, the sacrifice of the PFT. 'Put that bag down!' I command.

Histon looks up at me, smiles and continues to unzip the bag, a smart navy affair bearing the QPR logo.

I cannot believe it: openly defied, by the geek of the class, Histon, the fish-boy, the foetus whom I had spared and pitied. I step down from the podium and snatch the bag from the boy's hands. 'I said *put it down!*' I bark. 'Are you deaf, lad?'

Histon's eyes widen in terror. There comes a faint titter from the back of the class. A freckled hand shoots up, irritatingly, at the fringes of my vision.

'What is it, Spofforth?'

'Sir, he's my cousin, sir,' says Spofforth, helpfully. 'And, yeah, he is deaf.'

The lunch-time bell sees me scurrying towards the headmaster's office. I'd normally be heading to the MacKendrick Arms on the average Friday lunch-time, but today I've got a serious mission, a mission made all the more urgent by my earlier natter with the headmaster. He made it plain, while skirting gracefully around the issue and making me feel like an honoured guest at his wedding, that if I don't get him a reference letter soon,

I'm going to end up in charge of the lettuce at Burger King. And that, in turn, means I'm going to have to break into his office and steal some confidential information from him.

I'm not feeling great about myself as I head down the corridor. The way I handled little Histon has left a sour taste in my mouth. I tried to say something to him, but the first rush of boys down the corridor prevented this, and as his classmates rose in their lust for crisps, he vanished in the stampede.

The last classroom I pass as I leave the building contains Davenport, with one of his tiny sixth-form sets. They haven't rushed out at the first trill of the bell, and the sight fills me with envy. Davenport sits up on a desk, a yard of mottled flesh showing over the tops of his tan Chelsea boots. His sixth-formers sit round him in a circle, their books and faces open to him. Davenport says something and there's a chorus of laughs. He makes it all look so easy.

Crossing the courtyard, heading towards the headmaster's building, I put my regrets about Histon on hold. There'll be a time, I tell myself, a happy time when my job is safe, when I can go to the boy and make peace. I hold my breath as I enter and tread carefully, fearful of discovery. But I know it should be safe. The headmaster takes his lunch on first sitting and the secretary has been put on part-time due to some financial crisis of which few will openly speak.

I steel myself, glimpsing the brass door-handle of his office as I mount the stairs. This is the threshold of decency. Then my hand is trembling on the door-handle and my breath creaks in my ears.

Suddenly the door swings inwards and the headmaster stands in front of me. My first instinct is to bolt away and, if caught, deny everything. Luckily something prevents this.

The headmaster shows not a flicker of surprise. 'AKS!' he declares happily, as if AKS had rowed over from Friesland just for this meeting. Then he glances at his watch. 'I suppose I can call you Alastair. Since we're into the lunch recess. I assume you were looking for me?' Before I can answer, he sweeps me towards the staircase. 'Shall we natter as we walk? You were lucky to locate me. I normally take first sitting on Fridays.'

'Yes,' I say miserably, thinking only of the filing cabinets behind the retreating door and my thwarted mission. It's plainly not going to be as easy as I thought. Which shows that I didn't think about it enough.

'My wife has returned from an extended visit to Rotterdam. So we're going to grab a bite together. I assume you've come about the counselling sessions?'

This could be a useful cover story. 'Well, yes. I'm not sure about it,' I begin. 'I might not be very good at it. I've already managed to upset one of the—'

'That's splendid,' replies the head, patting me warmly on the arm. 'It was, was it not, Terhooft who said "the man who fears his limits has none to fear"?'

London is home to an especially confused breed of people – those who, in spite of dwelling in places such as Kensal Rise, refuse all food but sushi and recline each night on futons to read manga novels. The headmaster suffers from a similar sickness, but his psyche has not travelled quite so far as Japan. It might be called the *folie hollandaise* if more people suffered from it. Thankfully, they don't.

'Perhaps it was Bakhuizen van den Brink,' concedes the head. His mobile phone rings, playing a digitised version of 'Tulips From Amsterdam'. He answers it, then covers the receiver with a hand. 'My wife. You'll have to excuse me.'

He departs across the courtyard, seeing me off with a wave that could, in all senses of the word, be described as gay. I'm just thinking about heading back into his office, when Davenport attempts a rugby tackle on me from behind.

'What are you doing out here?' he demands. 'Bishing to the Archbeako?' And before I can answer this satisfactorily, or even at all, he deals me a dead arm. 'Coming to the Mac? Course you are!'

As we pass towards the main gates, into the shouts and clamour of the nearby building site, Davenport stops dead in his tracks, batting at my arm. 'School ghost!' he hisses.

We stop dead-still and watch while an angular boy drifts in through the gates, alone. He wears a shapeless grey suit, and his side-parted hair is damp, as if only recently tamed after a long sleep. Expressionless, he ignores us, though most boys wandering into the school at this hour would exude the guilty air of the truant.

I am transfixed, certain I've seen him before. 'Who is he?'

'Never found out what the little bleeder's name is,' Davenport replies, shaking his head as we watch the boy disappearing down the side of the Design and Technology building. 'Don't know who teaches him. Nothing.'

'I'm sure I know him . . .'

Davenport looks back at the departing boy. 'I doubt that. No one speaks to him,' he remarks, sadly. 'I just hope the skinny little sod *is* a ghost.'

An open-top roller-skate of a car now zooms through the gates. Its lady driver seems to have been designed by the same team responsible for the car. She's in her forties, ash-blonde, with a slim cheroot in her mouth and her hair flapping at us as she briefly glances in our direction. One of those women who have A levels in scorn. She returns her attention to the road and stares ahead, just a faint smile on her lips. She revs the engine a fraction too forcefully as she sears off down the path.

'Gizzler,' comments Davenport.

'What?' I ask, as we watch the woman park her car in the alcove reserved for the headmaster and the bursar.

'Dutch for Gisela,' Davenport elaborates, leading me away down the road. 'Gizzler. She's the HM's wife. Come on,' he urges, impatiently. 'You really oughtn't *stare* like that, chum. It won't get you anywhere.'

I deny all charges. 'I was curious,' I protest. 'I don't *fancy* her.'

'No?'

'Absolutely not,' I answer. 'Too old.'

'That lady,' he points over his shoulder in the direction of the car park, 'is the *Stuffit* princess. You know Stuffit Dot Com? The self-storage racket?' I nod. 'Her old man,' Davenport continues, while we cross the busy road, 'came to Holland from East Germany with a couple of salted herrings in his pocket. And look at her. You'd think she was born to it, wouldn't you?'

'You seem to know a lot about her,' I observe. Davenport's grasshopper mind rarely stays upon one subject for longer than a few seconds, and this potted biography of the headmaster's wife sets a new record.

'Ahh.' Davenport makes a vague, musical noise. Then he pats his belly. 'D'you know, I could eat a turd on a bun. That's how hungry I am. And I don't much care for buns.'

*

Afternoon lessons are approached in a haze accompanied by soft belches as my frame does its best to cope with a predominantly liquid lunch. Thankfully, the afternoon is a double period taken up by my sixth-form set. A collection of affluent peacocks, they never give me any trouble, instead treating me like some idiosyncratic handyman for whose services they are faintly grateful. This could have less to do with my teaching skills and more to do with the fact that the other sixth-form set are enduring the twin horrors of Northern Irish protest poetry and Mr Scarsdale. My lads – did I just call them that? – seem to appreciate what they have been spared.

We are working our way through the Ealing comedies, so that, by the end of the year, they will be able to grapple questions like 'Can old films have a message for modern audiences?' So I've arranged for the caretaker to set up the video recorder in the classroom. On the first two attempts, he brought a cassette player and then a beautifully preserved set of van de Graaff generators, but this week he's scored a bull's-eye and the TV's there on its stand, at the front of the room.

'Been in the Mac, sir?' says one of the set. This enquiry comes from Miller, a handsome, dark-haired youth whose friends call him Posey. Miller's father, I'm told, owns a string of pubs across west London and his son already lives comfortably from their fruits. He drives a brand-new VW to school and is always immaculate in a series of tailored suits. He could easily pass for twenty-five, as well as a bastard son of Tyrone Power. I often suspect that Miller has a highly paid job and merely calls into the school as a networking activity.

'I've been marking,' I answer, sternly. 'Lost track of the time.'

'That can happen,' Miller says, affably.

There's something about easy people that can make me very uneasy. Miller – whom I'd probably classify as one of the pupils I actually like – is one of these people. To cover my discomfort, I put the tape of *Passport to Pimlico* in the machine. There is a resentful murmur as Jerry Springer is replaced by a blank, blue screen.

'Watch carefully,' I remark, as the credits begins. 'I'll be asking questions on this.'

'Are we going to be marked on them?' asks Demetriou, a hawk-faced youth who is known to vomit if given unfavourable scores. I sigh inwardly. Of all my sixth-formers, I feel the least affection for Demetriou. He is a twitchy, unimaginative sort, taking Media and Cultural Studies as a fifth A level, it being his aim to follow his brothers to some respected business college in the States. He shows no interest in anything other than the marks he can score, and his opinions in class are distressingly unremarkable.

'Just try to enjoy it,' I counsel.

Demetriou looks profoundly puzzled at the idea.

Passport to Pimlico was released in 1949, a year when Britain was still preoccupied with the privations of war. This theme, of a community united by suffering, runs through the entire film. The opening sequence is a shot of some ration books, encased in a memorial wreath, with the words 'Dedicated to the Memory of . . .' displayed above. I wonder if anyone will see fit to note this down. To my surprise, Demetriou is waving at me. Joy of joys!

'Yes?' I ask, hopefully.

'Why do we have to watch another old film?'

I clench and unclench my fists a few times, hoping this might calm me down. Unfortunately, it merely fans my desire to see Demetriou pegged out in the staff car park, ravens pecking at his eyeballs.

'Not everything old's crap,' Miller retorts. 'Is it, sir?'

I feel a stab of warmth towards Miller, who has unwittingly hit upon the core issue of the whole course. 'Why do you say that, Miller?'

'My dad's got a 1978 Jag,' Miller offers. 'And it cost him a packet.'

'That'll be why you like wearing flares,' interjects the boy next to Miller. This is Booth, a colossal boy with a permanently open mouth and a big, rubbery face. He often reminds me of something dredged from the snows of a glacier.

'When have I worn flares?' Miller demands to know.

'Last Friday,' Booth declares. 'In Bar Cuba. I was *with* you, man!' He turns his case over to the class. 'Big, like, velvet loons, man. A total batty-man.'

Miller's face reddens as a gale of mocking laughter wafts his way. 'They were *wide-leg*,' he hisses, angrily. 'So you can wear them with a Cuban heel.'

'Flares, man,' repeats Booth, belligerently. 'Total, like, bait flares.'

In answer, Miller grabs Booth by the neck, tucking his head under one arm in a flawless move. '*Bwoy, a gwan buss up ya fierce!*' he declares, and proceeds to knuckle-jab his victim in the mouth.

Sensing I may have lost control here, I shout that nobody in my class is to buss up anyone's face, thank you. Surprisingly, this works. Miller releases Booth, who sits back, rubbing his thick neck resentfully.

'Thank you, Miller,' I say, aware of sounding very teacher-ish.

'Least I don't think Ermenegildo Zegna's, like, the total, like, height of style . . .'

'That's *enough*.' I turn the volume up on the TV and, gradually, order returns to the room. Demetriou, I notice, now has his arms folded in a sulky, resentful way.

There's a knock at the door. Irritated, and expecting to find some small boy sent on a fictitious mission by Davenport, I go over and open it, and find the headmaster there, smiling like the sort of people sent round by very modern churches.

'Sorry to intrude, AKS, but I wonder if some of your young gentlemen wouldn't mind lending the caretaker some assistance?' He shifts aside to reveal the caretaker behind him in the corridor, grunting as he tries to push a large grey filing cabinet along the floor. There are several other filing cabinets waiting for the same treatment.

'What's happening?'

'I'm moving our financial archive down into the old Cadet Force stores. There's no sense in them cluttering my office . . . Why are you smiling like that?'

'No reason, Headmaster.'

I collect myself and turn back inside the room, calling for a few volunteers. To my irritation, they all volunteer. As he troops past me, taking his jacket off, Miller taps me on the shoulder. 'Can I tell you something, sir?'

'What?'

'Those brogues of yours, yeah? They're, like, way too good for that suit.'

'I just feel like, I dunno, like everyone's talking about me.'

'What are they saying, Brenard?'

'They're gonna kill me. Put rat poison in my sandwiches. That kind of thing.'

I've sat here, alone in the Geography Room, a full half-hour, waiting to give counselling. I was about to leave when this rosy-cheeked sixth-former dashed into the room with the air of one pursued. He's now sitting at the desk, quivering, hands trawling through his long, flaxen hair.

'Have you talked to your parents about it?'

'They're in on it, too.'

I'd expected that, if boys came to see me at all, it would be to tell me about lost homework, or unfair treatment at the hands of Scarsdale. And I'd felt myself ill equipped to deal with even those woes. But this boy is on the brink of psychosis.

'I think we should think about getting you to a hospital,' I say quietly and calmly.

Brenard shakes his head. 'They'll keep me there.'

'They'd help you.'

Brenard considers this. 'How long would it take?'

I think it advisable to pretend. 'A fortnight maybe?'

'Can't tonight. I'm going to Bagley's.'

'Can't you tell this Bagley you'll see him another night?'

The angelic face wrinkles into pitying cynicism. 'Bagley's is a club, sir. In King's Cross. It's Ayia Napa II: The Reunion tonight.'

Something dawns now as I look at Brenard, at his carefully styled, floppy haircut, the manky coloured bands knotted round his wrist. 'How often do you go to these clubs?'

A diffident shrug. 'Two, three times a week. Why? And why've you got a plate of, like, rotting salad on your desk?'

'It's not important. Do you ever –' I wonder how to phrase it – 'has anyone ever suggested you should take drugs at any of these clubs?'

Brenard treats me to a megawatt of adolescent pity. 'I'm nearly eighteen. Why would anyone have to *suggest* it?'

'So you *have* taken drugs?'

'They're not drugs.'

'What aren't?'

'Trips. Love Biscuits. That's not drugs. Drugs is, like, brown and crack and that.'

'They *are* drugs, Brenard. And they can make some people very unwell. In the mind.'

'Governments just put that stuff out, sir, because they don't want people to, like, take it. It gives them insights, sir, makes them perceive reality more clearer.'

I give a sigh, having heard this argument a dozen times before, and usually from the same sort of people who tell you that *The Magic Roundabout* contains subliminal messages. They are to be viewed as the enemies of truth and reason.

'And this reality you're perceiving more clearer – I

mean, more clearly – that includes people trying to poison you, does it?'

'You wouldn't understand, sir.'

I assure him strongly that I do understand. I've been to raves, I say. Brenard laughs at the word. I've smoked cannabis, I say. Brenard looks interested.

'Has Mr Davenport ever smoked it, sir?'

'I don't know.' I instantly regret my earlier candour. 'Why?'

'It's just I know you share a place, sir. I could sort you both out, sir. If you fancied. Some nice skunk.'

'No.'

'How about some Librium? Help you unwind, sir.'

The conversation continues in this vein for a few minutes, until I see that it's pointless. In the end, I stuff a few leaflets into Brenard's pocket and bundle him out of the door – just as Brenard is offering me first refusal on a set of Bang & Olufsen speakers. I return to my desk and look at the clock. Almost five. I start to pack up my things. The door opens a crack and I look up at the sound.

The school ghost lurks shyly in the doorway. He rubs his nose with an ink-stained finger, then tidies his hair. It's this gesture, of brushing a recalcitrant little strand of hair to the left, that makes me realise I *have* seen him before today. In the vestibule at Mrs Danischewsky's, shimmering in the gentle light.

'Come in,' I say, encouragingly.

The boy looks briefly behind him and then drifts into the room. He looks at me mistrustfully, with large, grey eyes.

'How can I help?'

The boy shrugs. 'What makes you think you can?'

I am relieved, the shrug and the rude answer being

evidence of the boy's worldliness. If he is a ghost, at least he is a thoroughly modern, teenage one and not something conjured up from the cutting-room floor of Ealing Studios.

'Want to sit down?'

'Will it help you if I do?'

'I rather thought it might help you,' I reply.

'Why?' he demands crabbily. 'Why would being in a chair make it any easier for me than being vertical? Don't you think it might have more to do with you not wanting to be lower than me, which you will be if I remain standing? A notional concept, i.e., social status rendered concrete by its imposed relation to physical locus?'

'Possibly . . .' I falter.

'So you admit you want me to sit down because it will help you,' the boy declares, triumphantly, sitting down and crossing his legs neatly. I rub my eyes and try to smile encouragingly. The boy stares back, vaguely affronted, as if I'd invited myself into his home and demanded to look up his rectum with a light-pen. The silence grows uncomfortable, and it grows incumbent upon me to break it.

'You don't have to talk if you don't want to. That's the whole point,' I say, warming to my theme. 'It's OK.'

'Hardly OK me coming if I don't say anything,' comments the boy, reasonably. 'Unless you're going to tell me that it's in the silences that we truly come to know ourselves. Which I wouldn't advise you to do. I read everything about Zen Buddhism over the summer. It's nonsense. Just a gross popularisation of pre-Shinto mysticism.'

In addition to feeling confused, I'm, now starting to feel extremely thick. 'What's your name?' I ask.

The boy gives a delicate half-smile. 'Blundell,' he answers. 'Anthony Blundell.'

'So,' I say, 'Anthony. How's life?'

'Pretty crap,' Anthony replies, baldly. 'Since you ask.'

'OK,' I say, nodding. 'That's a good start.'

Anthony treats this to a mocking laugh. 'Oh, *please*,' he says. 'It's all *ow-kayy*,' he continues, parodying me. 'I'm Not *Ow-kayy*.'

'Well,' I throw back, testily. 'You're *not*, are you?'

'How do *you* know I'm not? Maybe I just came up here for a map of East Africa. Here you are forcing me to have psychoanalysis and maybe all I wanted was to fetch a map.'

'Did you want a map?'

'I've got no interest in East Africa.'

'But you *did* want a map of somewhere?'

'Stop putting words into my mouth. Counsellors are supposed to listen, aren't they? Isn't that what Freud was on about — the transference setting of the analytic hour, suspension of the norms of dialogue?'

'So there is something you wanted to talk to me about?'

Another shrug meets this. I swallow down the urge to shout something rude, and take a long look at the boy. It occurs to me that this Anthony, with his sharp little nose and old-fashioned hair, might be the target of bullying. He is clearly intelligent, and I know enough of boys to understand this can be a burden, particularly when topped off with an attitude like a sandpaper Durex.

'Are there . . .' I'm broaching the issue sensitively, 'is anyone giving you a hard time?'

'Apart from you? No. And what's that plate of old salad doing on your desk? It stinks.'

'I don't know what it's doing. I found it in my locker. It wasn't in there this morning.'

'Why don't you throw it away?'

I feel a faint throbbing at the temples. If only I could be in the MacKendrick now, taking a deep, oblivion-affirming draught from my first, frosted pint of beer. But I can't even go there tonight, can I? Perhaps, I think, smiling inwardly at the prospect, I'll do something highly unprofessional, buy a can of lager and swig from it on my way home. Perhaps that will help, rinse me clean of my encounter with this weird, maddening, intransigent boy.

I start again. 'Problems at home maybe?'

Anthony blows a raspberry and replies, 'I'm eighteen,' which I try to see as slight progress.

'You live close by, don't you?'

Distractedly he polishes the desk with his hand, spreading out long, thinly ridged fingers, like a team of grubs. 'Why say that?'

'I've seen you,' I reply. 'Don't you remember? In Mrs Danischewsky's Bed & Breakfast. You don't live there, do you?'

'God, you're just like everyone else,' says Anthony, uncrossing his legs. 'Aren't you?' He stands up abruptly, smoothing down his grey trousers.

'Where are you going?'

'Home,' replies Anthony, bitterly. 'I *was* going to tell you something, but you've stuffed it up now.' He looks at the odorous mulch on the plate at my elbow. 'No wonder people put rotting food in your locker.'

All At Sea

'Blundell, eh? Can't say I know the name. Probably did German.' Davenport shifts in his seat and, after checking his watch for the hundredth time, takes a mighty fistful of peanuts. 'Funny thing, that,' he continues. 'Every time you get a new second year, one of the bleeders sticks up his paw and says Sir, why do we learn Latin? So of course, you say: Well, Gospratt, or whatever your name is, Latin will help you when you come to learn languages like German, which have a case system. Yes?'

I nod and Davenport continues, brushing salt from his meaty hands. 'Thing is, the way it's timetabled, no one who does Latin ever *learns* German. So it's a load of hogwash. *I* don't know why they have to learn Latin. Don't give a skinny one, actually. Teaching you, Gospratt, Latin keeps me, Davenport, in ale. That's what I should say. *Quid pro quo.*'

Davenport has changed from his customary hairy green suit into a fawn one and, after a hasty shave, daubed the assaulted skin of his neck with a brackish cologne. He is also, regardless of being kept in ale by the likes of Gospratt, drinking wine by the glass – a curious feat for a man with hands like a Maori prop forward. Rough-hewn though Davenport is, he looks to me like a man on a date. But what sort of a girlfriend is called Corky?

I silence these thoughts, easing into my chair as the first pint takes effect. An arm – in my imagination anyway – encircles Rosie Kastrafitis' ample Mediterranean waist, and waiters are smashing plates as *rembetika* music plays us straight into bed. I know it isn't going to be her, of course, but that doesn't stop it from being a very satisfying vision. And I still don't understand why Davenport is being so shifty. Perhaps he likes Rosie Kastrafitis himself. Perhaps Corky *is* Rosie. It's all too hard to contemplate.

A modest clack comes from the balls on the snooker table and Davenport looks round. I do likewise, seeing nothing but elderly, overweight men in the company of slightly younger, and far thinner, women. The room is chilly and subdued, people sitting in their overcoats at little tables, listening, without much passion, to a trio of pensioners in the corner, who are playing white jazz and looking like they'd all rather be at home with the shipping forecast.

The door at the side of the bar opens. The breath catches in my throat as a tall girl wearing a very short, very tight dress enters the room. She waves at us. I'm wondering if this is Corky or if, better still, it's the mystery date. I start making meaningless adjustments to my hair and my shirt as she strides over on heels that make cross clicking sounds with every step. She is still looking our way and life, I think, might have dealt me the winning queen.

She flicks a cold glance downwards as she goes past our table and proceeds to kiss the bald head of the elderly saxophonist. Davenport catches my eye. 'Pitched your sights a little high there, Alastair.'

To hide my embarrassment, I drain my pint of Carlsberg and announce my intention to visit the bar.

Davenport shakes his head. 'Sorry, old man. Only members can buy drinks.'

'Well, how about getting them in?' I suggest, putting my wallet on the table – a European purse-like affair which Martha bought because she was fed up of watching me dredge my pockets. I rarely use it. Davenport makes a pained expression.

'I'm not exactly what you'd call a member either,' he admits, tweaking a pudgy ear-lobe. 'It's just that Corks is on the committee . . .'

The door opens again, and now a middle-aged woman wafts in on the breeze, wearing a long dark coat with an astrakhan collar. Davenport stands sharply, as if summoned by fanfare. 'Here she is,' he grunts.

The woman smiles over at Davenport, but before walking towards him she pauses a while at the bar, shaking hands and receiving respectful kisses on the cheek. I'm astonished. Expected Davenport's girl – if not Miss Kastrafitis and if an alternative creature could be expected at all – to be some hearty, plump figure, probably in jeans and a mountaineering fleece, the sort who list *après-ski* as a hobby. Corky, by contrast, looks well into her fifties, thin and elegant as she makes her way slowly round, receiving the tributes of various stewed knights on bar stools. With her dark hair tied neatly in a bun, and silver droplet earrings, she resembles a Roman dowager, such as might be found on the back of an ancient coin.

'You might stand up,' Davenport urges me.

Before I can obey this bizarre entreaty, Corky has come across to us. Davenport kisses her clumsily on each cheek and then waves a hand towards me, as if presenting something he's captured in a war.

'Boot's told me so much about you,' she says, arranging

herself delicately on the edge of a seat. Like Davenport, she speaks a fraction too loud, presumably because she grew up in a very large house. 'Get me an orange juice, sweet,' she tells Davenport, who then rather pompously attempts to hail the barman to our table.

'Boot?' I query, as Davenport accepts the inevitable and lumbers away to the bar.

'It's his father's nickname for him,' she says. 'Thick as a boot.'

'You know his family, then?'

Corky blinks at me in surprise. 'I'm his mother,' she says. 'Who did you think I was?'

I decide not to answer this in depth. But if Corky is Davenport's mother, then who is the mysterious lover that he insists he has?

That's the grandfather of the evening's revelations for me, but many lesser cousins follow. In Corky's magisterial presence, I learn more about my friend than I have done in a whole month of living with him. I discover, for instance, that he was delivered in the back of a taxi – his mother's waters having been broken, so legend has it, by a stray champagne cork at White's.

Another puzzle: I discover from Corky that Davenport, far from being adrift in life, as he is given to pretend, is writing a Ph.D., on the Roman poet Catullus.

'You never said,' I remark.

Davenport flushes. 'People think it's flaky,' he mumbles. The mumbling is yet another new trait, one simultaneous with Corky's arrival.

'No, they don't, darling,' replies Corky.

'Well, we know *someone* who does,' Davenport murmurs sulkily. I've never seen him this way before. In addition to the mumbling, there are coy smiles, a habitual teenage flicking of the hair and, in conversation, a need for constant encouragement. It's as if the boozing, cynical Davenport has been replaced with one who radiates insecurity. I've seen this before, when Tara once introduced me to her mother. There'd been lots of *darlings*, a brace of cold kisses and a flurry of patted arms. And behind it the same, unspoken sense that the parent was very much still in charge. This must be what the rich do with their offspring: give them a life of unfettered advantage, but keep them small in return.

Corky glosses over her son's last moody comment by saying her husband is a businessman and hardly has any time to read poetry, least of all dead Romans. Then she turns her full attention to me. 'I knew a Strange once,' she notes, sipping her orange juice with thoughtful poise. 'Passport Officer at the Embassy . . . in Vienna. Very handsome boy.' She makes an exquisite frown as some faint memory occurs to her. 'Actually, I always thought he was a spy. What does your father do?'

I answer, as truthfully as decency and the Official Secrets Act permit, that my father is just a retired teacher, the alternatives seeming, for the moment, far too ghastly to explore.

Corky smiles. 'Following in his footsteps. Fathers do like that sort of thing.'

At this point, Davenport clears his throat and says they ought to be getting along. 'Don't mind do you, old chum?' he asks, meaning I'd better not.'

'What about this girl you're introducing me to?' I object. 'You can't just leave me here.'

Davenport seems all set to offer some carefully argued and irresistible set of reasons as to why I should sit and wait in some club to which I do not belong, and where I can't buy a drink, for some girl I will not recognise. But Corky intervenes on my behalf.

'Don't be ridiculous, Boot,' she says, sternly. 'We're not going anywhere until Gisela comes, so you may as well get Alastair another drink. And you can fetch me a spritzer.'

'Gisela's coming, is she?' Davenport asks, vacantly.

'She's all on her own tonight so I've asked her along.' Corky frowns at her son. 'Now *stop* doing that thing, dear. You look like Uncle Bartholomew. Where's your tie?'

Davenport mumbles something about having left it on the bus. Corky tuts and opens her handbag. 'Lucky I picked one up for you in Sulka's.' She proffers a flat snake of silky fabric, which her son takes wordlessly from her hands. Then, seeming to have tired of Davenport, she turns back to me with a gracious, Princess–Di–in–leper–colony smile.

'Do you know Gisela Harpenden?'

'The headmaster's wife? I've seen her around.'

'She's a very dear friend of mine,' Corky notes. She looks round at her son, who is chewing his fingernails intensely, even though there are plenty of peanuts left.

'Boot,' his mother snaps, irritably tapping her glass with a sharpened fingernail. '*Spritzer!*'

As one, Corky and I watch his wide, sweating back as he picks his way to the bar. Corky mouths private words to herself, shaking her head. 'Sometimes, you know,' she remarks, leaning in towards me, 'I completely agree with his father.'

I don't think it prudent to comment on this, and nor does Davenport have the chance to reach the bar. The door opens suddenly and in walks a familiar figure –

slender and dark. The old shags at the bar neglect their gins as their stares are drawn to her. As are mine.

'Now you see why I couldn't tell you . . .' says Davenport, speaking with a faintly guilty air as he ushers Ann Gorley over to our table. Corky blinks, as if recently struck in the face with a wet bream.

'Oh God, you?' Ann asks, three syllables combining surprise, alarm and disappointment.

'Now, now, don't be all coy about it, folks,' says Davenport, rubbing his hands together, 'Go out and *have some bloody fun*!'

We're descending the steps of Westminster Pier before I can bring myself to mention our lost afternoon in Ealing and what may have happened thereafter. It's a chilly, damp night and she stumbles a little on the slimy stone.

'All right?' I hold out a hand to steady her. She ignores it, but smiles vaguely.

'Bloody foot,' she comments, as we join the small queue of people waiting on the quayside. She points to her left ankle, bulked out by a bandage under a black gypsy skirt. I wonder if the bandage is black too. Everything else is, tonight: black raincoat, black shoes, black blouse, even a necklace with a tiny black stone at her throat. She looks good – less of the Northern–Goth–toned–down–for–work, more of something else. Perhaps it's the real Ann, unveiled at last.

'How did it happen?' I ask, biting the bullet, and also setting aside a tentative vision of Ann in black underwear. 'Your ankle, I mean.'

She pincers her bottom lip with big teeth. 'I just fell down stairs one night,' she says, quietly.

'One night?' So not with me? Not after me?

'She makes a sheepish face. 'I was actually going out for a smoke. Sandra and Daisy've banned fags in the flat.'

'Oh, that's good,' I say, for some reason relieved I'm not implicated. 'I mean, well, it's *not* good. Not at all.'

She gives a bemused frown. 'What are you on about?'

On the count of three. It has to be done. 'It's just that, that time I was with you, in the flat . . . You fell over, you see, and I tried to help, but I thought you might have . . . You seemed to be very upset.'

'Oh, *that* . . .' she says, dismissively. 'I was just a bit tipsy, that's all.'

Tipsy describes your mum when she's been over to the neighbours' house at Christmas and some racy fellow in a golfing sweater has pressed her to a third thimbleful of port. If nutting yourself out cold on the door-jamb is what Ann Gorley calls tipsy, heaven help the man who's with her when she's drunk.

'It was sweet of you to be worried about me, Alastair,' she says, then adds: 'that is, if you *were* worried about me.'

'Of course I was. Hardly slept a wink.'

'Don't push it,' she says, affably, touching my arm again. She seems less brittle than I remember her – almost familiar. Desire begins slowly to twitch and fidget within, like the scrabblings of creatures in a forgotten forest.

'I shouldn't have drunk that second bottle,' Ann confides as the queue for boat tickets inches forward. 'I just got a bit upset. I think it was talking about Danny that did it.'

'Danny? Your ex-boyfriend?'

'*Late* boyfriend,' she says, darkly. She seems on the verge of offering more, when we are shoved from behind. A clutch of Italian tourists, disdainfully festooned in furs and Prada, stands behind us. And in front of us, a party of aged Americans. When these goodly folk, arrayed in jump-suits of every imaginable hue, have bought their tickets, it is our turn at the desk.

'Two for the river cruise, please,' I say. I notice with some consternation that the man selling the tickets is dressed as a Beefeater, but try not to give this too much attention. My thoughts are of Ann, edging closer to me on the cold journey down-river to Greenwich. That's why, on Davenport's advice, I chose this boat trip. It is to conclude with a drink – or hopefully several – in a pub next to the Cutty Sark, where there is, according to Davenport, live jazz and sufficient atmosphere to make even me look groovy.

It's an open-air craft, but there are two seats alone at the front, close to one of those roaring, mushroom-shaped gas heaters which you occasionally find in the beer gardens of badly appointed pubs. We settle ourselves here and look out at the river, the lights of London glinting in the dark water. A very pretty spectacle, marred only slightly by fumes from the heater. Ann sniffs.

'It was four months today,' she comments. 'Danny. Four months to the day they found him. On the common.'

A few things are emerging from the mist. A sordid tale told, with barely concealed glee, by Tara. Some cryptic references from Davenport. The late departed teacher of the Ferals, found dead in Versace drag. No wonder Ann's a mess. Or *has* been a mess, at any rate.

The boat engines bark, there are shouts on the quayside and the Beefeater jumps on as we depart down the river.

'Sorry,' she says, clearing her throat. 'Shouldn't keep going on about him. I just can't help it. I end up telling complete strangers and it's not . . . well, it's not the sort of thing . . .'

'No, I shouldn't imagine it is.' I fill in the gap for her.

She gives a wan smile, accepting that I must have been told the tawdry details, and rummages up her right sleeve. She brings forth a crumpled knot of tissue paper and dabs at her nose. 'We were just about to get a flat. How can you be just about to get a flat with someone and be keeping all that a secret? That you're putting a dress on every Thursday night and going down the common to . . .' She pauses, sucking in air. 'The *bastard*!' She blinks a little, halted by her own outburst. 'I'm sorry. I shouldn't have come, but Lawrence kept going on about how I needed to get out and start living and then he said he'd got this brilliant bloke lined up . . .'

As we move out into the centre of the river, the boat engines go quieter and I'm reminded why I like Davenport so much. Not because of him describing me as a 'brilliant bloke' – you can write that off as sales pitch – but as someone going out of his way to cheer someone else up.

'He's a good lad our Lawrence,' I say.

A chilly breeze is blowing in from the sea and Ann shivers. 'He speaks very highly of you,' she says, pulling her dark coat tighter around herself.

'Does he? I can't quite . . .'

'Can't quite what?'

'Well, I just wouldn't've thought you two would've had much to talk about. I mean, Lawrence is quite . . . traditional, isn't he? I can't really imagine you being friends with him.'

Ann shrugs. 'What I like about Lawrence is he's honest. There's no side to him. D'you know what I mean? Not like – well, not like some other people I've known anyway. Plus he's not a snob, even if he talks like one.'

'No.'

Ann smiles. 'You see. That's why I came tonight.' She looks inside her little patchwork bag and pulls out a half bottle of whisky. 'But I bought this in case you turned out to be awful. Then at least I'd be sure I could still get a bit pissed.'

Everything is suddenly looking quite good, not least because, as that brilliant bloke Davenport predicted, Ann is nudging herself closer to me as an antidote to the cold. I take the bottle and swig from it.

She's found something else in her bag. 'Here,' she says. 'Listen to this bit.'

As she pulls the cover back, I see it's the collected poems of Larkin. So she didn't send it to her stabbed friend in Bradford. 'I couldn't,' she says with a laugh, flashing those big white teeth. 'I kept thinking of that joke you made in the pub.'

She starts reading, reciting clearly in a School Assembly voice. *'Don't read much now: the dude / Who lets the girl down before / The hero arrives, the chap / Who's yellow and keeps the store, / Seem far too familiar . . .'*

'Get stewed,' I finish the verse for her: *'Books are a load of crap.'*

'I thought you didn't like poems.'

I don't, generally. But this one has blipped up from the fog of the past, its passage oiled by the swig of whisky. I had an English teacher who was fond of this poem, that and the one about your mum and dad fucking you up. He used to quote them at us when we were fifteen. Now, a teacher myself, I realise he possibly didn't like the poems that much, it was just that they had swearing in them, and he used this as a device to seem a bit cool in front of us. Still, I always liked the poem. What Larkin did with books, I did with soap operas and I knew I was doing it, even at the time, so when I first heard the poem, I thought, Hey, this guy's like me, an actual poet, just like me. That being sort of the effect poets go for. And this being, I now realise, why I like Ann – because she reminds me of things, in the way the Ealing films do: bits about the past that weren't bad at all, like a few nice evenings with your dad or realising you liked something you'd read at school.

'I like getting stewed,' I remark.

'Getting stewed,' she echoes, passing me the bottle.

'I'm . . . I'm very glad it turned out to be you,' I say, images of Rosie Kastrafitis withdrawing into the river's mist.

'Bless,' she says – which we'll overlook. 'Why?'

'Well, I didn't know what Lawrence might have in store. I was thinking it was someone else. No,' I steady my tongue, not wanting to confess my withering affections for the Maths teacher, who might, on reflection, be Davenport's girl after all, 'I mean I thought it might be some scary fashionable person who'd want to go to some bar in Soho or something . . .'

She chuckles softly as we chug past the London Eye, its pods illuminated, like eggs held up to candlelight. '*Some bar . . .*'

'Well, you know what I mean. Absinthe and people with blue hair.'

'You don't like people with blue hair?' she asks, amused more than affronted.

'Well, I . . .' I realise this could be the wrong avenue, with a girl who clearly dyes her hair. Then I take another swig and suddenly think, *Sod it*. 'No, I don't like blue hair.'

'What else don't you like?' she asks, a funny half-smile on her lips.

'What else? I don't know. Sushi? People who like sushi? Films with Robin Williams . . .'

She claps her hands, almost cheerful. 'More!'

'The World Cup. That "Pass Notes" column in the *Guardian*.'

'*Last of the Summer Wine*?' she butts in.

I nod. 'Kiss FM.'

'Men who wear shoes with buckles on them! An' grey shoes! An' Siamese cats. An' Wonderbras.'

'I quite like Wonderbras,' I can't help musing. Then, anxious to regain some ground, I add, 'John Sessions. Clapham.'

'Places that sell forty-eight kinds of tea,' Ann enthuses, big doleful eyes gleaming as she gathers steam. 'An' . . . an' cappuccinos with froth on them . . .'

'But cappuccinos are supposed to—'

'Oyez, oyez, oyez!' interrupts the Beefeater suddenly, in ground-glass-and-tuberculosis tones. To my dismay, I see he's stepped out of a little doorway at the front of the boat and has a microphone in his hand. The tannoy speaker above rattles with the force of his voice, rendering all other communication impossible. 'Welcome ye to the River Cruises of London a-boat a-trip!' He goes on, in accents suggestive of gin palaces and mudlarks. 'My naime is a-Glen, and oi shall be your goide for the next . . . a-seventy-foive minutessss.'

Shit on wheels. Just when things were getting good. Nobody told me there was going to be a commentary. I glance at Ann and she's shaking her bobbed head in bafflement. 'Maybe this is just a little gimmick,' I mouth to her over the noise.

'Hif yew carn 'ear me at the back, raise your 'ands,' Glen recites blandly, like some bingo caller who first began to get sick of his job round about the time of the Winter of Discontent and hasn't changed his mind since. 'Hif yew carn 'ear me, don't come to the front of the boat . . .' A studied pause. 'Cos if you do, we'll sink.' A ripple of laughter comes from those able to understand English. 'There are pur-lenty of loife-jackets on board, but if yew should 'appen to be German . . .' He clears his throat. 'Then oi ope yew can swim.'

'Christ,' Ann groans. 'Did he say seventy-five minutes?'

'Hif yew look over to the chimbleys on your right 'and soide . . .' Glen continues, turning a dial on a machine at his elbow, so that his commentary now has a sick-inducing echo effect, 'yew will be a-lookin' at the former a-Dewhurst Match Factory, now a luxury development housin' a number of famous stars, such as a-Billy Ocean and a-Brian Cant.'

Ann, her face an inscrutable mask, takes the whisky bottle back from me and drinks deeply from it. The jinx is with us still.

'Do you know that guy? He's waving at you.'

'What?'

'Do you know that guy?'

'Did I?'

'Have you gone deaf? I asked you,' Ann leans in to my left ear and bellows the words, warm spittle, like champagne fizz, flecking my ear-lobes, 'do you know that bloke?'

Since Glen's commentary began, my fortunes have been

heading steadily towards the bowels of the earth. Ann descended into a pained silence as we chugged eastwards, and the chilly wind forced her deep within herself. Whenever I caught her eyes, she'd manage a smile, but it was always a dry cream cracker of a smile, not the chocolate éclair I'd been aiming for. She finished the bottle of whisky on her own.

Hoping we'd fare better on dry land, I remembered Davenport's point about the pub next to the Cutty Sark and led Ann inside. But there is no live jazz and less atmosphere than at an outpost of Starbucks. It's noisy – you can barely hear anything except The Communards – quite full, almost exclusively of men in combat gear, and, if Ann is to be believed, one of them is waving at me.

I follow the direction of Ann's finger to a tall, thin man with a blunt wedge of blond hair at the front of an otherwise bald head. He does seem vaguely familiar, I have to say.

'*Elleicester!*' he cries delightedly, coming over to us, clutching a short bottle of lager.

Now I know him: Darren Krajic, the young Australian who interviewed me at the Hammersmith OneStop JobShop. The meeting ended with me telling him to get himself a proper job.

Darren looks quizzically from Ann to me. 'Who's this?'

'Ann Gorley,' I say, in a doom-laden voice, waving a hand ineffectually between my two companions. 'Darren Krajic. He's my JobStart counsellor.'

'*Was*, matey,' Darren breathes. 'I took your advice. Told my mum the truth: that I wasn't happy at the JobShop. And d'you know what she said?' He chatters indistinctly, possibly under the influence of some terrible powder. 'You'll never believe it. She said, "If you're not happy, son, change the tapes." Just that. Can you believe it? Change the tapes. My old ma. So I did. And guess what?'

'What?'

'I'm a guide at the London Aquarium. Having the absolute time of my life.' He turns to Ann, touching her lightly on the arm. She recoils slightly, but Darren doesn't notice. 'This guy's *brilliant*, you know. My little Northern agony aunt.' Then he turns back to me. 'You're not really dressed for the occasion, are you?'

'What occasion?' Ann interjects, stonily.

'Friday nights. Boot camp,' replies Darren, tartly. 'Strictly leather and uniforms. I can't think why they let *you* in. Must have thought you were the drag act.'

After glancing briefly at the crowd around us, Ann directs a thunderous glare at me. 'This is one of those puff pubs, isn't it?'

'Is it? I didn't know . . .' I avoid Darren's questioning eye, and hers.

'You said to me,' she continues, accusingly, 'when we were getting off that stupid boat, "There's a nice little pub I know." That's what you said, Alastair. How can you *know* the pub without knowing it's a puffs' pub?'

As she raises her voice, people – hard, muscular people – begin to stare our way.

'Ann, please. It's not very polite to talk like that. I didn't actually know . . .'

'Look at these people. There's someone over there in a camouflage skirt! And he's got bigger muscles than my dad. It's disgusting!'

'They're allowed to wear whatever they want, Ann. I think it's called a free country.'

'Don't patronise me, Alastair!'

'I'm not patronising you. I'm—'

'And why are you standing up for them?' She folds her arms and looks at me. 'No. Don't bother answering. I can guess.'

'Guess what, for God's sake?'

'Not you as well, Alastair,' she says, disgustedly. 'Not you as well.'

Turned Out Nice Again

I awake to the sounds of Davenport, declaiming as he drags his World War One Admiralty telescope into my bedroom.

'Hail the rosy-fingered dawn,' he intones, as he and the heavy brass object, mounted on a tripod, inch across the carpet. Cinna, ever at his master's heels, leaps around, giving tiny barks and panting, suspecting – for whatever doggy reasons I know not – that the whole affair is just a preamble to his being given a side of beef, or perhaps some poodle to rape.

'Yes, that's right, feller,' Davenport croons, as Cinna's tail entwines itself in the legs of the tripod. 'You're helping me, aren't you?'

I groan, rubbing the crust of sleep from my eyes and look at Davenport. He's wearing his old St John Lorimer's tracksuit, a purple affair, straining at the seams. I have seen this tracksuit before, and know it augurs ill.

'Raise the torches high, O boys! I see the flame-hued veil approach. Lo, sing together in tune. Ad seueros migrate.'

'What?' I ask weakly.

Davenport peers down at me, faintly upset that any man should be in bed at 8.30 a.m. on a Saturday. 'Thought you were in the bog,' he says, by way of an apology for waking me. 'I said you should join the ranks of the sober.'

This causes me to give another, quieter groan. It's as I feared. Davenport has entered one of his frequent binges of self-discipline which often follow a Friday night on the sauce. He must have ditched his mother at some early point and gone off to get soused. But who with?

'No more,' declares Davenport stoutly. 'I've already jogged to the bottle bank and back.'

'What's with the telescope?'

'Going to start logging the heavens again,' grunts Davenport, as he heaves the contraption with all his weight, dragging it to the window. 'Fellow needs a decent hobby, Alastair. Stop him from pissing his life up against a wall.'

I look down at the little Persian rug, a relic of the Martha days, which has become hopelessly knotted around the base of the telescope. Why couldn't Davenport have left the device where it was, covered with a dust-sheet, in his own bedroom?

'They've put that blasted mobile phone mast in the way,' Davenport explains. 'So I thought I'd stick it in here. Knew you wouldn't mind.' He starts to fuss with a lever on the side of the instrument.

I say nothing, reminding myself that this particular whim of Davenport's will not last beyond the weekend. It is common for my housemate to wake up full of self-loathing, particularly at the weekends, when he cranks up his intake of booze from the small-fishing-smack level to that of the twelve-funnelled transatlantic liner. In the resultant hangover, he will rise early and subject himself to violent exercise. He will then move through the house, eighteen stone of bloodshot ginger whirlwind, cleaning and tidying. Whole rooms will be rearranged, attic-loads of junk sent in bags to the charity shop, yet the house becomes no less cluttered.

I tend to sit, sipping Alka-Seltzer, at the centre of the storm, as Davenport thunders around me, sweating and denouncing his former self, declaiming in Latin and announcing the dawn of a purer, sober age. By mid-afternoon, he will collapse in his ancient armchair, shivering. He will wake a few hours later, lethargic and depressed, declaring that the thing he most needs now is a small glass of sherry. Which, thankfully, signals the end of the affair. At least until the following weekend.

'Best part of the day's already gone, you know,' Davenport comments critically, training the telescope out of the window. He brushes a pile of neatly folded shirts off the little wooden chair by the window and sits down. 'Good Lord,' he exclaims, peering through the telescope.

'What is it?' I kick the duvet off, my bladder bursting, and pad across to the window, picking up the shirts.

Davenport gives a chuckle. 'Look.' He twists the telescope round so I can see.

I look through the lens at the patch of scrub-land shared by the houses in our little quadrant. 'It's that pit bull from number eleven,' I remark, puzzled. 'Taking a shit.'

'Not *there*. Here.' Davenport nudges the telescope thirty degrees to the right so that I gain a clear view, through the trees, to the old tennis courts. There are several pairs of girls from the local convent school out there, practising, their cheeks flushed pink with the cold.

'They're from Holy Ghost.'

'*And Holy, Holy, Holy is the Lord of Hosts,*' recites Davenport, I take my eye from the lens and look at him. A rapturous smile creases his meaty face, and he shakes his curls in awe. 'Did you ever glimpse a sight so lovely as the Holy Ghost sixth form playing tennis?'

'It's a good job they don't let you teach them.'

'Stop hogging it,' replies Davenport, snatching the telescope back. He jams it to his eye again and gives an exquisite moan. 'Bouncing,' he breathes. 'Bouncing *womanhood*.'

'Is this why you've put the telescope in here?' I ask, sternly.

'That,' replies Davenport loftily, 'is a comment that does not do you justice. I suggest you take a cold bath and think about how much you have hurt me.'

I say, walking back to the bed and pushing Cinna off it, that I'd prefer a hot one.

'Well, there isn't any hot water,' Davenport replies. 'Gave all the windows a good splosh-down. Which reminds me, you got any plans for the day? Why are you bloody here anyway? You should be eating toast and honey off Ann Gorley's marble-white backside.' He takes a deep breath and starts to recite again. '*Like myrtle flowers are the odours of her virgin bed, like the spindrift shores of Illyria my lady's coves and crannies . . .*'

I'd just been pondering the extreme oddness of Davenport saying he'd cleaned the windows, wondering if the universe had entered some sort of cosmic meltdown. His mention of Ann recalls me sharply to earth, where a tidal wave of regret promptly knocks me down. A short film-reel of memory skewers my head to the pillow – Ann flouncing, full of righteous fury, into the Greenwich streets; Ann hailing a cab; me explaining, becoming angry with her, insulting even as she stepped in alone. And the cab driver's advice, useful then, as now, as they drove away: 'Best leave it, son.'

'It didn't go very well,' I comment, carefully, trying to extricate Cinna's head from my crotch.

Davenport shakes his head, as if I'd just addressed him in perfect Etruscan. '*Not very well*?' he echoes. 'Don't talk rot, man. You know what your trouble is?'

'Stop it, Cinna! What?'

'Don't take it out on Cinna,' Davenport admonishes, standing up abruptly. 'You think women are just like men. And they're not.'

'I had noticed a few points of divergence.'

'I'm not sure you have. Chap like you spends all his time wondering what a girl's *thinking*. Imagines they're going through all the neurotic little thought processes that you are. But they *don't* think. You know what they say. *Sed mulier cupido quod dicat amanti in vento scribere oportet aqua.*'

'I don't believe I do know that one, no.'

'Nevermind. But that's the wonderful thing about them, though, you see. Can't waste time wondering, etc.'

'I'm sure Germaine Greer would be very interested to hear this.'

'Shut up. No, not you, Cinny-cins, Papa didn't mean you to shut up. I meant the nasty man.' Davenport puts one hand on his hip, wafting the other in the air as if lecturing me on the finer points of the ablative. 'When a lady takes a shine to a chap, or even when she doesn't, it's got no earthly rationale. You can say something perfectly irrelevant, like you've got to get some new shoelaces or something, and she'll suddenly go all gooey on you and tell you what a sweetheart you are. Agreed?'

'Well, sort of . . .' I really wish, at this point, that Davenport would drop the subject and leave me alone so I can have a good wallow and tell myself what a luckless arse

I am, doomed to wander the earth with a permanent hard-on.

'Alternatively, you can tell them how much you love them, and they'll simply turn round and tell you to stop being boring. Because it's got nothing to *do* with their heads. It's all about hormones and cycles and glands and suchlike.'

'Wouldn't that be a sort of earthly rationale, then — these hormones and glands?'

'God, man, why do you always have to quibble so? Point is, if you say your date with Ann went terribly, it's a sure sign to me that she's lying in bed right now, writing your name in the dust on her bedside table. And wishing you were . . . well, you know . . . *up* her.' Davenport grins in an upsetting way, as if imagining the scene.

Can I face confiding in Davenport about the events of last night? Can I tell him about her refusal to answer the phone when I rang her flat in the small hours of the morning? No, I cannot, even if it's partly his fault.

'It's no use lying there staring at the ceiling. I suggest you get up, make yourself presentable and get round there with a hundredweight of johnnies.'

'No.'

'Well, suit yourself,' Davenport declares, huffily, preparing to exit the room. 'But whatever you do, I'd seriously prefer it if you'd take yourself out of the house for the morning. I'm finding this negativity of yours a great strain.'

'Yes, I know, *Cinny-inny-bum-chops*, nasty man won't take him on his walk.'

Cinna takes a series of gnashing leaps around us, jaws snapping like a taunted crocodile. Davenport is making matters worse by dangling the lead in the air – holding it out to me in a doomed attempt to be rid of his furry friend for a few hours.

'I can't possibly take him in the Co-op, can I? Apart from anything else, all the till girls are Asian.'

'What of it?'

'Davenport,' I say firmly, batting lead and dog aside, 'you know as well as I do that that dog is a confirmed *fascist*. He goes for anybody who's not an able-bodied white male.'

'Poppycock.'

'He does. He goes for black people, Asians, people with limps. Last week, just by the shops, he went for that old guy with the zimmer frame, the one who looks like Wilfred Hyde White.'

'Probably just wanted to chase him around a bit,' Davenport pleads, subjecting Cinna to a vigorous rubbing. 'Gets frisky when people don't take him on enough walks.'

'He's your dog. You take him.'

'*I'm* cleaning the house.'

'I'll clean it with you.'

'I want you to go out.'

'Why are you so keen to get me out of the house?'

'Not keen to get you out of the house, Alastair. Don't be so Northern. I simply think you'd prefer being out in the sunshine.'

'It's raining, Lawrence.'

'You said yourself we needed some groceries. So where's the harm in taking Cinna along for a little adventure?'

'Possibly because Cinna's idea of an adventure is most people's idea of a massacre.'

At mention of his name, Cinna sets up a series of blood-chilling howls, making my very bones throb, and reminding me of the need to depart.

Davenport sniffs and raises his chin, as he always does when feigning hurt. 'Just for the record, Alastair, this *dog*, as you call him, is a Christian and a socialist. Three weeks ago, he laid an enormous turd right outside Buckingham Palace. Not that I exactly approve of that, but it shows he has a mind of his own.'

'He does enormous turds everywhere. Including,' I add, shooting Cinna an extra-dark look, 'my bed.'

'That's because he likes you,' says Davenport, attempting to shut the door in my face and only succeeding in pinioning Cinna's tail.

There's a call-box at the end of our street and, since I've been rudely turfed out of my own house, there are a few things that need to be done. I find a twenty-pence piece and dial my parents' number. I haven't spoken to them for a fortnight. My mother sounds grateful to hear my voice – a touch too grateful.

'I've tried calling you a couple of times,' she says, a high, fluttery note of anxiety in her voice.

'We got cut off. Lawrence forgot to post the cheque.' I make a note publicly to forgive Davenport for this.

'Oh dear. You'll be in trouble now.' My mother has a very archaic vision of the world, in which transgressions such as neglected bills and elbows on the table can incur the wrath of the law. I spent the first ten years of my life in constant fear of arrest. 'Like father, like son, I suppose.'

'What?'

'Your father's got to go to court,' my mother continues, distractedly. 'It's been in the *Clarion* and everything: "Pensioner on Burglary Charge".'

It transpires, from my mother's faintly gloating account, that my father has been employing a little too much of his MI6 training. In an attempt to persuade the local MP of the necessity of joining the Neighbourhood Watch, he decided to stage a break-in.

'Forgot how much weight he's put on, silly man. Got stuck in that silly little window at the top of his porch.'

'You haven't got a porch. You live in a flat.'

'Not us, dear: Mr Arlidge. The MP. *His* porch. Your father was trying to burgle him. The policemen thought he was a terrorist because of that speech Mr Arlidge made about Palestine.'

'Oh God.'

'They kept him in Bootle for seventy-two hours under that Prevention of Terrorism thing and he had to have coffee from the vending machine, so he's been running backwards and forwards ever since. I told him to have a cheesy scrambled egg, bind him up a bit, but of course he won't listen. They get very stubborn when they get old. I think he's going a bit gaga, bit confused . . .'

My mother is two years older than my father, and has always been twice as confused, but she's never been one to let facts stand in the way of a good theory.

'Can I speak to him?'

'Oh no, dear. He's gone for a walk.'

I should think he has. Tramping the beach, in those gales that come straight from Greenland, rather than face my mother's scorn. She can keep it up for months on end – deliberately not wearing make-up and lashing her hair up high on her head to underline the point. I still remember that Christmas when he bought her a calorie counter, thinking it was a cookbook. It was Easter before he was allowed back to the marital bed.

'So how's Martha?'

Back in the late 1980s, it was possible, with a short-wave receiver and a length of copper wire dangled out of my window, to intercept broadcasts from Radio Tirana. These broadcasts usually consisted of a rather terrifying lady reciting bauxite production figures for the Gjirokastra region, interspersed with lengthy eulogies to Enver Hoxha. The thing I liked about these broadcasts was that Enver Hoxha had been dead for several years. But they never mentioned it. It was as if they thought it an unnecessary detail.

Unfortunately this is also the attitude my mother has to Martha. Within moments of my telling her we were splitting up, she'd asked me whether Martha had considered ScotchGuarding the new sofa. And on all occasions since, our conversations have been marred by a studied refusal to accept that we are not together any more. It's as if my mother has filed me away now, in a drawer marked MARRIED, and the administrative costs of relisting me are too great to consider. It's one of the reasons I haven't phoned in two weeks. And one of the reasons I find myself pretending I've run out of change.

In fact, I've got to make another call. But there's an attitudinous girl in a white tracksuit and a noodle perm waiting outside the box and I'm in no mood for conflict. I head across the common, drizzle pricking my skin, and thinking of hot coffee.

The FullaBeenz has recently installed an old-style red phone booth in its uppermost corner. Clutching something called a short skinny *latte*, I pick my way through the steaming fug of Saturday shoppers and make a call.

Tara answers in a trance-like state, presumably roused from dreams of Cap Ferrat or a new pair of Manolo

Blahniks. There are awkward questions to ask, questions that are making me quiver slightly and the coffee spill over the edges of the cup. I bend down and place the *latte* on the floor at my feet.

'What are you up to, Tara?'

'I'm still in my pyjamas,' she says, sleepily. 'Amjie's in Delaware. I don't know why.' She gives a big yawn. 'I was just having a q. lovely dream . . .' I hear a faint smacking of the lips down the receiver. 'You were in it.'

'I hope I behaved myself.'

'You never behave yourself in *my* dreams.'

This, regrettably, has to be written off as merely an example of Tara's basic sales patter, something she learned in the womb. And there are hard things to be said. 'I was actually ringing about the reference thing . . .'

'Yes?' A wary note has entered her voice.

'Well, it still hasn't come. And I was just wondering if there'd been a problem.'

There's a horrible pause. Then she speaks. 'There's no problem, Alastair. But you've got to fulfil your end of the bargain first.' Her voice sounds completely different – clipped and joyless. Not unlike the Radio Tirana announcer. 'No info, no letter. I thought I'd explained that.'

'Well, I *have* tried . . .' I say, thinking of my recent attempt to burgle the headmaster's office. 'But it's not easy. I mean, it's coming, and they've just moved all the archives, which ought to make it easier, but I was wondering if I could sort of have the letter in advance . . .'

'Just get on with it,' she snaps. 'You help me, I help you, sweetheart. *Quid pro quo.*'

A click. She's hung up. I take a step back in shock, wondering exactly how my friend and saviour has managed to turn so effortlessly into a paid-up member of the Blackmailers' Guild. All sorts of paranoid fancies begin to crowd in. I wonder if that first meeting on Kensington High Street wasn't just by chance, but a deliberate set-up. Perhaps she was looking for the perfect dupe and I fitted the bill? This can't be right, and it can't be right to think it. Madness lies this way.

There's a hot damp feeling around my ankles. I glance down and groan. The coffee cup is resting on its side and a pool of steaming grey liquid is lapping around the floor. When I step out of the kiosk, the rivulet of coffee follows me, onto the café's pine floor. It reaches a smart brown paper bag by the knees of some resting shoppers and, gaining purchase there, begins creeping up and spreading outwards.

At the table a block-shaped, youngish man, with one of those chins that were popular with Battle of Britain fighter pilots, frowns at me. I mutter a few words of apology. His companion looks up. A small cat-like face with a neat, pointed nose regards me.

It's the girl from the bus.

She blinks, knowing she knows me from somewhere. She holds up the bag, its bottom dripping brown liquid. 'Fuck,' she says, simply.

'Yes,' I reply. 'Sorry about that.'

'Well, sorry's not good enough, mate,' says her companion, whose square-cut, captain-of-rugby jaw I would instantly love to make less perfect with any item of heavy iron to hand. 'There was a candle and a birthday card in there. We'd just bought them.'

'It was an accident,' I say, gesturing feebly to the phone booth behind.

'I accept that. But the bag's ruined. The card's ruined.'

I accept that. Tosser.

'The card's not ruined, Jay,' the girl says, a hint – or so I fancy – of weariness in her voice. 'I put it in my bag.'

Jay ignores her. 'And sometimes, you know, accidents have to be paid for. Like the sign in the china shop says.'

I gaze down at him, realising on closer inspection that he's not what I thought at all. This is no punchable Sloane, nor the sort of Dagenham psychopath whose pints I invariably manage to spill. It's worse than that. His chin might be on the wrong side of statuesque, but his face is open and honest, with a slightly crooked nose. He looks like he might have made an ugly adolescent, might have had as much trouble getting someone to snog him as I did. He's got a flat, slightly Bristol accent, like he worked hard to get into college and when he got there he divided his time between working even harder and being sensitive to his first girlfriend and being a thoroughly likeable bloke down the bar. And he's reasonable. A reasonable, regular, decent guy, the sort you can't possibly dislike. Who's with *her*. And, God, I hate him.

'I said the card's in my handbag, Jay. Look.'

'Well, what about the candle, then?'

'If I'd broken your candle,' I say, with as much dignity as I can muster, 'I'd offer to pay for it. As it is, it's just got a little coffee on it. You can wipe it off.'

A pained look enters his eyes. 'Look, mate, I don't want to be a twat about it, but you're seriously out of order. *You* spilt the coffee.' He looks down at the floor and groans. 'It's all over my shoes and everything . . .' He pauses, trying not to lose his temper. '*You* bloody well wipe it off.' He thrusts a serviette towards me.

'Jay . . .' says the Bus Girl, testily. 'Take it easy, OK?

You don't have to make everything into a goddam stand-off.' She looks up at me, embarrassed. 'Forget about it.'

'I already have,' I say, taking the serviette from Jay's hands. I wipe down my jeans with it and place it back in his hand.

Bus Girl turns slightly, catching my eye as I walk out. And even with her hand covering her mouth, even through the steam of the coffee machines and the damp shoppers, I could swear she's smiling.

I didn't exactly look at the house when I left this morning, but now, as I pick my way down the driveway and look up at the windows, I see it's true. Davenport has cleaned them. Unfortunately, this now means everyone can see the state of the curtains, but it's an improvement on the solidified cobweb.

The inside has also undergone a transformation. I suspect the bulk of the gentlemen's club clutter has merely been gathered, by the armful, and stuffed in my room, or the room Davenport refers to as his 'study', though I suspect the only thing he truthfully studies in there is pornography. But still, you have to take your hat off to the man.

On the mantelpiece sits a little toadstool-shaped oil-burner, belching the scent of sweet bergamot into the room. If I'd been asked, on that Mr-and-Mrs-for-flatmates gameshow they're running on Channel Five, which of the two − a scented oil-burner or a rocket launcher − Davenport was more likely to possess, I'd have plumped for the latter. And on top of the bergamot smell there's something else − some heavy, foreign scent that's certainly not aftershave. There's also the remains of a snack on the table.

One thing's the same: Davenport's been eating dad-food again. My housemate has a predilection for the sort of delicacies usually only eaten by people's dads. Dark chocolate, Bath Olivers, potted crab, anchovy paste; food so pungent and costly that only men of means, with jaded palates, would consider eating it. There are two plates, both with remnants of food on them. And next to them, an empty bottle of Perrier-Jouet. Davenport, like many who pace the foggy hinterland between drinking and dipsomania, is a creature of a confirmed habit. He could never have polished off a whole bottle by this time of day. Not on a Saturday. Not alone.

Davenport emerges from his study, sweat glistening on his brow. He's wearing his dressing gown. 'Oh, hello,' he says, casually. 'Nice morning?'

'Curate's egg,' I respond, watching as my housemate hurries over to the mess on the table.

'What was the good bit?' he asks, gathering up the plates.

'Interesting encounter with someone.'

'Well, we all like those,' he says airily, padding off towards the kitchen.

'Two plates, Lawrence?'

He freezes. 'Sorry?'

I point at his burden. 'You've got two plates out.'

'So I have. One was there from the night before, I suppose.' He frowns. 'Why are you so concerned about my patterns of crockery usage?'

I don't answer, but I follow him into the kitchen. Cinna is out in the garden, joyously tearing a hawthorn bush to pieces.

'And why are you wearing your dressing gown? You were wearing your tracksuit before.'

'I had a bloody *shower*! Why are you giving me the third degree?'

'Has someone been here? Is that why you wanted me and Cinna out of the house?'

'No one's been here, Alastair. This is in your mind. And why should it matter if someone had been here?'

'It doesn't. I was just wondering who. And why you won't tell me.'

Davenport slams the dishcloth with unnecessary force into the sink and looks at me. 'All right! I confess. I had somebody round. A lady. Is that so awfully wrong?'

I lean up against one of the chairs. 'So you had your girlfriend round?'

'Ye-es,' he says, as if some invisible cardinal of the Inquisition was tweaking his nipples at the same time.

'The one you won't talk about. The one I've never met.'

'Alastair, you *are* behaving very oddly. What makes you think there's some sort of jiggery-pokery going on?'

'The fact that I have to be pushed out of the house so she can come round? The fact that I don't even know her name?'

'I don't mind you knowing her name.'

'What is it, then?'

A hunted expression flashes across his meaty brows. 'Erm . . .' His eyes dart around the room. '*Rosalind.*'

'Rosalind.'

'You've some objection to her being called Rosalind, have you?' He gives me a dark look and then raps on the kitchen window. 'Cinna! Stop that!'

He bustles out into the garden, where Cinna is attempting to tunnel under the fence into the garden next door. This is a garden that contains both children and bunny rabbits, so it's neither surprising that Cinna should want to get into it, nor that Davenport should want to prevent it. But I can't help feeling he's taken a convenient escape route. And I've got an idea that I know why. There is no Rosalind.

Davenport returns, dragging Cinna by the collar. He tosses a few frozen fish fingers onto the floor and the dog eagerly sets about them. Davenport gives me an awkward, guilty look. 'Sorry. They were your fish fingers, weren't they?'

'I don't mind.' I take a deep breath and plunge in. 'It's Rosie, isn't it?'

'Rosie?' Davenport gives a hollow laugh and wipes his brow. 'Rosie Catastrophe? Why on earth should you think that?'

'I don't know. *Things.*' Things like Davenport coming up, under pressure, with the name Rosalind. Like Mr Scarsdale saying that Davenport loved her and Davenport making just a little too much fuss to the contrary. Davenport forcing me, who perhaps might have had the sliver of a chance with her, into a date with Ann Gorley.

My housemate sits at the kitchen table, listening to this. Cinna starts gnawing at Davenport's toenails, but his master does nothing to prevent it. His eyes are troubled.

'You've cornered me. It *is* Rosie. I'm sorry.'

'You don't have to be sorry. And I didn't mean to corner you.'

'Well, I know you sort of thought . . . I thought you might . . . you know, *mind*. That's why I didn't want to say.'

'That's why you've been so cagey about it?'

'Well, yes,' he says, with the sudden ease of a man who has made a clean breast of things. 'That and . . . some other things. We don't want to go public on it, you see, staff-room gossip being what it is. You won't say anything?'

'My lips are sealed.' Then a thought strikes me. 'On one condition.'

'Name it.'

'You'll get the phone reconnected. And you'll take that telescope out of my room.'

He darts me a look combining surprise and awe, as if I was the school geek who'd inadvertently batted a six. 'Quite a steely little fellow underneath, aren't you?'

'Oh, you know, Lawrence. *Quid pro quo.*'

Kind Hearts and Coronets

Mr Scarsdale beetles into the staff room, his jacket bearing the vinegary tang of the canteen. 'Where was Davenport off to in such a rush? He practically knocked me over. And was he really wearing a cravat?'

'I think he had an urgent appointment,' I say, carefully, because I am somewhat distracted by the sight of Rosie Kastrafitis trying and failing to get a Diet Coke from the vending machine. Her already sizeable bosoms seem to be involved in some sort of competition with her hair, each expanding by the hour so that she is, at present, a creature composed almost entirely of breast and hair. This spectacle is so diverting that it's almost possible to forget that Davenport has just departed for some unspecified lunch liaison, reeking of cologne and dressed like an eighteenth-century fop. And if Rosie is standing in front of me, as she indeed is, and Rosie is meant to be Davenport's girlfriend, then who has Davenport gone to meet?

'We'd better get going,' Scarsdale says to me. He's right. It's a wet Wednesday lunch-time and we are on duty.

Our exit is interrupted by a bleeping noise from Scarsdale's jacket. It's his pager. He fought a vicious campaign to prevent the headmaster from issuing these and, once that failed, fought another campaign to ensure that he was the first person to get one.

'The bastards!' he exclaims, looking at the little screen. 'Look at that!' He shows me the pager – currently flashing the digital message *R Soul*. 'That's the seventeenth I've had today!'

In recent weeks, Mr Scarsdale has appeared to be sliding inexorably towards mental haemorrhage. He's now to be heard referring less often to 'the lads', and more regularly, as now, to 'the bastards'. His fiery outbursts (known as 'meltdowns' by the boys) ricochet round the school at half-hourly intervals, and he reeks permanently of stale sweat. Davenport is unconcerned, assuring me that this sort of crisis affects every teacher in turn. But I'm not so sure. Only last week, so it is rumoured, Scarsdale threw a copy of *Paradise Lost* at a boy in his class.

Being on duty is a joyless state, whether one passes it alone or with Scarsdale. It means you spend your precious lunch-hour in circuit of the school, turfing reluctant boys out into the cold and dealing with all manner of adolescent absurdity, from lost teeth, through nudity, to attempted murder.

Scarsdale loves it. As we start to tread the main corridor, the little man swaps his bottled-foetus glasses for a huge Soviet-administrator pair and, with these in place, begins to sniff the air, as if breaches of the school rules had a specific odour, one which he is uniquely skilled in detecting.

The task fills him with such pleasure that he forgets the pager message and starts relating a story to me. The details are irrelevant. Scarsdale only has one kind of story. Its basic title is They Didn't Know Who They Were Dealing With. It begins with someone – corporate or individual –

dishing out substandard service to Mr Scarsdale. It ends with that someone seeing the error of his or her ways and sending Mr Scarsdale a case of conciliatory champagne or ten thousand air miles. I suspect the walls of his house are decorated with framed reimbursements from Virgin Railways and grovelling letters from British Telecom.

The tale is cut short when Scarsdale breaks off to accost some boys wearing trousers better suited to crack dealers in south-central Los Angeles. He leaves me to my own devices, whistling a little tune to myself. And by the time he returns to my side, he's forgotten the story. We start the long haul down towards the library.

Rather than risk any more stories from Scarsdale, I decide to ask him a question – one that's been bothering me since last week. 'Anthony Blundell. Do you know him?'

'Bright,' Scarsdale acknowledges gruffly, his beard crackling against the edges of his neck brace. 'Tutoring him for his Oxford exam. Why?'

'Do you think he'll get in?'

'*I'm* tutoring him,' Scarsdale repeats, irritably. 'And he's in my MCS set. His insights into the Siege of Derry poems are . . .' He licks his grey lips, searching for a suitable compliment. And settles upon: '. . . good enough. Why the interest?'

The opportunity to reply is rendered obsolete as we reach the doorway of Room 8. Scarsdale glances in, spying a shifty knot of boys gathered round the teacher's desk. 'You sweep the library,' he says, nodding curtly to me. 'I'll take this lot.'

I would sooner go on holiday to Jamaica with Combat 18 than enter the library, kingdom of Ann Gorley. But there's little choice. As I push the wooden doors open, the librarian in question appears right at my elbow, knocked aside by my entry. She's been poking at the lock with a can of oil. 'Sorry,' I mumble.

By way of an answer, Ann shoots me the sort of look you could expect from an Albanian hill-tribesman whose brother you'd just accidentally shot some moments after marrying his pregnant sister. She turns, drifting haughtily back to her desk.

The library is the only room the boys are allowed legitimately to occupy during break-times, and it's always crowded, the air foetid with Monster Munch and hard-boiled eggs.

I approach Ann's desk as she enthrones herself. 'How are you?' I enquire, breezily, hoping to repair relations after our date.

Ignoring this preamble, Ann busies herself with her lunch – a spartan girls' collation of green apple and LoTaste yoghurt.

'Look, Ann,' I cut to the chase, lowering my voice, 'I'm sorry about what happened. It was a . . . a misunderstanding.'

'It's forgotten about,' she answers, lowering her eyelids.

Given that, since last Friday, the only contact between Ann and myself has been a few sharp looks of the pox-on-your-house variety, I can't help seeing this as progress. So I try following it up with a chummy smile. 'Friends, then?'

She bites her lip. 'Not really, no. I just meant let's try and get through the rest of the year without any bother. I've had enough of weird blokes to last me a lifetime.'

My anger rises at this point. 'What do you mean "weird blokes"? You think I'm weird just because I take you to a pub and it happens to be a gay pub? You think I'm gay now, do you?'

'I never said you were gay. But you talk about it as if it doesn't matter, Alastair,' she says, softly and severely. 'You obviously think that sort of thing's all right, or something. I'm just glad I found out what your views were before I got too involved.'

'My views?'

'That sort of thing,' she pronounces, piously, 'makes me feel sick.'

'Well, that's your problem,' I retort hotly. 'I don't know how you can even say things like that, Ann. What about your friend? The one who got stabbed?'

'He got stabbed because he goes round Bradford wearing a cape. He's a Goth, not a pervert.'

'How can you go on about your mum and dad being narrow-minded when you come out with crap like that? For God's sake, Ann . . .'

'Actually, I'd prefer it if you didn't use language like that,' she says, tightly.

'Like what? God? Oh no . . .' A sense of dread washes over me. 'Don't tell me you're . . . You can't be, surely. Not you.'

'What?' she snaps. 'A Christian? Why not? What if I have started going to church? What's it got to do with you?'

'I'm just saying—'

'Well, just stop *saying*,' she interrupts. 'Be quiet. This is a library.'

With that, she picks up her book – some cheery, cartoon-illustrated manual for the Alpha Course – and proceeds to ignore me. Feeling lost and hopeless, I look around the packed library, cheered slightly to see that no one has paid us any attention. The boys are crowded round wooden tables, six or seven together, engaged in a variety of unscholarly pursuits, of which eating crisps and sniggering are probably the most innocent.

Then, to the left of me, in a little alcove devoted to periodicals, I see one boy sitting alone. Like a young Alec Guinness, he's a whey-faced, bony individual, with gold spectacles perched on the tip of his sharp nose. He's engrossed in a large, plastic-backed volume, eyes blinking as he scans its pages, pausing only to scratch feverish notes on a little pad. Sometimes I think Davenport's ghost metaphor isn't quite right for Anthony. He often seems to me more like a bird, with his tiny, pecking movements and sharp grey eyes. But today there's almost something machine-like about Anthony Blundell – the way he scans each page for a few seconds before flicking over, the mechanical jerks of his pencil.

'How's it going, Anthony?'

The boy looks up, a skinny professor, enraged at having his most secret experiments disturbed. Blinking violently, he puts his pen down. 'If you mean how's the work going, I could reasonably say it was going quite well until about two seconds ago. And that it's not going too well now. But thanks for asking.' He picks up his stubby pencil and resumes his position, hovering over the notepad and waiting for me to go the fuck away.

Perhaps that's why he sits here alone: he's a boy blessed with a singularly unfortunate manner. Yet I feel this powerful urge to establish contact, not least because there was something he wanted to tell me last week, interrupted when he ran from the room. 'What are you reading?' I ask, peering down at his books.

'*The Trumpet Shall Sound,*' he answers resentfully. 'It's about millenarianism in the South Pacific. Cargo cults, chiliasm, that sort of thing.'

'Is that on the syllabus?' I ask, warily.

Anthony rolls his eyes. 'Of course not. I just thought it might be useful for the Oxford exam.'

'Oh yes. I'd heard about that. I gather Mr Scarsdale is tutoring you.'

Anthony puts the pencil down again. 'If you can call it that.'

'Well, that's pretty good,' I falter, simultaneously trying to keep the conversation open and regretting ever starting it.

'It'll be *good*,' he says witheringly as he stares back at the book, 'when I get in. And not good at all if I don't. So a bit premature, on your part, the good thing.'

I'm just contemplating bringing the entire shelving unit crashing down on top of Anthony's quibblesome, objectionable little head, when I remember that he came to see me of his own volition. Something on his mind. And it's my duty to help. Even if I'm a rotten teacher, a crap date, all these and worse, I can at least try to get one thing right. 'Anthony. When you came to see me last week . . .'

'*Noise!*'

This bizarre interruption, meaning that there is noise and that it must stop, has been issued by Mr Scarsdale, a man who has never needed a loud-hailer, although he often carries one. These one-word sermons can be commonly heard across the school, *Ties!* and *Litter!* and *Hair!* being among his favourites.

Scarsdale enters the library proper and scuttles over to me, wiping his glasses on the end of his polka-dot tie. Sighing, I file my hopes of a reasonable conversation with Anthony in a personal drawer marked UNLIKELY. It contains many items right now – like drinking only at weekends and getting Davenport to take the telescope out of my bedroom.

'What have you been doing in here?' the hairy disciplinarian demands, staring belligerently up into my face. 'It's like Bedlam.'

Scarsdale has a fondness for Bedlam. And Grand Central Station. And Beirut and Aberdeen-at-chucking-out-time and thousands of further metaphors for a slightly noisy room. I often wonder why he even pretends to get cross about boys being noisy. For a start, they just *are* noisy, in and of themselves, so getting in a stew about them is rather like being annoyed about the chimes of Big Ben. And secondly – why won't he just admit it? – Scarsdale thrives on noise and all other infringements of the school's Decalogue. They give him a hard-on. On those rare, precious days when class trips to the Museum of Mankind and raging viruses render the corridors as empty as a junkie's larder, Scarsdale lapses into a state of twitching misery, precisely because there are no boys to shout at.

I mumble something feeble, which Scarsdale dismisses and interrupts, pointing at a little tribe of sixth-formers on a far table.

'Go and see to them,' he rasps.

'See to them?'

'*Look at their ties!*' he hisses.

There is currently a custom among the sixth form to knot their ties back-to-front, so that the thin portion remains uppermost while the fat end is stuffed into the shirt. It's known as 'hard tie', on the grounds that only the most daring are prepared to flaunt one. Mr Scarsdale is a sworn enemy of hard tie – it sits on his database of sins somewhere between hair gel and being out of bounds.

As I approach this group of alleged miscreants, I see to

my annoyance that it's composed exclusively of my own Media and Cultural Studies class, the ones I largely like and get on with. Round the table loll the dashing Miller, resplendent in a dove-grey Italian suit, tapping with a fountain pen on his folder; his sidekick, the Stone Age Booth, dribbling onto his folded arms; and in between them, tapping out a text message on his mobile phone as he chews bright green gum, the beaky-faced Demetriou.

I'd never imagined these three to be close friends. But that's the surprising thing about Sinjun Lawmaahs, an institution of immense aesthetic contradictions. Each day, huge lumbering Jutes and Saxons clash bags and share desks and swap gum with almond-eyed Ganymedes of near-offensive beauty. There are boys who look like fish and locusts, and others whose mere grins send the Holy Ghost girls into a damp ecstasy when the two schools collide on the Green. It's a little Ealing-style community, I suppose, except that there are some, like Anthony, who do not take part at all.

'Ties, fellers,' I say, approaching the table and wishing various untreatable viruses upon the head of Mr Scarsdale.

'Sir?' Miller asks, playfully.

'Just do them up properly, please,' I say wearily. 'Then we can all get on with our lives.'

Slowly, resentfully, the trio down pens and mobiles and begin to comply. 'Why are *you* bothered?' Miller mumbles, quietly picking at the knot of his tie. 'Trying to please the Arsehole?'

'What did you say?'

'Talking to Booth, sir,' he responds, grinning brightly up at my face.

I walk back to a grimly nodding Scarsdale, now wishing I could fashion a garotte from a few dozen school ties and hold a most satisfying Assembly: one in which Scarsdale, albeit briefly, would be the star.

'That's the hard core,' Scarsdale observes in a low voice, nodding back at the sixth-formers. 'Miller and Booth. A little cell I've yet to crack. I keep petitioning the Head to get them excluded, but of course he won't have it.'

Looking back at this so-called cell, now cackling over something on Demetriou's mobile phone, I ask Scarsdale why, if they're so dangerous to the fabric of the school, the headmaster won't see his point of view.

'Because they're *rich*!' Scarsdale splutters in my ear. 'Can't exclude them, because we need the fees. Same with some of the staff. Take Davenport . . .'

'What about him?' I ask, leaping to my friend's defence.

'When he was in the sixth, Davenport turned up for the Cadet Force parade with "Born To Kill" written on his helmet. Now he loafs around with his hands in his pockets all day, teaching them dirty poems. And why? Because he's not like you and me. I warned you about him when I first met you, didn't I? People like him own the ground you're standing on! And they think they can walk over everyone else! He'll walk on you in time, you mark my words.'

Scarsdale is growing agitated now, the fruity tang of sweat issuing from his dirty neck brace. I feel an overpowering urge to run away from him, screaming, only returning when I've filled a rugby sock with nuts and bolts. He rails against privilege, this sweat-stained goblin, but it's not on grounds of socialism, just pure covetousness. He cannot wait to knot power and privilege around his own neck and wear them like a hard tie.

We pass out of the library, at which point Scarsdale treats me and the surrounding air to a metallic belch and says he's going to his office. I expect there are some boys queuing up there to be shouted at. 'You can do the rest on your own,' he offers, ungraciously, as he veers off to the right. 'And watch out for hair gel. It's difficult to spot when you're outside. You'll have to sniff them.'

I have, of course, no intention of sniffing boys, now or on any other occasion. Once I am free of Scarsdale, I lower my head – for no reason other than believing that this makes me less conspicuous – and make a bee-line for the old storerooms, where the accounts are kept.

I grinned like some local inebriate when I first discovered the accounts were being moved to the storeroom. I thought this would make them easier to steal. But on the two occasions I've tried since then, my mission has had to be aborted at the last minute – once because I got as far as the door and heard the headmaster and the bursar within, conducting a very earnest conversation, and the second time because a strange illness gripped me as I was skulking through the dimly lit entrance. I think they call it conscience.

Today the coast should be clear. The bursar is in the Cayman Islands and the headmaster is in an all-day meeting. It's now or never.

Not that my conscience is keeping any quieter. As I cross the quad, the off-white bungalows of Ealing Studios hover into view and I feel that what I'm doing is an affront to them. This was where, in 1939, they made *Cheer, Boys, Cheer* – a film that sums up the Ealing ethos in a single stab. A quirky, family-run brewery is about to be overrun by a vast, faceless corporation. Its fate rests in the hands of one man, a spy sent from the big brewery to infiltrate and destroy the smaller one. But, of course, he falls in love on the way, and hilarious consequences ensue. No such cheer for me.

I head downstairs, into the darkness and the musty, jumble-sale aroma of the storeroom. The filing cabinets, dozens and dozens of them, stand in formal rows like resting soldiers. This theme is heightened by the presence of various bits of obsolete military equipment leaning against the walls: webbing and netting and camouflaged mess-tins, the assorted bric-à-brac of warfare.

I go for the most recent archive, because I assume this will contain the sort of information Sammaddi wants. Getting that information out of the filing cabinet, however, is not such a picnic. Real spies, and spies in films, go equipped with skeleton keys and crowbars. My toolkit consists of desperation and a greasy spanner I found on the stairwell.

In my mind's eye, there's always been a drawer marked TOP SECRET FINANCIAL INFORMATION and it will open in a single tug. This turns out to have been highly fanciful. I tug the top drawer and all the drawers under it, and of course they don't move. I try various manoeuvres with the spanner, making a great deal of noise and succeeding only in toppling the entire cabinet to the floor. A domino effect then ensues, further cabinets smashing to the ground in the fashion of drunken sentries.

This would be a good moment to do a runner. But I don't. Not just because there are smashed filing cabinets in the way, but also because some of them have burst open. Their treasure has spilled out, buff folders and typed sheets lying on the floor like so many beckoning sirens.

I reach down for them, panting slightly indecently, like a boy putting his hand on his second pair of female breasts.

I hold a folder in my hands for a brief, delicious moment. And then a low groan makes me drop it.

I freeze. The groan comes again – a long threnody of despair, only partially human. I look around the dimly lit room, seeing nothing but camouflaged rucksacks and filing cabinets. Then, from the darkest corner of the room, from underneath some sort of tent designed for desert warfare, there is a scrabbling.

A slender hand shoots out from under the canvas and pats the floor. There's a grunt, a cough, and then the headmaster emerges slowly, painfully. He sits up, ashen-faced, his shirt hanging out of his trousers. 'AKS?' he croaks, looking up at me with the eyes of the damned. 'What on earth are you doing in here?'

'I was – I thought I heard a noise. Are you all right, Headmaster?'

'Yes, I –' he looks around him distractedly – 'I had a terrible headache. I must have fallen asleep.'

'You were sleeping down here?'

'I like it down here. The phone doesn't ring. It's dark and . . .' he gives a little sigh, staring at his knees, '. . . safe. I suppose that seems a little odd to you.'

I help the headmaster to stand up, but as soon as he does so he declares the need to sit down again. He executes this, heavily, squatting upon an upturned filing cabinet, with his head in his hands.

'My meeting with the auditors finished ahead of schedule,' he says, in a bland, detached voice. 'There wasn't a lot to be said.'

He proceeds to tell me, unprompted, with breathless concentration, that the school is facing imminent financial collapse: a collapse not unrelated to the nearly completed Sports Centre.

'It's too late to halt the building work apparently, and anyway Mr Warren's final instalment is just about to go through.' He looks at me, his jewel-blue eyes suddenly warm and frank. 'I'm sorry to be burdening you with this, Alastair. It's really not fair. But I'm afraid it could be all over. All over.'

'Are you sure about that?'

He lifts his head towards the bare lightbulb and sighs. 'I've never understood why some people should have things and other people not. I wanted everyone to use this place. Like they do in the Low Countries. Not just the sports complex. Everything. I thought we could have summer schools. Let people use the language labs and the Auditorium.' He clenches his slender fist. 'Make this place into a . . . a real *hub*.'

'A hub?'

'Yes — a hub for the community. That's what's missing round here. There's nothing. But try telling that to those faceless, number-crunching . . .' He searches for a word. '*Wallies*. They're more than happy for me to spend money on guard dogs and closed-circuit television. But what about *giving* people something? Giving them something to use, so they don't want to break in and smash it up? Is that such a silly notion?'

'No. I don't think it is at all.'

He looks at me with affection. 'I love this school, you know. My wife says I love it more than her. Sometimes I think she might be right . . .' He trails off into silence. He takes a breath and smooths down the knife-edge creases of his trousers. 'But when you love something, you can't just stand by and see it destroyed, can you? You'd want to fight on?'

'Of course . . .' I say, a thought flickering at the edges of my mind, then blossoming into Technicolor. 'Maybe there's a way of saving the place . . .'

He looks at me sharply. 'Such as?'

'Well. Erm. You could try and raise money for a start. That church down the road has a car boot sale every weekend.' I stop speaking, aware that the headmaster is looking at me with mounting blankness.

Suddenly, he claps his hands together. 'Exactly!' he exclaims. 'I see what you mean. A bit of fighting spirit.' He stands up and starts pacing round the paper-strewn floor excitedly. 'I'm going to do everything I can to save this place. Car boot sales, summer fairs . . . I'm going to make jam and stick two boys from Ten L outside the gates every lunch-time to sell it. We could have a tombola!'

'You could do vintage-car rallies at the weekend.' I'm getting rather into this brainstorming. 'Or do historical reconstructions on the playing field. You know, like the Battle of Naseby.'

'Well, perhaps not that.'

'No. Sorry, Headmaster.'

Five minutes later, I'm heading back to my lessons. I feel like waving to the Ealing Studios behind the fence, but settle for a surreptitious nod in their direction. They have relieved me of a great burden.

You couldn't really ask for a clearer manifesto of Ealing than *Cheer, Boys, Cheer*. Plucky little Greenleaf Breweries, run by a cheery old soul who collects tankards, versus the tyrannical Ironside Corporation. Small, eccentric and cosy versus huge, humourless and ruthless. Merry England versus the looming threats of Germany and Russia.

And, of course, the simple faith of Steven Harpenden versus the scheming octopus of Tara and Mr Sammaddi. An octopus that can get knotted. Because I won't be helping them. Why should Sammaddi get his hands on the school when it can be saved without him, made into a hub, as Harpenden says?

There are those Tennyson lines going round in my head as I head towards the cloakroom to fetch my briefcase, the lines that lent their name to the Ealing title. *Kind hearts are more than coronets, / And simple faith than Norman blood.*

Opening my briefcase, I'm less pleased to discover that some kind heart has filled it with fresh dogshit. However much I might be on the school's side, it seems someone in the school is not on mine.

Next of Kin

'Just give the Annster a nudge up there, would you, there's a chap?'

I bend down, making a step of my linked hands. The angular girl wordlessly puts a tall, laced boot into this fleshy platform and I heave her upwards towards the hinge at the top of the library door. Her crimson backside rests against my burning cheek.

'It won't budge!' Ann exclaims. I let her down gently and as we straighten ourselves we bump into each other.

'Leave it out, you two,' Davenport quips, in a maddeningly jolly voice. 'Laws against that sort of thing. Save it for later.'

Ann stares darkly at the floor. Davenport has now begun picking at the lock with a bunch of keys. He's an expert lock-picker, apparently, a skill much in use around the school, since the caretaker doesn't know one end of a key from another. That's why Ann called us over to take a look at the door − or, more specifically, called Davenport over, with me as the highly unwelcome addition.

'Always been a sod, this one.' Davenport grunts, squinting into the keyhole. 'When I was in the Lower Remove they pulled me out of a Greek Unseen to open it. Prince Philip was coming to have a gander.'

'The royal lock-picker, eh?' Ann says, in a friendly voice. Davenport chuckles. Feeling frozen out, I start to drift away up the corridor. There's a loud crunch and a cry of 'Bravo' from behind me. Shortly after this, Davenport comes thundering up the corridor, wheezing with the effort of catching me up.

'Talk about on a plate!' he exclaims, punching me between the shoulder-blades. 'My dear chap, I sometimes worry about you. I fix it up for you to cradle Gorley's rose petal of an arse in your hands and you just drift away. She was clearly bitterly disappointed.'

I turn to face him. 'Lawrence, you've got to stop.'

He looks hurt, but there's no other way. In the past three days, Davenport has employed every stunt in the matchmaker's bible, short of shackling Ann and me together, naked, in a lift. I know he only wants the best for me, but there's a desperate urgency making his plans fail twice as miserably as they were doomed to in the first place. Worst of all was him sending us both pager messages on Wednesday, telling us that a Mr Q. Pidde urgently wanted to see us in the photocopier room. When we both arrived there, we found each other, a bottle of Cava and – oysters being presumably beyond Davenport's end-of-month budget – two packets of prawn-cocktail crisps: a sight which, in spite of the melt-in-the-mouth quality advertised on the side of the crisp packets, failed to melt Ann's heart.

'Don't look at me like that. You may as well know: Ann hates me. And I'm pretty sure I hate her, too. It's as simple as that. We're not going to get together, whatever you do.'

Davenport gives me a watery-eyed look, the sort Cinna gives when you've denied him the opportunity to savage some limping child. 'So there's no chance you'll be seeing her tonight, then?'

We head together into the auditorium, where the boys are slowly filing in. We make our way up the steps, me talking in a low voice. 'None at all, I'm afraid.'

'It's just I could take OMG aside for a BFW . . .'

'*Who* for *what*?'

We ease our way onto the row at the back where we always sit.

'Our Miss Gorley, for a Brutally Frank Word. Sometimes it takes that final push. I mean, I wouldn't want to blow my own cornet or anything, but I have had a few minor successes over the years. Tara, for instance. I fixed her up with her first beau at Durrers. Did she tell you that? Of course it was merely to prepare the ground for having a crack at her myself, you understand . . .'

I've been trying not to think too much about Tara, who has left a number of messages on our answerphone at home and is evidently still expecting me to spy for her. I haven't quite managed to tell her about my change of heart. Or begun to consider how I'm now going to get a reference letter, with that particular avenue being not so much closed as converted into a full-on minefield.

'I just can't understand for the life of me,' Davenport chunters on in my ear, 'why you didn't get on with her.'

'Because she's fucked up!' I say, too loudly, and several rows of boys turn round. 'She refuses to have anything more to do with me,' I continue, lowering my voice, 'because I took her to a gay pub. It was the one you suggested, incidentally.'

'Really?' Davenport comments, vaguely. 'That's quite interesting.'

'Is it?'

'Well, yes. I've always fancied myself as a sort of amateur psychoanalyst of the gender divide, as you know. And I suppose you could say Ann's trying to make you into another Danny Laycock.'

'The dead bloke?'

'Exactly. You know – she wants to think you're probably a closet pansy so she doesn't have to risk getting mixed up with you and possibly getting hurt again.'

'Fascinating. Does that mean she's not fucked up, then?'

'Oh no – she's obviously howling mad. But then, they all are, slightly, aren't they, ladies?'

'I can't understand why you're not doing this as a career, Lawrence.'

'Thank you. But what's troubling me is the thought of you loafing around all lonesome on a Friday night. Shocking waste of a handsome buck.'

I now glimpse the reason for Davenport's urgency. 'Do you want me out of the house?'

'Well . . . I wouldn't mind, old boy. Not for the reasons you think, either. We're trying an experiment. She's going to paint me.'

'This would be Rosie, I take it?'

'Rosie?' Davenport clears his throat. 'Well, yes. Who else? Terribly good little artist, actually. Won prizes for it. I think every gentleman should have his portrait done at least once, don't you? And my looks won't last for ever . . .'

I'm prevented from discussing this further by the ringing of the bells. Silence fills the auditorium.

This morning sees a break from the established routine. The headmaster has gone to a conference, 'Pedagogy – a Jungian Perspective', in The Hague and the school rises today to the sight of Mr Scarsdale trotting onto the stage, his head thrust high into the air by a gleaming new neck brace, and his gown trailing on the floor behind him.

'This should be good,' murmurs Davenport.

It is indeed an entertaining spectacle. Mr Scarsdale stands on a pile of hymn books in order to peer over the lectern, and announces in a mournful, cancel-all-the-doves sort of voice that there will be no reading today, no music, no congratulations. He pauses, letting the silence take hold. Then he begins again. 'There are certain boys,' Scarsdale declares, huskily, 'who are sailing dangerously close to the shore.' He glares down at the auditorium, causing a few sinless Year Sevens to gulp. 'Certain boys,' he continues, 'who find it amusing to abuse the services provided by British Telecom, by sending offensive messages.'

He says that these boys are *skating on thin ice*. They are not only breaching section 4.8 of the 1987 Public Communications Act, they are breaking school rules. The fact that there is currently no rule forbidding boys to send offensive messages to people's pagers does not mean it is OK. It is far from OK.

'There is no school rule forbidding treason,' Scarsdale rasps to the tensed auditorium, 'but any boy trying it would swiftly find himself in detention. As will any boy I catch sending offensive messages to my pager. For your information . . .' he continues, pointing into the audience, 'and, believe me, I *know* who you are, boys, ho yes, and for your information, I have changed the number. But if I ever catch the persons who were doing it . . .'

This tirade is interrupted by a trilling sound from his pocket. Scarsdale stops, mid-sentence, and retrieves the pager from his pocket. Reading the message, he flushes an emergency-red colour and flings the little box to the floor.

Then he jumps from the pile of hymn books, landing right on top of the pager. It splinters like dry bones. He continues to jump up and down, until there remains only a pile of shards and screws. I am wondering if someone should intervene, and am almost about to do so, when Scarsdale stops jumping and turns to face the hall. He points again into the auditorium with a wobbling finger, as if warding off a spectre. 'You will not win!' he screams, in a hoarse monotone. I am reminded strongly of Peter Sellers playing various dictators, including himself. 'You will not win!'

He then bolts from the stage and out of the doors, leaving the shocked school behind him. A few embarrassed titters break out here and there. A few wags in the sixth form start a round of applause, but it does not proceed very far. Davenport silences them, which proves that even he is disturbed by the event.

I decide that normality must be resumed swiftly. I rise to my feet and tell the boys to start filing out as usual, a process only obstructed by Miss Kastrafitis arriving late, trapping her hair in the main doors and having to be rescued by the Fire Brigade.

At lunch-time, Davenport and I emerge from adjacent classrooms on the main corridor and walk together towards the staff room. It's normally a cross between Sarajevo and the January sales at this hour, but today it seems as if the pensive hush of Assembly still hangs around like a subduing cloud.

'Here's one,' Davenport exclaims. 'I'll get the first round if you can top it. Scarsdale in a spangled leotard, mud-wrestling with Fatima Whitbread.'

Although this game normally occupies a large chunk of our daily lives, and is played with great vigour by both participants, I find myself now bereft of a response. All I can say is that I almost feel a bit sorry for Scarsdale. Last week, I spent an entire evening rinsing my briefcase with Dettol and it still smells of dogshit, so I know what it's like to feel persecuted. And to be persecuted by persons unknown is even worse. I saw in Mr Scarsdale's frantic outburst a chilling prophecy of what might happen to me if I don't get to the bottom of the matter quickly.

Davenport brushes my point aside. 'Quite different,' he says. 'Thing about Scarsdale is he never had what it takes.'

'And what's that?'

'Simply a matter of—' Davenport halts mid-sentence as we come across a dark, chubby boy of eleven, standing alone outside the Music Room. He is making a series of deeply unattractive shrieks, like a dingo being raped. 'Oh glory,' Davenport says. 'One of our little WUBs.'

WUBs – or With Us Brieflys – are a recently labelled category of boy, so called because when they are introduced to their new classes the teacher invariably has to say something like 'With us briefly this term is little Anton Sergeievitch Telushkin who doesn't speak much English . . .' WUBs tend to be the sons of diplomats, or the sort of Eastern Bloc businessmen who have become suddenly and inexplicably rich. The school charges elevated rates for giving them a desk for a term or so, before they are whisked off to some new life in Brooklyn or Jedda. Speaking little English – and none of that curious hybrid of posh, patois and MTV employed by the boys – they make a rather pathetic spectacle, wandering the corridors friendless and confused, a sitting target for those of their peers who profit from the theft of dinner-money. Just last week a WUB approached me, sniffing, with the words 'Please ken you hellup me?' and I almost felt like a father might feel.

'Abuladze, why are you making that godawful racket?' Davenport asks, bending down to the child.

'*Veech van?*' asks Abuladze, revealing a tongue bright blue from the toxic confection he was rolling around his mouth.

'That shrieking sound,' Davenport continues, in a studied voice that is almost a parody of his own. 'Why are you doing it? Or let's look at it another way: why *do you think* you are doing it?' He gives me a sly wink.

Abuladze screws up his face for a moment, the very picture of youthful concentration. It is the face every teacher wants to see. '*Eastern Soul act caught my otter,*' says the boy. At least that's how it sounds to me.

But Davenport seems to understand. Nodding wisely, he says, 'East and Sollak have got your jotter, eh?' He turns his head to me. 'Heard of East and Sollak?'

I shake my head, having never encountered these boys. They sound like a pair of Davenport's SW1 shirtmakers.

'Where are they,' Davenport continues, in the manner of an aged QC who knows exactly what a crowd-puller he is, 'these boys allegedly in possession of your jotter?'

'*No fuck Sir Ron the gay ogre feel drip.*'

'If East and Sollack are in Norfolk, on the geography field trip with your jotter,' Davenport probes, gently, 'then why are you, Abuladze, standing outside the Music Room making a noise like a brace of banshees? Is it going to get your jotter back?'

Abuladze gazes up at Davenport, unblinking, mesmerised. 'No, sa.'

'Well, then, run along and stop howling.'

The boy departs, humming, and Davenport turns

proudly to me. 'See? Couldn't have come along at a better time. That's all it takes. Discipline, control, respect. Just a bit of acting.'

Davenport has a point, I think, as we part by the staff room. It's all a matter of acting, and the best teachers are those with a sense of drama. To assume control, one simply has to pretend that one has it already. The boys are not fooled, but they reward you for playing the game. Scarsdale, on the other hand, has suffered because he genuinely wants control and the boys, knowing quite how much he wants it, are equally determined he should not have it. Teaching isn't a gift, it's a game.

I see this, quite clearly, as I go to check my locker and find a deeply unflattering cartoon of myself pasted to the door. The artist has not only technical skill, but an unsettling ability to pinpoint my darkest insecurities. I am depicted emerging from the MacKendrick Arms, wearing an outsized overcoat with its lower hem in tatters. My cheeks are flushed red and my ears buffoonishly large. All around me are little bubbles, the sort cartoonists employ to suggest inebriation.

'That's very good, isn't it? Did you do it yourself?'

I turn round and find myself looking at the olive-skinned and perpetually troubled face of Miss Kastrafitis, whose locker is next to mine. A clump of her dark curly hair is missing thanks to the Fire Brigade.

'No. I think someone's playing tricks on me,' I say, about to screw it up.

'Like who?' she asks, blinking very quickly. I look away, because sometimes Rosie's blinking has the unfortunate effect of making me blink at the same speed, which can result in disorientation and nausea.

'I don't know, Rosie. The Ferals are the prime suspects. Ten L, I mean.'

'I can believe that. Which ones in particular?'

'Not sure.' Then a thought strikes me. I found him and apologised, of course, in the end, and it seemed to be accepted. But perhaps it wasn't. Perhaps it's a real old-fashioned vendetta. 'I did manage to offend that quiet one with the large head. Peter Histon. Maybe it's him.'

Rosie shakes her head. 'I doubt that very much. He's a lamb. And besides . . . may I?' She takes the drawing from me and examines it from various angles. Then she shakes her head again, making the gold hoops in her ears jangle. 'No. Somebody older did that. Definitely.'

'How do you know?'

'I'm a teacher, Alastair,' she says, simply, but not disguising a faint rebuke. Perhaps I was wrong. Perhaps some people are born to teach after all. She hands the drawing back and starts pulling exercise books from her locker. 'I've always wished I could draw,' she muses. 'I hated art when I was at school. I got paint thinners in my eyes and they had to take me to hospital to have them rinsed. And then of course there was that time I got locked in the kiln . . .'

My last lesson before lunch was with the dreaded Ferals. I was – Socratic debates with Spofforth aside – encouraged by their apparent industriousness, their compliance, their apparent readiness to sit still and not set light to things. I fancied I was getting through to them at last. And perhaps that's true. And Miss Kastrafitis is doubtless right. The drawing didn't come from 10L. But this knowledge no longer cheers me up because it's still true that, elsewhere, I have enemies.

As my sixth-form set files in after lunch, they are

surprised to find me already in place. They are also miffed to find the TV absent, and a pile of photocopied sheets on the table.

'Thought we were going to watch that Pimlico film, man,' says Booth, smoothing his thick thatch of hair. Today he resembles some scary Inca carving, all huge mouth and primordial eyes.

'Not having a test, sir, are we?' This from a worried Demetriou as he throws his bag into the corner of the room.

'Just sit down and be quiet,' I say, in a cold, quiet voice. 'Yes, Miller, that means you too.'

My class take their seats with a puzzled, aggrieved air. I regret what I'm doing, but can see no other way out now. Who were the most feared, least abused teachers when I was at school? Those whose lives — and sometimes their gender — remained a mystery; those who, you always suspected, spent their breaks reading *Chalk and Marker* magazine, and folded themselves up inside their lockers at the end of each day.

I can see my part in the game. I've been too familiar with the boys, let them take liberties. I saw where that mocking round of applause began in Assembly this morning. It was with Miller and Booth and their coterie of designer-clad acolytes. Miller, who made that quip about me being in the MacKendrick. I also know that they have a score to settle with me now, over the hard ties, and there's no doubt in my mind that the salad, the dogshit and the cartoon stem from them. Time to be a man of steel.

Easier in the long-term, too. The nice guys, the ones who'd let you eat your crisps and would happily bitch with you about the deputy head, they were the ones you took for granted. But the fierce ones were wiser. They'd spend most of the term walking round in a foul, boy-hating fever, until the last day, when, with a carefully executed bit of PR, like dressing up as Santa Claus to hand out fun-size Mars Bars or dropping a huge chunk of sulphur in some water, they'd suddenly become kindly uncles, with everyone saying afterwards what cool blokes they really were. That's what I've got to do – be hard and keep it up until the end of term, when I'll, I don't know, hand out Special Brew and Rizlas.

'I can't believe there are still people talking at the back.'

'Yes, you can,' says a voice. This makes me fairly angry. But I decide to leave it alone. After all, the voice has a point. Of course I can believe there are people talking at the back. Because people always are talking at the back. People were talking at the back when Socrates was marking homework. That's why people go to the back. To talk. Why do teachers even say things like this? And, more frightening still, why have I started saying them?

I start again, more sternly. 'I don't particularly like finding rotting food in my locker. I don't particularly like . . .' I decide to bypass the indignities of the dogshit for now '. . . finding nasty little drawings in there either. And I want it to stop.'

The class stare back at me, innocently. Just as I expected. They were hardly going to break down and confess.

I ransack my brains for more words, for my last lines were the only ones I've prepared. I recall a phrase that Brother Constantine was fond of using. 'I'm just doing a job,' I say, more reasonably. 'You'll all be doing jobs one day. Some of you already are.' Here I look pointedly at Miller. 'And it's hard enough, frankly, dragging yourself out of bed some mornings, without having to cope with harassment. Is that understood?'

'D'you want us to sort them, sir?' asks Miller.

'What?'

'Whoever's doing it. We'll give them a kicking, if you want, sir. Take them out.'

'Clip them, sir. Pull the trigger.'

The class gives a chorus of nods and approving noises. Booth offers to give the culprit a dead leg. Demetriou says he could lend me his brother's Ninja sword, if that might help. Someone else – who *is* that chubby one who looks like Herbert Lom with acne? – says he knows someone whose brother knows someone else who can get people shot. Which I doubt.

'Cut it out. I'm just warning you. That's all. Now look at your sheets.'

No one moves. The boys glare at me, hurt and affronted. 'You mean you think it's us?' says Miller, fiddling with the knot of his tie. It's done up the wrong way round again.

'I'm just giving a general warning, Miller.'

The noise of a dozen teeth being kissed sounds around the room. 'So you *are* saying it's us?' Booth chips in, digustedly. '*Raas*!'

'Look at your sheets,' I repeat. 'This is from a book called *Ealing Studios*, written by a gentleman called Charles Barr. Get ready to take notes.'

A long, heavy silence follows. Resentfully, the boys pull out pens and paper, with a great deal of slamming desk-lids and muttering.

'We're going to read the marked passages on page forty-three,' I say, pale with the exertion. 'Miller, you can start.'

Miller flips through his photocopied booklet with

studied slowness. He takes a deep theatrical breath and begins. 'It. Is. The. Coming. Together. Of. These. Three. Currents . . .' He reads the words blandly, falteringly, like the sort of local unfortunates my mother would delicately refer to as *backward*.

I give a weary sigh. I'd underestimated their capacity for protest. 'Read it properly, Miller.'

Miller looks up from the book. 'We liked you,' he says, '*sir*.'

'I've heard all about you,' says a voice, echoing in the post-Friday quiet of the Geography Room. Anthony Blundell has appeared in front of me, like a vision. Whiter than usual, it seems, clutching a shapeless green kitbag.

'Do you always creep up on people?' I say, crossly.

'Imprecise,' Anthony replies. 'Creeping up on people says more about the people's reactions, you see, doesn't it, rather than my intentions? If you meant to say, Do people normally get a fright when you walk into the room, then I could have answered you truthfully, or at least more accurately. Yes. Yes, they do. I can't seem to help it. Sorry. In fact, not sorry, since I can't control your actions, can I?'

I compose myself. At least someone appears to trust me, however desperately, skin crawlingly *logical* he happens to be. 'I didn't think you'd come back,' I say.

Anthony shrugs, dumps the bag on the floor and sits down. The bag is partially unzipped; bulging from the top is the scholarly tome he was studying the other day. 'If I tell you something,' he says, solemnly, touching his milky, almost luminous face, 'you can't say anything to anyone. All right?'

I nod, encouragingly. 'It's all in confidence.'

Anthony looks over his shoulder. Then he stares at me closely for a second, his grey eyes giving nothing away. Again I understand why he has no friends. He has a spooky manner: he creeps up on people, holds their glances too long on some occasions, and on others will not meet them in the eye.

I shiver, involuntarily. It's as if the boy might be scanning my soul. And Lord knows what festering toadstools he will find.

'You got the wrong ones,' he says, simply.

'When?'

'It wasn't Miller, or any of them,' Anthony says, in a low voice.

'Who was it, then?'

Anthony shakes his head. 'I don't know. I'm just telling you. People don't notice me. So I always know what's going on. And it wasn't them. They're after someone else, Miller and that lot. And they like you.'

'But you must have an idea who it might be.'

Another ponderous, hypnotic stare. 'I don't know. Honestly. Maybe you've offended someone.'

'That narrows it down.'

'You're on your own there. I'm sorry.'

'It's not . . . it wouldn't be you, would it? I mean, we did slightly get off on the wrong track last week.'

'Did we?' He looks surprised. 'What most people seem to call getting off on the wrong track I would usually call a reasonable conversation. What happened?'

'You got worked up, when I said about seeing you at this B&B place down the road.'

'Ah . . .' He rubs his pointed pencil nose. 'Well, I needed to tell you about that. You see, you *did* see me there.'

'I know I did.'

'But it's not like you think,' he says, glancing at his shoes. 'My family . . . we own it.'

He's lying. 'But I know the owner, Anthony. Mrs Danischewsky. She and her husband bought the place with his compensation money.'

'And we bought her out,' Anthony answers sharply. 'We own lots of them, actually. OK?'

'OK.' A dead-end street, if he wants to lie to me. It's not even relevant – I don't care whether he's living in the back of a Transit van. I lean forward across the desk, placing my palms upwards. 'Why did you *really* come to see me last week?'

Anthony makes a frustrated grunt. He's like some crabby old inventor who can't understand why the world doesn't want his perpetual-motion machine. 'If that's what you want to know,' he snaps, 'why bother with all this stuff about where I live? It doesn't come into it, does it? It's of zero relevance. Why can't people just stick to the point?'

'Go on.'

'People always say I'm quibbling. I just want everyone to be precise. What's so bad about that?'

'The reason you came to see me, Anthony . . .' I prompt.

'That girl,' he says. 'The one who brought round the books and things.'

'Martha?' I exclaim, slightly startled.

'I don't know her name, do I?' he cries, irritably. 'She wasn't wearing a badge. The point is, she was very upset. Crying. Bridget – Mrs D had to give her a cup of tea.'

'What was the matter with her?'

Anthony gives an insect-twitch of a smile. 'She asked

me to give you a message. But then she changed her mind, and said she didn't want you to know. And Bridget said it wasn't our business to go passing things like that on. So I wondered about it. And then I thought I'd better. But you knocked me off my stride last week, with your rather laughable attempts to be Sigmund Freud. And then I spoke to my sister—'

'What was the message?' I interrupt, on the verge of performing a karate stunt on the desk.

'She's pregnant,' Anthony says.

'Excuse me?' But there's no need for him to repeat it. And Anthony knows that from my expression. 'So that's why you came to see me,' I reflect numbly, barely aware of his presence. 'Martha's pregnant.'

'Not exactly. There was something else.'

'Go on.'

The gaunt boy points his chin thoughtfully in my direction. 'Would you — do you think you'd be at all interested in going out with my sister, sir?'

'*What*?'

'It's a simple enough proposition. Would you go out with my sister? You know, ask her out. Take her to the pictures. Be her boyfriend and so on.'

'But . . . but I don't even *know* your sister.'

'I know. But you'd like her if you did. She's a nice girl.'

I rest my head in my hands, feel the cool of my damp palms on my fevered brow. 'Anthony,' I'm speaking in a monotone, 'I'm in no position to go out with anyone's sister right now.'

'Why not? You're not with this Martha any more, are you?'

The door opens and Mr Scarsdale appears in the

doorway, cracking his knuckles like some gnome with a grudge.

'Ho, it's you, Mr Strange,' he grates. 'I thought I saw a boy going in here. Strictly out of bounds, this is.'

I point a finger at Anthony. 'Counselling hour. I'm Not OK.' Which is true. I'm not at all.

Trouble Brewing

'Thing I realised a while back. What's wrong with a lot of young men, in my view. Young women, probably, too . . .'

'*I'm not here. Leave a message after the beep . . .*'

She's re-recorded the answerphone message, erasing the father of her unborn child from her life. I put the phone down and look at Davenport, resuming the conversation he started ten minutes ago, before disappearing into his study. He's returning with a flower vase and a table-cloth.

'If you could just shift that lager tin for me, there's a chap. Thanks. What was I saying?' Davenport proceeds to throw the table-cloth over the table.

'Young men,' I respond, gloomily.

'Oh yes. Far too judgemental. Spend their whole lives looking for someone who looks like them, talks like them, went to the same sort of school. Think it's all about shared commonality, you see. "Do you remember the time the *Blue Peter* garden got trashed?" "Did you have a Showaddywaddy album?" That sort of thing. All bollocks.'

'Is it?'

'A failure to understand the true and mystical nature of love,' Davenport pronounces.

My housemate is bare-footed, in a vest, an apron — depicting leeks and pointy hats and various other emblems of Wales — tied round his green suit trousers. For the first time I notice how muscular and hairy his forearms are, like those of some sadistic dentist. Behind us, in the kitchen, a distinctly flavoursome stew — another of Davenport's buried talents — is bubbling away on the hob. Beyond that, outside the back door, in fact, Cinna howls pitifully and taps with a paw on the glass, having been ejected into the rain so that Davenport can fumigate his basket. And all because Miss Kastrafitis is coming round to paint his portrait. Or so Davenport says.

'That's the thing about almost every filly I've ever stepped out with,' Davenport says, returning from the kitchen tasting a wooden spoonful of the stew. '*Iucundi acti labores*,' he exclaims, smacking his lips. 'Where was I? Oh yes. More or less nothing in common at all. Always disagreeing. Like that slightly slutty one with the small moustache at college. Can't remember her name now.'

'There've been that many?' I ask, with gloomy irony.

Davenport ignores it. 'First time she came over to my rooms, she said: "I'm not getting under that duvet, Davenport, it's filthy . . ."'

'Your girlfriend called you Davenport?'

'Well, no,' Davenport says, flushing slightly. 'She called me . . . well, never mind. Point is, I stood my ground. Said, "Look here, toots, it's a gentleman's bed. It's for farting and ejaculating and scratching your nads in. It's not some lady's bed, where you lie in your scented cotton shroud and dream about Lord Rochester being cruelly sensitive to you. So you either get in or fuck off."'

'And what was the outcome?'

'Well, she fucked off for a bit and I had to go out and buy a new duvet. But the point is—'

The phone rings and I leap for it, to prevent my

housemate, in this deeply reflective mood, from saying anything he shouldn't into the receiver.

'Hello. You just rang my number. Who are you?'

How typical of the new, efficient Martha to dial 1471 and then a 3: the sort of move only performed by brisk, careerist folk afraid to have missed some hi-urgency call from New York.

'Martha. It's me, Alastair,' I say, taking the phone out into the hallway and sitting on the stairs.

'Oh.' Not a frosty *oh*. Just a light, matter-of-fact one, as if I was the carpet fitter ringing back with a quote. 'How are you, Alastair?'

'Fine.' How do I say it? What's it going to be – a boy or a girl? Can we call it Rex? Can we not send it to St John Lorimer's? For some reason, none of these things come out of my mouth; instead, the brutal question: 'Are you keeping it?'

There's a pause, a tired exhalation. 'They told you, then. I asked them not to.'

'They thought I should know. I must say, Martha, I agree with them.'

'Why?' she demands, sharply. 'What's it got to do with you?'

'Oh, sorry, Martha,' I exclaim, slipping into the familiar argument-groove. 'Maybe you don't think it's particularly important that you're carrying my child.'

'I'm not carrying your child.'

'You got rid of it? Without telling me?'

'It's not *your* baby. How could it be, Alastair? Think!'

As with most men, my understanding of the mathematics of conception, and particularly the female end of the business, is a bit foggy. It always seemed to me there was some kind of scatter-gun principle when it came to

Martha's menstrual cycle, or more like the London Transport principle, in fact, in that you'd get weeks and weeks of nothing, then a whole load of periods came along at once. Made even more confusing by the fact that Martha always said she was regular as clockwork. So I know we weren't doing a lot of procreation in the last few months, but we did kind of manage it once or twice and the pill's not 100 per cent effective. That at least is the theory I've worked out in these last, panicky hours, trying to vacuum the carpets and wash up, all the while lost in a rush-hour of emotions, half-terrified and three-eighths miserable and somewhere, in all of that, about 0.125 milligrams proud and fascinated to find that nature actually *works*.

'It's Tim's, Alastair. I'm having Tim's baby.'

Fury and wisdom begin an elaborate tango in my mind. Of course she is. Why didn't I see it? Now it all adds up: not just that stumbling attempt at a kiss outside the winebar, but all the late nights, the nights when she came in with wine on her breath, saying, 'We cracked open a bottle of Chardonnay, just to keep us going'; the restaurants we had to visit, on the grounds that 'some guy' at work had been there and said it was A1. Some guy, my arse. Some bug-eyed tit called Tim.

'Don't be like that, Alastair. We weren't going any-where. You admitted it yourself. And Tim was so nice, and he'd been going through a terrible rough patch with Kitty ever since the twins were born . . .'

I'd like to take Tim through a further rough patch: that thistly bit on the edge of Ealing Common, where the junkies throw their needles, Tim bound hand and foot and tethered to the back of a Harley, driven by a drunken and hopped-up-to-the-eyeballs me.

'I was meaning to get in touch, actually. We're going to get married, when Tim's divorce comes through. We wondered if you'd do a reading in the church?'

'What reading? A little something by Sid Vicious?'

'Please try to be a bit grown-up about it.'

'Please fuck off.'

She loses her patience, a click of the tongue signifying that Reasonable Martha has swapped places with Well Fucked-Off Martha. '*You* fuck off. It's all your fault, not mine.'

'What's my fault?'

'You just sat there on the sofa for months, watching those stupid old films,' she says, her voice becoming shrill. I can picture her on the other end, her eyes flashing, hair glinting as she flicks it angrily from her forehead. 'And you didn't even look at me. Why do you think I had my hair cut? Why do you think I lost all that weight? Because of you! I wanted you to look at me. And you didn't. You didn't even do anything when I was sleeping with Tim.'

'I didn't know you were sleeping with Tim!'

'You just didn't want to see it. You could have stopped it happening any time. All I wanted was you to *do* something. You could have told me not to change and I wouldn't have done. But you didn't do anything. So it's all your fault and you're a tosser, Alastair, a complete tosser.'

'I see.'

After replacing the receiver with considerable calm, I sit, head in hands, at the foot of the stairs for a few minutes. There it was, I think. 'Notice Me' – a game for two players. Another of those high-stakes games we play – and I had to go and lose the piece of paper with the rules on.

I return to the living room, where Davenport is seated

in the armchair, hewing shards of Edam-yellow skin from his feet with a penknife. 'Personal grooming,' he quips. 'Cripes. You look like you've seen a ghost.'

I sit on one of the hard dining chairs, saying nothing. I don't think I can face one of Davenport's homilies on the miracle of childbirth or the esoteric manner in which a man can lose a woman yet gain a deeper understanding of the universe. I've already gained that understanding, in about five minutes flat, and I don't like it one bit.

There was a time, I remember, quite early on in our relationship, when Martha and I had been walking along the King's Road. And Martha was talking but I'd not been exactly listening to her, attention drawn, just momentarily, to one of those improbable hologram-type women you see drifting around the Chelsea boutiques. And Martha had realised what I was looking at, and kicked me on the shin with the words: 'What makes you think you could have her, you little shit?' before vanishing into the traffic. Because – yes, she was having a bad day. But more than that, she always wanted me to notice her. And she never stopped. I thought she was pulling away – with her busy haircuts and designer tableware. I began to believe, in the last days of our relationship, that I could have brought home Maltese waiters and sucked them off in the shower. And providing no one left any wet towels on the floor, Martha wouldn't have given a stuff. I was wrong. She just wanted me to notice her. And what might have happened if I had noticed her? If I had known my part in the game? None of this. I could have been with her still. That baby could have been ours. It might have been good. Who knows?

Davenport pads bare-footed over to me with a bottle of cooking sherry and places a kindly hand on my shoulder.

'Get yourself a dose of that,' he counsels. 'No, no, not in the mug, please, Alastair. I'll fetch you a sherry glass.' He pads into the kitchen, where he lets Cinna in and then returns with possibly our one unblemished item of glassware.

Mechanically, I pour myself the largest measure possible, only stopping when the sweet fluid runs down onto my fingers. Davenport nods approvingly and returns to his seat. Cinna assumes a dutiful posture at his master's right elbow, so excited by the odour of feet that he starts to get an erection.

'If you ask me, you've taken on far too much with that counselling nonsense. Always in a terrible mood afterwards. What happened today?'

I force my thoughts towards a subject I can speak about, thinking this will perhaps help. 'Not a lot.' Then a memory occurs. 'I know why the school ghost's a ghost.'

'Because he's dead?'

'He's living in a B&B. I think he's moved out of home. I don't know why.'

'Why do people usually move out of home?' Davenport grunts, resuming his home chiropody. 'Because they don't get on with their folks.'

'I don't think Anthony really gets on with anyone.'

'Seems to have a certain degree of affection for you.'

I look back at my housemate, now feeding strips of the skin from his feet to Cinna, who is, in turn, swallowing them with relish.

'Man and dog, united in a circle of symbiotic harmony,' Davenport declares, delightedly. Then he frowns at me, slightly hurt. 'There's no need to do that disgusted look.'

It's not a disgusted look. If anything, seeing Davenport feeding his own dead skin to his dog has helped me slightly. That and learning about Martha's impending lovechild have made me realise that this bachelor half-life holds no more joys for me. I've got to find a woman – fast. And not screw it up this time.

Davenport glances at the clock. 'I don't want to chivvy you, but you did say you were going to the pictures. And it's going to get a tad crowded in here, what with easels and paints and so on.'

'Yes, all right,' I say, at that moment remembering something else. 'I was talking to Rosie earlier on, actually.'

'Oh yes?' Davenport says, with more than a soupçon of shiftiness.

'She said she hated art. Couldn't draw for toffee. I thought that was a bit peculiar under the circumstances.'

Davenport suddenly becomes incredibly fascinated by a dark patch on his left trouser leg. And when the business of scratching it and sniffing his fingers and wiping them on his apron could not possibly be repeated one more time, he gazes into the middle distance. 'Yes, well,' he pronounces carefully, 'she's her own harshest critic, you see.'

The doorbell rings and Davenport dashes for it with all the alacrity of a Levantine carpet salesman who's just spotted a coachload of elderly Germans. Cinna goes mad, leaping into the air and letting out a series of Stygian howls. The noise is so loud, I can barely hear the tense, urgent conversation at the door.

There's a clanking sound as an easel comes into the front room. Behind it, clutching an immaculate set of Louis Vuitton luggage, is a tall, slender woman with a Perma-Tan. Her exquisitely made-up face is streaked with dampness.

A distinctly tortured-looking Davenport proffers a

quivering hand in her direction. his voice hoarse and dull. 'Gisela. Have you met my housemate? This is Alastair.'

She ignores me, her gym-perfected body racked by a sudden sob. 'I've left him, Lawrence. I'm not going back.'

'Going to pour any hot beverages on me today?'

'Sorry?'

It's the Monday-morning bus and a grey day. She's sitting in the seat opposite, her blonde hair loosely hanging down from under a Forties hat that looks like a little meringue. Maybe she works in a theme restaurant? Called Blackouts or Blitzes, serving powdered egg and whale-meat to the strains of Vera Lynn.

'No, I'm sorry,' she says, fiddling with the zip on a little red, kettle-shaped handbag. 'I'm sorry about him talking to you like that. In the coffee-shop. He can be a bit . . . you know. We were having a bad day.'

'That's OK,' I say now, with a half-smile and noticing, once again, and almost in spite of myself, these great green eyes of hers. Big, where everything else is neat and small, but not huge − not like those of fish-boy Histon, and not like Anthony's, which are grey and far too wise. 'We all have days like that.'

'It was a whole *weekend* like that,' she says, with a tiny laugh. 'It was a relief to get back to work.'

'What do you do? For work, I mean.'

'Do? Oh, I'm a solicitor.' She says it '*sollissidor*'. 'I work in Hanwell. Well, I work half the week in Hanwell and half the week up in Finsbury Park. I do Mondays, Wednesdays and Fridays here one week and Tuesday, Thursday there, and then swap round and do Mon—' She stops herself, biting her hand. 'Sorry. Very boring.'

'Not at all. I'd never've had you down for a solicitor.'

Her eyelashes flash up and down, like those of some cartoon character that's also available as a pyjama case and rucksack. 'Don't say it like that! What's wrong with being a solicitor?'

'Nothing,' I add hastily, embarrassed. 'Just not what I imagined, that's all.'

'What you imagined?' she comes back, her eyes narrowing. I'm reminded of Joan Greenwood, the languid and throaty starlet of a dozen Ealing flicks. 'I don't understand.'

'It's just I . . . well, I had a sort of game. In my head. Guessing what different people on the bus do.'

'Oh, I do that at the doctor's. My dad taught it me. You get extra points if you can get them to, like, actually tell you.'

'You do that one too? I thought it was just me. Anyway, I had you down for a . . . for a . . .' My voice trails away. It seems faintly ridiculous now, telling her I thought she was an actress, when she just does a spot of conveyancing.

'For a *whut*?'

'Well, you've always got those crime books, you see.' I point to the one on her lap – a luridly jacketed library book, entitled *Dames Don't Float*. 'I thought maybe you wrote them. And then there's the way you dress, so I thought maybe you were an actress or something.'

'Something wrong with the way I dress? Can't I dress how I want?'

'Of course. I just didn't think you'd be a, you know, a solicitor . . .'

'Oh, well,' she says, stroking the middle of her throat with a red fingernail, 'sorry to disappoint you.'

'Not at all.'

She looks away, out of the window. The bus lurches on and we lapse into a forlorn silence.

Quite an enigma, all things considered. I didn't mean to sound rude about solicitors. This one's definitely far from average, dressing as she does like a vintage movie star, with that half-American accent and a passion for crime fiction.

'I like these clothes,' she says suddenly. 'That's all. Maybe I just don't want to go round looking like that guy.' She points at a man leaning against the Met Police 'Rat on a rat' poster. 'Even if I do have a boring job. What job do you think *he* does?'

I've seen the man before – one of those people who manage to be entirely grey. Zip-up briefcase and a mac, balding, sucks Tunes all the time. The man they put in adverts to emphasise the sheer hell of life without Lemon Zest or Anusol ointment.

'I don't know. A businessman?'

'But I thought you said you spent all your time trying to guess what jobs people did?'

'I don't do it with everyone.'

'Well, who do you do it with?'

'Erm – just you, actually.'

'Oh.'

That *oh* – shocked and slightly wary – means that silence reigns between us again and she starts to read the jacket blurb on her book. But then, looking out of the window, a new thought occurs. It's born, partially, out of a Friday night sitting in alone in the MacKendrick, waiting for Davenport's gruelling negotiations with Gisela to come to an end; out of a weekend doing washing, wrestling alone with a new duvet cover and feeling generally, horribly single; and then, most propitiously, of gazing across Ealing

Broadway right now to that little independent cinema, where they're showing *The Sweet Smell of Success*.

'Look,' I say, trying simultaneously to flash her my best, I-don't-collect-comics-or-spend-my-evenings-on-the-internet smile and remain on my seat while the bus veers violently to the left, 'I hope you don't think this is rude, but I wondered if you'd . . . if you knew they were showing *Sweet Smell of Success* at the Royal? It's just that I'm going, you see, and . . .'

In the movies, the dialogue progresses seamlessly from the initial I-think-you-dropped-this to a shot of Her laughing uproariously in the crowded station coffee bar and showing a bit of stocking as He tells Her that hilarious anecdote about His landlady and the Frenchman in the blackout. Not in life, buster. My own attempt could be best described as plaintive, and possibly criminal. I shouldn't have bothered. Desperation gives off its own repellent musk.

'That's your best effort, is it?'

'Huh?'

'I'm supposed to roll over now you've actually deigned to speak to me after all these weeks of pretending you're not looking at me?'

'I'm not sure I——'

'Yeah, sure,' she says, blowing a little raspberry through her lips. 'The old Hugh Grant number. All "terribly sorry, but I wondered if you'd . . ." Chuck in a bit of stammering. Honestly. British men.'

Burriddish men. 'Well, I didn't realise it was such an insult,' I say, a touch haughtily, 'asking someone out.'

'I'm not insulted,' she replies, brushing bits of hair behind her ears. 'Just disappointed. Because I know exactly what *you* do.'

'Oh you do, do you?' She's really got me riled now – right under the skin in that special way, like an over-long movie on a full bladder, or people sitting behind you in such movies, who won't blow their noses, even though there's a whistling sound coming out of them.

'Sure. You probably sit in some office all day, surrounded by girls. And you spend your whole day thinking up new ways to get them to massage your little ego. Little sad intrigues and schemes. And then not doing them, because the reason you keep conkers in your pocket, fella, is you've got no balls.'

'Well, I'm sorry to let you down,' I say, my voice rising to a quivering shout, 'Miss Aren't-I-A-Bit-Mysterious-In-My-Veronica-Lake-outfit, but you're completely wrong. In fact, I don't think anyone could ever be so completely, prize-winningly bloody wrong about me. I don't sit in an office all day and I'm not surrounded by girls either.'

'No?'

'I wish to Christ I was. But I'm surrounded by boys, actually. Noisy, irritating, malodorous boys. I'm a teacher. So stick that in your vintage handbag!'

Composing a vast war poem in my head, consisting of all the things I despise about the Bus Girl and am going to tell her I despise when I next see her, I duck through the gates with my head down. Bunny Warren is outside his Portakabin, talking to one of his builders, a much smaller man in a lumberjack shirt. Bunny's poking a finger at the smaller man, actually jabbing him with it. With each blow, the man jerks back slightly. There's a frightened, embarrassed look in his eyes.

I scurry on, sensing there's something going on here, something I'm not supposed to see. I also don't want to get talking to Bunny. Most mornings entail him ambushing me with great rambling accounts of Bruce Forsyth's legendary barbecues or the time he did the tango with Carol Vorderman. They always make me very late.

Inside, Davenport is standing, frowning, picking a blob of bubblegum from one of the tall wooden tribute boards. 'Hello,' he says, glancing round. 'Think you're too good for Assembly these days?'

I ignore this, knowing full well that Davenport's mood is solely because Gisela has gone back to the headmaster's bed instead of staying in Davenport's. It's all to be expected. And, all things considered, Davenport has made a good recovery for a man who was declaring his intention to enter a monastery on Sunday night. 'The bus was late. Anything important happen?'

'No. Oh there was one thing. *Steve* . . .' he says the name with studied disgust '. . . announced the Prizegiving guest. It's that little celebrity arsehole Rick Reed.'

I've heard of the aforementioned Rick. He's one of the new breed of 'Brit Lads', a movement of novelists and dramatists unified by a fascination for football, of both the pub league and intercontinental kinds, football violence, football as played in the past, football matches set on distant planets and all matters otherwise football-related. You can occasionally see black-and-white pictures of Rick on the front of *Time Out*, big-eyed and shaven-headed in a Ben Sherman shirt, and looking like a sensitive Rottweiler. He is chiefly famous for having head-butted a *Times* journalist who called him middle-class.

'Know what we used to call him?' Davenport asks, as we head towards the staff room. 'Dick Weed. He's an Old Boy, which means they'll probably make me take the bugger out to lunch beforehand. I wonder if he's still allergic to everything,' he muses on. 'Used to be one of those sods who always had a note.'

'Have you seen his play?' I've seen posters for it. *Shoot, Jerry, Shoot* – a three-hour extravaganza based upon the legendary football match played in the trenches.

'My hatred of Rick Reed, Alastair, precedes his entry into the canon of Eng.Lit.'

'What's wrong with him? Apart from his preoccupation with football?'

Davenport shakes his head, pursing his lips. 'You wouldn't understand.'

This is a regular observation, Davenport feeling that a St John Lorimer's education is far more than just that. It irritates me profoundly. We near the staff room, where Anthony Blundell, with smudges of dirt on his shirt collar, is telling Mr Scarsdale that he's forgotten his homework.

'Better prepare the crash team,' Davenport comments.

'Have you actually done it?' Mr Scarsdale asks, in a quiet voice. This studiedly hushed tone is an integral part of the Scarsdale meltdown procedure: it lulls the victims into believing that everything might be all right.

Anthony – his grey eyes mesmerised by fear, like a rabbit in car headlights – nods. 'Yes, sir. It got sick on it. From my, erm, little brother . . . so it's drying out on the boiler.'

Scarsdale, who has deliberately chosen a pair of glasses that magnify each of his eyes to the dimensions of a small moon, places a hand on the boy's bony shoulder, presumably as a prelude to snapping his neck. I feel an inexplicable urge to jump in and protect Anthony.

'All right, lad,' he says gently. 'Get it to me tomorrow, OK?'

Anthony scuttles away, glancing behind his shoulder all

the while as if it might be a trick. There's a deflated atmosphere in the crowd as everyone moves off. And one of increasing unease for Davenport and me as Scarsdale bows at the staff-room door to let us go in first.

'After you, lads.'

We enter the staff room, where Miss Kastrafitis has got herself into trouble with a broadsheet newspaper. Scarsdale asks if anyone would like a cup of coffee. Davenport and I watch in silent suspicion as Scarsdale, whistling a little tune between his teeth, goes over to the coffee-pot. 'Are you feeling all right?' Davenport says, at last.

Scarsdale meets this with a grandfatherly smile. 'Why?'

'You do seem rather . . . different,' I venture.

The old man turns his radiant beam upon me. 'I caught Miller and Booth calling my new pager last night,' he says, his teeth gleaming like those of some rodent surprised in a dark tunnel. 'So I gave the head an ultimatum. Them or me. So it's over, you see.' The staff room offers him half-hearted congratulations as Scarsdale comes across with a tray of coffees. 'Now I can get on with phase two,' he announces, happily.

'Phase two?' asks Davenport.

'The school magazine,' Scarsdale replies, sipping the steaming drink.

'We've already got one,' objects Davenport. '*The Old Lorry.*'

Scarsdale interrupts him. 'What we've got, Davenport, is a shoddily produced *stab* at a magazine, which is totally under Harpenden's editorial control.' Here, Mr Scarsdale places a heavy Seventies NHS set of glasses on his nose, making him look like Michael Caine after a long illness. 'I'm setting up a rival. It's going to be out in time for Prizegiving. And it's going to have double the circulation.'

'How can it have double the circulation?' Davenport queries. 'Every boy gets a copy anyway.'

Scarsdale waves this aside. 'You're welcome to choose your side, Davenport,' he warns, ominously. 'Just don't expect you can change your colours.'

The little man sips his coffee noisily and then gazes over the rim of his mug at me. 'I meant to tell you, Strange. Headmaster's looking for you. He seemed a bit agitated. Something to do with your references.'

The Feminine Touch

'*Een ontbijt voor de draam, en geen koffij nach de schlaam.* Sorry, I must introduce my wife. Gisela – this is AKS, who's been implementing some thrilling new initiatives on our new MCS course.'

I'm standing in the headmaster's office, shaking Gisela's limply outstretched, much bejewelled hand and trying to pretend, just as *she* is, that we've never met before. A glassy smile is fixed on her rust-painted lips but, otherwise, she's the picture of innocence. Not a muscle is giving away the fact that, a few days ago, I was standing in front of her in our front room, while she sobbed and told us she was definitely leaving her husband for good. A husband she has now blatantly not left at all.

'A pleasure to meet you.'

'Do sit, Alastair,' the headmaster bids me, brushing some imaginary flecks of contamination from his black suit. This morning he is neither chat-show anchor nor underpant-model, but closer to the *maître d'* of some Mayfair restaurant that has no phone number. 'Just a couple of points. Firstly, I wanted to update you . . . I've received a letter of reference from Mr Sammaddi.'

'Have you? I mean, you have?'

The room spins in front of me, the immaculately dressed Harpendens at the centre of the vortex like some lurid Aquascutum advertisement, the bookshelves behind them whizzing in and out of view. How can this have happened? I gave Tara nothing, and then, when she gave up calling me, gave up trying to explain to her. I've spent the last week just waiting for the inevitable to happen – the call to the office, the P45 in the buff envelope.

'Yes.' He frowns delicately. 'I've been paging you since seven this morning. Perhaps your batteries are running low?'

I say nothing, this being the first time anyone has mentioned that the pager needed batteries. No wonder Scarsdale said the head was getting agitated.

'Well, it's all highly commendable. I won't bother you with the entire text, and the handwriting is really rather poor, but he says you'll be a credit to my organisation.' He looks up from the letter and gives me a measured smile. 'But I knew that already. Some of your fund-raising strategies were most innovative. I've already begun to implement a few.'

I nod, numbly, wondering all the while what ghastly game of chess Tara thinks she's playing with my life, and what her next gruesome move might be. One thing's for certain: there's going to be a move. And I'm not going to like it.

'So I thought,' the headmaster continues, 'as Edmund Schietekat once put it, we might grow fat from your granary of worthiness, sir.'

'Sorry?'

'If you wouldn't mind chaperoning Rick Reed when he comes to do the Prizegiving. That would be a great boon to us.'

I'm just about to say that I'm not really cut out for escorting Brit Lads, particularly not ones who – if gossip columns are to be believed – get coked up at the Booker ceremony and call Melvyn Bragg a bollocks. But the Head holds up a slim, tapered hand to quiet me.

'ARS has recently presented me with his mid-term report.' He looks up at his wife. 'Mr Scarsdale has been showing young Alastair the ropes.' This is not entirely untrue – but it's a rope, singular. One fashioned into a noose, bearing the legend 'Attach head here'. 'Any man who can win a few words of positive feedback from ARS has my undying respect, Alastair. I realise it's not at all easy working under him. And strictly between you and me, there are *moves afoot*, as the Dutch Premier once said . . .' Gisela rolls her eyes and lights a cheroot, a gesture that causes her husband to tug, neurotically, at his Adam's apple, a worried look in his deep-blue eyes. 'Moves afoot to, shall we say, ensure that a certain teaching operative's tenure of that post is not extending beyond a point where its functionality and exercise have become disagreeable to those who formerly were appreciative of and, er, yes, of it.'

So Scarsdale is for the chop. Well, I don't much care, even if he did say a few nice things about me. And even if the head has started talking like a Jane Austen character.

'Secondly, the Pickle Night.'

'*Pikkelnacht*,' adds Gisela, flicking ash onto the floor.

'A little custom from the Low Countries,' the head explains, passing Gisela a ghastly ceramic ashtray, which looks like a dissected eye and probably won its creator a few prizes. 'On the night of Queen Juliana's birthday, it's customary for a little festivity. Employers invite their employees over for pickles and genever. Perhaps a hand of whist.'

'Sounds nice.' An evening of card-games with the

Harpendens, eating pickles and drinking stuff that tastes quite like whatever the pickles were pickled in. No wonder they're called the Low Countries. A person couldn't be much other than low after a night like that.

'Of course, we lay on a somewhat more substantial spread, don't we, dear? Some cold *haaringsbroodje* usually, and a few *olliebollen*.'

Gisela doesn't answer this, she merely stabs her cheroot into the bowl with unnecessary force. I get the impression that she's not intending to have much to do with the *olliebollen*. Or much else.

The trilling of a mobile diverts the headmaster's attention and he hunts in increasingly unbalanced fashion for it in his pockets and on his desk before realising that he's left it outside in his coat pocket. He darts away, leaving Gisela and me in stiff silence. She has the look of a woman who lives exclusively on tiny, expensive breakfasts – yoghurt and fresh figs and crispbreads – and I haven't a clue what to say to her.

She takes the lead. 'He sweats when he eats, you know.'

'Excuse me?'

She gives a dry swallow, fiddling with her wedding ring. 'Lawrence. When he eats, he sweats.' There is a long silence after this. Outside, we can hear the headmaster using the unctuous voice he uses only on the wealthiest parents.

'Oh. I see,' I say at last. 'Is that why you've gone back to your husband, then?'

She glares at me. 'Stupid. It's why I love Lawrence. He's like my father was, you see. How do you say it? *Stocky*? Kind of like a bull, you know, rushing around everywhere? Makes a lot of noise.'

I say, for want of any better response, that I've heard the

noise myself. It sometimes keeps me awake. Meanwhile a snatch of the headmaster's conversation drifts through the door. 'I understand at least one of the Whittaker twins was carrying tear gas at the time . . .'

Gisela gives a disgusted click of the tongue. 'You think Steve makes any noise?' she asks, her perfect, fine-boned face contorting with some deeply felt but indistinct emotion. 'In Holland we have a saying, "He smells of steam." You understand that, Alastair? Steven is like this. Nothing. But Lawrence smells of . . .' Her breast rises and falls. She gives me the sort of civilised glance that makes me realise Britain will probably never form a functioning part of Europe. 'You think it's bad, me and Lawrence, I think.'

'Well—'

'Yes, you do. Well, tell me. You think it's right I should love a man who loves only his job? Only this school?'

'Well, no. Not really . . .'

'It was his father's sixtieth birthday party,' Gisela interrupts, with a husky sigh. 'This was when I first knew I loved him. He's outside the restaurant, your friend, smoking a cigarette. And I came out for a minute. And I saw him. Giving money to a man. A beggar, you would say. And for that moment I thought it was my father. I thought: Yes. You are a strong man, Lawrence. I love you. You see?'

'So why aren't you with him?'

She takes a breath, about to say more, when the headmaster reappears, beaming as he clicks his phone off and tries, unsuccessfully, to put it into his smallest pocket.

'Well, that's super. Friday night. And please tell LSD as well, will you? I'd so like our Mr Davenport to experience a little Dutch culture. And Gisela will be unveiling some of her latest watercolours, won't you, dear?'

Gisela shakes her head at me, mouthing something that looks quite like *No*.

I find myself quivering as I go to my next lesson. It's the sixth form, and although I composed an apologetic speech to them last night in the bath it seems to have been wiped by intervening events. In any case, the expulsion of Miller and Booth has rendered it pointless. The rest of their clique will doubtless think me implicated in some way, and hate me even more.

I stare down at my scuffed shoes as I enter and a hush descends upon the classroom. 'I said some things last Friday,' I say, quickly, not daring to look up, 'and they weren't fair. And whatever's happened since then, I want you all to know that I was wrong, and I'm sorry.'

I look up. The class is a pinkish blur before my eyes. '*Blud!*' exclaims Miller's voice. 'Safe, yeah? Forget about it.'

The haze clears and I now see Miller, sitting at a desk, wearing a purple velvet lounge suit. 'Miller?' I croak. I clear my throat. 'I thought you'd been excluded.'

Miller waves a hand affably. 'Well, I have. But I didn't want to miss the end of *Passport to Pimlico*. We are still watching it, aren't we?'

'You don't mind, do you, man?' This is from Booth, seated next to Miller in a matching suit, but still looking like something from the Pleistocene era whose chief achievement was the use of stone hammers. 'Only, we start work tonight, so it's the last chance.'

I ask them numbly what work they are planning to do. A shame, to think that a bit of youthful rebellion has condemned them to a life of patty-flipping in Burger King. I realise that I'll miss them.

'Oh, we're opening this bar. In town.'

'Half-price cocktails tonight, sir,' adds Miller. 'If you fancy it.'

I say that I just might. 'Dress to impress, sir,' cautions Booth, passing me a flyer. 'But we'll stick you on the guest list.'

Lunch-time sees me doing a different thing. Namely, swimming. This is for a variety of reasons. Firstly because I'd rather stick my head underwater than think about anything. Under ANYTHING are currently filed dogshit, cartoons, and salads, Martha's baby, Tara's spooky game-playing, Ann Gorley and that irritating Bus Girl – the list is endless and has recently expanded to re-incorporate the ghostly Anthony Blundell, who doesn't live at home but now appears to have a little brother who gets sick on his exercise books and a sister in need of a boyfriend. Secondly because a month and a half of living with Davenport – a lifestyle fuelled by Herculean quantities of ale – has resulted in a dangerous expansion of the waistline. And somewhere in my unconsious mind is a link between me losing control over reality and me losing mastery of my trousers.

There's a little clutch of Ferals by the gates, engaged as part of the headmaster's fundraising drive in the process of accosting passers-by and forcing them to buy raffle tickets. Choosing 10L for the job was an inspired move on Harpenden's part because, even if half the money goes missing, these boys are threatening enough to ensure that no one dares to walk by without throwing them a few quid.

They seem to be in a fairly human mood for once, and as I go past they say things like 'Sir, sir,' and 'Going for a smoke sir?' to which I manage a don't-push-it smile and tell them I'm off for a swim. This gets a laugh or two.

There's no point going home for swimming trunks. I don't own any and I wouldn't risk putting anything of Davenport's that close to my most precious organs. And Cinna will think I'm a burglar. I'll swim in my boxer shorts and borrow a towel from the Lost Property box. No one will see.

After doing a few lengths, I'm interrupted by the sound of a door slamming. I quickly exit the pool and head for the changing room. There's no one around. 'Hello?' I call out. There's no answer. There is, however, a quantity of chlorinated water in my ears, lending the interior of my head an echoing effect, like a big balloon with a few dried peas rattling round inside.

I shrug and head for the bench where I left my clothes and towel. They are gone. I stare vainly all around, check under the bench, then check under all the other benches too, saying over and over again things like 'Calm, calm' and 'deep blue ocean'. Then I scan the showers. And those offering no solace, I begin to wonder if my memory is perhaps failing me, and maybe I did leave my clothes by the pool after all. So I splash once again through the green disinfectant puddle at the entrance to the pool, strewn with wiry hairs and verruca plasters, and head back in. I walk all round the pool, shivering. My clothes are gone. This is no joke.

Except, I realise, as I sit, despairing, on a bench, it *is* somebody's joke. Clearly, I am still being victimised. And this is the most brutal assault to date.

I look up at the clock. Only ten minutes until afternoon

school. There could be boys in the changing room any minute now, if they're still using the place. Crazily, I wonder about hiding in the showers until darkness falls, but then I remember that I have three lessons to teach.

As goose-pimples form on my legs, and my penis shrinks to a peanut, a plan forms. There is, I know, a brambled path at the back of the pool and, on the other side of it, a fence. It is made of wire, but I'm pretty certain I could scale it, given enough desperation and urgency, feelings I now have in ample and mounting quantities. From there, it's only a swift dash, across the old tennis courts, over another smaller fence and into the back garden of my house. I'll break a window and get more clothes. Give Cinna whatever's in the fridge to shut him up and keep his jaws off my leg.

Outside, I gasp as cold air hits flesh that rarely see the sun. Steeling myself, I start to run. The rough leaves of the path scratch and pull at my feet, but I'm surprisingly fast when I need to be. Now I'm before the fence where it dips slightly – this has to be the only crossing point. Thinking of my safety, I lay the thin, damp towel over the wire and clamber over. Some ragged points of wire jut up through the towel and into my boxer shorts, tearing at them and pricking my scrotum. I swear and topple naked onto the ground the other side.

Leaving my only pretence at dignity shredded on the wire, I plough naked through the bushes, towards the tennis court. As I emerge into the light, like some long-forgotten prisoner of the jungle, a series of short, high screams pierces the air.

There are a dozen girls in tennis skirts on the court, rackets in their hands, transfixed, staring at me. A stout nun is bearing down upon me, waving her racket like a scythe. I wonder how she might respond to my immediate re-conversion to Rome. I need God right now, more than I need underpants.

I grope through my afternoon lessons, having cut my hand breaking the glass on the back door and scarcely had time to dry myself before Cinna, scenting the blood, barged through my bedroom door and bit me on the right ankle. Now, I am cold and aching, hand and ankle performing a carefully executed duet of throbbing and my mind haunted by a host of hairy spectres.

I never viewed the final bell with so much boyish pleasure. I belt from the classroom before the first of the boys and make a bee-line for the warmth and safety of the staff room.

As I run in, Davenport's assisting Miss Kastrafitis with the picking of the weekly Lottery numbers. He wrinkles his shaggy eyebrows at me, amused. 'Here he is,' he quips. 'The Sinner.'

I stare at him, heart beating. What does Davenport know? Surely, that old nun couldn't have had any idea who I was, I bolted from the tennis court so quickly, and no one followed me. Or did they?

Scarsdale looks up sternly from some form he's filling out in painstaking detail. 'I want a word with you,' he says.

'It's not like it seems,' I gabble.

'Ho,' Scarsdale sings, sarcastically. 'Isn't it?'

'Someone's been playing tricks,' I explain.

'I know that,' spits Scarsdale, standing up to face me, and just about reaching the bottom of my ribcage. 'It's *you*. Sneaking behind my back, poaching.'

'Poaching?' I query, deeply confused.

Scarsdale stands right on my toes, his loo-brush of a face glaring fiercely upwards. 'That's what I'd call it. Stealing my pupils off me. Well, you're welcome to him. *You* can hold his hand through the exam. And see how well he does.'

'Who?'

'Blundell!' shouts Scarsdale. 'Oojer fink? Creeps up to me this afternoon and says' – here he alters his tone to a high, mocking lisp – ' "Thir, I want to be in Mr Strange's class. I don't want to do the Belfast poems any more. I want to do the Ealing comedies, thir. With Mr Strange." The little skunk!'

I shake my head, insisting I know nothing of this.

'Jew fink I just come over on the S.S. *Gullible*, sunshine?' Scarsdale enquires, brutishly. 'Asking me questions about him! All those cosy little chats you have with him on Fridays.'

'Yes, but I assumed—'

'When you *assume*,' Scarsdale recites, from his vast liturgy of teacher-twaddle, 'you make an *ass* out of *u* and *me*.'

I glance towards Davenport for help. But my friend merely puffs out his cheeks, helpless.

'I don't blame you,' Davenport says later, in a kindly but woeful tone. 'You wouldn't necessarily know, not being a Lorry's man yourself and all that. But poaching another chap's boy, that's just NTDT, old boy, strictly NTDT.'

'What?'

'Not The Done Thing.'

'I needed to see you, Alastair.'

'I was just going out.'

'Don't go out. Please. It's f. important, darling. Stay in.'

It's seven o'clock. I was just heading out, with a hefty nimbus of misery over my head, to go and eat pickles with the Harpendens. Davenport, needless to say, has bowed out of the proceedings, giving some very shaky set of excuses which included both blinding headaches and tickets to an ancient Greek performance of *The Frogs*. And I was picturing in detail the evening ahead like an Arizona dirt-track. A desperately weak gin and tonic, perhaps two, but certainly not enough to anaesthetise me against the acute facial pain of smiling and looking politely captivated for at least four hours. Hand after hand of Flemish card-games, tailing off into studied yawning at the appointed hour, and offers of a taxi before being pushed out into the unwelcoming night, just five minutes too late for Last Orders.

And then the doorbell rang. I answered it, lumbering grumpily to the door in the fashion of a fairy-tale troll, and found, standing in front of me, Tara, wreathed in Siberian bear-fur, her neck bare except for a string of glittering stones.

My dark ex-friend gives me a smouldering look that manages to be both meaningful and meaningless as I let her into the hallway. I offer to take her coat, thankful at least that Cinna has gone with Davenport to whatever function he's really attending, and is therefore not on hand to attempt coitus with said coat. But Tara says she wants to keep it on.

She stands in the centre of the living room, teetering on a pair of shoes fashioned from a few threads of leather, gazing at her surroundings as I fix a drink. She smells like the lobby of the sort of hotel I'd never be allowed into, not even to deliver a package.

'I see Lawrence is still living in the eighteenth century,' she remarks, as I hand her a glass of whisky. She flops down heavily in the armchair, revealing a tapering expanse of smooth, bare leg, which I try, and fail, not to stare at.

'Yep,' I say, curtly, wondering what she wants. I just don't trust Tara any more.

'So how are you, Alastair?' she asks. 'Enjoying the job?'

'Yes, thanks.'

'Met anyone nice?' she asks, carefully.

'Look, Tara, I don't want to be rude, but what do you want?'

She looks hurt. 'Why are you being so horrid? I got you your letter. Well, I mean, I *forged* the beastly thing actually, but it worked, didn't it? And you don't even have the good manners to thank me for it. It was q. bloody hard, you know.'

'All right, all right. Thanks. Thank you.'

'Don't say it if you don't mean it,' she replies, sulkily.

'I don't know why you sent it! First of all you say you're not going to help me unless I risk my neck for you. Then I don't, and you do it anyway. What's your game?'

She sighs, takes a sip of her drink and gives me a molten look over the rim of the glass. 'I've been q. naughty,' she says, in a tiny voice that I recognise as the one she uses for persuading men to do various things. 'Misled you a little.'

'What do you mean?'

'It wasn't really a case of me helping you. It was the other way round.'

'Tara, I'm just a teacher. In fact, I'm not *even* a teacher, am I? What could you possibly have ever wanted from me?'

'You're my friend,' she says, plaintively. 'You always *used* to be my friend. When we were at work. Didn't just stare at my tits and make crappy comments like most boys.'

I keep silent, remembering that I *did* stare quite a lot at Tara's tits, and the rest of her; I just did it with a little more subtlety than the builders over the road. Or perhaps the word should be dishonesty. But it's true what she says. We were friends. We used to help each other.

'I *am* your friend. But what's going on?'

She arches her neck back, scratching it with a single fingernail. It's the sort of gesture I've seen the Bus Girl doing equally well, making me think that women must have to practise a lot of things in the mirror.

'I realised it was v. silly of me to ask you to go and steal things. I mean, it's impossible. You could have got into trouble.'

'You're right. That's one of the reasons I'm not doing it.'

'One of the reasons?'

'The other reason being it's a shitty thing to do. And I don't want your husband to buy the school. I think it should just stay like it is. There are a lot of people who like it that way. There's Lawrence, for one. And he's my friend, too.'

She nods solemnly. 'You're right. I realised that. That's why I came round, you see. I just wanted to say, you don't have to do anything, Alastair. I'll have to work things out on my own.'

'What things?'

'Well, you don't need to know, do you? I mean, don't worry about me, or anything. I'm used to looking after myself. I've been doing it ever since I was little. Well, you know I have. I often used to think that was one of the reasons we clicked, you and me. Wasn't it? You with your spies. Me not knowing who my real father was for all those years.'

'I suppose so.'

She makes a brave face. 'You know he's in prison? Daddy?'

'I didn't.' Although the knowledge is no surprise. Tara's natural father – an elderly hooray by the name of Ben Fielding – the boss of the vanity publishers we worked in, was a man who relished defrauding people in the way others of his class enjoy chasing foxes.

'It was in all the papers. A while back now. That's where the problem started, really. Amjie was mortified. I mean, he sort of takes it personally. You can see why. He thought he was getting a little slice of England, marrying me. Upper-class English rose and all that. Then it turns out to be a rose that stinks. That's how he puts it, anyway.' She smiles faintly. 'Always did think he was a poet.'

'Hardly your fault.'

'Of course not. But he's . . . he's so obsessed with being this perfect English gentleman. That's why he's been trying to buy all these things. You know, the newspaper and the schools. He wants to join the club.'

'I wouldn't have thought England was the kind of club people wanted to join any more. Particularly not successful Indians.'

'Well, you don't know anything about it, do you?' she retorts, sharply. 'Sorry. The point is, I've let him down so. That's how it all started. Those awful Browning brothers gazumped him for the *Evening Herald*. The government won't let him buy that Dome thingy. So I thought, if I could just do one thing for him, he might . . . you know,' she looks down at the floor, 'start liking me again. It could all be like it was when we met.'

Looking at her, hearing her voice as it goes so small and feeble, my anger starts melting into pity. 'Tara, you haven't let him down! You can't help your dad being in prison. How can you sit there blaming yourself? If you want to know what I think, your husband sounds like a bit of a shit. He married you to make himself feel better. In fact, not even feel better, that would be too honest: just *look* better, to other people. And now you haven't measured up to his little fantasy, he doesn't want you. You should tell him to get lost. If he wants a status symbol, he can go and buy a Bentley.'

'I love him,' she says, firmly.

'You shouldn't love him, Tara. Find someone who can love you back.'

'There were plenty of times I wanted to tell you to stop mooning over that ... that *cold*, fucked-up Martha girl who was never in a million years going to make you happy,' she snaps. 'And I never did. Do you know why? Because you can't help what you feel. No one can. So you can tell me a million times not to love him. You can tell me all the reasons why I shouldn't, and I'll still love him. I just do. It's like Ben Nevis, or ... or something. You can't knock it down, you've just got to build a road around it. It's just there.'

I feel chastened. 'OK, OK.' My mind flails around for some solid ground upon which to continue. 'But have you considered something: maybe if you just stopped trying so hard, he might come round?'

'He won't! I know him. Once he gets an idea in his head, there's nothing I can do.' She straightens herself, in the time-honoured manner of a plucky film heroine rising to the challenge. 'I'll just have to keep on trying for him, that's all.'

'But we're talking about a tenth-rate little private school in the west London suburbs! What would a multimillion-aire want with it?'

'He's not as wealthy as people think,' she says. 'Not any more.'

'Isn't he? Why not?'

'You'd only be bored if I told you,' she says, hastily.

There's a pause and I sense she doesn't want to explore this avenue. So I fill her glass and wish her luck. There doesn't seem much else I can do.

'There is one thing, Alastair.' She looks at me directly, almost sternly. 'You could say you'll always, I don't know, you'll always believe in me. Not believe any of the things other people say about me, whatever they say.'

'What things? What people?' I'm tempted to say she's not making much sense, but that's never tended to go down well with any of the girls I've known. 'Who's going to say bad things about you?'

'No one. I mean . . . I didn't mean that . . . I just mean . . . if you, for instance, didn't hear from me for a while. I mean, a long while. You wouldn't, you know, be spending all that time thinking awful things about me. I mean, you'd stay on my side. That's all I want to know.'

'You've got it.' I'm up now, bending over her, hugging her inside the fragrant fur. I have only the faintest idea as to what I've agreed to, and an even fainter one as to what might be passing through Tara's mind. I suppose, I can *only* suppose, that she inhabits a pretty paranoid universe, and she just wants to know that she has a friend. We all want to know that, sometimes.

She pulls away and winks at me. 'Excellent. Now, is there anywhere in this suburban *nightmare* we can go for some supper?'

Spare A Copper

'Three hundred acres, apparently. Not that I've ever
been entirely sure how big an acre is ... The
Prince of Wales used to go up there all the time. I expect
we'll have his bedroom. Who knows, if you're a good boy
I might bring you back a stag ... Alastair, are you even
listening to me?'

An unusually chirpy Davenport and a reasonably
troubled me are walking down the main corridor after
Assembly. I've been worrying about Tara all weekend –
certain, for reasons I cannot explain, that there were
darker things troubling my old friend. Things she wanted
to tell me, but didn't, or couldn't. After our long talk, we
went out for a pizza and she got gaily, wildly drunk. So
drunk that she tried to smoke a bread-stick and kissed the
cashier. At the end of the night, I folded her into a cab,
like some toy that had had all the air let out of it, and she
mumbled just one thing as she kissed my neck. A small
thing, but one I've not been able to forget.

'I'm in so much trouble,' she said, in a bright Nursery
voice, as if she was saying something quite different. 'Bags
and bags.' When I asked her to repeat it, she just looked at
me and said, 'Poor Alastair.' Then she went back to Eaton
Square.

'You might show a bit of interest, Alastair,' Davenport

exclaims, forcing my thoughts back to the present. 'This is my one little oasis of joy in an otherwise bleak landscape. Soon as I get back there'll be Prizegiving and Dick Weed and all manner of untold turd to cope with. Talking of which, where are you taking the little shit for his literary luncheon? Somewhere that'll give him a good wallop of *e. coli*, I trust.'

'What exactly have you got against Rick Reed, Lawrence?'

It transpires, with prompting, that back in his own sixth-form days Davenport had written a 'brilliant' little playlet – a biting satire on the Classics teachers for the House drama competition, an institution now defunct, the headmaster having abolished the House system in his first week here, as being 'unnecessarily divisive'. And that the script for his work of genius had gone missing just before rehearsals were due to begin.

'Had to make do with some miserable little one-acter out of one of Scarsdale's books. Bombed, of course. Then Dick Weed's play comes on. He'd robbed mine, word for stinking word. Bosworth House stole the Cup from Flodden and now Reed's making it big in the Smoke. On the back of other people's bloody talent.'

I venture to suggest that this is hardly the case. 'He's written one play about a football match. And now he reviews other plays for that free paper they give out on the tube. Hardly the big-time, is it?'

Davenport shakes his coppery curls. 'He won the Miss Gay-Knight Cup for Drama, man! That sort of thing opens doors for you, everywhere.' He stops talking as I, glimpsing the headmaster a few yards ahead of us, drag Davenport into an empty classroom. 'What are you doing, Alastair?'

'The head,' I whisper urgently. 'I'm avoiding him. I didn't go to that sodding Pickle Night.'

'Oh, didn't you? Oh well, I shouldn't worry too much. I know for a fact that Gisela wasn't there either. Well, of course she wasn't. She was with me. A most energetic reconciliation,' he adds.

'Good for you,' I say, feebly.

Davenport claps me on the back. 'Anyway, chum, I'm off now. Only came in to pick up my Barbour.'

'But what about your lessons?'

'My dear fellow, haven't you listened to a word I've been telling you? I'm wagging off for a couple of days. Got a note from my mother.'

It emerges that Davenport does, quite literally, have a note from his mother, who is an osteopath in Harley Street. Thus exempted from work, he is meeting Gisela at King's Cross and going to Scotland to stay in a castle recently purchased by her father.

'Enjoy the cross-country!' he cries brightly to me as he veers off towards the staff room. Fortunately he doesn't hear my response.

I'm not surprised to find my sixth-form set don't have a lot of time for *Hue and Cry*. This sort of *Boy's Own* adventure plot went out with the ZX Spectrum and the fluorescent sock, if not before. It's a fanciful yarn about a gaggle of schoolboys who read adventure comics. Then they discover that these comics are being used by a gang of criminals to communicate covert messages about raids they're planning all across London. So, boys being boys – in Ealing Studios, at least – they set about foiling the crims.

I can't help liking it. It's that little-guys-trounce-the-big-guys formula. But beyond that, it's saying that dissent and rebellion are important. If it weren't for the kids, disagreeing with the adults, not listening to them and not obeying them, the criminals wouldn't get caught. That's why I mourn the passing of Miller and Booth – the boys who chafed under Mr Scarsdale's rule-book. It's why I can't look at Demetriou, and all the other boys who worry about tests, and have embossed their exercise books with plastic, without experiencing a shudder of distaste. It's the same shudder I get on Saturday mornings watching young fit banker-type couples going for a jog.

I've got a lot of affection for the *Hue and Cry* era. I can just about remember the power cuts in the Seventies, the sense of excitement that everyone in our street, our town, my class, was conquering the same adversity: eating by candlelight and going to bed with a torch. It was the last outing for the spirit of the Blitz, the all-hands-on-deck ethos that dominated every Ealing screenplay.

It does not, however, dominate the Ealing classroom of today. Demetriou is staring at the screen with an affronted expression that reminds me of the Duke of Edinburgh being forced to sit through an hour of naked tribal dancing, while his classmates are arranged in various attitudes of despair. The Herbert Lom boy is lancing spots with a compass, and the skull-faced creature next to him is filling in an UCAS form.

The tall, red-faced boy with the head of a dwarf gives a defeated yawn. And as it finishes, the classroom door opens. A few sweet papers blow in on the breeze. Anthony Blundell stands in the doorway, his hair neatly plastered down with soap or other unguent, his face giving no clues as to why he should be twenty minutes late.

'Anthony?' I say. He looks at me blankly as he wafts

into the room, a green US army kitbag slung over his shoulder. 'It's generally polite to apologise when you turn up twenty minutes late . . .'

Usually I couldn't give a tinker's about what's 'generally polite'. I'd rather we all sat here and made up rude poems about Scarsdale, and homework was painting them on his Vauxhall Nova. It's just that I'm anxious, in light of recent events, not to lay myself open to accusations of favouritism.

'*Sorry*,' Anthony says, sardonically, standing under the strip light. His face suddenly looks hard and pinched. Maybe he's not eating enough?

'Why were you late?'

'Didn't feel like getting up.'

'I wish I could just absent myself every time I felt like not getting up, Anthony.'

He gazes at me coolly. 'I expect lots of other people wish you could too.'

This is too much. He transfers himself to my class and I get it in the neck. Then he turns up late, doing a Clint Eastwood impression. I should blow my top about this.

'Just . . . just find a seat, Anthony.'

He looks around him. The assembled class look back, not moving a muscle, no one shifting aside to make room, even though there are plenty of spare chairs dotted around, especially with the departure of Miller and Booth. He's quite clearly a pariah, our Anthony, but why? There are boys who look, and are, weirder than he is, even in this room.

'Here,' I say, pushing aside a pile of my own books and papers. 'Sit there.'

He obeys wordlessly, withdrawing a cheap notebook

and a stubby pencil from his pocket. I make up my mind to have a word with him, at least offer him some decent paper and pens.

Soon, Anthony's entrance is forgotten and everyone is once again immersed in his own private *ennui*. Except for Anthony: I notice him, scribbling away at his notepad, while everyone else is quite still. He has that B&B smell again – washing powder and baby oil; it hangs about him as he jerks his arm across the pad.

We've just reached the point where the boys go to visit the famous author of the adventure stories, Felix H. Wilkinson, rendered by a sinister and slightly fey Alastair Sim. He utters his great line, 'Oh how I loathe adventurous-minded boys!' and I notice a ripple of laughter across the class. I stop the video, curious. They haven't laughed at anything else, though the script is bristling with so-called jokes.

'Why are you all laughing?'

There's an embarrassed silence. Demetriou coughs. 'He's a batty-man, sir, innee? Gay.'

'Nonce, more like,' says the giant-dwarf boy. Cahill, they call him, I think. Anthony sighs and looks up at the ceiling.

'They're synonymous, are they, Cahill?' I ask, imperiously.

'Who's anonymous?'

I give up. 'I'm not sure that was the film-maker's intention,' I say, turning the film back on. Suddenly it's not so hard to see why Anthony doesn't fit in round here.

At the end of the lesson, to a chorus of groans, I give out the homework. 'What views of post-war Britain have you gained from *Hue and Cry*?'

'Sir, sir, are we—'

'No, Demetriou, you're not going to be marked on it. Just tell me what you thought. And tell me,' I add, raising my voice above the scuffle of feet and scraping chairs, 'tell me if you actually liked it. And why.'

I turn to Anthony, with a smile. 'Think you can manage that?' And it's at this point that I realise I'm talking to an empty chair.

'*Der wazzon Dutch Boyne* . . .'

'What?'

I blow my nose. 'I said, there wasn't much point me waiting for the next lesson. To hand your essay back, I mean. It was very good . . .'

I'm standing on the narrow landing outside Anthony's B&B room, nose streaming and eyes watering. I would seem to have caught a case of bubonic plague from my spell on Ealing Common, marshalling the cross-country. But some things must be said.

Wordlessly, giving nothing way, the sharp-featured ghost boy waves me into his desperately small room. The smell is at its most pungent now – like a Chinese laundry. Behind me, still on the threshold of the door, Mrs Danischewsky gives what she fancies is a discrete cough.

'Shall I make you boys some tea?'

'That would be nice,' Anthony replies, with a solemn, cultured nod, like some old priest to a housekeeper he has come to love. Mrs D declares, inexplicably, that she doesn't blame us, and then goes away. I can hear her transit down the stairs, trilling some joyous ditty about a colleen from Skibbereen who did awful things to a bard's heart.

Anthony perches, very formally, on the bed. He's wearing grey trousers and a blue, round-necked jumper, full of holes. His feet point in the opposite direction to his body, like those of a Forties heroine in a long tight skirt. He offers me a seat. I can choose from three options: the armchair, a red felt-covered affair, draped with shirts and socks: the hard wooden thing next to the table with the piled books on top; and a tiny, yellow plastic affair, best suited to midgets and children who have just learnt to stay upright.

I plump for the chair, moving aside a sort of clockwork skull on wheels and setting it on the mantelpiece above me. On this coffee-stone structure, above a two-bar electric fire, there are few adornments – a little travel clock and some meaningless crayon scribbles on a piece of paper.

Anthony's room is nowhere near as bleak as I'd imagined. There's a big poster of a smoking Clint Eastwood on the wall above the fireplace; on the opposite wall, a faded flag of California – 'Bear State'. Over by the bed, a little South American-style rug, ochre and azure stripes, picked out no doubt from among the lanterns made from olive-oil cans and the papyrus birthday cards in that shop opposite the Broadway Centre.

Then, as my eyes grow accustomed to the dim light, I arrive at an even greater anomaly: a large wooden cot, underneath which are scattered various sticky renderings of pterodactyls and Sherman tanks. Odder still, inside the cot lies the short and softly breathing form of Joe, clad in a pair of red dungarees, his skin shining in that way only very new things can.

'So you found us, then?' Anthony says, quietly, folding a tiny Power Rangers T-shirt.

'Us?'

He points to the cot. 'Me and Joe.'

I rub the top of my head and then, that having failed to produce any enlightenment, start biting my thumbnail.

'But I thought . . .' I try to recall what Mrs Danischewsky said about Joe. Her sister's cousin's brother-in-law's niece's . . . It's all too hard.

'He's yours?' I exclaim, wide-eyed as the truth hits home.

Anthony nods, silently, now picking a plastic knight's helmet from the bed and stowing it under the cot. 'I shouldn't have lied really, only it's all so complicated. Me being here. And him. They'd probably chuck me out, wouldn't they?'

'Not if they don't find out.'

He acknowledges this with a nod as he adjusts a lime-green blanket over his son's sleeping body. Then, sitting back on the bed, he squints at the pile of books I brought with me, resting now on my lap. 'What are they?'

'Oh, er . . .' After the rush of courage it took to come here, I'm suddenly embarrassed. Immediately as my last lesson ended, I went and ransacked the headmaster's selection of counselling literature. Only as I was crossing the common did I realise how meagre a library this was. A leaflet entitled 'So You Think You've Got Chlamydia?' A booklet about cannabis, executed in that let's-talk-to-the-kids cartoon style, called 'Paranoid Pete and the Munchies'. Something else, brick-sized and intimidating, about Overcoming Shame. I might keep that for myself. And then the book at the top of the pile – a miserably bad choice.

'Why are you giving me that?'

I look at the title of the slim volume, printed in San Francisco, entitled 'Twice Blessed: Jewish and Gay'. 'Oh dear.'

Anthony's bony, prematurely aged face breaks into an incredulous smile. 'So that's why you came? To reach out to the lonely boy? The boy with a secret love, the love that dare not speak its name?' He flashes me a look of utter condemnation. 'I'm not *gay*!'

'I know that. I came to see you,' I reply, swallowing down little waves of annoyance, 'because you're living here. And you never have a decent pen. You always look tired. And no one seems to talk to you.'

As if in contradiction of my last charge, Mrs D then knocks at the door. Admitted, she bustles in, mad and laughing, with tea-things, full of questions about Anthony's sister and the looming Oxford exam. All of which is a source of deep, private amusement to her, as if perhaps she has some saucy translation device in her head, and all our responses are turned into *Carry On*-style obscenities, like knickers and knockers and nookie.

'Well, no one at school talks to you, anyway,' I say, when she's finally been dispatched.

Joe makes a murmuring sound and Anthony stands up, bending over the cot and making a few, instinctive adjustments, which result in a deep sigh from the sleeping child. Then he looks solemnly across to me. 'Well, now you know. I just keep myself to myself. To be honest, I'd probably be doing that even if I didn't have Joe. I don't . . .' He gives a pained sigh. 'I don't seem to get on with people much. I just wind them up. I don't know why.'

'You don't wind me up,' I say hotly.

'Be honest,' he replies, cupping the mug between his long, white fingers. Mrs D's tea, true to form, tastes like mutton fat, but it's always served with such charm that you forget this until the first sip. Anthony winces and puts the mug down.

'Good as ever?'

'I just want to do my work, pass the exam and get us out,' Anthony says, ignoring my joke. 'It's only a few months and then we'll be free. There's facilities there, you know at Oxford, for single parents.'

Together, as if he is the central hearth of the room, we glance at Joe again, now letting out a delicate snore. So much is settling into place. Anthony's unique smell, like the smell of the new mothers on the bus. That premature weariness that hangs around him like a cloud, setting him apart from his classmates. Of course he doesn't get on with anyone – what would Anthony have to say to people like Demetriou and Brenard, whose chief worries are whether they'll lose their virginity before the release of *Grand Theft Auto IV*?

But how did someone like Anthony come to produce an heir? A boy, or rather a *man*, like Anthony can't hold a conversation without it turning into a Talmudic debate. And who, for that matter, would invite Anthony to a party, let alone offer him a drunken shag?

'It was an inter-schools debating contest,' he explains. 'In Winchester. There was a lot of wine. I'd never had any before. And I wanted to try it. Not wine. I mean, you know, *it*.' He gives a private laugh at some grisly memory. 'Well, everyone does, don't they?'

'But what about . . . what about his mother?'

'*Emma*,' he says, not bothering to disguise his opinion. 'Feverishly awaiting the results of her interview at Warwick, I should think. I don't know. It wasn't exactly what people call love. It was just a stupid thing. Lot of fuss about nothing, really, isn't it, in the end? But she wanted to keep him at first, and then after about three months she couldn't handle having him. And her parents were old. They wanted to foster him out. So we stepped in.'

'Your family?' To which he gives a nod. 'So what are you doing here, Anthony? Trying to bring a child up in some crummy bedsit?'

'You assume it's all so *Dickensian*,' he says, waving his hand in the air, now back in Distracted Academic mode, lecturing me. 'Me in some awful boarding-house. It's not like that at all. We like it here, me and Joe. Bridget . . . Mrs D has him in the daytime. Lets me work at the table in the dining room. She's family, you know. On my mum's side. And we do go *home*, you know.'

'Do you?'

I've got it very wrong, it seems. Anthony gently lifts Joe into his arms, where he sits, grizzling and red-faced, like some elderly uncle unduly disturbed from his crossword. 'I know, I know. I'm sorry,' he murmurs, as the child wriggles and protests, waggling arms and legs in a complicated octopus-dance. 'If I don't wake him up now, he'll never get off tonight . . .'

Expertly, he shakes Joe up and down a few times. Suddenly I'm seeing the kernel of Anthony Blundell, split from its awkward, prickly husk. A man, tender and capable and strong. Not a lonely geek, but someone who works hard and stays out of the way because he has to.

'It's true what I said. My mum lives in Hammersmith. I just don't get on with her partner, that's all. And he doesn't like Joe. So I took him away. Set up here. Everyone keeps on at me to go back, of course, but I won't.' He strokes Joe's fine hair. 'We're all right here. Everyone helps out. Most people, anyway.'

This is all so foreign to me, it might as well be in the realms of sci-fi. Teenage scholars with baby sons. Mothers and fathers who seemingly don't care, and others, barely equipped for the part, who do. 'Mum's a bit crap,'

Anthony says, waving a plastic halberd at Joe, who seizes this murder weapon happily in a fat fist. 'I mean, she's flaky. Won't do anything to upset *him*.'

'Your stepdad?'

'Her boyfriend,' he corrects me. 'So it's better like this. No arguments. And my sister's just down the road. We go there, too, when she's not in a mood with me.' He gives a private laugh. 'I wind her up, too.'

Released onto the floor, Joe starts to attack his yellow dwarf-chair with the halberd, burbling some highly meaningful nonsense to himself.

I stand up, reaching for my wallet. 'I shouldn't really be doing this,' I say, proffering a twenty-pound note, 'but it struck me you might have a use for it. Especially now.'

'I don't *need* money.'

'I'd like to help, Anthony.'

Anthony gives me one of his looks. Meanwhile, Joe waddles nimbly over to me and rests his fat chin on my knee. A second set of pale, mistrustful eyes scour my face, as if I'm about to let him down. 'So what about going out with my sister, then? You never did give me a proper answer.'

I give a long groan. 'No, Anthony, please. Not this again.'

'What do you mean "not this again"? Why not?'

'Because . . . Because. Well, why *should* I? Why are you even asking me, for God's sake?'

'Because she's had a run of bad luck lately. Some idiot who used to work in her office. *Jason*. Keeps breaking up with him and then getting back together with him. It's killing her. Bad pickers, you see. Her and Mum. It'd be really great if you'd, you know, step in. Boost her self-esteem.'

'Anthony,' I say, patiently, as Joe clambers onto my lap and sneezes in my face, 'the world doesn't work like that. It's not some scientific equation.'

'Isn't it?'

'No! You can't just slot people together. Your sister might not want me boosting her self-esteem. And she certainly wouldn't if she knew her little brother had asked me to.'

'Aah, but she wouldn't have to know that, would she? Not if you didn't tell her. And besides, she *would* want you. I know she would. I could fix it all up. You're exactly the right sort of person.'

'How do you know that?' A question slightly ruptured as Joe puts a foot into my groin.

'All she needs is someone who'll give as good as he gets. Someone she can respect.'

I have to prevent myself from uttering the sort of unhinged laugh that can get a man arrested. 'But what makes you think that's going to be me?'

He looks at me solemnly. 'You don't shout at people. You don't throw things. Did you know, you haven't even got a nickname?'

'Haven't I?' The thought, diverting as it is, rather pleases me.

'No. And even when you're wrong, you say sorry. Do you know how many teachers do that? You're just what she needs.' Anthony points at Clint Eastwood on the wall. 'A stand-up guy.'

I, too, look at Clint Eastwood, and think I've never felt less like him. And it has nothing to do with lacking ponchos, cheroots or extremist politics. 'I'm sorry, Anthony. I just can't do that.'

His mouth sets in a hard line. 'But you *promised*.'

'I did no such thing!'

'Yes, you did,' he exclaims, rising and snatching the child into his arms. Both glare at me, hot and defensive, as if I was a marauding social worker. 'You said you'd like to help. And now you're going back on it. So you're a liar!'

Whisky Galore!

'It's not that I particularly mind your lack of attendance. But a simple fax or e-mail would have been polite. As it is, the evening was an unmitigated diaster. Miss Kastrafitis slipped on a herring and sprained her ankle . . .'

'I'm sorry, Headmaster. It was an unexpected family crisis.'

He's caught me, as I knew he would. Men who are being avoided know it only too well, and the knowledge gifts them with invisibility. I was just checking my pigeonhole – with some degree of trepidation – and thinking that, whether it contained a nasty surprise or not, I would treat myself to an hour in the chilly calm of the MacKendrick Arms. Then the headmaster manifested himself, like some Savile Row-outfitted djinn summoned by my footfall from a tiny crack in the floorboards.

'Yes, well . . .' the headmaster bristles. 'As it happens my wife wasn't able to attend herself, so I suppose it doesn't really matter.' He shoots me a fierce look. 'You don't know where she was, I suppose?'

'Your wife? No, I don't.'

'No, of course you don't,' he says, sheepishly adjusting his herringbone tie. 'I do apologise.'

I look at the headmaster, suddenly feeling immeasurably sorry for him. In recent days, he might not have seen much of me, but I've watched him enough to detect a new, slightly crumpled aura, one that haunts not only his suits and shirts but also his whole posture. He's started to resemble an item of once-smart luggage whose owner no longer takes it anywhere glamorous.

'How's the fund-raising going, Headmaster?'

His mouth droops even further. 'I believe it was H. D. Dodewerd who first said . . . Never mind.' He gives a deep sigh. 'Not terribly well, Alastair. I keep thinking that what we really need is to locate a benefactor. A sort of latter-day St John Lorimer who wouldn't mind injecting some fluid reserves.'

'But then you'd have to run the school their way, wouldn't you? You couldn't do all the things you wanted to do with it. You know . . . a butt for the community.'

'A *hub*,' the headmaster corrects me gently. 'Well, I don't know. Provided we could show an investor that he or she would get a reasonable profit I'm not sure he or she would mind how socially responsible we were.' He laughs quietly. 'Capitalists tend to be predominantly interested in capital, as the term would suggest . . . Anyway, this is hardly germane. How are *you*, Alastair?' He gives my arm one of those little squeezes which leave me feeling somewhat violated. 'Are you looking forward to Prizegiving? I'm sure you'll find it great fun.'

'I'm sure I will,' I reply, wondering how this could ever be so, unless I take strong drugs. And then a miraculous vision occurs to me: a way of saving two troubled souls at once. 'I was thinking, actually . . . You could perhaps find room on the platform, Headmaster, for an extra guest.'

'Who would that be?'

'Well, it was just a thought.' A stupid thought. I should have kept quiet.

'Come on, AKS, come on. Think out of the box.'

'Excuse me?'

'*On dreams do we build sure castles of stone.* Wasn't that what Bindelwijk said?'

'I thought it was Shakespeare.'

'Who? It's not important. What were you thinking?'

'Well,' I start hesitantly, 'it's just that I'm quite a good friend of Amjit Sammaddi's wife.'

'He point-blank refuses to understand the difference between the gerund and the gerundive. And his only comment on *Oedipus Rex* was that he didn't find it very funny . . .'

This judgement, barked out by an irascible Davenport, several rows behind me, floats across the gymnasium. It's Parents' Evening, and we're all seated at little folding tables, the sort with one wonky leg that become terribly irritating when you're doing an exam, but are still quite irritating in all other situations.

I've not been as busy as Davenport or the others, with me teaching what's known in the trade as a 'non-core subsidiary'. This is tactful, headmaster argot for something taught only by the fat boys in life's cross-country race. But even if I'm largely idle, I understand something of my colleague's mounting frustration. There seems to be some principle at work whereby the parents of the nice kids, the ones who listen and look vaguely interested in things, just sit down for a second or two, or don't come at all; whereas the progenitors of the dull, the witless, the plain criminal, they want the full half-hour and the thirty-page bound report, plus flow charts. And instead of hanging their heads in shame and offering me bottles of Scotch and sack-loads of used tenners in recompense for having foisted their little walking nightmares upon decent men like me, they want to have an argument. Make me understand that their child's genius is simply being mishandled.

I had a QPR footballer up just now. And when I told him that his son had behavioural difficulties – namely, that he can't sit still for forty minutes without hitting someone or saying he's got an erection – the man just blinked at me, astonished at my lack of compassion. 'Can't you just give him a ball and let him do skills?' he asked, plaintively. 'He's good at skills.'

Mind you, I've not been entirely blameless. There was the moment when I told the parents of little Min Huoc Ba that his essays lacked imagination. His mother looked at me briefly, conducted a little conversation in Vietnamese with her husband and then looked back. She informed me in clear, Australian-accented English that they'd escaped their home country on a boat, along with two hundred others. And that, as far as they were concerned, little Min Huoc Ba's essays didn't need to have much imagination in order for little Min Huoc Ba to make a life more decent than their own. His grandchildren could maybe do that, she said, the imagination–thing. I felt rather ashamed of myself after that.

'Excuse me. I'm looking for Mr Strange?'

I look up at the sound of a faintly familiar voice – clear, with an accent at the edges. And right into the face of Bus Girl, scrubbed and pink and slightly bothered. '*You?*' I say this too loudly and at the tables around me people look up, interested. As if perhaps we once had a torrid affair in Tangier, and she's come to introduce me to our child.

She blinks, faintly affronted, a small hand at her equally fun-size bosom. 'Last time I looked. Is that your way of saying hello, or your way of saying Mr Strange is over there, third row from the right?'

'No, it's me. I mean, I'm him. Or he's me,' I stammer, sitting up in my chair. 'Whatever. Please sit down. You do recognise me, don't you?'

'The teacher on the bus,' she says, seating herself, neatly. 'Sure.'

She's in a mauve outfit tonight – a little jacket, drawn tight over her breasts, and matching skirt that fish-tails out at the bottom. Dressed as if to snare some unsuspecting GI with her cigarettes and hard patter. But she's brought the briefcase with her, I see – must have come here straight from the office. But why, specifically, has she come here? Can't possibly have a son here, can she? Oh God, please don't let it be one of the Ferals.

'You're teaching my little brother,' she says, placing fur-lined gloves on the table. Short, ringless hands.

'Who would he be?'

'Anthony Blundell.'

I do my very best to deal with this, while the floor beneath me lurches up and down and she turns into a wobbling being of pure light. This being (a) her, the moody sister down the road. The one Anthony asked me to ask out, and now won't speak to me, won't come to my lessons, because I wouldn't. And this being (b), unbeknown to Anthony, the girl I'd already asked out because I'd been staring at her on the bus for months, and got a megatonne of withering scorn in my face in return. Mary.

'I'm sorry I went off at you like that,' she says, apparently reading, my mind. 'I'd—'

'Anthony told me,' I interrupt, holding up a placatory hand.

She frowns. 'He told you I'd seen *Sweet Smell of Success* twelve times?'

'No, erm, not that,' I say, reddening under the collar. 'Never mind. So what brings you here?'

'You mean why am I here, and not my – our – mother? Or how did I get here? I came on the bus.'

My knuckles whiten as they clench the edge of my seat. That same, maddening obsession with clarity and detail. That little tendency towards autism that sometimes makes me want to hurl heavy objects at Anthony. And of course she'd have it, wouldn't she? She's a *sollissidor*.

'Our mother's not well,' she continues, returning my attention to the matter in hand. 'So I came instead. That's OK, isn't it?'

I tell her that it is, before moving on, with a degree of professional aplomb – quite remarkable in the circumstances – to telling her that there's not a lot to say about Anthony. He's clever, and he'll do well, provided no one introduces him to pot and the wonders of Pink Floyd. And given that he's already shouldering the kind of responsibilities most thirty-year-old men would sprint from, screaming and into the nearest ale-house, this is a pretty unlikely scenario.

'Well . . .' she answers, leaning her little head to one side. From her cheekbones, there's a certain way in which the skin sweeps down to her top lip, like some beautiful carved thing. 'I knew all that. It was more that we thought we should say thanks. You know. For being kind to him. Not letting on about . . . you know.' She lowers her eyes, prettily.

'About Joe?' I say, trying to stop wondering how she manages to look so striking without any apparent use of make-up. 'Well, I haven't really—'

'Well, OK. Whatever, Mr Strange. But you've shown more interest in him than most. And I know he doesn't look like he's grateful, but he is. We all are.'

'Your family?'

She gives a faint waggle of the head – a 'maybe' gesture. Another thing I've seen Anthony do. It's like being transported into a live version of *Kind Hearts and Coronets*, with Alec Guinness's bony face cropping up as assorted duchesses and aged priests.

'In fact we – Mom and I –' she begins, lifting the briefcase onto her lap and opening it, 'we thought you might like this.' She produces a bottle packaged in glossed cardboard. 'I don't know if you're a drinker . . .'

'Oh yes,' I say, taking delivery of the bottle and thanking her. 'I'm one of them.' Someone just made my night. And Davenport's – if he behaves. Emboldened by the presentation of gifts, and the nervous smile she gives me, I mention something that's been bothering me. 'I couldn't help noticing. You sound a touch American sometimes . . .'

'A touch American . . . ?' she echoes, tartly, as if to say, in best Bette Davis fashion, 'OK, Buster, I'll chew the fat. But push it, and I'll stick a thistle up your ass.'

'I grew up over there,' she explains. Whereas Anthony just blinks, in the manner of some crabby don whose proposals for the college herb garden are falling on deaf ears, Mary has this way of unfolding the eyes slowly. Like time-lapse photography of a budding orchid, tropical green and lovely. 'In LA. My dad was a writer. He and Mom went over there to work.'

'But they came back?'

She makes a flat-mouth, sardonic gesture that answers my pointless question. 'My dad died over there. And

Mom couldn't get enough work. She wanted to be an actress.'

'A glamorous background,' I say, stiffening slightly, not because I want to, but because I'm aware that there are parents waiting behind, shifting from foot to foot and coughing.

'Not really.' *Nhat rilly.* That accent again. Amazing how you can get used to it, like it even, not be reminded of stiffs in baseball caps talking about Phi Beta Kappa or flunking Math. 'Not when there's no money. It was fun, though.' She gives a tiny little shrug at this point, hugging herself in, and I'm reminded of something we sing in Assembly – some faintly paederastic Victorian ditty about that which is small being that which is also beautiful. Small boys, no, there's precious little of beauty to be found in them. They chew gum and they're basically vicious as wolves. But in a small woman, you'd be surprised how much beauty there is.

'I gather Anthony's not too fond of his . . . your stepfather?'

'They don't get on. He's—'

She seems on the verge of offering me more, when the cosy little nimbus of our conversation is blown aside – vaporised, in fact – by the noise of a desk being toppled behind us. Rubber feet dragging on pine. And then, on top of this, Davenport's voice, loud and close to break-down: 'Word I'd use, Mrs Bender, is *not* under-stimulated. Word I'd use is *thick!*'

'"Metaphor and Pain in the Later Works of Gaius Lucretius Catullus". It's my Ph.D.'

'Have you started working on it again?'

Davenport pats the thick brick of typewritten pages

with a doleful expression in his dark brown eyes. 'Finished it years ago, old son. Could get it published any time.'

'Why don't you?'

He performs a boyish shrug. 'It's probably a load of crap.' He gives a heavy sigh, scratches an armpit and then stands up. 'Come on. Let's not stand around in here. It depresses me.'

I found him, when I came home from Parents' Evening, sitting in his study with the door open. He was fingering his Ph.D. – an object I'd assumed to be highly theoretical – with a dazed, melancholy expression. There's something heavy going on.

And when I've given Davenport a slug of Mary's whisky, and he's sitting in his favourite armchair doing his favourite thing – which is scratching his crotch with one hand and scratching Cinna's ears with the other – he tells me that he's had some news. 'Seems old Gizzler's up the duff,' he says.

I sit up in astonishment. 'Is it yours?'

My chunky friend tuts, affrontedly. 'Of course it's mine! You don't think *Steve* could come up with the business, do you?'

'I'd never given it any thought. Anyway, do I congratulate you or what?'

''Fraid not,' he says, glumly. 'Gisela's going to flush it.'

'Oh dear. Sorry.'

He shakes his foppish curls. 'Don't be. I mean, *I'm* sorry enough. But it's not really down to the chaps, is it? Can't reasonably tell a lady what to do with her own innards, can you?' He downs the whisky and reaches for the bottle again. Cinna, annoyed at the lack of attention he is receiving, pads haughtily out of the room.

'I suppose not. But where does that leave you and her?'

'Oh, she says we're all right enough,' he says, with a leaden sigh. 'And I suppose we are. But it's different. Do you know what I mean? Something's happened and I can't quite figure out what it is. It's like I've let her down or something. Does that make any sense?'

'Sort of,' I reply, remembering what I felt like in the dying throes of my days with Martha. I felt exactly that.

'It was all going so swimmingly. Scotland was an absolute *dream*. That's when it happened. Something about all that baronial splendour. Log fires; going round in tweeds; blasting the buggery out of animals. Made me absolutely horny as hell. Thought I'd found my little niche. Thought we could just hole up in a castle, me and her, and breed till we dropped . . .' Davenport twirls the whisky round the glass. 'I can't stop thinking what it might be *like*. That's why I was taking a dekko at the old PH in the study. Something else that might have been. Anyway, I don't know why I'm being such a girl about it. My father was a complete *cunt* to me, and who's to say I'd be any different?'

'Because you want to be?' I suggest, reaching for the bottle before all the whisky vanishes. 'I mean, not many people are deliberate cunts. Most of them just don't know the rules of the game. They don't know what they're supposed to be doing. You could be different.'

Davenport gives me a wan smile. 'Perhaps. You've gone very philosophical all of a sudden. Is Alastair Strange in love?'

'Fuck off.'

'Not that blonde piece who gave you the whisky, is it? I must say, if it is, I'll kick your shins, you lucky bugger.'

'No.'

'She certainly seemed to have a liking for you,'

Davenport adds, his eyes shining with renewed brightness as he returns to one of his favourite themes. 'Way she kept sticking her hair behind her ears. Leaning forward, poking her baps at you across the table. And most of all, *that*.' He points at the whisky bottle. 'What do you think that's supposed to mean?'

'Someone saying thank you?'

Davenport grunts as he rearranges his testicles. 'Take my advice, old boy. Might Have Been is a load of bollocks. You're damn right about things being a game. And if the ball lands in your lap, you bloody run with it . . . Hello, my little furry chap. He likes his blankey, doesn't he? Loves his new blanket.'

Cinna has returned, dragging a length of stained brown fabric from his slavering jaws. I look at it distractedly. 'That looks like my coat.'

'Really?' Davenport exclaims, vaguely. 'I wasn't sure whose it was. I just came down this morning and saw that Cinna had rather claimed it for his own.' He gives an indulgent laugh. 'Put his little liquid stamp of ownership on it, if you catch my drift. Didn't think any chap would be wanting it after that.'

'Lawrence,' I ask sternly, 'why have you cut up my coat for your bloody dog?'

'*Try* not to call him that, there's a chap. Try thinking of him as a sort of retarded brother.'

Train of Events

'I know it doesn't work. It's not supposed to. You need your 108.'

'What's a 108?'

The goitred functionary who runs the Photocopier Room holds up a plastic card with a magnetic strip down the side. 'Like this,' he explains, without affection. I wonder why people like this man – with his medieval torturer's haircut and his name badge that says NIGEL – FACILITIES SUPPORT – always end up manning Customer Care desks and helplines, when they blatantly neither help nor care. 'It activates the machine and then it stores your copying history on a personal database.'

I reach for the card happily, aware that I've only got ten minutes to photocopy thirty sets of exam papers for my lesson with the Ferals. I've wasted fifteen already, sweating and cursing the machines while Nigel watched me from behind his copy of the *Ealing and Hanwell Courier*.

He snatches the card away. 'You can't have this. It's a sample.'

'Well, where can I get a proper one, then?' I cannot prevent a high-pitched note of despair from creeping into my voice.

Nigel chuckles, as if the idea that I could obtain such a card is only marginally less ridiculous than us running away to Barbados together to run a beach bar. 'You were issued with one at the start of term. Everyone was.'

'Well, I wasn't. So what do I do now?'

A charmless shrug follows, during which I gaze hotly at Nigel's name badge and start wondering exactly which facilities it is he supports. The facility for turning decent men like myself into axe-murderers, possibly.

'The only machine that doesn't need a 108 is over there.' Nigel jabs a thumb over his shoulder towards a vast humming plinth that resembles a particle accelerator.

'Well, can I use that one, then?'

Nigel shakes his head with gloomy satisfaction. 'Staff aren't authorised to use that one. You have to leave the job with me and I'll deal with it.'

'Well, we'd better do that, then. How soon can you get it done?'

Nigel opens a hardbacked log-book with studied nonchalance and runs his finger down a column of figures. 'Next Monday?'

'*Next Monday*?!'

Nigel blinks indolently. 'Best I can do,' he pronounces, tapping a pile of documents wrapped in brown paper on the ledge next to him. 'I've got the final proofs for the new magazine to do before Prizegiving. If you want to jump the queue you'll have to speak to Mr Scarsdale.'

Seeing instantly that this taking place and ending in a favourable outcome is about as likely as my being selected for the next NASA mission to Mars, I settle for a bit of forehead slapping and general swearing. Nigel watches me, unmoved. He then emits the sort of fart that sounds like a small motorbike passing by and departs in the direction of the toilet.

It takes only a few more blows to my forehead and a

few more curses flung in the direction of the heavens for me to realise that I've got to take charge here. I've planned this lesson – and without the sample exam questions in front of them, the Ferals will descend into a state of restlessness that makes the Toxteth riots seem like a Baptist coffee morning. I look over at the big photocopier. Its various banks of lights are blinking and twinkling like an air traffic controller's console, and I'm filled with a dangerous sense of my own abilities.

It's dangerous, because no sooner have I located and lifted the almighty lid of this device, and placed the exam questions underneath, than the computer screen to the left of me flashes a highly discouraging message. ENTER AUTHOR CODE, it says. And when I fail to do this and press the more helpful-looking orange button marked 'Start', it says ILLEGAL OPERATION. Panicking slightly, and reminded unavoidably of back-street abortions, I press a few more buttons – ones with arrows on them and bearing further sanguine legends such as Go, and 'Activate'. These result in little, other than a few indications on the computer screen that I am about to be turned into a trace of gas and the local police will be informed by e-mail. I deliver a mulish kick to the front of the machine, which results in a panel falling off, to reveal yet more buttons.

'Having trouble, sir?'

I look round, and the mists of confusion clear to reveal the suavely grinning form of the recently excluded Posey Miller. Crooked in the arm of his black Nehru suit is a pile of glossy magazines.

'Miller? What are you doing here?' I had been thinking about saying something along the lines of him not being allowed on the premises, but stopped when I realised that I, too, am not supposed to be where I am.

Miller gives me a dimpled smile of disarming insouciance and pats his stack of magazines. 'Oh, just cleaning out my locker, sir.' He nods across to the machine. 'Looks like you're in a spot of bother there.'

'I can't get this sodding thing to work.'

Miller comes across to me. 'It's not that hard when you know how. My dad's got one of these.' The boy puts the magazines down and studies the computer console. He makes a clicking sound with his tongue and then presses a few buttons. While this goes on, I try not to look at his magazines, which are strictly top-shelf or under-bed material with titles like *Afro Buns* and *Rodeo Slaves*. 'How many copies do you need, sir?'

'Thirty,' I answer. 'There's not much time. I was supposed to be there two minutes ago. There'll be all hell breaking loose by now.'

Miller waggles a pair of perfectly arched eyebrows at me. 'Ten L, is it? You'd better not be late.'

'No,' I say, with feeling, 'I'd better not.'

'Tell you what,' Miller says, kindly. 'You go on and start the lesson. I'll get these finished in about five minutes and bring them round to you.'

'Well . . .' I begin, all sorts of inchoate objections about teacher–pupil protocol hovering in my mind, along with others that remind me that Miller is not a pupil any more and I am not much of a teacher either.

'Go on,' he urges. 'It'll be fine. Where are you? Room 8?'

'Yes.' The mere mention of Room 8 depresses me. It was where, just yesterday, my teaching lectern toppled to the floor along with me. I suspected the Ferals but, as with all the other villainies recently enacted upon my person, I could prove nothing.

Miller seamlessly takes charge, tapping buttons and enchanting the machine into a song of industrious humming. I realise I'd better do as he suggested, and thank Miller for helping me.

'No worries,' he says, giving me a wink. 'And don't forget to drop by the club if you're ever in town.'

Leaving Miller, but with the faint, troubling sense that he's up to something, I cut round the front of the school towards Room 8. And it's here, on the wide gravel walkway that takes me past the playing fields and the building site, that I encounter an usual sight: Anthony in his blue mac, the sort of thing no boy since 1955 would be square enough to wear in public; Bunny Warren in his bright yellow waistcoat and white hard hat; and on the ground, a short, curly-haired man, in jeans and jumper, writhing in agony. His workmates are gathered around there too – the assorted Bosnians and Albanians and Abkhaz, their clothes streaked with dirt, their faces pained and nervous, flinching as the man lets out another roar of pain and surprise.

I run up to them. The man on the ground has a wound to his head and gouts of claret are spilling onto the asphalt. '*Pozvanitye!*' he shouts. '*Vrachu! Pozvanitye pazhalusta!*'

'Shurrup,' Warren replies, irritably. He looks up at my approach, a slightly worried glance crossing his luncheon-meat face. 'Had a little accident,' he says.

'Have you called an ambulance?'

'It's not that serious,' Warren replies, in light, nervy tones. 'I'm just getting the car brought round. I'll take him up the 'ozzie.'

'He shouldn't be moved!' Anthony exclaims, furiously. 'I've told you.'

'My arse, Ant'ny,' Warren replies, stiffly, and reaches down for one of the man's arms. He lifts it, trying to pull him upright. The man lets out a chilling roar, his face turning the colour of minerals. Warren appears surprised at this and lets him drop back to the floor, where he twists and groans some more, breathlessly murmuring Slavic agonies.

'Anthony's right,' I say, breathless and nervous from the blood and shouting. 'You could do him real damage if you pick him up. He needs an ambulance.'

Warren makes a pained face and shakes his head. The plastic helmet wobbles from side to side, like a badly fitting wig. 'It'll be all forms filling in and that. Police asking questions. *Carnavit*. Got to get this place finished.' He gestures to me with his head. 'Come 'ere. Give us 'and with him.'

Anthony steps in, snatching Warren's mobile phone from his waistcoat pocket. There is a murmur from the gathered labourers, one of surprise and support. 'It's got nothing to do with getting the place finished,' Anthony spits, tapping at the phone. 'It's because you've got illegal workers on this place. They're not insured. They haven't even got hats.'

Warren snatches the phone back, then grabs Anthony by the lapels. The thin boy is pulled, limp and doll-like, towards the man. Warren breathes hard through his nostrils, a bull preparing to duck and charge. 'Listen lar,' he says, in a sour voice, six-inch nails corroding in acid. 'I've had about enough of you. You don't give a flying fuck about these blokes. You're just doing it to get at me.' He raises a thick hand and delivers a sharp, smacking blow to the side of Anthony's head. A noise – meat hitting bone.

'Leave him alone!' I shout, pushing hard at Warren's chest with both hands.

Warren drops the boy and stares at me through narrow eyes, surprise turning into a plan. He licks his lips. 'Oh aye? Come on then, Southport. Come on.' He motions to me, palms upwards, fingers doing a little dance in the air. Head cocking, like an Indian dancer, first right, then left. Meaning *fight me*.

Inside my head, tiny grasshopper voices are wondering just how this is supposed to have happened. Others are asking what I intend to do. How do I fight a man with gold bracelets, arms like two sides of Bootle's thickest beef?

Suddenly, Warren's face wrinkles up in pain and he buckles to the ground, cursing. Anthony stands by, a thick piece of wood in his hands, smiling thinly as Warren rolls on the floor, clutching his left knee.

'You little fuckshite!'

'Get his phone,' Anthony commands me.

Half an hour later, when ambulances have come and gone and Warren is conducting an earnest conversation with two policemen, Anthony and I start walking back into the school. The windows of every classroom are filled with faces, boys and teachers watching the spectacle. In various different places, I see the silhouettes of Scarsdale, Davenport, Miss Kastrafitis, turning and calling for order.

'All in a morning's work.' My gaunt companion appears unshaken by the events, merely saddened.

'You were very brave,' I reply.

Anthony responds, with a shrug, 'I've never taken any crap off him. Mum and Mary, they creep round him all the time. Have to whisper when he's in a mood. "Bunny's had a bad day. Got to be careful." I won't do it. Argue back. And, of course, Joe's not going to keep quiet, is he? He can't.'

'Not much chance of you going back home now, I suppose.'

Anthony rubs the tip of his nose, showing an inch of dirty cuff. 'We never were. Mum's going to leave him. Says she is, anyway. Me and Mabs are working on her.'

Mabs. I like that − a fitting name for his sister. Mabs the bad picker. Like her mother, presumably, picking Bunny Warren.

'Shouldn't have thought it needed a lot of work,' I comment, as we enter the main building.

'You don't know Mum. Well, of course you don't. You don't know anything about us really, do you?' Anthony says.

'You've not really told me much.'

'She thought he'd get her work, because he knows all these celebs. Except of course he doesn't really. Just sniffs around them in a rather odious manner . . .' He stops himself and falls silent, thinking.

We stand outside the staff room, preparing to part. Notices flutter in the corridor breeze. One, penned and signed meticulously by Scarsdale, catches my eye: WILL THE BOY WHO . . .

'I suppose I should be getting back to—'

'Ever seen a film called *The Great Twinkie Challenge*?' Anthony asks, abruptly.

'I don't think so . . .' I say, wondering how this is relevant.

'Doesn't matter. It's crap. Got Goldie Hawn and Burt Reynolds in it. Anyway, my dad wrote it. Well, someone called Chip Trachtenheim wrote it, but it was my dad's idea.'

'Oh. I see. I'm not sure I—'

'You said you wanted me to tell you something about us,' Anthony interrupts, irritably. 'Well, there you are. I have. It was supposed to be the last Ealing comedy,' he continues, earnestly. 'It was supposed to be about the London to Brighton car rally. But then they shut the studios. And when we were in America my dad showed it to some producers. He thought they were his friends. But he was wrong. They turned it down. And it was the last thing he wrote. And then the *Twinkie* thing came out. It was exactly the same plot. It finished him off.' He nods slowly, looking at me, gauging my reaction. Not for the first time, it seems like he's looking into my soul. Scrubbing it clean with a Brillo pad. 'So you see, I can't stand people who aren't honest,' he says, pointedly. 'Nor can Mary.'

'What's that supposed to mean?'

He pauses for a moment, frowning under the light outside the staff toilet. It's on the blink, once again making the boy look like a projected image from an old film. 'You like her, don't you?'

'Your sister? Well . . .' I recall her appearance at the Parents' Evening, bearing gifts and dressed to kill. 'Did you fix that up, Anthony? Her coming to the Parents' thing?'

He shakes his head. 'Mum really was ill. A migraine. So you might say it was pure chance. Except I don't believe in chance, not really. I believe in facts and forces.'

'What forces?'

'The attraction of bodies in flux. A kind of Brownian-motion-meets-Keynesian-economics. Supply and demand.

Mary needs someone to get her away from this Jay person. So do you, evidently.'

'How do you work that out?'

'Your ex-girlfriend comes round telling us not to tell you she's pregnant. Now you live in a spare room in Mr Davenport's house,' he replies, witheringly. 'Nobody would live with him if they had a better offer, would they?'

'I like Mr Davenport.'

'Why won't you just ask her out?' he demands, exasperated. 'I assume it's the sort of thing you've done before.'

'It's not only the sort of thing I've done before, Anthony, I've done it with your sister before. Asked her out, I mean. Before you even mentioned her to me. She gets on my bus in the morning.'

I thought this might shock Anthony into silence, but he gives an interested waggle of the eyebrows, as if he'd perhaps stumbled upon some new theory in a dusty book. 'And what did she say?'

'What didn't she say? She said no, a lot of times, and fairly loudly. Along with delivering a rather misinformed attack on my manner of asking people out.'

'Misinformed?'

'She accused me of being some sort of office Romeo. The sort who tries it on with everyone. Which I am definitely not.'

He gives a biscuit-dry chuckle at this – a little scientist who's just grown a new type of mould. 'Well, there you go. That's exactly what this Jay is. She was taking it out on you, that's all. Displacement, Freud called it. But she's more or less over him now. Jay, I mean, not Freud. Says so, anyway.'

'Well, I'm deeply pleased for her,' I say, beginning to weary of this absurd wrangling. 'But really . . .'

'You know she bought a car a month ago?' he interrupts. 'She only gets on that bus because of you.'

Went The Day Well?

In the taxi on the way to the abbey, I try a little small talk with Rick Reed, mentioning that I've read some of his theatre reviews. This doesn't please him much. He takes a Capstan from a little brass case, but lacks the courage to light it. 'The theatre's bullcrap,' he pronounces, in the moody fashion of someone who is very glad to be interviewed, but equally concerned not to seem it. 'I'm doing novels now. Kind of post-post modern historical stuff.'

Reed is about my age, with bulbous, stary eyes which never quite focus on my own, making me think there must be a kidnapping going on just behind my shoulder. He sports a boxy pair of tinted sex-offender spectacles, and carries one item of luggage – a Kwik Save shopping bag, presumably bulging with bitter insights into the human condition.

He is coming to present the prizes, he tells me, not out of any affection for his alma mater, but because his publishers have arranged for his first historical novel, *The Bishop's Boots*, to be sold in the abbey's foyer. This in no way interferes with his very emphatic view that his publishers are also bullcrap.

'Somebody took my words,' he says, leaning back in the seat and showing me his soft, pink hands, the tools of his writer-craft, 'and bound them up in card. That's all it is. Bullcrap.' He speaks every sentence as if to a crowded auditorium.

'What was your first novel about? I think I've seen it around.'

Reed puffs out his cheeks and says, 'Starvation. Tuberculosis. Mass emigration. That sort of thing.'

This surprises me. 'No football, then?'

''S about that, too,' he elaborates: ''bout a Gaelic-speaking football team during the Irish potato famine.' He goes on to tell me – rather angrily, and as if it might be my fault – that this work has met with a tepid reception, on account of the reading public being (a) bullcrap and (b) not willing to learn Gaelic. He then hands me his rail tickets and proceeds to pester me about claiming expenses. To distract him from this, I broach the subject of his new historical novel. But Reed lowers his fleshy eyelids, shaking his head. 'It's big,' he hints, darkly. 'Massive, in fact. I wouldn't want it getting out.'

'Any football in it?' I probe.

'Mostly not,' he says, swallowing a couple of Rennies. 'Well, some.'

The plan was to take Reed to the abbey first, to leave his things. But seeing as he doesn't have much in the way of things, and knowing as I do that Mr Scarsdale is currently pacing up and down the abbey with a clipboard, shouting at people, I decide to head straight for our lunch destination, a cheap trattoria round the corner. Reed, however, has other plans. 'Is the Abbot's still going?' he asks.

I cheer up when Reed says this. Because the Abbot's Tabard, a small ale-house close to the Italian place, has recently been revamped into the sort of establishment where gourmet sausages are sold in greater quantities than beer, which means, in turn, that Davenport will be somewhere else. I have received strict instructions from Davenport to keep Rick Reed away from him at all costs, and I agree wholeheartedly with them. For reasons not unrelated to a 3 a.m. call from the headmaster's wife, Davenport has been in a shocking mood all morning.

Reed finally puts the Capstan back in the case. 'I like the Abbot's. It's *real*. Know what I mean?'

Once inside what might be described as one of London's least *real* pubs, I steer my charge to a vacant corner and then go off to the bar with the intention of being served some drinks, sometime. But Reed, to my surprise and relief, says he doesn't touch alcohol. He also appears not to smoke. He accompanies me to the bar, in order to see what soft drinks are on offer.

Reed deliberates many minutes over the soft drinks, in the same manner as a bedouin choosing a camel, or a lady in a shoe shop. Finally, he makes his decision. 'I'll take a glass of pineapple juice,' he declares, in the tones of someone announcing the birth of a new literary movement. 'To start with.'

This coincides with my first hope-shattering glimpse of a sweating Davenport, who has shouldered his way through the crush on the other side of the bar and is motioning to the barmaid with an outstretched twenty. He glances up, peers through the steam rising from the dishwasher and sees us. His bloodshot eyes narrow and I see him muttering something.

This is bad, awfully bad. But not irredeemable. Perhaps I can sandwich myself between the two of them and prevent bloodshed. Perhaps Davenport has cheered up. 'Thought you'd be in the Mac!' I call out, breezily.

'Shut for refurbishments,' Davenport snaps, as he rounds the corner of the bar. Reed turns to face him and gives a delicate burp. 'I'm surprised you had the balls to turn up, Reed!'

'Ginge!' Reed says, with a faltering pretence at *bonhomie*. 'You're looking good, man.'

Davenport scowls and, reaching right across me, yanks at the rough fabric of Reed's worsted suit. 'What have you come as, Dick Weed?' he asks. 'Lady Chatterley's lover? No. That'd be too honest for you. More like the Artful Dodger.'

'Come on, Ginge,' Reed replies, plainly terrified. 'Come and have a drink. On me.'

'It'd *choke* me,' Davenport declares nobly.

In the interests of a quiet life, I intervene here, saying I'll buy Davenport a drink. Two drinks, if he cares to give me that twenty back. But even this, an offer usually seized upon with charmless haste, is ignored.

'I'm sorry, Ginge,' the novelist continues, pitifully. 'Never slept properly since. I sold the drama cup, you know. Gave the money to Militant Tendency.'

Davenport says that he doesn't care a hoot about the Miss Gay-Knight Cup for Drama. Ever since Prep One, he says, venomously, Rick Reed has been a low character. 'You bished on Bubnik-Kasterlitz and got my brontosaurus confiscated,' Davenport thunders, a charge to which Reed hangs his balding head in shame. 'And you cribbed your way into Lower Remove. You had the irregular verbs in your jotter.'

A small curious crowd has gathered round us now and the noisy pub has fallen silent. I notice the barmaid dialling a number on the telephone.

'Does any of this really matter?' I remark, uneasily.

'You wouldn't understand,' the novelist replies.

'You're right there, Weed,' Davenport concedes gruffly. 'He never does. Not a Lorry's man. Comes from the North.'

'A smudger,' Reed pronounces, looking disdainfully at me.

'Oik,' Davenport corrects. 'Smudgers were the grammar school.'

'Gosh, you're right,' Reed says, with a faint laugh. 'I'd quite forgotten.'

'We had some laughs, didn't we?' Davenport murmurs. 'Before it all went sour? Do you remember Billinge?'

'He was the one who always had spare underwear in his desk, wasn't he?'

Davenport gives a little chuckle. 'No, that was Beamish. Billinge was the one with the sister.'

'Gosh, yes. Billinge's sister. Do you know, she was the only girl I ever met who actually *enjoyed* . . .'

'I know. Me too.'

The two men are now locked into the sort of cosy familiarity that old ladies enjoy at bus stops. The crowds cease to be interested in us. The barmaid replaces the receiver and comes up to the bar. 'That's twelve eighty,' she says to me. Which seems quite possible. I say that it's got nothing to do with me. I turn to Reed and tell him I'll be back to pick him up at a quarter to two.

'Make my own way there,' Reed says, haughtily.

'Fine.'

'There's no need to get all girlish, Al,' Davenport says. 'Stay and have a dram. You might learn a thing or two.'

'I wouldn't want to get in the way,' I say icily, turning away.

Davenport follows me, pulling me back by my elbow. 'Have we done something to offend you, old boy?'

I survey my thickset friend in his crumpled suit, the strained waistband of his green trousers curling in on itself. 'Five minutes ago you couldn't stand him,' I remark, glancing over at Reed, who appears to be practising his signature on a nearby beer mat.

'Yes, well, Alastair, you must understand: some loyalties go back a long way. *Lorry's contra mundum* and all that.'

'Fine. Just make sure he's not late.'

'Oh, he'll be safe as houses with me,' Davenport replies, patting me on the shoulders.

I got her work number from Anthony this morning, pretending it was important for me to have 'contact details of his guardian', that sort of guff, of which, pausing to scribble a number on a notice torn from the Ninjitsu First XI noticeboard, Anthony believed not a word. He said, grinning broadly, that I should try not to ring her in the mornings. 'Always in a mood in the mornings,' he said.

'Well, I won't need to ring her,' I replied, irritable at being so obvious. 'Unless there's an emergency.'

'It looks to me like there might be,' Anthony replied, slinging his American kitbag over a shoulder and vanishing into the usual post-break-bell enactment of Gallipoli.

She winds me up, just as her brother does, with her conversational *non sequiturs* and barbed responses. Not like anyone I've ever wanted before. But I do want, in spite, or maybe exactly because, in the midst of all the teeth-grinding, eye-popping frustration she seems to induce, there's something else. Like a feeling of blood running, at last, in an arm you've leant on for too long. A humming, an alive feeling, prickly pins and needles being far preferable to sod all.

Plus there's a sense of hope today, regardless of Davenport's recent betrayal. A feeling of things coming together – a jigsaw forming itself without human intervention. It was confirmed by the little card I received from Tara this morning, thanking me for arranging an invite to the Prizegiving for her husband. There was no writing – just the imprint of a pair of red lips. But I knew what it meant. And I knew that the decks were clear now.

Down a quiet street some yards away from the abbey, I step into one of those ultra-modern phone boxes, internet and fax and possibly teleport combined, with the instructions listed in every imaginable language, except English.

'*Fiendish Dolan Suzuki.*'

'Mary Blundell, please.'

The receptionist, possibly an automated device with a Kiwi accent, responds with a click. The closing bars of 'El Watusi' give way to Beethoven's Ninth. I rehearse a few lines under my breath. 'Just wondering if . . .'

'Mary Blundell.'

'Oh, hello, Mary,' says a curious, high-camp voice – my own, suddenly turned into a slightly sinister seaside entertainer's. 'It's Alastair Strange.'

'Oh,' she replies, swallowing some mouthful of *sollissidor*-sandwich, *ciabatta* and *lollo rosso*. 'Hello.'

Not giving a lot away – sounding like she can't imagine why I'd be calling her, or that she can't remember anyone called Alastair Strange, or that she can, thank you, and doesn't much care to.

'How are you?'

'A bit busy, actually.' As in *so shag off*.

'Oh, sorry. I can maybe call you back—'

'No, it's not your fault.' The voice changes gear. 'I'm just in the middle of buying a house. And it's going a bit crazy. Dutch auction.'

I make sympathetic sounds, trying to imagine what a Dutch auction might be. A sale of giant, circular cheeses, perhaps. 'I thought you'd be good at all that. Conveyancing and so on.'

'You did, did you? And why's that?' A pause. We're back in the wintry wastes of Ice World.

I take a breath. 'Never mind. Look, I was just wondering if—'

She gives a laugh or a cough, interrupting my flow. 'What? If I wanted to see *Sammy Going South* at the BFI?'

Well, there's an idea. 'Would you?'

'Saw it last night.'

Christ. This prickly stubble-rash of a girl. Why exactly am I bothering? I know why I am bothering.

'Well, perhaps not that, but I thought you might like to go for a drink. Maybe. Some time?'

There follows a silence just long enough to harvest a pound of horse hair, knit it into a garment, wear it for a while and put it on a long wash. My mood turns from yellow, through black, to a disconsolate, turned-down blue.

'Where?' she asks, finally.

'Do you know the MacKendrick? They've got sixty different kinds of whisky.'

'I like whisky.'

'I know. I mean, I thought perhaps you might.'

'Well . . .' There's a muffled sound, perhaps a hand over the receiver. I can hear her say 'Thanks, Kim', then the muffle goes away and she's back, saying: 'Oh *fuckeroo!* This is it! Alastair, the fax came through. Shit on wheels. I'll call you back, honey, OK?'

Before I can say 'Sure', or any such monosyllable designed to make her feel I'm easy and cool to the point of being comatose with this, the whole calling-back jazz, there's a click. I'm alone, facing a little symbol of a Welsh dragon and the words *Telefon: cwm llheoidol gwllad wyf 192*. She can't ring me back: I'm in a call-box. And if she looks for my home number, she won't find it, because I live with Davenport, and he pays the bills. Sometimes. I might as well be back at square one.

The abbey is a bazaar of smells. On the first three rows holds sway the musty odour of the teachers' gowns, in the spectrum hues of every British university. Behind them, a miasma of cheeseburger and bubblegum from the twelve rows of assembled boys. And beyond them, the costly musk of their proud parents. Added to these are the fatty gases of the candles, the damp of the abbey stone and a thousand Polo mints. I am feeling sick – but then I would be, however the air smelled.

Up on the platform the headmaster is speaking, resplendent in the sort of gown that would not disgrace the Milan catwalks, its hood fringed with a snow-white band of fur. Next to him sits a skeletal, liver-spotted figure, sporting no adornments at all, save for a Rotary Club pin in the lapel of his mildewed suit. This, I assume from the notes in the programme, is the chairman of the Governors, though it might be St John Lorimer himself, disinterred for the occasion.

To the right of him sits Tara's husband, Mr Sammaddi, a slight, delicate man in a double-breasted suit, his black hair immaculately waved and parted. He frowns in an effort to seem interested in the speech. To the right of Mr Sammaddi is a single, horribly empty chair, its occupant absent. This – this naked, mocking space – is why I can take no joy in Sammaddi's presence.

The teachers are seated in the first two rows. Behind us, there are scurrying movements. Mr Scarsdale's long-promised magazines arrived here late from the print room and, even as the platform party began to troop onto the stage, the proud editor was desperately attempting to distribute two copies to everyone in the abbey. But Scarsdale's desperation was nothing compared with what I now feel, as I sit on the hard ecclesiastical seat and contemplate the space where Rick Reed is supposed to be, and plainly isn't. I have descended into my own whirly pit of misery, every few seconds checking the vestry door for signs of movement, starting in hope every time a pew creaks or a programme is dropped to the stone floor. But no one arrives. I have screwed up: screwed up, as some of my pupils would put it, *bad-style*.

'It was, I believe, the contemporary Dutch philosopher Marius Hoogstraat who coined the phrase "information super highway",' the Head notes, making a tiny, seamless adjustment to his microphone as he speaks. He is interrupted by the digitised warble of a mobile phone, way back, among the parents, followed by a ripple of abashed laughter. 'And I see we are very much in the fast lane here,' the head quips, like a seasoned stand-up dismissing hecklers. A burst of sycophantic mirth follows. Mr Sammaddi touches the corners of his mouth with a silk handkerchief. 'But our founder, Sinjun Lawmaah, beat Mr Hoogstraat to that notion nearly a century ago,' the head continues. 'For what is a school but a six-lane freeway of information exchange? What are our boys, gathered here today to receive the honours for which they have toiled so hard? What *are* they but miniature Eddie Stobarts, or Norbert Dentressangles, zooming at breakneck speed to their chosen careers, with a heavy and precious cargo of knowledge?'

The head pursues the motorway metaphor, comparing the classrooms to Trusthouse Forte service stations, the teachers to the RAC. Sammaddi has begun to wear a pained look, either troubled by his bowels or beginning to wonder why he bothered coming. Next to me, Miss Kastrafitis sighs, as copies of the magazine are passed down along the row. She licks her fingers and starts to read.

Suddenly, just as the headmaster is folding up his speech and returning to his seat, Davenport squeezes himself beerily along the row of seats and taps me on the shoulder. 'Mission accomplished!' he whispers loudly. Unfortunately, this is uttered within range of one of the little drop-mikes hanging from the rafters, so that his encouraging message is broadcast to the entire abbey. The platform party shoot hostile, mackerel-eyed stares down at us. But I don't care. Rick Reed is making his way up the steps to the platform. It's going to be OK.

There's a tuft of frayed carpeting at the edge of the stage platform and Reed trips, dropping a kebab from his hands. 'Fuck it,' he mumbles, kicking curled shavings of onion and meat onto the front row. Swaying dangerously, he stares at the platform party, as if about to report that they have looked in an unwelcome fashion at his girlfriend and must now be prepared to step outside. He then rummages in the pocket of his suit. I notice, somewhere in the midst of all this, that Sammaddi has started to smile.

With a mournful flash of amber, Reed withdraws a quarter bottle of whisky, uncaps it and takes a deep draught, before lungeing at the lectern, twisting the microphone close to his mouth, like Johnny Rotten on the verge of toasting the Queen. There is a soft ripple of surprise across the abbey. 'Headmaster,' he begins, with that mixture of piety and concentration used when the very drunk are trying to seem otherwise. 'Barents, Poys. *Dear* Poys.'

I see the headmaster's jaw shoot forwards a centimetre, the first time he has ever registered anger. A pair of azure eyes gleam out towards the third row, towards me, scanning the teachers. I shuffle down into the depths of my jacket.

'It's not your turn to speak!' I can hear the headmaster hissing at Reed. 'It's the chairman of the Governors first. Then it's you. Didn't AKS brief you beforehand?'

Reed turns, takes one look at the chairman of the Governors and bursts out laughing. Then he gazes back out at the audience. 'How many . . . h–how many of you slags really know what it means to have a soul!' Reed cries. 'Hmm?'

There is a polite silence across the vast hall of stone, as if Reed has raised a contentious issue at a dinner party and no one has quite had time to find out what they're saying about it on Radio Four. Nobody moves – except for Sammaddi, whose slight body is now shaking with spasms of mirth. I dread to think what Tara's going to say.

'How many you boys know wad your precious founder was? Sinjun Lawmaah. Hmm? I'll tell you. And those of you too fucking dead to listen can read it in my next novel! Simeon Lodzinski, as he called himself when he first landed here from Lithuania, was a loan shark and a . . . a *pimp*!' A slender bolus of spittle shoots from Reed's lips, flashing in the light as it arcs down to the front row. 'A rack-renter, preying on decent working-class people!'

He reels from the lectern and, pausing only to steady himself with the chairman's zimmer frame, gropes his way towards the table where the prizes are stacked. There, he picks up the most ostentatious trophy and holds it aloft, the Grail captured from the Saracens. 'See this?' The Founder's Cup for Integrity? Want to know about the founder's integrity? Do you?'

'Yes!' Sammaddi calls out, clapping his hands together. He is perhaps the only person here enjoying himself.

Reed glances round from the lectern, trying to focus on the platform party, but gives up fairly quickly. 'The coroner's report said he died of a perforated bowel, neglecting to mention that he perforated it him-fucking-self! Lowering himself onto a wine bottle, in front of a terrified brostitute. I mean prostitute.'

Reed loses his train of thought. He wipes his brow and swallows, opens his mouth a few times, gulping the air. But it does him no good. Noxious gas bubbles up from somewhere at his core, expanding his cheeks. He lets out a long stream of grey, lumpy vomit, which splashes into the Founder's Cup for Integrity, overflowing and dripping rudely around his wrists.

This might, in itself, be enough to cause a stampede. But no sooner has Rick Reed toppled from the stage, arms flailing, sick trailing, into the gowned ranks of the staff, than Miss Kastrafitis, some way behind and next to me, emits a shrill cry. 'The magazine!' She shoots up, trembling, a copy of Scarsdale's magazine in her hands, its pages open at the middle. 'Look at it!' she cries. She turns to me, her mouth opening and shutting, wheezing for breath. I take the magazine from her. Davenport leans in too as the shocked stillness of the abbey turns to uproar and people all around us urgently open their magazines. In the corner of my vision, I can see Scarsdale, the neck brace fallen from him, vaulting with surprising agility over a row of seats as he tries to seize a copy of his work. Rick Reed staggers to his feet and leans forward also, sick-spattered fingers reaching for a glimpse of the offending item.

The middle page is entitled 'The magazine's founder, Mr Scarsdale, at home with his wife'. Underneath it is a grainy picture evidently transplanted from an adult magazine. It pictures a short man, naked save for a pair of cowboy boots, his head buried between the doughy thighs of a woman.

'That,' slurs Rick Reed, like a man politely excusing himself, 'bakes me veal kwai ill.'

The Ship That Died of Shame

'Stick a copy of *Hotspur* down your strides and you'll be fine,' mutters Davenport dealing me a bruising blow to the bicep as he passes on by.

Heading towards the headmaster's office, I say nothing, thinking that, should any copies of *Hotspur* be available, they'd have gone up Davenport's anus a week ago, along with some broken bottles and the end of my boot.

Several days have passed since Prizegiving, and normality is still a distant mirage. Mr Scarsdale is on indefinite leave. The story of Rick Reed's outburst in the abbey has hit the national press, resulting in a PR disaster for the school and Rick Reed being offered a six-figure sum for his next novel. And from Tara there has been only the ominous silence of someone too angry to get in touch.

I've been waiting for Davenport to offer a few, halting words of apology, words which have failed to appear, even when, on our way to school this morning, I received a pager message summoning me to the head's office for a briefing. Not a 'natter', not a 'chat', but a briefing, a term suggestive of harsh words and summary dismissals, if not the rack and scold's bridle – instruments which should rightly be applied to Lawrence Sacheverell Davenport, MA, for feeding the Prizegiving guest five pints and three double Scotches in the space of an hour.

As I walk in, Harpenden is pacing the floor and speaking to his secretary. 'Get me fanny shots, will you?' The secretary raises two pencilled eyebrows at this, unsure whether she should commit the words to her notepad. 'F-a-n-n-y S-c-h-o-t-z,' the head spells out, impatiently running a hand through his metallic hair. 'Of Carter Schotz. She's handling the libel action.'

He dabs at his tanned brow with a silk handkerchief, a faint tremor in his movements, and then turns a permafrost gaze onto me. 'You'd better come in.'

Within the inner sanctum, I am offered neither coffee nor a seat. I stand before the desk, head bowed, as my employer tells me that he is 'intensely dismayed'.

'I didn't know he was going to get drunk,' I plead in defence. 'Davenport assured me he'd get him there on time.'

'It was a simple task, Alastair,' the head replies, crisply. 'And you let everyone down. The saddest thing is, you know who you've let down the most?'

I make an inspired lunge at the answer expected. 'Myself?'

'No. Me. I'd only just been telling the chairman of the Governors what a focused team player you were. The great strides you'd made with the MCS course. And then you do this.'

The headmaster pours water from a filter jug into a glass tumbler, adds two pink tablets and pauses as they dissolve. He looks at me, twirling his wedding ring on a russet finger, pondering his next move. 'I received an e-mail from Mr Sammaddi yesterday,' he continues, shuddering at the memory, 'saying that he still had absolutely no idea why we'd invited him, and thanking me for one of the most hilarious afternoons of his life.'

'Did he offer us any money?' I ask hopefully.

'What do you think?' the headmaster shouts, slamming his palms on the desk. 'Of course he didn't!'

There's a pause while the headmaster collects himself and feels his pulse.

'I don't see how I can be held responsible for something Rick Reed chooses to do on stage,' I plead. 'I was just escorting him.'

'And whom should I hold responsible?' the head asks, releasing his wrist and taking a deep breath through his nostrils. 'My wife perhaps? A randomly selected member of Ten L?'

I shake my head. 'No, but—'

The Head interrupts. 'You leave me no option but to place you on weekly report.'

'Report?'

The head reaches for a sheet of paper on his desk and pushes it across to me. 'If you'd care to read and sign.'

This is one of the head's flashier innovations, known as a TBI, or Targeted Behavioural Initiative, wherein offenders are obliged to put their signatures to a range of earnest promises, which are then posted up on one of the school's main noticeboards. I am presumably the first member of staff who has ever had to sign one.

The final paragraph worries me more than all the others. I look up at the headmaster, who's waiting, silently thumbing through a thick, vinyl-bound document entitled 'Fluid Pricing in the Education Sector'. 'It says here, "I agree to take charge of the forthcoming school trip to Étaples." Is that supposed to be in here? I thought Mr Scarsdale was doing it.'

'As I'm sure you're aware, Alastair,' the head says, giving a delicately poised cough and then examining his hand, 'Mr Scarsdale has been temporarily out-contracted. In fact, surface-level at least, it looks like being a permanent arrangement. Especially in the light of what's occurred this a.m.'

'What's that?'

'His legal team has consented to abandon his compensation suit against the school in return for a modest redundancy settlement. Well, they couldn't really do otherwise, considering the fact that he was seen jumping all over the place without his neck collar.' The headmaster folds his hands neatly together and gives a pained smile. 'Not that that's stopped him faxing me doctor's letters every five minutes.'

Numbly, I bend down to sign the agreement. As I scratch my signature, the headmaster suddenly lunges forward like a cobra, snatching the pen from my fingers. 'Where did you get this?' he demands, sharply, holding the pen aloft.

It's a stubby, cigar-shaped fountain pen, something I picked up from the kitchen table this morning. I had assumed it was Davenport's.

'I just picked it up somewhere . . .'

The headmaster glares at me keenly, then subjects the barrel of the pen to extra scrutiny, as if appraising some precious jewel. 'This is my wife's. I had her initials put on the clip. Now, *where* exactly did you pick it up?'

'Caught us at a difficult moment,' says my father. 'Got a few of the lads round . . .'

Sitting alone in the staff room, I look askance at the phone receiver, wondering if I've heard right. 'The *lads*?'

'Yes. Akko and Vinny and a very nice young fellow called Headache. At least, I think that's what he said.'

My father was awarded 180 hours of community service for his attempt to burgle the local MP. He started today, he told me, dismantling part of the town's pier along with a hand-picked selection of the local juvenile mafia. A number of his fellow offenders are currently in my mother's kitchen, eating Dundee cake and watching the afternoon re-run of *Neighbours*.

'Akko's, ah, helping me to install a burglar alarm,' my father enthuses. 'Knows all about them, apparently. They run an installation course in Fylde Prison. Rather makes me wish I'd been given a stretch. You know, I frequently look back on my time teaching German O level in Walton Jail as one of the happiest in my life.'

'But you almost got killed in Walton. A rapist threw a chair at your head when you asked him where he was going for his holidays.'

'A little misunderstanding. There's something so very *refreshing* about the criminal classes. My handler back in the Bucharest days used to say that a healthy streak of criminality is the finest thing a young agent can have on his c.v. Quite true. I'd always hoped you might have leanings that way yourself.'

'Did you?'

'You always fell asleep during those ridiculous Ealing comedies on the TV. As a matter of fact, so did I. All that sentiment and moralising. I took it as a very healthy sign that they bored you so much . . .'

'But I thought you liked them.' I say, in a plaintive voice. This had always been the one fact I thought I definitely knew about him – a little raft of certainty in an ocean of enigma.

'Oh no. I was always abroad when they came out at the *Kinema*. And I just remember watching them all one time your mother was in hospital. Still makes me shudder. My wife was ill and I was trying to look after a small and rather difficult boy. Oh dear. I suppose that was you, wasn't it?'

Some moments later, I put the phone down and take Mary's work number out of my pocket. I've never had such a clear vision of the way ahead, perhaps because the past had once again become so murky. All these years I've thought there was that one slender bridge between my father and me. Some films we both dozed our way through, decades ago – meaning everything to one person, less than nothing to the other. Sometimes, it seems, the past means as much as we want it to. And that, in turn, makes the future all the more inviting.

'If you are in custody, and require legal assistance, you may call the duty clerk on 0780 . . .'

I do think for a minute about ringing the duty clerk and asking whether he or she thinks Mary's the sort of girl who'd prefer to go and see a film, something obscure and debate-worthy at the NFT, or whether I should just cut to the chase and get her blind drunk. Then the bleeps go and I'm just about to leave a message for her, when Davenport enters, a pile of exercise books under one arm and a plaster bust of Cicero under the other. He smiles sheepishly as I replace the receiver.

'Still here?'

'It would seem that way, wouldn't it?' I reply, stonily, replacing the slip of paper in my pocket.

Davenport dumps his wares on the table and moves to the coffee cups. 'Fancy a couple in the Mac?' he asks. 'Supposed to be hooking up with Gizzler at eight. Could do with a spot of Dutch courage.'

'I'm going home,' I reply quietly. 'And staying in.'

Davenport gives me a curious, wan look as he bends to

the floor. 'If you don't mind me asking, Al, are you for some reason in a bit of a huff with me?'

I sigh and look at Davenport. The man's wobbling like a small performing elephant as he tries to tie his shoelace, his face puzzled, hurt and entirely without artifice. It is hard to be angry with him. That said, I still am.

To break the silence, I switch on the television. An actor briefly famous for playing an East End wife-batterer now invites me to celebrate the union of butter and olive oil. This being an unlikely cause for festivities in my view, I turn away from the screen to face Davenport. 'You don't even *know*, do you?'

'Well, plainly not. Only, I thought we were chinas.' Davenport, realising that the zip of his Rupert-the-bear trousers is undone, attends to it, leaving a little flag of his blue shirt poking forth.

'I'm pissed off because of Prizegiving,' I explain. 'Reed turns up clutching a half-eaten kebab and a bottle of Stag whisky. So I get the blame for that. And to round it all off nicely, Lawrence, the headmaster very nearly got the impression I'm screwing his wife.'

I tell him about the fountain pen. How I had to lie to Harpenden, claiming I picked the pen up in the car park, intending to put it in Lost Property.

Davenport looks worried now, his cheeks assuming a marbled effect, like some ghastly offal blancmange. 'You didn't, you know, say anything you shouldn't?'

'No. He believed me. He even apologised. But all in all, *old chum*, all the crap that's falling on my head should rightly be on yours. And, yes, I am in a bit of a huff about that. I think you'll find most people short of Jesus Christ would be.'

Hearing this, Davenport sits down sheepishly on the

sofa and lights a foul-smelling cheroot. 'Dearie doo,' he says, pushing the offending piece of shirt back into his fly. 'You must rather have taken against me lately. And quite right too. I've been completely bloody to you.'

And as much as this is true, I realise there's not much point in continuing to be angry with my housemate. It would require an effort, and I'm far too tired. 'Let's just forget it.'

'No,' says Davenport, piously puffing clouds of dung-scented smoke in my direction. 'It's not on. I behaved like a total blunderbus and I ought to jolly well make it up to you. Afraid things haven't been going terribly well for me lately, see? Trouble with the old girl and such.'

'I thought you'd sorted it all out.'

'So did I.' He gives a pained, impotent shrug. 'I mean, she tells me she's up the stick and she doesn't want it. And so I say, "fair do's, I'll stick by you," and so on. And that just seems to have put her in an even worse mood. Didn't even remember my birthday, you know.'

I experience a pin-prick of guilt and shame. 'When was your birthday? You didn't say anything.'

Davenport makes a miserable face. 'Didn't feel like making a fuss this year. Everything's so bloody rum right now. You know, Al, I've got a terrible feeling we might be on the skids, Gizzler and I.'

'Maybe it's for the best,' I offer, trying to sound both kindly and wise, and failing spectacularly in both camps.

'But it *isn't*,' Davenport insists, staring at his shoes. 'She doesn't love Steve. I can't explain it to you but we were *meant*, you know, we were meant to be together . . . I mean, look at it. There's Steve . . . speaks fluent Dutch, practically lives off cold herring. Got a bloody photo of Queen Beatrix in his lav. He'd sell his wedding tackle if he thought it'd make him more of a Dutchman. And Gizzler doesn't want him. She wants me. She *did*, anyway.' He gazes at me intensely. 'And I want her.'

'But why? Don't you think things might be easier if you just forgot about it?'

Davenport makes a short growl of anguish in his throat. 'I *can't*! You don't understand.'

'Try me.'

Davenport gazes awkwardly at the carpet, his brow furrowed. 'If you were a small woman, Alastair, you'd have no trouble finding someone big to look after you. It's terribly easy. But what if you were a large man? What if you were me?'

'Well . . .' It's hard to respond to the revelation that Davenport would prefer to be a small woman.

'That's what she does. She might not look big, but she is. She's a lot bigger than I am. And when I'm with her, I just feel . . . sort of . . . *safe*. I don't get into bother. People are nice to us, you know, when we go out to places, people talk to us. Do you think people are like that when I'm on my own?'

'Aren't they?'

'No. They look at me like I'm . . .' he flaps his arms like some disconsolate turkey, '*this*. This stumpy hooray with a loud voice. That's what people think of me. But when I'm with her, it's all right. Like the day we got together, outside the Miramont. It was the old man's birthday and Corky asked her along. I'd gone out for a smoke. And I got into this . . . spot of hoo-hah with a tramp. Came up and started hassling me, you know, and I offered him some cash. But he didn't want it. Just wanted to take a swing at me, see? Didn't like the cut of my jib. And I thought, Heigh-ho, here we go, more of the usual. Time for me to receive my monthly smack in the kisser. Then *she* came out and he just disappeared. And it's been like that ever since, you see. There's never any trouble when I'm with Gizzler. All just melts away . . .'

His voice suddenly changes tack, an urgent gleam in his eyes. 'I know she's talked to you, Al. She said she had. Did she say anything about what's going on? Anything at all?'

'I'm afraid not. She just said you sweat when you eat.'

Davenport gives a joyless, private laugh, but says nothing.

'I think that meant she loves you,' I add. 'In fact, I'm sure she does.'

'Hmm,' Davenport says. Then he shakes himself and rubs his knees briskly. 'Not your problem anyhow. I owe you a good turn or two. I know! Why don't I take the Froggy trip for you? How's about that?'

I look into Davenport's ruddy face and see that he means it. I weigh up the offer, which is, in itself, a highly attractive one. I could have a day off – perhaps spend it with Mary, if I can get hold of her. No dawn coaches down the motorway, no hordes of bickering boys falling off the ferry or running away to Amsterdam. But there's something else on my mind.

'I'd sooner you just got that telescope out of my room,' I point out, pressing my advantage. 'It's been there weeks now and I can't do it on my own.'

Davenport nods fiercely, rubbing his hands together. 'Say no more, old boy. Plus I'll throw the Froggy trip in as a bonus. I could get Gizzler some eau-de-Cologne or . . .' His voice dies, as he becomes transfixed by the television screen. I follow his gaze. '*O saeclum insapiens et infacetum,*' Davenport murmurs.

'What?'

'Latin for "How did that cocksucker get on the goggle-box?" '

It's an appropriate question. Rick Reed is on the TV, the guest of an early-evening chat show. The presenter, a frenetic ginger-haired man who is either on drugs or has live eels permanently up his arse, is warmly pumping Reed's hand as he takes his seat next to a Page Three model. Reed is dressed much as he was for the Prizegiving, but to underline his new celebrity status he has added a flat cap and a pair of blue-tinted sunglasses.

We listen to the interview for a few minutes, but Reed is treating the studio to such a stream of invective that most of his words are obscured by bleeping sounds. This, arguably, makes things more bearable.

Davenport starts pulling his coat on. It's time to go, he says. 'I'll see you back at the ranch, I guess. You going to be in?'

'Yep. Do you want me to take Cinna for his walk?'

Davenport looks touched, but shakes his head. 'No need. Afraid Cinna's in exile at the moment. Spending a little time with his grandparents.'

'Really?'

'Yes,' Davenport responds, gravely. 'Poor chapster got rather excited over Gizzler's new Manolo Blahniks. Had a little accident. Perfectly natural – young dog, lady's shoes, time of the year and all that. But she was on at me to get him, you know, *snip-snip*. So I smuggled him out to the folks' place. He's in a terrible state – won't talk to me at all. But what else could I do? I've got to get Gizzler back somehow.'

I lingered a while in the staff room. Tried watching *Neighbours*, but soon gave up. The Ealing comedies might have lost a little of their sheen in the last hour, but I still can't go back to soaps, not with their easy clichés and their quick fixes to life's endemics. I liked them once: when I was stuck in an armchair all the time, they were an ersatz life, the Silk Cut Ultra Low of real existence. But now they're about as captivating to me as visiting some small, locally funded museum. I know the drill too well: the new beefcake, who nearly runs over the feisty blonde on his first day, and, after six weeks of loathing, subsequently skips down the aisle with her. The teenage double-act, Geek and Romeo, whose crackpot schemes are rumbled by the gruff storekeeper. Like Larkin said – just a load of crap; get stewed instead.

It's submerged in thoughts of getting stewed and how best that might be swiftly and cheaply achieved that I walk up the pathway to our house, hearing shouts from the tennis courts behind. A slender, dark figure lurks in our doorway, startling me as it turns round. 'Where's Loz?' it asks.

I peer into the gloom and make out the shape of Ann Gorley in black leggings under a long dark skirt. 'Lawrence? He's gone out. Can I help?'

I open the front door and let us in. A warm, piny smell greets my nostrils, welcome if entirely unexpected, and undoubtedly due to the absence of dog.

Ann hovers on the threshold, uncertain, picking at the wooden toggles on her duffle coat. 'I lost my keys, didn't I? I was hoping Loz could pick the lock.'

In the kitchen I put the kettle on as Ann tells me, sniffing faintly, how she had a row with Mr Smaut after he enticed her along to a meeting of his local church, over in Acton.

'This great big black guy gets up and starts saying how

there's someone here crying out for salvation. Someone who's got a drink problem. Next thing I know there's three of them kneeling on my chest and Adam's speaking in tongues.'

'Were you . . . were you involved with Mr Smaut, then?'

'A bit. I thought he was going to be different,' she says, bitterly. 'That was why I started going to church. I thought I'd meet a better kind of bloke. What is it about me? Why do I have to keep on picking nutters?'

'I'm not really the one to ask, am I?'

'I'm sorry. I didn't mean that. You were the best one of the bunch. I mean, you weren't like any of the others at all. I wish I'd realised that at the time.' She gives me a long, rather serious look and takes a few steps towards me.

'Did you say tea or coffee?' I ask, stepping back, embarrassed. Something crosses Ann's face – anger, shame, something she makes every effort to hide with a bright smile. I busy myself with the milk.

Some minutes later, when we're in the front room drinking tea, she removes a mobile phone from her crochet handbag as I start leafing through the *Yellow Pages*. 'There are lots of these locksmiths do twenty-four-hour call-out. Probably charge you a bit, though. Are you all right for cash?'

She bends her long neck wanly to the floor. 'I only had spare change, and I put all of that in the collection box.'

'I can lend you some. And put your phone away. It'll be cheaper calling from here.'

She narrows her eyes. 'You don't have to be so nice, you know. I've been pretty horrible to you.'

She's right, I'm being over-nice. But I feel bad, because I think she wanted something back then in the kitchen –

an embrace or more. And I couldn't give it to her. It's not just that someone else has stepped into Ann's place. It's also that I feel awkward with her now, as if liking her was something childish, like needing the light on in the hallway to get to sleep. I liked Ann because she was dolorous and Northern, because she had a great long personal catalogue of the things she hated, because she reminded me of where I came from, what I used to be like. I think the word for it is 'narrow'.

'Have you got anything to drink?' she asks.

There's sherry in the fridge. A case of Wincarnis Tonic Wine – a beverage I thought could only be found under the beds of Sussex ladies who resemble Margaret Rutherford – next to Cinna's basket. And the bottle of champagne I bought as a belated birthday present for Davenport, still in its tissue paper in my briefcase. It'd be easy to put all my plans on hold, get smashed with a familiar face.

'Don't think we have. Sorry.'

We're like two people who'd been friends in another decade, happy to loaf together round the war memorial, in their neon socks and their gel-spiked hair. Now they meet in another decade, another town. And there's a certain fondness, but more of the awkwardness, the embarrassment, a desire to occupy separate stretches of pavement.

Later, as she's upstairs in the bathroom, cleaning herself up, I call one of the locksmiths in the book, a firm triumphantly calling themselves Ennytime, Ennywhere.

'Englebert speaking,' says a chirpy, Cockney-sparrer-type voice. 'Locks and glass. Ennytime, Enny—'

I cut him short. 'Is there any chance you could come and get my . . . erm . . . friend . . . into her flat? She lives in the parade.'

Enny treats me to an almost indulgent laugh. 'Ealing Parade, d'you mean, mate?' he asks, in the kindly fashion of a bus conductor rousing a confused drunk. 'By the common?'

'Yes, that's right.'

'The Parade by the common?!'

'That's what I said.'

'Oh dear. *Mate.*' Enny's voice suddenly goes distant. 'Naa, naa – bok choi, I said. And get some more of them lickle spring rolls while you're up.'

'What?'

Then he's back with me. 'Sunday.'

'I'm sorry?'

'I said I'll get someone over Sunday. Can't say when, like. Between six and six.'

'But it's Wednesday night! You *said* you do twenty-four hours.'

There's another burst of laughter, this time with other, raucous laughs in the background. I think I can make out the clinking of glasses. I hang up angrily, leaving Enny and company to chortle long and hard over the hilarious story of the muppet-who-wanted-something-doing.

I wonder what the next step is. Maybe I should call my father. Perhaps Vinny or Akko could tell me how to pick a lock. I hear Ann's heels on the bathroom lino above my head. Sitting down on the sofa, I move her black duffle coat onto the arm. A tuft of bright synthetic blue sticks out from the pocket. I pull at it, and instead of it coming away as I'd expected, the tuft turns out to be attached to a plastic troll. I pull the troll out of the pocket and there's a jangling sound. A keyring emerges, attached to the troll's feet, and attached to the keyring is a set of keys. Ann's keys.

So she hasn't lost them at all. Maybe she didn't know

they were in her pocket. I lift them up and down a few times, testing their weight in my fingers. It'd be hard not to know they were in your pocket.

'Ann?' With the little blue-haired troll jangling in my hand, I mount the stairs to the landing, past the potted fern that smells of dog urine, and the forbidding sepia snapshot of some long-dead Davenport. The bathroom door is wide open – the tap dripping as it always has. A light shines from under my bedroom door. Nervously, I push the door open, the hinges creaking. 'I hope you're ashamed of yourself!'

Ann stands by the window, facing me, hands on her narrow hips. Her expression is shocked and angry. 'Sorry?' She points wordlessly to the telescope, its lens trained out of the window.

'It's Davenport's,' I explain. 'Says he's logging the heavens.'

'A likely story,' she explodes. 'You bloody degenerate! I bet you creamed yourself when they put the floodlights in.'

She moves back to the window and brushes the curtain aside. A white, magnesium glow comes from the sky outside. Still perplexed, I join her at the window. 'I've been reading about that flasher in the paper,' Ann says, in a low, fierce voice. 'Then I come up here and find *this*.'

There's a shout from the tennis court. Figures leap on the clay, almost incandescent in the harsh lights. The convent girls are practising late, as they do most nights. I sometimes wrap my old scarf around my eyes, just to keep out the glare.

'For God's sake, Ann, you seriously think I'd—'

'I wasn't wrong about you at all, was I? To imagine, I came round here thinking we could—'

'Hang on,' I say angrily, advancing on her, the keys still in my hand. 'Let's get this straight. You think I'm a degenerate because I don't mind people being gay. *And* you think I'm the flasher. *And* you think I look at the convent girls through a telescope? So I'm a sort of generalised pervert, am I? Any job considered? Where's the logic in that?'

'Sex maniacs don't have any logic.'

'*Sex maniacs*?' My voice cracks. 'At first I thought you were just a bigot. But now I know what you are. You're 100 per cent stark raving mad, aren't you? You don't need a boyfriend, you need help! Look! What are these?' I dangle the keys in her face, the troll swinging back and forth on its metal chain. 'Your bloody door keys. You hadn't lost them at all, had you? You just invented some reason to come round here. And why? What's going on in there?'

I come to a halt, breathless. I let the keys drop. We stare at each other. Perhaps I came on a little strong. Or perhaps it did some good. Ann's got a thoughtful look on her face. Maybe we're about to get to the truth.

'Let me out, please,' she says, folding her arms across her breasts, 'or I'll scream.'

The Night My Number Came Up

Wincing as he picks at the crotch of his new Burberry-pattern long johns, Davenport slams the phone down as I'm coming down the stairs. There's a sour look on his heavy face.

'Not that heavy breather again?' I ask. Since this morning, we've had a dozen calls of the nasty and silent variety – some nameless nose-breathing creature waiting until there's just the right pitch of anxiety and fear in our voices before clicking off. My persecutor has recommenced hostilities, and I have the lurking sense that showdown might not be far away.

But Davenport shakes his head as he stomps, barefooted, into the living room. 'It was Gizzler,' he mutters, glumly.

'She OK?' I ask, following his mottled back into our front room.

'Gisela can go to hell,' Davenport replies, moodily pouring himself a large glass of a concoction he calls his 'winter nip' – Cava, Wincarnis and brandy in equal doses. It's Thursday night and we've been drinking it steadily ever since we got in. He sits down in his favourite armchair, wincing. 'These buggering long johns. Evidently designed by a woman. I only got them because Gizzler said she liked them.'

The long johns in question were purchased a couple of days ago from a boutique on the Fulham Road. The word BOY is written in gold letters across the waistband, and Davenport says they're all the rage. This would appear to be true: one paper I read said that Rick Reed has been offered a million pounds to star in their poster campaign.

'Are you going to come tonight?' Davenport asks, pulling a pair of stiff socks from the radiator behind him.

'I really can't think of much worse. I spend all day surrounded by boys. Why would I want to go for a drink with the sixth form? And anyway, which sixth-formers are you talking about?'

'Oh, I don't know. That druggy one with the floppy hair, Brenard. Few others.'

'I wouldn't have thought the MacKendrick was Brenard's taste.'

'It's all been done up, Alastair. Not the MacKendrick any more. Got a sort of surgical theme. Barmaids in nurses' outfits, medicine cabinets, that sort of thing.'

'It sounds like the lowest realm of Hell.'

'Stop being such a fogy!' Davenport tuts. 'You're young. We both are. If you want to know why I'm going out with the boys tonight, *that's* why. Because we've been wasting our youth, mooning over women that don't bloody deserve us . . .' He examines his drink for a moment. 'Could do with a drop more Wincarnis in this . . . Anyway, where was I? Yes. We need to get out and live a little. Besides,' he adds, rising and treating me to a full frontal of his custard-coloured belly, 'I don't notice your little blonde besieging you with offers.'

This is true, if uncalled for, and makes me sink into a pool of self-pity for a few seconds. I've rung Mary and left her four messages, each one sounding more pitiful than the last. Just a few moments ago, I wrote a stern note on my left hand, reminding me not to ring her again.

The phone trills again, and as I rush to answer it Davenport calls after me: 'If it's Gizzler, tell her I just went out with a quartet of well-stacked teenagers.'

I don't know the origins of Davenport's most recent dispute with Gisela, I only know it's making for a mighty moody evening. As I pick the receiver from its cradle, I whisper a fervent prayer. Hail, Mary, sister of Anthony, blessed art thou amongst the lustful, and blessed shall be the fruits of thy phone-call.

'Hello?' A metallic silence greets my ears, then I discern a faint, nasal breathing in the background. 'Look, who are you?' I say, sternly. 'Stop ringing me up.' More silence, followed by a wet sound, perhaps lips forming into a sadistic smile. 'Look. I *know* who you are . . .' This is not even close to being true, although Ann Gorley is now prime suspect. I was merely hoping to freak my persecutor into saying something.

'No, you don't' – so it worked, sort of – comes a muffled voice, familiar at the same time as being hopelessly unrecognisable.

'You're being very stupid,' I say.

'*You're dead, Strange!*' shouts the voice, before its owner slams down the receiver.

Davenport – apparently recapturing his youth, but currently in the midst of donning a pair of baggy cords best suited to the gardening pages of *Country Life* – seems unconcerned when I rush back in and head straight for the booze.

Gripping the mantelpiece, my hand trembles, more from outrage than fear. The voice, I'm more or less certain, wasn't one of the boys'. But it could well have been Ann's. It now seems clear that she was at the root of all the tricks against me: the rotten salad, the dogshit, the drawing and the stolen clothes. She could have known that the telescope was in my room, set up the whole business of coming round and seeming to be friendly, just so she could have the showdown she wanted to have with Danny, accuse me of being what she wanted me to be. She's easily mad enough to be the one behind it all. What did she say? 'Why do I have to keep on picking nutters?' Because she's the real nutter.

'It'll just be boys,' Davenport opines, soothingly. 'It's always happening. Scarsdale once told me he has to disconnect the phone for the entire duration of Christmas. And they still send pizzas round.'

'But they don't send death threats,' I point out, slamming the drink to the back of my throat. This was one development I really didn't need.

'That's exactly why you should come and have a few jars with the lads. Get to know them as friends. Break down a few barriers.'

I'm just about to launch into the subject of what I'd like to break – namely, the ankles and skull of whoever's just been on the phone – with a monkey wrench, when it rings again. Davenport and I look at each other.

'Well, I can't answer it,' Davenport says, now pulling on a tweed jacket that should have been, perhaps was, buried along with whichever ancestor originally hunted foxes in it. 'It might be Gisela. And I'm making her suffer. Giving her a hard time.'

'I'm going to just ignore it,' I say, sitting down on a footstool.

We try this for a few seconds, both maintaining our teachers' well-practised, I'm-not-going-to-give-them-the-satisfaction expression, but the phone's persistence goes right up my spine to my teeth, drilling away at the tartar of my resolve. Eventually, I haul myself up and belt out into the hallway.

'Hello?' There's the tinny silence again. The God of Fury ignites a fierce, blue blowtorch at the base of my brain. 'Look, just fuck off, will you!'

'That's nice.'

'Oh God. Mary. Sorry. I thought you were someone else.' I wipe beads of condensation from my brow and lean against the wall – the only solid, dependable thing in my life, it seems.

'Evidently. So who is she?'

'It's not a she. Well, actually, it might . . .' I don't think I can face going into this right now. I take a few breaths, listening to the noises on the other end of the phone: a rushing roar, clamouring voices, a tannoy delivering gloomy news. 'Where are you?'

'Charing Cross,' she says. 'I've been on a course. Just picked up my messages. I was wondering if you still fancied that drink?'

Death threats, Davenport and the multiple ignominies of the past days suddenly withdraw, imploding to a point the size of a mosquito's egg, which I cheerfully brush aside. So she hasn't been ignoring me. She wants to go for a drink. With me, tonight. Hail Mary, Mother of Good.

'Do you want to go to the MacKendrick?'

'When you say "you", I take it you mean "I",' she responds nimbly, as if dismissing police evidence. 'As in *you'd* quite like to go to the MacKendrick.'

I bang my forehead gently against the wall before speaking again. 'Well, where would *you* like to go?' This interminable tennis match over wheres and whens is twice as bad when you're apparently dating a cross between Confucius and Perry Mason.

'Well, I don't think you'd like the Mac much now,' she says. 'I went past it the other day. And I'm already in town . . .'

'Up west . . .' I couldn't help a note of despair creeping in there.

She laughs. 'Don't be such a suburban putz. Come on.'

'A what?'

'Never mind. Just get on a bus, feller. I'll meet you in the French. You *do* know where that is, don't you?'

'Oh yes,' I lie.

With that, she's gone and Davenport is at my side, sniffing the air and looking betrayed. He hands me a full glass of winter nip. 'Down this in one if I were you,' he observes, bitterly. 'Condemned man and all that.'

'. . . Measles maybe, that time, or mumps. But Dad was standing there with this red medicine in a bottle. And Anthony was sitting up in his bed – he was maybe five or six. And I remember him saying – you know that little cross professor voice he does . . .'

I nod at Mary as the waiter takes our plates away. We're in an Italian place off Old Compton Street, pitching our voices above the roars of the strolling crowds outside and Frank Sinatra inside. She's dressed oddly, oddly for her, in a grey suit that's only ten years out of date and a white blouse. Her face fresh, there are just those two high spots of colour on her cheekbones. Together, we look almost like everyone else, but that's not what bothers me.

' "You might have poisoned me," he said. And we were all laughing. But Dad was trying to be serious, so he sat on the edge of the bed and showed him the bottle. And he said, "Look, you know, it says, one teaspoonful for little boys. And that's what I've given you." And Anthony just looked at him and said, "Your spoons might not be their spoons." '

We share a laugh at this, she leaning her head to one side and showing me a pearly set of doll's teeth. It was the perfect Anthony anecdote, mistrustful and spiky even at that age. We've spent most of the meal talking about him, in fact. His obsession, at the ages of two and three, with road accidents. His sorry catalogue of childhood ilnesses, the classic history of the average genius. The time when, in his first week at St John Lorimer's, Mr Scarsdale shouted at him for completing a spelling test in green ballpoint. And Anthony stood up and said: 'I don't appreciate you speaking to me this way.' He sat down to a chorus of catcalls and mocking arm punches, which gave way to six years of solitude and obscurity. I wish I'd known all this before, but at the same time I wish we could actually stop talking about Anthony and start talking about his sister.

'What's the matter?'

'Nothing,' I say hastily, looking her right in the eyes. 'Just I think we should stop talking about Anthony.'

She frowns. 'Well, what *do* you want to talk about?'

'People usually talk about themselves.'

'Yeah,' she observes tartly. 'That's what makes me sick about most people.'

A little sigh catches in my throat. For the bulk of this evening – ever since I arrived at the pub and there wasn't anywhere to sit down – I've been thinking that things aren't what we'd call groovy. It started badly as I waited for her out on the pavements of Dean Street and a red-headed woman obviously on a blind date came up and asked me if I was Terry. Her look of relief when I said I wasn't took me quite a few fathoms deep. Then Mary came along, small and gleaming from some recent argument with a cab driver, and I was expecting the old jinx to budge. But somehow it hasn't.

It's not a disaster, not one of those nights of limping starts and conversational dead zones, but nor has it turned out like I imagined. Perhaps I did far too much imagining. One of the things I imagined, reasonably enough, was that I'd get some clue from her as to whether I was wasting my time. That seems to be how it is – men make moves and women make hints that the moves are or aren't going to be welcome. But Mary seems to prefer her own game, a game largely based on watching the balls I knock over the net and sending them straight back, plus a dangerous spin.

'OK,' she says, tapping a tiny front tooth with a red fingernail. 'Ask me a question, then.'

'All right. Who was that bloke in the coffee-shop with you?'

She barely blinks. 'An asshole. A semi-asshole, anyway. Well, no. Someone who can sometimes be an asshole, just like anyone else. Just like you.'

'So was he your boyfriend?'

'Yes,' she says, carefully. But before my spirits can sink right through the floor and entomb themselves in the soft mud of centuries, she adds, 'He was.'

'*Was?*'

'Was.'

This has a swift warming effect, like the first drink of the night. 'Good.'

'Why good?' she asks, playfully.

I decide to start playing back. 'I don't know. Because girls like you usually are going out with assholes.'

She raises her chin, as if levelling some pretty howitzer in my general direction. 'What do you mean, "girls like me"? You hardly know me. Maybe I'm an asshole too.'

'Possibly.'

'No, believe me, Alastair. I am. Card-carrying.'

This makes me laugh and she joins in and the waiter comes up and pours the last of the wine into our glasses.

'What about you, Alastair? Are you seeing anyone?'

'Nope.'

'Why not?'

'Fuck off.'

'I just don't understand it, Alastair. Single and yet so charming.'

'Extraordinarily good-looking too.'

'Except you've got no ass.'

This seems a little uncalled for. 'What do you mean "no ass". I mean, arse?'

She giggles, biting the top of her hand again, a gesture she performs so often there are small teeth-marks around the knuckle of her index finger. 'Your back just kind of tapers into the top of your legs. And then there's just this pouch in your trousers where your ass is supposed to be.'

'No, there isn't.' I'm beginning to get a little miffed.

'There is! I don't mind, Alastair. It's very sweet.'

That word. Fine when you're into true relationship territory, but a gruesome signpost on the first night. Sweet equals pet hamster, little brother, best friend's dotty old dad. Sweet equals all the things she's probably not and never going to sleep with. Sweet induces a sour earwax taste in the mouths of lusting men.

'It's even more sweet of you to get in a sulk about it.'

'I'm not sulking.'

'You are.'

Something in me snaps and I slam the glass down on the table, making her jump. 'Is this the only game you can do?'

Her eyes narrow. 'What do you mean, "game"?'

'This – this – stupid wind-up thing? Is it the only way you can have a conversation with someone? By having an argument?'

She blinks at me, a hurt, surprised, almost damp expression in her eyes. One which then turns frost-hard as her jaw shoots forward. 'Why shouldn't I?' she asks, in a quiet, indignant voice. 'You'd rather we just sat here and talked bullshit, would you? I agree with you all night just so you'll take me home? *Forget* it!'

'Maybe we *should* just forget it,' I say hotly, pushing the coffee cup away from me. There follows a rather serious pause in which Mary does cross things with her hair and the couple at the next table – he bald, married, forties, and she none of these things – stare at me. I try to catch the waiter's eye so I can get the bill, but he's the only one not remotely interested in us.

'What's so great about agreeing?' she blurts out suddenly. 'You know who you remind me of? My mother.'

The tocsin sounds again. I've never been compared to anyone's mother before. And when you hear it from someone you've been planning to get naked with, it must be the final death knell. But hearing it almost relaxes me. It's the peace that descends upon a man who knows he's blown it, who can now stop trying at last.

'I'm like your mother, am I?'

'She's such a *girl*. You know? Never says what she thinks. She just works out what the loudest man in the room's saying and says it right back. It's pathetic. I'm sure as shit not going to be like her.'

'You're close, then?'

Mary ignores this. 'We used to have these big screaming rows. *You're going out dressed like that? You think you're going to get a boyfriend dressed like that?* I'll tell you something . . .'

I sit back in my metal chair, letting her go on. It seems preferable to shouting.

'There was one time . . . This was, like, the worst thing she ever said . . . I was sixteen . . .' She contemplates eating a fragment of stale bread-stick and then thinks better of it. 'And this horrible guy from my class kept calling round. Looked like Kissinger with a pony-tail. And she encouraged him. So one time, I just sent him away at the door. And she came out with tea-things and she went ballistic. She said, "Who do you think's going to come calling for you, sweetheart? Sal Mineo?"'

'Who's he?'

She looks at me, eyes widening in frank horror. 'You don't *know* who Sal Mineo is?'

I can't help laughing. Because this could be one of the most ill-fated dates since Henry VIII was introduced to Ann Boleyn. But I don't mind. I'd never have noticed Mary if she wasn't the way she is tonight. Exactly the person I need to be with, tonight and in theory beyond. Spiky, argumentative, thoroughly unsuitable. She's got me hooked.

My Learned Friend

'I just don't *understand*, Alastair, how any supposedly intelligent adult can be so goddam complacent! There are people still dying for the right to vote!'

'Where? Where exactly are all these people dying for the right to vote?' She says nothing, lets me go on, smiling a suspiciously pretty smile. 'It sounds to me, you know, like that thing people say when you mention some actor who hasn't been on the telly for about ten years. People always say, "Oh, he's doing a lot of theatre."'

'Your point being?'

'Well, do they *know* that? Have they actually seen him doing, I don't know, *Noises Off* at the Lyric or is it just a way of coping with the fact that he's probably propping up some bar in Muswell Hill and not actually doing much of anything?'

'You're fucking impossible, aren't you? And don't be rude about out-of-work actors. My mother's one, remember?'

We're standing at the arse-end of a long line of people in Beak Street and still, after twenty minutes, on the subject of politics – one we started long before the bill was paid. I have managed to reduce Mary to a state of quivering indignation, her eyes shining with outrage and her nose aglow with converted zeal. She looks good that way.

'I just don't see how voting makes a difference,' I toss this casually in, just to keep her ticking over. 'How can any individual make a difference?'

'Gnn-gnnggaah!!'

We are trying to gain admittance to a club called Attitude. Outside the restaurant, Mary and I took a brief interlude from our wrangling to discuss the issue of having a drink elsewhere. And while rummaging in my pockets for some change to give to a man playing 'Hava Nagila' on the steel drums, I'd found a crumpled club flyer.

'So what about Anthony?' Mary demands, poking me in the chest as the queue inches forward and a pair of large, pig-tailed women in gymslips and wicker stetsons try to push their way in.

'What about him?'

'If you're so convinced no one can make a difference, why did you bother trying to help him?'

She's got me stumped here, so I can either admit it or think of something facetious in response. She doesn't give me a chance, but steams in, prodding me in the ribs.

'See? This is what you do. You try and make out everything's just a game. But you looked out for Anthony. You made a difference to someone, didn't you?'

'Yeah, well. I'm one of the good guys.'

'No, you're *not*. There aren't any. But you're real. All this is real . . .' she insists, waving an arm around her and in the process knocking into a shifty little crew of Hilfiger-clad bother-merchants. 'Sorry . . . *Dickhead*.' She looks back at me. 'I mean . . . it's not Cowboys and Indians, feller.'

'What?'

'I think . . . yeah, I think I only know one truly good guy in the whole world.'

'Who?'

'Anthony. He never lies. Never hurts anyone – not on purpose anyway. And look at him. He's my brother. I love him. But he's not exactly normal, is he? *You* are. *I* am . . . Oh fuck. What's the use?'

'I don't know. I don't get you.'

Mary gives up on whatever knotty point of philosophy she's trying to convey, half because she isn't getting anywhere and half because the people in front of us are admitted as one vast block, and we're approached by a white-haired girl in a bomber jacket, a pilot's headset around her ears. Her face manages to convey equal quantities of fury and indifference.

'Yeah?'

Rather stunned by this post-modern approach to the greeting, I say, 'Two for the club, please.' The girl, who also has a number of drill bits in her face, and presumably on purpose, gives a joyless laugh and points to a sign on the wall. It says NO OFFICE ATTIRE. She then flicks a cold glance at Mary.

I recognise her now. She's one of that cohort of gum-chewing lady-Gauleiters, who always migrate to jobs that involve saying No to a lot of people, and usually lurking sensibly behind booths of bullet-proof glass. You will find these humanity-hating creatures as doctor's receptionists, secretaries, ticket clerks – and, of course, you'll find them outside night clubs. But you won't usually find me there.

'Can you get out of the way?' Ms Attitude says, adding 'Please' by way of an additional insult, and pronouncing it like one too.

'Let's just find somewhere else,' Mary says, pulling gently at my sleeve.

'Best listen to the lady,' Ms Attitude quips, nodding and waving through a pair of boys in shimmering catsuits. 'Or do you want me to call Security?'

'So you're not Security, then?' I remark, as a wand-like girl dressed as an Israeli paratrooper is also admitted in front of us. I've decided to have an argument now, even if I'd sooner slit my throat than give the Attitude Club so much as a Manx shilling.

'I'm the style consultant,' replies Ms Attitude, cocking her head upwards, as if inviting me to land a punch on her jaw, which would be nice, I think, but inadvisable. 'I decide who's right for the atmosphere of the club, and I'm not having any suits. Awright, Kai?' she adds, exchanging a high-five with a fat man who has, on appearance at least, just knocked off from the Apollo Mars mission.

'Why not?' I ask, pointing at Mary in her grey suit. 'What's wrong with people in suits, for crying out loud?' I glance down at Mary, who has fallen quiet, her neat little mouth set into some forbidding expression. I should probably cut my losses.

'Cos they start hassle. Pissed-up City boys with fat wallets. Groping girls and that . . .'

'Does she *look* like she's going to be groping any girls?' The spirit of Anthony is upon me. I am the Meister Quibbler, devoted to my art.

Ms Attitude treats me to a shrivelling appraisal. 'Are you gonna get out of the doorway?'

'So you mean to say,' I declare, warming to my theme, and encouraged by the interested patch of spandex-clad onlookers now nodding our way, 'that in our supposed Western democracy the decision as to who can and who can't come into a public place of entertainment rests with you?'

'Just fuck off, mate,' she says, as a crackling burst issues from her headset.

'So if we came back in thousand-quid trainers and . . . I don't know, dressed as a pair of thirteenth-century Persian rabbis, we'd be all right, would we? You'd let us in?'

This gets a laugh from the crowd, two of whom are uniformed policemen, or perhaps just masquerading as such.

Ms Attitude flicks the metal spike in her lip. 'Not now, I wouldn't, no. I know your face, mate.'

'But you would have. And why – because people dressed like you are bound to be all right? And people in suits are not?'

''Ere, Sanjay,' says an approving voice from the crowd. 'Come an' check dis. This guy's *classic*.'

'So what about all the people who might wear trainers and snowboarding trousers to work and then go home and drown kittens?'

'Which people go home and drown kittens?'

'Well, I don't know. People. And all the people who have to wear suits to work who might be all right inside, in spite of their suits?'

'Lettim in,' declare a couple of foxy Asian boys, dressed in Bakofoil and cycling shorts.

'Go on. Let him in.'

'Yeah. Stop being such a bitch.'

Ms Attitude ignores me and the crowd, leaning her head back into the booming interior of the club and shouting, '*Troy!*'

'You know what you are?' I say, calmly, stepping back and smiling. 'You're the worst kind of Fascist.'

This seems to rile her. She steps down from the porch and pokes me in the stomach. 'Don't you call me a Fascist. My boyfriend comes from Cuba.'

'Yeah, exactly. So you've got your Cuban boyfriend and your metal face-spikes and your dolphin-friendly, save-the-rainforests shower gel, and you think that makes you all right. And inside you're just another . . . another bloody Ann Gorley!'

'A what?'

'I mean you hate *life*. You make up all these rules about who's good and who's bad because that's easier for you.'

'Troy,' she shouts into her microphone. 'We've got a Code Red out here. Kicking off bad-style.'

Mary, whose presence I seem regrettably to have forgotten, tugs hard at my arm and drags me out of the queue. 'I think we'd better get you home,' she says.

Just then, a man appears in the doorway. Slim and wavy-haired, Tyrone Power in cream jodhpurs and a shirt like a circuit diagram. 'Hello, sir.'

'Posey?'

Posey Miller makes a faintly wounded face. '*Troy*, please. What are you doing here?'

Moments later, Mary and I are inside the mad crush of the club, Posey Miller forging a path through the sweating space aliens and the transvestites. 'Sorry about that,' I shout in Mary's ear, as the music pounds like fists into my stomach. She says something in reply, without smiling, and I get the strong impression I've blown it.

Miller makes a slick motion to one of the girls behind the bar. A bottle of Krug is passed back to us in an ice-bucket. 'Thanks,' I shout. Riotous mambo music has just replaced the banging techno, and the dance floor to the left of us starts to pullulate with hot bodies.

'Caught you a scout with Gable!' Miller bellows back. 'What?'

He leads us away from the bar and through an archway, to a barely lit area with low marble tables and leather sofas. 'I'll sort you out with a table.'

After another wordless motion to one of his staff — a ladyboy dressed as some Tudor mugger — Miller has us seated. He fusses over Mary, lighting her cigarette and all the while making pointed, congratulatory eye-contact with me.

The Attitude Club seems to be an odd mixture of Cuba and ancient Rome — stone pillars and fading Communist posters among statues of various gods. All around us, terrifyingly fashionable people are looking like they're enjoying themselves.

'You seem to be doing very well for yourself,' I say to Miller.

'So do you, sir,' he returns, with an easy smile. 'Did you enjoy Prizegiving?'

Looking at Miller's enigmatic grin in the flashing club lights, I have a memory of the last time I saw it: in the photocopier room, hovering over a stack of lurid porn. He'd been trying, quite clearly, to get me out of the way so he could enact a sweet revenge on Mr Scarsdale. A warm smile takes possession of my face. They shouldn't have expelled Miller. They should have given him the Founder's Cup for Integrity.

Miller's mobile phone trills at this point and he bows away with excuses. A member of the *Miss Saigon* cast has just insulted Bruce Grobbelaar in the cloakrooms.

Once Miller has departed, I suddenly find myself embarrassed by the champagne and the VIP treatment, lacking anything to say. And Mary, folded neatly away on a very distant corner of the sofa, seems on the verge of a lip-chewing exit from all future forms of fun. Inexpertly, I pour some of the drink into our glasses. It fizzes over and down my sleeve. This, at least, seems to amuse her.

'All right there?' I ask, handing her a glass.

'Good work out there,' she says, taking a sip and looking at me over the glass rim. 'I really hate those fashion-fucks. You really stuck it to her.'

'I thought you were pissed off.'

'Oh no,' she says, crossing her legs and leaning back in her seat. 'I was just wondering why you said you didn't understand me when you obviously knew what I meant all along.'

But I'm still not sure I do. I shift a little closer to her, about to speak, when she suddenly frowns, gazing intently into the heaving crowd ahead of us. 'What's up?'

She nods over towards the archway. 'Isn't that your friend?'

I glance across. In the epileptic rainbow lights of the dance floor, a stocky, shirtless man is being levered away between bull-necked bouncers. I rub my eyes and look more closely. The man is dripping with sweat and has a dark woolly hat rammed over his ears. Around his neck hangs a whistle on a string. He moves out of vision, and I shake my head.

'Couldn't be,' I say, glugging back some more of the alcoholic sea-water. 'Not Davenport. You'd never get him in a place like this.'

She nudges my knee with hers. 'I wouldn't have thought I'd get you in a place like this either.'

It must be one or two in the morning now and we're lying together, hot and exhausted, in the darkness of my room.

For a small person, Mary gives off an astonishing amount of warmth. Every point at which our bodies are touching, and that's most of them, is the temperature of newly served soup. The only cool things are the silky sheet of her blonde hair, draped across my damp chest, and for some reason, doubtless related to an unhealthy lifestyle and incipient deep-vein thrombosis, the tips of my toes. Seeking to warm these, I shove my left foot under her smooth calf.

Mary gives an electric jolt, her neat limbs disturbed by the sudden cold. 'You freak!'

'What a romantic thing to say.'

She sits up now, flushed skin almost phosphorescent in the darkness, adjusting her hair, whose flaxen tips brush the top of her breasts. She makes a face at me, a slack-jawed, goggle-eyed stare.

'What's that supposed to be?' I ask.

'You.'

'Nothing like me.'

'Yes, it is. You were doing it all night.'

'Well, only at you.'

She ignores this and reaches down for her bra.

'Going somewhere?'

'I've got to get back,' she says, hands fastening behind her back, her small chin on her breastbone.

'What? Why?' I ask, in confusion, wondering why a couple of cold toes under the calf should suddenly spell the end of a glorious night. 'Can I see you tomorrow?'

She sighs, makes a serious face, seems on the brink of saying something, when, from downstairs, there is an almighty crash.

'What the—' She jumps up, eyes wide with fright, grabbing clothes from the tangle on the floor.

'It's OK,' I say, reaching out to her. I'm well used to loud crashes in the night. They usually signify Davenport's uneasy transit from sofa to fridge or out to our neighbour's rhubarb patch, where Davenport often urinates, to the great welfare of the rhubarb, which has won prizes locally. 'It'll just be my flatmate. Come back to bed for a bit.'

'Look—' she says, stepping into her skirt, but she is interrupted by the sounds of Davenport's sepulchral bass, singing as he thunders up the stairs.

'*Vestigis minimis*,' he sings. Then there is a loud sickening thud, followed by a bout of what could be whimpering, before the song and the laboured footsteps recommence. '*Vincimus orbem. Servos opiumque apportantes . . .*'

'What the hell is he doing?' Mary whispers, pausing in mid-dress. We wait, listening to the silence. She's just bending down carefully for one of her shoes, when my door crashes open, a shaft of light splintering the darkness.

'*Ad te scola amabilis!*' Davenport bellows, as he staggers into my room and collapses on the vacant portion of the bed. He's half-naked, a whistle tangled in the thick wiry undergrowth of his chest. His face and arms are smeared with mud and blood and other nameless matter. He looks like he's tunnelled his way home, through sewage and concrete.

Later, after we've switched the lights on and arranged the gibbering Davenport in a vaguely upright position with pillows behind his torn and bleeding back, Mary says we should call an ambulance. I disagree. 'He's just had too many, that's all. He'll be all right.'

'All right?' she spits. 'Look at him, Alastair. Look at his goddam eyes. He looks like he's been drinking neat lysergic acid all night.'

I gaze into Davenport's eyes, bulging and haunted, as one who's apprehended the true purpose of existence and discovered it to be pretty disagreeable.

'Davenport,' I say, slowly and carefully, remembering now where Davenport said he was going, who he was going there with, 'have you taken anything?'

Davenport responds with a sweet smile. He puts a beefy arm round my neck and attempts to kiss the side of my head. 'I have metamorphosed,' he pronounces happily, as I extricate myself from his sweaty grasp, 'into a being of pure light. By dawn, I shall no longer be visible to the naked eye.'

I glance at Mary in panic. To my dismay, I see she's got her jacket on. I stand up and go over to her. Meanwhile, Davenport starts scrabbling round underneath the sheets. 'You can't go now,' I say, taking hold of her arms. 'I'm sorry about what's happened, but—'

'No, I'm sorry,' she says, sadly, giving my hands a quick hot squeeze.

I'm starting to feel rather puzzled. 'What do you mean?'

She bites her lip. 'There's no easy way of saying this, Alastair. I shouldn't have come. It wasn't fair on you.'

'Not fair?'

'That guy in the FullaBeenz?' she asks. 'He's not my boyfriend. Not any more. He's my fiancé. We just got engaged.'

'But—'

'I told you I was a card-carrying asshole.'

She bites her lip, pulls away from me and hurries out of the door, out of my reach. I am left, staring distractedly at Davenport, his cheeks now wet with tears.

'*I* think I'd make an awfully good father,' he sobs. 'Don't you?'

★

'So what does bugger-lugs get up to in here, then? No, don't tell me. Sod all.'

'It's his study, actually.'

'His *study*? The only thing that bugger's ever studied is his bloody navel.'

It's around dawn and the Earl of Chertsey and I are in Davenport's study. Birds are just beginning to sing outside, the darkness giving way to a grey, shabby light – one which aptly matches my mood.

After Davenport wound the bed sheet, toga-style, round his stately form and headed out into the road – purportedly with the intention of visiting his ex-beloved – I decided it was time for some action. Ambulances seemed out of the question, as he was (a) the son of a nobleman, (b) a respected teacher and (c) tripping, in common parlance, his very nuts off. So I called his parents, who groggily told me to get him indoors and await their arrival.

Now, Davenport is in bed upstairs, sleeping fitfully, his brow tended by an ashen-faced Corky. And I've been making tea with the Earl of Chertsey. There couldn't be a man less like his son; he's a neat, sinewy creation standing no more than five feet tall, his dark hair slicked back behind a Fifties quiff. He looks like someone bred to work down coal-mines, rather than to own them.

'And what's all this meant to be?' the earl asks, roughly picking up a pile of printed papers from the desk.

'It's his Ph.D.' I reach forward and put the papers back in order.

The earl sits down in the chair and grunts with obvious surprise. 'Never thought he'd get round to starting it,' he observes gruffly.

'He's finished it.'

The earl pauses in mid-yawn and fixes his bloodshot

eyes on the Ph.D. It seems for a moment that something big might be dawning on him. Then both eyes receive a vigorous rubbing before their owner looks blearily at me.

'He'll never send it off, you know. Never make owt of himself. He's always been t'same. No staying power. Ah remember when he were a little lad. He'd not just started Cub Scouts three weeks and he's on about leaving. Ah remember saying to him, ah said, "Listen to me. You're a Davenport. And Davenports don't give up . . ."'

'Well, he didn't give up, did he?' I say sharply. 'He finished that bloody thing at least. And it took him years.' I falter, catching from the earl the sort of look that his ancestors must have used to prevent peasants from revolting. I dimly wonder if you can be flung in the Tower for swearing at the minor aristocracy. 'I just don't think you're being entirely fair, Your Honour.'

The earl extracts a white glistening object from his bottom teeth and examines it. 'Why'd you call me that?' he asks. 'I'm not a judge, ye know.'

'Sorry. I don't know what you're supposed to call earls.'

He blinks at me in bafflement. 'I'm not an earl. Where did you get that from?' He jabs a thumb up at the ceiling, in the direction of his psychotic son. 'Bugger-lugs been giving you more of his bloody fairy-tales, has he?'

I shake my head numbly, remembering. Davenport has never actually once said his father was the Earl of Chertsey. It all came from Tara. In fact, perhaps it didn't. I can no longer remember anything clearly.

'Somebody said—'

'I'm *Lord* Chertsey,' he grunts.

'Oh, I see,' I say, trying to sound like I understand the difference, which is apparently enormous.

'I'm a Labour peer. Ah just picked Chertsey cos that's

where we live. Should be Huddersfield by rights, but the missus took against that . . .' He trails off into a moody silence, reflecting upon some distant, or possibly constant, dispute with his wife.

The stillness is broken by a hoarse cry from the upper reaches of the house. '*Terribilis. Terribilis est locus iste!*'

Davenport's father swears under his breath, rising awkwardly from the chair. 'One thing after a-bloody-nother with that lad,' he mutters. 'You know what he needs? A girlfriend. Not that he's got a bastard's shite's chance of getting one. What's the point of leaving home if you need your bloody mam to come round every five minutes?'

'But she never comes round here.'

'She pops over every bloody night.'

'No, she doesn't. She's never been round in the whole time I've been here.'

Lord Chertsey's face assumes the startled look of an ancient fertility mask. 'Well, I'll be . . .'

I head swiftly for the door. 'I'll go and see if they want more tea.'

Davenport's father accepts this, drifting into the front room, patting his quiff and making various disgusted sounds about the furnishings. I run upstairs and, opening the door to Davenport's fever-pit, find him in bed with his mother.

He's sweating profusely. Curls are plastered like sea-weed to the side of his head and ginger hairs are clustered in damp whorls across his pectorals. I realise here that Corky, whose arm is around her son, is fully dressed in a powder-blue twin-set, but that does little to diminish the grotesqueness of the sight.

'It's him,' Davenport croaks, pointing a finger at me in the doorway. '*He* did it.'

I try giving Davenport a weak smile. This is a smile that sometimes causes toddlers to burst into tears, and its effect on Davenport is similar. He groans and buries his head in his mother's cardigan.

'Were you with him last night?' Corky asks me, in a voice redolent of chilly marble cathedrals. 'What happened?'

'I don't know. I think his drink might have been spiked with something. Drugs, you know.'

Corky shoots me the sort of glare you could expect if you laughed during a memorial service held in one of these aforementioned barely heated cathedrals. 'Which drugs?'

'I don't know,' I answer, pitifully. 'I don't know much about drugs.'

'No, of course not,' she replies, nastily. 'Not a boy from Merseyside.'

'What the hell's that supposed to mean?' I exclaim, indignantly. '*I* didn't give him anything.'

'No, you'd be too clever for that,' Corky replies, arranging the duvet around her son's chest. 'But you're a bad influence. The very worst kind,' she adds, now piously fingering a crucifix around her neck. 'You're a fellow traveller, Alastair, an egger-on. I've seen the way you two boys drink.'

'And how would that be?' I ask, harshly. 'Other than from a glass?'

'Lawrence drinks in a way that's not happy,' she answers, cryptically. 'I've seen it in other men, too. But not you.'

Before we can delve into the unhappy fashion in which

Davenport and other men drink, while others do not, and both groups have had the misfortune to be seen doing this by Corky, Davenport stirs from his latest acid-rictus and fitfully murmurs something about staples.

'What's he saying?'

We both listen. 'I think he's saying Étaples,' I say, at length. Then, with appropriate doses of dawning dread and regret, I realise why. 'Oh Christ. He's supposed to be taking the school trip. Well, I mean, I was doing it, but he . . . he agreed to go instead.'

'That's what he's like,' Corky replies sonorously, leaning her head against his. 'Trusting. Too easily led.' Then she glances up at me, twenty centuries of fiefdom and unquestioned authority. I am a serf, on the brink of being banished for a year and a day. 'Well, you know what you have to do, Alastair.'

I've got my passport. A few notes in my pocket. And I have a plan. To get on the school coach and then, once safely in foreign territory, to abscond. Hitch a ride to the sunshine and stay there until everyone's forgotten me. There's no other option.

I pick my way down the front path, narrowly avoiding a few of Cinna's dark brown legacies and feeling a little better as the cold morning air knocks some calm and reason into me. I check my watch. It's 7.20 – plenty of time to catch the coach.

As I turn right, I'm aware of footsteps behind me. I continue on, past the entrance to the tennis courts, aware that I'll never see them again, never twist my ankle in the little pothole by the gate-post. The footsteps grow heavier, quickening in pace as I approach the bus stop. This reminds me briefly of Mary, all the mornings I stood here, all toothpaste breath and damp hair, eager for a glimpse of my mysterious solicitor.

Maybe I was just a necessary experiment, as she sensed her freedom fading. Maybe she was testing to see whether she could actually find someone else, and then, reassured that the goods on offer were pretty shop-soiled, taking that confetti-strewn plunge into the matrimonial rock-pool. I can't brood on that now, I think, as I hear heavy, wheezing breaths at my shoulder. I'll worry about it when I'm stuck in Thonon-les-Bains or Pissy-Peauville, poached in rotgut vino. But what a cow, all the same.

'*You filthy bastard!*'

This hoarse cry shatters the morning air as a pair of slim hands grab me from behind and spin me round. Grey-faced and unshaven, the headmaster punches me in the mouth. I stagger backwards from the lip-stinging blow, banging into a lamp-post. The headmaster then charges at me like a cuckolded billy-goat, buffeting into my stomach with his coiffed head.

'I said I'd kill you, Strange. And, by God, I will. Even if I have to do penal servitude for it.'

'Wh-why?' I bleat, feebly, as the headmaster puts soft, trembling hands round my neck.

'Oh yes, it had us all taken in, that innocent look,' he spits, his deep-set eyes burning with a gas-blue flame. 'When all the while you were . . . having it . . . engaging in intercourse with my wife.'

'But I wasn't,' I protest, trying to pull his hands from my throat.

'Don't try it,' he grates. 'I browsed the Received Calls database on her Ericsson. And the Numbers Dialled menu. Hundreds and hundreds of times, your number.'

He starts to squeeze more heavily and I can see little flashes of starlight at the corner of my vision.

'It was Lawrence!' I sorry, as the light dims.

'Try again! No Lorry's man would behave like that!'

'So you see, I wasn't exactly *flashing* at anyone. It's all circumstantial. That's the word, isn't it?' The detectives don't answer me, or give any sign of encouragment, but let me continue. 'Ann Gorley's just cooked the whole thing up. Don't ask me why.'

'We're not asking,' Philip says, a little irritably. He taps the folder in front of us again. 'I couldn't honestly care less about cartoons and dogshit in your locker.'

'Briefcase,' Gerald interrupts. 'The dogshit was in his briefcase.'

Philip ignores him. 'We want to know about your association with this woman. The girl in these photographs.' He flips the folder open.

One of the black-and-white photographs was taken in the FullaBeenz coffee-shop. Another was taken in my driveway. All of them feature me and the sort of girl you wouldn't expect to see me featured with, unless I'd known her a long time. And I'm now getting the strong sense I barely knew her at all.

'Why are you interested in Tara?'

The two detectives glance at each other. Philip folds his hands. 'We were contacted by a Mr Amjit Sammaddi in January of last year,' he says, 'concerning some serious discrepancies in his accounts. Money not where it ought to be, that sort of thing. Money completely absent, in fact. Our investigations led us to this young lady. His wife.'

'Pretty girl,' Gerald observes, removing his glasses and wiping them on his tie.

'It seems Tara's been siphoning off a nice little retirement fund for herself. And she was last seen at Heathrow, purchasing a one-way ticket to Costa Rica. You maintain that you know nothing about that?'

'But she said –' my voice assumes a hollow quality, as if played back to me on an answerphone message while even drunker than I was when I recorded it – 'she said she loved him. That's all I can tell you. Every conversation I had with her, she'd say it again and again. How much she loved him.'

'Sometimes the dog barking the loudest is really a cat,' Philip says, mysteriously. He looks at Gerald. 'No, you don't have to write that down.'

'I wouldn't know,' I say, miserably tired and confused. 'She just said he had his heart set on buying the school and she wanted to do anything she could to make it happen. You know all that. And I didn't do anything to help her. Not really, anyway.'

'But you seriously believe she had his best interests at heart?' Philip asks, sceptically. 'She had you hooked good and proper, didn't she? You must be one of the most trusting souls I've seen in a long time.'

'If someone tells you something, you believe it.'

'Do you?' Philip gives a biscuity chuckle. 'Sorry. It's just that we tend not to, in our line of work.'

'Well, I do. And what was Tara doing wrong? I don't understand.'

They say nothing. But Philip shifts a little in his seat and I can see his watch. I realise I've been here a long time now and I still only know their first names. There's a tape machine to the left of me, but they haven't switched it on. Did they tell me who they were? 'Who *are* you anyway?'

One or other of the detectives gives a discreet cough. I

look at them both — at their bland, instantly forgettable faces, their dowdy clothes. And a scary thought occurs: a man like Sammaddi — a billionaire Indian politician, a businessman with interests everywhere — might have some big people interested in his movements. Powerful people who can photograph you anywhere, snatch you off the street and lock you away for a long time.

'You're not . . . you wouldn't be MI5 or something like that?'

'*I wish*,' Gerald interjects, with feeling. 'They turned me down. I reckon it's just because I stood for the Greens when I was at Warwick.'

'Thank you, Gerald. No, Mr Strange, we are not MI5. We are the Fraud Squad.'

'Oh.' I can't help sounding a little deflated, because it doesn't have quite the same cachet to it. You can't, after all, imagine a team of armed men kicking a door down and shouting, 'Freeze! Fraud Squad!'

'Perhaps a little less glamorous, but nevertheless a vital component of the modern police service,' Philip says testily. 'And I believe you asked us a question. So if you'd let us answer it, that'd be appreciated.'

'All right,' I say, sheepishly. 'Sorry.'

'In layman's terms, Alastair, Tara nicks money. But she's got a clever way of covering her tracks.'

'Well, you'd expect that, wouldn't you, girl like her?' Gerald interrupts. 'First Class Honours in Maths, you know. From Durham. Good university, that. It was my first choice, only I couldn't get a B in Statistics.'

Philip winces slightly, but continues. 'She acts as hubby's business adviser. Hubby likes that. Hubby thinks, "Pretty girl, cut-glass accent, perfect ambassador", see? And Tara likes that too. Tara gets hubby to invest his money all over the place. She'll do half a dozen legitimate investments and then, little treat for herself, she'll get him to sink his cash into a few things that are on their last legs. Millennium Dome. Ailing newspapers. See the similarities? When something's going down, you've got money all over the place – hard to watch until the vultures fly in. Perfect way to cover her tracks, you see. She can say to hubby, "Bad luck, old sport, some you win . . ." eh? Meanwhile she's filching all the choice scraps for herself. Cleaning up nicely. Hence Costa Rica.'

So that's what Tara meant when she said she was in trouble; why she told me her husband wasn't as rich as people thought: the one peppercorn of truth in a night of lies. No wonder she had to get so drunk. And no wonder her last words were 'Poor Alastair': in the midnight of wickedness, a lone lighter-flame of conscience. She was lying to me, but somewhere, buried deeper than all the money she'd squirrelled away for herself, there was a tiny stab of guilt.

'You'd think a man like Sammaddi would have more sense,' Gerald observes.

'Well, that's where you'd be wrong, Gerald,' Philip says, happily, pointing the stem of his pipe at him. 'You'll see this time and time again in the job. This Sammaddi guy's straight as a rail. Opens hospitals for little orphans in Rajasthan. Never put a foot wrong. But he trusts her.' Philip looks back at me. 'Loves her, you see. You probably loved her a little bit too – otherwise you'd have asked yourself a few more questions. Asked her a few, as well.'

I can't think of a suitable reply, possibly because Philip's right. But Gerald chimes in with a helpful observation. 'It's a bit like what happened to Macbeth,' he says.

'Gerald is one of our graduate fast-trackers,' Philip adds, witheringly.

'But what about me?' I yammer, some instinct for self-preservation at last taking charge. 'I mean, I didn't exactly do anything wrong, did I? I just got him an invite to the Prizegiving. You can't arrest someone for that.'

'No,' Philip admits, forlornly. 'But I'm sure we could get you for something. What was all that about flashing in the swimming pool?'

'If you'd care to sign here, sir,' says the old, pigeon-chested desk sergeant, passing me an envelope. He empties it onto the desk, showing forested forearms and smudgy tattoos. 'One wallet, contents twenty-nine pounds and twelve pence. One handkerchief – soiled.'

'What's happening?' I wonder why these are being handed to me, if this is a prelude to being clapped in irons and shipped to Wormwood Scrubs.

'We're checking you out, sir,' says Gerald. 'No charges.'

'Hang on . . .' The sergeant sifts through a pile of papers. 'Young lady came for you but she couldn't wait. Said to give you this.'

Standing in the air-conditioned warmth of the station lobby, I read the note – nutty ink scrawls on the back of an arrest sheet.

Dear Alastair,
 Anthony saw them taking you off and he rang me. I said I'd act for you – whatever it is you've done now – but they said they were letting you go. Mazel tov. Sorry I had to split.

'A cracker, she was,' says the sergeant reflectively. 'Made me wish I was your age again.'

I sit down on an orange plastic chair, beneath a poster that says 'Pallet Theft – Together We Can Crack It'. I rub my eyes and start again.

I'm going to stay with a friend in York. The train's at half eleven and I've got to call into the office first. I really didn't mean to hurt you last night. It's just there's a lot going on right now. If it makes you feel any happier, I think what happened made me realise I'm doing the wrong thing. Maybe. That's what I've got to work out. I'll call you when this has all blown over and maybe we can finish all those arguments!

I fold Mary's letter in half and put it in my trouser pocket, staring at the digital clock on the wall. It's just after nine. Assembly should be in full flow by now, the whole school packed, red-eyed and resentful, into the Auditorium. Except there's no headmaster today, no Davenport, no Scarsdale. No Posey and Booth. Somebody else won't be there, too. It's Friday, the day of Anthony's exam. He'll be starting it right now. Or, more probably, finishing it. Handing it in, beaming that donnish grin of his.

'Sorry, sir. We do try to keep the reception area clear for safety reasons . . .'

I look up. The old desk sergeant is bent over me, his purple-veined face wrinkled in polite concern.

'If you wouldn't mind just moving on now, sir. One of our forecourt staff will be pleased to find you a cab . . .'

There Ain't No Justice

'"Just a little bit of jotter paper, it is. Stick it under your tongue." So I did. And then I said to them, "This is a load of tosh, lads. Doesn't work. Give me a couple of dozen." And they all said, "Wait a bit, sir." So I did. Sod all. Swallowed the lot. And then they ran out, and I was still only feeling vaguely tight, and then that Brenard chap said something about Special K, which *I* thought was a breakfast cereal, but apparently not, eh?'

Davenport sits, dishevelled and shaking, on the floor of his bathroom, clad reassuringly in his old, bottle-green suit and one of my T-shirts. By his bare feet rests the dozing form of Cinna, returned from exile and dribbling onto the linoleum.

'Sorry about the lack of seatables,' Davenport says, as I look round for a place to rest my own aching limbs. Finding nowhere, I perch on the toilet bowl.

The traces of last night's drug-hell have not quite loosened their spooky grip on my housemate. He's a more delicate shade of pink than usual, with a jittery air and a tendency, during conversation, to stare into the beyond. He's also taking regular sips from a tooth-mug of booze, dosing himself every time the darker memories threaten to take him over.

'Afraid I've been through a bit of a hoo-hah,' Davenport tells me, ruffling Cinna's head-fur with an outstretched hand. 'I can only apologise. It can't have been pleasant to witness.'

'What happened?'

Davenport leans his damp ginger frizz against the wall and stares at the ceiling, indulging in a deep, theatrical sigh. 'People quite often don't mean what they say. Have you found that? Sometimes they say the exact opposite of what they mean.'

I sit still, watching little knots of pubic hair and navel fluff blow across the floor like tumbleweed. Tara didn't exactly say the opposite of what she meant, she just lied through her teeth. And Mary lied too – for some different reasons which I'm not clear about. But I understand the point.

'Take Gisela,' he muses. 'Tells me she doesn't want this sprog, but then goes right *off* me, like I'd made her do something terrible against her will. Like I was the one making her get a – you know, have an abortion. Took me all this time to work out what was going on.' He looks directly at me, through puffy, wonderstruck eyes. 'Do you know, I'm almost grateful to those boys for giving me drugs. If I hadn't gone and taken them, I'd never have seen it . . .'

I could think of few things worse than listening to someone else's drug experiences. Winning an all-expenses-paid trip to Chad, perhaps, or going to a talk by a local artist. But somehow, because it's Davenport, I keep listening.

'That was the odd thing. Wasn't a bit like being tight at all. Didn't want to fuck anyone, didn't fancy a pizza. It was more like everything was *desperately* normal, but it was all so terribly funny at the same time. I realised nothing was what it seemed. Nothing at all. Not even your own reflection in the mirror. And it was all a great big joke, because we walk round all day, most of us, not realising what anything's really like, what's really going on. I kept thinking of that black-and-white flick you showed me – you know, just after you moved in. One of your Ealing jobs.'

'*The Lavender Hill Mob*?'

'No, not that. The war one. The one where Thora Hird's playing a nymphet and the Royal Gloucestershire Regiment turn out to be German spies.'

'*Went the Day Well*?'

'Bingo!' Davenport declares, slapping his palm on the lino. 'The very same. Kept thinking of it all night. Like Gizzler and me, you see.' He leans forward, urgently. 'You do see, don't you? You don't think I've just gone do-lally?'

'Erm. So you've split up then, you and Gisela?' I ask, confusion now enacting some primordial battle with fatigue and discomfort.

Here, Davenport makes a constipated-grandfather face. 'Good Lord, no! I mean, nothing's what it looks like! I realised what she was on about, see?'

'Which was what?'

'She wanted me to tell her what to do. Don't you see? Even big tough people like her sometimes want someone else to be in charge. Tell 'em what to do. She just wanted me to tell her to keep it. So I did. And she is. She's coming here, and she's walking out on Steve and we're going to have it. We're going to have the baby.'

'Congratulations.' It sounds a bit lame, particularly

echoing round the toilet, but I do mean it. Someone deserves some luck round here.

'Thank you. Though it does rather bring me to an awkward subject, Alastair. Be needing the old spare room, you see . . .'

'That's all right.' I don't really mind, particularly as I'm probably out of a job by now. I seem to be out of a lot of things, including Hope and Future Plans.

'Good man, good man. 'Course, you'll be sorely missed,' Davenport chunters on, his dilated eyes moist with sentiment. 'You're a true original, you know.'

'Thanks.'

'And thank *you* for the champers,' he replies, raising his mug to me. 'Jolly decent of you. No. There'll never be another Alastair Strange. Never seen a new bug take so much ragging without losing his mettle. But you stuck it out, didn't you, you plucky little sod?'

'Stuck what out?' I could just about cope with his account of drug-induced enlightenment, but he's lost me now.

'The ragging, Alastair. The *japes*. You know: the salad in the locker, the drawing, stealing your swimming trunks . . .' Davenport chuckles at the memory. 'Gosh, I had some fun with you.'

'*You?*'

Davenport looks upon me as if perhaps the drugs had taken hold again and I've now revealed myself to be a toadstool or an eighteenth-century Flemish milkmaid. 'Well, naturally it was me, old son. Who did you think?'

'But I accused . . .' My voice has taken on that quality again, of being not merely faint but also coming from the other side of some vast, rain-swept valley. 'I accused pretty much everyone, Davenport. I never had the faintest idea it was you.'

'Ah well,' Davenport says, his chest swelling with pride. 'Just goes to show you, doesn't it?'

'To show what?' I ask, limply.

'Lots of things not being what they seem . . .' He loses his trail as Cinna staggers to his feet and wanders determinedly into a far corner of the room. 'Spot of doggy Feng Shui, eh, boy?' Davenport exclaims delightedly, as a stream of the dog's yellow urine echoes tinnily against the radiator. 'Staking his little claim.'

Averting my eyes from this touching spectacle, I unfold Mary's letter and look at it again.

''Course,' Davenport continues, in my direction, 'I'll see you right, old chap. References and all that. You could even maybe hole up at my folks' place if you fancy it. They've got hectares going spare . . . Alastair, where are you *going*?'

I am experiencing one of London Underground's cleverest weapons in the fight against free movement: namely, a narrow corridor filled exclusively by wide-bottomed, slow-moving women in floral-print dresses. They are ambling, arm in arm, towards the exit, with that easy air of a couple taking a Sunday stroll round an art gallery. It's eleven twenty-two and I have eight minutes to get on the train to York.

'*Get out of my sodding way!*'

Wobbling scandalised chins turn away from me, full of Home Counties censure. 'This is why I never come up to town any more,' says one lady, dolorously. 'Lager louts,' says another. 'National Service,' says a third.

The escalator, at first sight a vertical stretch of a few

hundred feet, turns into a creaking silver odyssey, Mount Fuji executed in slow-moving steel, as soon as I'm on it. I start bounding up the steps, three at a time, past baleful pictures of Rick Reed, simulating masturbation in his checked long johns.

I don't know what I'll say once I'm in front of her. Perhaps I should have plotted it out before I dashed from the house and into the street. I only know this: that once Mary's been up North and thought about everything, she'll make the wrong decision. She'll ring me, all right, maybe even deign to have a nervous half of lager or two in my company. But that'll be it. Or it might be.

What Mary said in the Attitude Club was right. And what she said outside it, too. I understand it now. Life isn't a game of Cowboys and Indians. If it was a game, there'd be rules, winners and losers. But there aren't any, can't be any.

They understood it in Ealing. It happens at the end of *The Man in the White Suit*. Alec Guinness is Birnley, the zealot-scientist who discovers a self-cleaning, everlasting fabric. He remains what he is, right up to the closing minutes of the film – blinkered, unaware that his invention has dire consequences for the mill-workers, determined that science must conquer. Until, pursued by a mob of striking workers and panicking capitalists, he bumps into his old landlady, a local washerwoman. She refuses to give him refuge, saying snottily, 'What about my little bit of washing, what's to become of that?' This is Birnley's epiphany, where he sees that dogma and science, the rules, everything that trades in blacks and whites, like the dodgy creeds of the war era, must be cast asunder. The real, full-fat, high-tar world isn't that simple.

Acid burned this truth into Davenport's synapses last

night. Lots of things are not what they seem. Nice people can do rotten things – like Mary did to me, like Tara's doing to the man who loves her. A bluff, towering figure like Davenport, bull and bear combined, can still want someone to look after him. And people who seem hard and strong, like Gisela, can still want someone else to tell them what to do, sometimes. To change their minds.

I'm going to change hers. Because the only thing left, if we're all swimming round in this casserole of maybes, is to hope and to try and do what we believe in and to trust we'll be all right. You never know.

The only problem is that platform twelve has now receded to a distance at least as far away as Ealing and I've only a minute to spare as I run through the people, vaulting carefully strewn clots of baggage and sleeping bodies. Perhaps because of the blood rushing through my ears, there's a dull fizzing sound inside, giving way to a still quiet. I approach platform twelve in this muffled sound-scape, skilfully skirting a team of strategically placed Hasidic Jews as I run down the concrete gangway and through the barrier. An astonished man in uniform mouths urgent words at me as I shoot past him and towards the waiting train.

I'm inside now and we're moving. Save for the two First Class coaches, which are deserted but for a glowering conductor whose job it is to prevent anyone from sitting there, the train is crammed to the luggage racks with humanity. As I thunder, sweating and distracted, from one carriage to another, it's like I've stepped into heaven's waiting room. There are row upon row of patient nuns, people being earnest into their mobiles, couples and families engaged in various modes of homicidal bickering. God knows what York's got, apart from the Jorvik Viking

Centre and the Railway Museum, but the rest of Britain seems to be on its way there this morning.

I can't believe things have gone my way for once. But perhaps they always are going my way, always have been, and I just haven't seen it. It doesn't matter. I've seen it all now. And in a minute or two – in this carriage, or the next one – I'll find her, and everything will slot into place, like the final pieces of an almighty, celestial Airfix kit.

I reach the end of the final coach, where excitement starts sliding away into something more familiar. Doom settles on my shoulders like a silken cloak. I look around me, up and down the coach. My eyes scan the catalogue of heads – assorted orange peel and bottle-blonde and hamster hues – as if I'm looking for the dirty words in a passage of prose. And then it really hits me. A lurching, nauseating moment. Like coming downstairs in buoyant spirits the morning after some party and noticing, for reasons you cannot remember, that everyone hates you.

She's not here.

Perhaps she missed the train; perhaps she never seriously intended to get on it. All I know for certain is that I am on it now, and the doors are locked, and it's taking me somewhere I don't want to go. Via a lot of other places I don't want to go, like Stevenage. On my own now, today and into the conceivable future. There ain't no justice. Not once you step outside of Ealing.

She's not here.

I lurch uneasily back towards the centre of the train, looking defiantly at anyone who catches my eye. At least I tried. And if the assorted homilies of the school assembly are to be believed, this is just as important as succeeding. For the first time, I can see why that might be true. And at least there was last night – good, if not great, in parts. There'll always be that.

Over a background of static whines and the crackling of distant shell-fire, the steward announces the opening of the buffet car. I'm not so interested in the BLT Zinger or the Turkey Tacos or the award-winning range of herbal teas. And to be fair, the steward doesn't sound like he's too interested in them either. But I am interested, indecently so, in the alcoholic beverages. By the time this train discharges me in Milton Keynes, I intend to be so drunk that I have to crawl to the toilet to be sick.

The steward, a cheery Afro-Caribbean doing his best to look like he doesn't mind wearing a straw hat and a candy-striped waistcoat, is opening big cardboard boxes of plastic cups. I'm the first customer.

'Just be about five minutes, mate,' he says. 'I've not got me float yet.'

I lean up against the side of the narrow corridor. Things could be worse. I might have lost my job, but then again, I might not. As I ran out of the house, Davenport was shouting something at me, about his enormous trust fund and how he was going to use it to rescue the school. But even if I have lost my job, I suppose I'll find another one. It's just a shame there won't be another Mary.

Underneath my feet there's a nasty squealing sound, a million mice caught up in some rusty flourmill. The train lurches and begins to slow down. I catch the steward's eye. 'First of many, eh?'

He squints at me, doubtfully. 'First of many what, bruv?'

'Delays. We've just stopped, haven't we?'

'Yeah. It's Finsbury Park overground, mate. We always stop here.'

I glance out of the window and see a platform full of people, waiting to get on. I didn't know the inter-city trains stopped here. I suppose it's a good thing, because I can get off. But as I move towards the door, I can't help wondering where I heard Finsbury Park mentioned recently. Someone was saying something, and I wasn't listening too closely, because I was looking at them and thinking of other things that had nothing to do with Finsbury Park or Ealing or unmarked homework or the bus timetable.

Then, as I'm grappling with the door-lock, I remember where I heard it. She said it.

She works here.

She said it to me. And leaning out of the window, because that's the proper way to open the door apparently, from the outside, I can see something good and true and just on the platform.

She's here. Just as I saw her all those mornings on the bus. Small and neat in her vintage costume, blinking in faintly affronted fashion at the sun. As if she'd like to start an argument with it. She'll have to settle for me.

I call out to Mary and she looks suitably astonished, but she waves back. Then she starts running down the platform towards the door. And people look at us, but not for long, because there are lots of other meetings on this platform, lots of trains passing this way. Soon our voices are just a tiny part of the endless soundtrack and the flickering movements of people and wheels.